# DETROIT BREAKDOWN

Also by D. E. Johnson

*The Detroit Electric Scheme*
*Motor City Shakedown*

# DETROIT BREAKDOWN

## D. E. Johnson

Minotaur Books ❧ New York

DETROIT BREAKDOWN. Copyright 2012 by D. E. Johnson. All rights reserved. Printed in the United States of America. For information, address St. Martin's Press, 175 Fifth Avenue, New York, N.Y. 10010.

www.minotaurbooks.com

Map courtesy of Michelle Johnson

ISBN 978-1-250-00662-2 (hardcover)
ISBN 978-1-250-01212-8 (e-book)

First Edition: September 2012

10  9  8  7  6  5  4  3  2

For Papa Dill, Mama Hand-me-down, their children, and, of course, Pearl, the cat. I only wish my imagination were half as rich as that of my girls and their cousins.

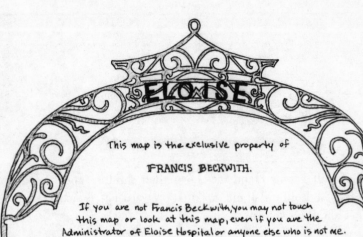

ELOISE

This map is the exclusive property of

FRANCIS BECKWITH.

If you are not Francis Beckwith, you may not touch
this map or look at this map, even if you are the
Administrator of Eloise Hospital or anyone else who is not me.

Anyone who touches this map will be subject to extremely painful
disciplinary measures!!!

# KEY to MAP

|||||| MICHIGAN CENTRAL TRAIN TRACK
∘∘∘∘∘ DUR TRAIN TRACK        ⅀⅄⅁⅃ WHEAT FIELD
⌒⌒⌒ FRONT GATE                ═══ ROAD
-+-+-+ BARBED WIRE            ↣↣↣ TUNNEL
· · · · · SIDEWALK            ∽∽∽∽ WATER PIPE

1 AMUSEMENT HALL          13 LAUNDRY
2 GAZEBO                  14 SCHOOLHOUSE
3 ICE HOUSE               15 ICEHOUSE
4 DUR TRAIN STATION       16 BOILER PLANT
5 CONSERVATORIES          17 DOUBLE RESIDENCE
6 WOMEN'S ASYLUM          18 PUMPHOUSE
7 COUNTY HOUSE            19 BARNS
8 BUILDING B              20 PIGGERY
9 BUILDING A              21 TUBERCULAR SANATORIUM
10 NURSES' DORMITORY      22 INCINERATOR
11 WAREHOUSE              23 WAREHOUSE
12 BAKERY

Do Not Touch This MAP!!!!!     THIS MEANS YOU!!!!!

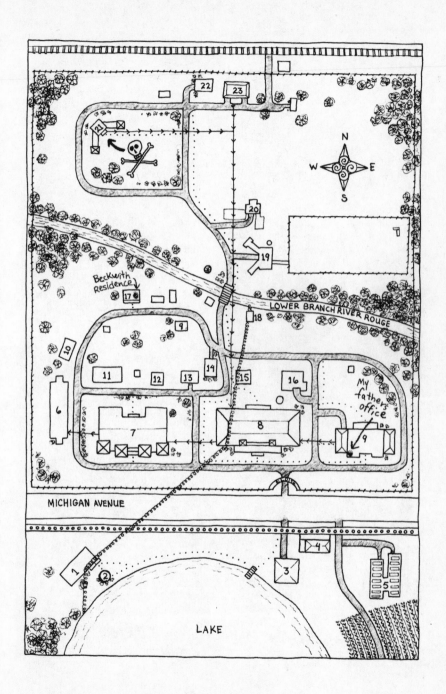

# DETROIT BREAKDOWN

# CHAPTER ONE

*Tuesday, August 6, 1912*

## Will

Elizabeth stepped through the little door in the bookcase and disappeared down the corridor. "You won't believe this, Will. Come on."

I stood at the side of her father's old desk, staring after her into the narrow passageway behind the bookcase. The unfinished boards and timbers contrasted with the smooth walnut inside the den. "Just a minute." I tried to drum up some courage, but it wasn't coming.

"Will!" Elizabeth called. "Where are you?"

I took a deep breath, stepped through the door into the passageway, and took four sideways steps before I froze. Sawn timbers pressed against my back, the wall in front of me only inches from my face. There was just enough light to see the murky gray of the raw wood and the ends of nails protruding through the boards in front of me. Droplets of sweat slid down my forehead into my eyes. Beneath my suit coat, my shirt was already soaked. Beads of sweat smeared from my knees to my trousers. I couldn't breathe. My heart pounded in my ears.

"I—I can't . . ." I hurried back toward the light of the den.

"Will?" Elizabeth called again as I stepped through the door.

Safely back in what had been her father's den, I bent over, gloved hands on knees, and panted, wrenching my thoughts into the present by focusing on the pain in my right hand and shoulder. The nerves in my hand still sent out messages to my brain that they were burning, even though it had been a year and a half since the acid scorched me. The shoulder was a newer pain, a bullet wound from the Gianolla gang. To be fair, I'd shot two of them first.

Elizabeth stuck her head into the room. "Will? What's wrong?"

I straightened and shrugged. "I can't. It's too close in there."

"But it's right around the corner. You were nearly to the room."

"There's no other way to get there?"

"No, but—"

"I can't do it, Elizabeth." I reached over and took her hand. "I want to, but I can't. It's the dreams."

"Oh." Her face fell. "The trunk?"

"Yes. I didn't want to worry you." I'd never been claustrophobic, never thought twice about plunging into tight spaces, but an incident earlier in the year had changed that. I'd been kidnapped and twice stuffed inside a steamer trunk. At the time, it was nothing more than uncomfortable, but the experience lived on in my nightmares. I wake inside the trunk. The air is stifling, and it's blazing hot. I'm squeezed inside, unable to move at all. With a certainty I seldom feel, I know I will die. The air thins. I try to conserve my energy, but I can't stop myself from gasping in as much air as I can. I hear nothing other than my ragged breathing. Just when my lungs can take no more, I wake myself with a scream of terror.

"I'm sorry." She stepped close to me and cupped my cheek in her hand. "You've looked . . . I wondered if you've been sleeping. Are you having them every night?"

"Yes." I fell into one of the club chairs opposite the desk.

Elizabeth sat beside me and took my hand again. "I'm sorry, my darling."

"I'm doing all right," I said. "Most of the time."

"That's fine. The hidden room isn't going anywhere. I just thought you'd find it interesting."

No one, not even her mother, had known about the room. Her father had had it secretly built when the house was constructed. A few days earlier, Helga, the Humes' maid, had found the hidden door while cleaning and alerted Elizabeth. She searched the room and found piles of cash and documents incriminating some of her father's co-conspirators, most of whom had died at roughly the same time he had. She'd already given the money to charity and burned the papers.

Finally calm again, I breathed more easily. "Lord," I said, feeling my shirt stick to my back. "I need a bath."

"Why don't you take one?"

"I don't want to leave already, Lizzie. I'll never get back on your calendar."

"Nonsense. Anyway, you can take one here." Her tone became playful. "I won't even make you use the servants' bathroom."

"I don't have a change of clothes."

"Oh, but you do. I haven't made it to the mission yet."

I'd given her a pile of clothing for the McGregor Mission, one of the many charitable organizations she supported. "Well, I suppose . . ."

"I'll try to make it worth your while." She leaned over and kissed me. With a giggle, she said, "Your mustache tickles."

I don't think I'd ever heard her giggle. I'd been working on a beard and mustache for about a week, and the results thus far were not promising. The mustache was coming in well enough, but the beard was thin, particularly on my cheeks. I thought I should probably shave it and just try for the mustache, but beards were fashionable. I didn't want to give up so easily.

I stood and pulled Elizabeth to her feet, noticing for the millionth time how beautiful she was. Sometimes she took me by surprise; her eyes green as holly, her high cheekbones and full lips, her beautiful auburn hair, short now. Each feature—lovely, but they added together in some exponential equation that ended in perfection. "I love you so much," I said. "I want you all to myself."

She pecked me on the lips. "And you know I love you. But you also know I have my work. Once the election is past, my time will be free."

"I doubt it. They won't let you go."

"There'll be nothing left to do. We'll have the vote."

"Perhaps," I replied.

"There's no 'perhaps.' We're leading everywhere." She turned and headed for the door. "Now come and take a bath, smelly. Everyone's asleep. We've got all night."

I arched my eyebrows. "Would you care to join me?"

Her eyes bulged, and her mouth formed a perfect circle. "Of course not," she whispered. "What if my mother—" She stopped when she saw my smile. "Oh, you are such a goop. Now go."

The bell on the telephone jangled, startling us both. "Don't answer it," I said. I could feel our evening disappearing into smoke.

The phone rang again.

Elizabeth looked toward the doorway and back at me. "It'll wake my mother."

"It's got to be a wrong number. Who would call this late?"

"Someone with bad news, that's who," she said.

The phone kept ringing.

"Then let it ring."

She made up her mind and strode to the desk, picked up the candlestick of the telephone, and put the receiver to her ear. "Hume residence." As she listened to the reply, little furrows appeared between her eyebrows and began to deepen. "Elizabeth." She listened again. "No, I'm her daughter. Who is—" A pause. "Wait—Robert Clarke, you said?"

Robert Clarke was a cousin of Elizabeth's who had spent his life at Eloise Hospital—the Wayne County insane asylum. I wouldn't have known that had her mother not gone to Eloise fairly frequently to visit him. I'd occasionally asked Elizabeth about Robert, but she always changed the subject. I stopped asking a long time ago.

I heard a muffled voice on the other end of the line but couldn't understand it.

"All right," she said. "I'll be there as soon as I can."

She started to hang up, but stopped and listened. "About . . . half an hour?" Pause. "I'm not sure *exactly* when. I'll hurry." She slammed the receiver onto the hook and turned to me. "Could I borrow your motorcar?"

"Of course, but why?"

"It's just . . . a problem I have to deal with."

"At Eloise?"

She gave me a tight nod.

"Why don't you let me drive? I can see you're upset."

"No. That's all right." Her words were short, clipped.

This was not like her at all. "What's the matter?"

She glared at me. "Can I borrow the automobile or not?"

"Yes. But let me come."

"Damn it, Will—" She stopped herself. Her eyes shifted from right to left, and then she looked at me again. "All right. Go start it. We have to leave now."

While I'd never seen Elizabeth act this way, it was obvious the phone call had shaken her to the core, so I decided to hold my questions until we were under way. I ran out of the den, down the hall, and out the door to my Model T Torpedo parked at the curb. The sweat that covered me chilled in the cool of the early August night. I set the spark and throttle, ran around to the front, and cranked the starter. The front door burst open, and Elizabeth ran down the steps. When the engine caught, we climbed into the car. Across the street, the Detroit River burbled and surged.

"Hurry," Elizabeth said. "Please."

With a sense of foreboding, I made a U-turn and headed west on Jefferson. The wind blew through my wet clothing. "It's on Michigan Avenue, isn't it?"

"Yes."

I'd never been to Eloise, and the thought of the place gave me the willies. Worse, I was certain the telephone call had ended the magical time Elizabeth and I had had over the last four weeks. We had been drinking one another up, physically, mentally, and emotionally, and were even closer now than when we'd been engaged. I suppose nearly being killed half a dozen times gives one a little perspective. We certainly understood how quickly we could lose each other.

I glanced at Elizabeth. "Are you all right?"

"I'm fine. Just drive faster."

I gave the Torpedo more gas. At eleven thirty on a Tuesday night, there were few vehicles out, and I sped down the street at forty miles per hour, straddling the middle of the road in case someone pulled out from either side.

Eloise Hospital was a sore subject with Elizabeth. When she and her mother returned from Paris last year, Mrs. Hume had been committed to Eloise by her brother-in-law, who was after his dead brother's money. It had taken Elizabeth a month to get her out. I couldn't help at the time. I didn't know they had returned, not that it really mattered since I was in jail.

The wind was bringing tears to my eyes. I fished around behind me for my goggles and handed one pair to Elizabeth before I slipped on the other. "Can you tell me what happened?" A truck pulled out in front of us, and I swerved around it, honking the horn as I did.

Elizabeth grabbed the dash in front of her. "The man on the phone said Robert was accused of killing another patient"—her voice broke— "and was threatening to kill himself."

"Oh, Lord." We roared down the street.

I wheeled around a pair of cars waiting at the Woodward Avenue intersection and squeezed past, narrowly avoiding a horse-drawn wagon. The river steamers at the ferry docks sat dark and quiet, shadowy behemoths motionless in the water. I turned up Griswold and accelerated, now hitting fifty miles per hour. The engine roared, the tires whirred, and the wind howled in my ears.

"I'm sorry," she said. "I shouldn't have spoken to you that way." I could barely hear her over the sounds of the car.

"That's all right, honey," I shouted. "I can only imagine how upset you are. Who called?"

"I don't know." She'd raised her voice now as well. "I think it was another patient."

"Why?"

"He sounded similar to Robert. Mechanical, forced. Like he was trying to disguise his voice."

I dodged a man on a horse and continued speeding down the road, hoping no members of the Detroit Police Department's "Flying Squadron" were in the area tonight. Michigan Avenue was just ahead, and I slowed to thirty-five to take the turn. The back end of the car skidded, but I corrected for the turn and opened up the throttle. Soon we were again up to fifty miles per hour.

"Wait," I shouted. "How would a patient make a telephone call this late at night? For that matter, I can't imagine they let patients make calls at all."

Elizabeth turned in her seat, leaned in closer to me, and put a hand up to keep her hair out of her face. "I don't know."

"Maybe it was just a prank."

"A prank? Virtually no one even knows he's related to us."

"Robert hasn't been violent before, has he?"

"No." She paused. "Well, not that I know of."

A streetcar was crossing the intersection ahead of us. I slammed on the brakes, sliding to a stop about twenty feet away from it. As soon as it was through, I jerked down on the throttle again, and we sped away.

"Tell me about him," I said.

"I don't really know that much about him."

"But you know something."

Her mouth tightened, and she looked away. "He got angry with us a lot. I think he's intelligent, but something just doesn't work right in his brain."

"What sort of . . . debility does he have?"

"The doctors called it dementia praecox. I don't know much about it."

"How long has it been since you've seen him?"

"A long time. Oh, God." Her voice caught. I glanced at her and saw tears running down her face. "I know I should have gone, Will. It's just . . . that place. I hate it."

The asylum's black iron gate cast a long row of shadows that swallowed us as we ran up to the entryway. I glanced at Elizabeth. The dark parallel lines slipped across her face as she moved, alternating with light cast by the flood lamps of the grounds. A huge redbrick building loomed in front of us, its twin cupolas silhouetted against a black sky. An iron archway hung above the gate. The institution's identity was revealed with a single word formed of simple block letters. One word was enough.

ELOISE.

Truth is, I wasn't any more enthusiastic about coming here than Elizabeth had been in years past. Eloise was a name that put fear into the hearts of every schoolchild—and most everyone else—in Wayne County. In fact, I couldn't recall ever hearing of a child in the Detroit area being named Eloise.

I tightened my grip on Elizabeth's hand, more for my comfort than hers, and strode toward the gate. Ahead of us, farther up Michigan Avenue, streetlamps lit a commercial area and, past it, a residential block. We turned up the short walk to the gate, where I released her hand and rang the bell. It made a loud, grating buzz. When I took my finger off the button, I heard men shouting in the distance. Their voices were indistinct, far enough away that I couldn't identify what they were saying. They quieted. Across the street behind us, the waters of a small lake lapped against the shore. A rowboat bumped against a wooden dock. On the other side of the lake stood a large building, a gazebo between it and the water.

Elizabeth's foot tapped against the pavement. We exchanged a glance, and I rang the bell again. Still nothing. She reached across me and pressed the button, holding it for a good thirty seconds.

A guard in a green wool uniform and cap walked out of the darkness between the building in front of us and another to its right. He was perhaps thirty years old, with a heavy beard and acne scars.

When he was close enough, Elizabeth took hold of one of the bars in the gate and said, "Robert Clarke is my cousin. I must see him."

The man stopped in front of us. He frowned and glanced behind him.

"I was told he was threatening to kill himself," she said. "If that's true, you must let me see him. He'll listen to me."

"I don't know," he said. "I got orders to—"

"Please." Elizabeth reached through the gate and took hold of his sleeve. "You must help me."

After looking at her a moment longer, he made up his mind. He unlocked the gate, grabbed hold of the bars, and leaned back, putting his weight into drawing the gate open a couple of feet. When we were through, he closed and locked it again. "This way." He ran off, down the dark sidewalk from which he'd come. We followed closely behind, Elizabeth a fast runner in her flat-soled shoes, and me just able to keep up with her. We burst out of the shadows and onto a street. The size of the complex was suddenly apparent to me. A network of roads and buildings spread out before us, lit by the glowing orbs of streetlamps.

The guard veered left behind the main building and ran to the entryway near the far end. Three policemen huddled on the porch with another man. Inside, a few people walked past the windows. None of them looked alarmed. They were just going about their business.

The guard stopped at the base of the steps and turned to us, panting. "Wait here. I have to ask—"

"I'll come," Elizabeth said. I was panting as hard as the other man, but she was barely winded. "There's no time to waste." With that, she hurried around him and up the steps, holding up her dress with both hands so as not to trip.

The guard gawped at me. I shrugged and followed her. By the time I reached the top of the steps, she was already inside. Two of the policemen looked at me with raised eyebrows, but I continued to the door, trying to convey an air of confidence I didn't feel. They let me pass.

I entered a reception area, a tall, unadorned room about thirty feet square that smelled sharply of bleach. The marble floor continued into long hallways to the left and right, with a shorter one leading to the front of the building. It was surprisingly quiet. A pair of orderlies ambled past me, talking idly.

How, I wondered, could it look like this when a man had just been murdered?

I heard my first evidence of patients—a long howl that cut off abruptly. My heart quickened as the voice echoed through the room.

Elizabeth had already collared a young woman wearing a black dress who was carrying a stack of bedpans. "Where is Robert Clarke?" she asked, in a tone that made it clear she would brook no hesitation or argument.

The woman pointed toward the hallway on the right, and we ran past dozens of closed doors. Ahead, a policeman leaned against a doorjamb, conversing with other men inside. Elizabeth stopped and looked—and drew in a quick breath. I peered over her shoulder.

Two men in suits knelt next to a man in a white nightshirt who lay crumpled on the floor at the side of a desk. His hair was cropped short and uneven, his face was bony, and the legs poking out from the bottom of the gown were as thin as sticks. I stepped around Elizabeth and walked into the room. The man's mouth was slack, teeth broken and irregular, tongue swollen, purple. He was clearly dead. Now I saw what the men were looking at: a deep burgundy welt, about an inch thick, circling the man's neck. He'd been hanged.

"What do you want?" the policeman asked.

"Robert Clarke," Elizabeth said. "Where is he?"

The policeman focused on her. "Why?"

"He's my cousin. I must speak with him."

He gave her a sly smile. "Don't know that you'll be able to without a séance. Said he was gonna kill himself."

She grabbed the front of his uniform in her fists. "Where is he?"

He looked startled, and for a second I thought he was going to hit her. I took a step forward, but all he did was meekly say, "End of the hall. Turn right."

She let him go and ran out of the room. I followed again. It was another hundred feet to the end of the hallway, and fifty to the end of the next one, where half a dozen men stood outside a room, trying to peer inside. A hysterical voice shouted, "Go away! I'll do it!"

"Robbie!" Elizabeth cried and pushed through the men jamming the doorway.

"Leave me alone!" the man screamed.

I shouldered my way into the room behind her. A man in a white nightshirt stood in the back corner, a serrated knife with a blade perhaps eight inches long in his hand. He was tall, dark-haired, thin. He looked exhausted, and sweat dripped down the sides of his face. His head turned back and forth, his wide eyes on the pair of policemen standing ten feet away from him on either side. One of them was fat, maybe twenty years old, the other thin and at least sixty. Both held revolvers.

"Here now, boy," the thin one said. "Hand it over."

Elizabeth slid in front of him. "Robbie, it's me, Elizabeth."

"Hey." The cop grabbed her shoulder. "Who the—"

"Lizzie!" Robert broke into a cry at the end of her name. "I didn't do it. It was the Phantom. I told them." His voice was mechanical, forced, like she said the caller had sounded.

"It's all right. I'll help you." Out of the side of her mouth, she said to the cop behind her, "Let go of me. I'm Robert's cousin. He'll give me the knife." After a second, he released her. She took a step toward Robert— nearly close enough for him to reach her with a swipe of the knife.

"Miss, you've got to get back." The thin policeman grabbed her arm, but she pulled it away from him and held her position. "Listen now," he said, a warning in his voice.

She glanced back at him and whispered, "Let me try."

He didn't respond. I moved to Elizabeth's side, just in front of her position. Robert looked crazy to me. I wasn't going to let him stab her.

"Will." Elizabeth's voice was dead calm. "Get back. We're fine."

I glanced at her and then back at Robert. His eyes were fixed on Elizabeth, his face contorted with fear or rage. "Okay." I took half a step back, still ready to pounce if he made a move toward her.

"I'm not going to the Hole," Robert said. "I'm not. I'm not. I didn't do it. Lizzie, help me. It was the Phantom. He did it."

"All right, Robbie," Elizabeth said. "You're going to be all right." She took another step toward him.

"Get back, missy," the fat policeman warned.

"No," she said. "He's my cousin. It's all right." She sounded like she was trying to calm down the cop as much as she was Robert.

"Lizzie, they're going to put me in the Hole. I'll never get out. I didn't do it. I didn't—"

"It's okay, Robbie," she said. "I'll help you." She took another step toward him. He could easily stab her now before anyone could react.

"Get me out," he pleaded. "Get me out of here."

"Just give me the knife." She spoke in a matter-of-fact tone, as if this were the most natural thing in the world.

"Step back!" the fat policeman shouted. Both cops now had their guns pointed at Robert's head.

"Elizabeth," I said. "Be careful." I edged to my right, working myself between Elizabeth and the fat cop, who sounded like he was on the verge of panic. The hammer on his revolver was cocked. He reached out and grabbed the shoulder in which I'd been shot, trying to pull me away. Wincing, I twisted out of his grip.

"Move!" His right arm snaked around me, gun extended, trying to find a target.

Elizabeth took another step closer to Robert, who raised his arms.

The fat policeman pulled the trigger, and his gun went off in a smoky explosion.

Robert fell to the floor, screaming, his hands up to the sides of his head. The knife clattered to the floor. I couldn't tell if he'd been hit. The policemen rushed him, shoving Elizabeth and me out of the way. The older one jumped on top of Robert and pinned his arms to the floor. Still screaming, Robert tried to wriggle out from under him.

"Stop!" Elizabeth shouted.

I leaned in to try to help the cop get Robert under control, but the other one cracked me over the head with his nightstick. Stunned, I fell to my knees. As Robert continued to struggle, the younger policeman reared back again with his nightstick and clubbed him over the head. He collapsed in a heap on the floor.

Elizabeth rushed in and pulled at the policeman on top of Robert. "Get off! Get off!"

He shoved her away, scooped up Robert's knife, and stood. My mind was still trying to catch up. The room seemed a blur of activity. Police, orderlies, and guards hurried in. Some shouted commands; others followed them. Elizabeth knelt next to Robert and felt his pulse, then looked him over. "I think he missed," she said. "I don't see a bullet wound."

I sat hard on the floor, wincing with pain, my good hand over the lump growing on the crown of my head.

Elizabeth touched my arm. "Are you all right?"

"I'll be fine," I gasped.

She stared at the cops. I could see she wanted to shout at them but was conflicted. Perhaps what they did saved Robert's life. I wanted to yell at them, too, but my head hurt enough already.

The older policeman put his hands on his hips and squared off on his partner. "You goddamned idiot. You could have killed somebody."

Elizabeth was looking at the hole in the wall where the bullet hit. It seemed awfully close to where Robert had been standing.

"He was going to . . ." The young policeman's voice trailed off.

"He was going to nothing," the other man said. "He was giving up. You're lucky you can't shoot any better'n a little girl."

Robert began to rouse, and the older policeman snapped a set of handcuffs on him. A pair of orderlies took his arms and began dragging him out of the room.

"Wait." Elizabeth stood and hurried over to them. "Robert? Are you all right?"

"I . . . I'm . . . okay." He was dazed, but he seemed to be coming to his senses.

The orderlies again began to drag him off.

She took hold of Robert's arm. "I'll help you. Don't be afraid." To the orderlies, she said, "Where are you taking him?"

"He's going to solitary until we hear different," the older policeman said. "Now, you." He pointed at me. "You're lucky he didn't shoot you. Hell, you're lucky I didn't shoot you, you dumb son of a bitch. Interfering with an officer of the law. Ought to shoot you now." He turned away and began ordering around the hospital employees.

Elizabeth bent down next to me. "Let me see your head."

"No. I'm fine." I levered myself to my feet. "Let's see what they're doing with Robert." I took a wobbly step.

"Whoa," the older policeman said. "We're going to need a statement."

"Can't we do that after—" Elizabeth started.

"Statement first."

She looked toward the door and then back at him. "All right. But then can we see Robert?"

"Ain't my decision."

We spent the next fifteen minutes explaining to him how we happened to be at the hospital and then giving our perspective on what had happened in the room. Elizabeth kept trying to sneak glances at what he was writing, but he tilted the pad away from her every time. Me, I just wanted to sit down with a block of ice on my head.

Finally Elizabeth folded her arms over her chest and said, "Shouldn't someone who wasn't involved in the shooting be taking witness statements?"

The cop scowled at her. "I don't answer to you, missy."

"Hey," I said. "There's no reason to—"

"Will." Elizabeth took my hand. "It's all right. Let's just get this over with."

When the cop finished with us, a nurse led Elizabeth and me away. Ahead of us were three men in suits, huddled together. Elizabeth nudged me. "The one on the right is the administrator—Dr. Stephen Beckwith."

He was a large, rumpled man of perhaps fifty years, wearing brown tweed trousers with suspenders and a wrinkled white shirt. His silver hair was long, his strong jaw stubbled with whiskers, though I'd have guessed he had shaved that morning. He was an impressive-looking man, the kind you wouldn't be surprised to learn was a Nobel Prize winner in science or something equally astounding.

The nurse turned up a hallway perhaps thirty feet in front of them. Elizabeth paused, and I thought she was going to continue forward and confront Dr. Beckwith. Instead, she followed the nurse who led us up the hall and ushered us into a large office with a pair of upholstered chairs opposite an antique walnut desk. A sitting area, with a leather sofa and another upholstered chair, was backed by a wall filled with books, at first glance all medical and psychiatric tomes. "Wait here," she said. "Someone will be with you soon." She left the room and closed the door behind her.

Elizabeth touched my left shoulder. "Let me look at your head."

"No, it's—"

"Sit."

I knew arguing wouldn't change how this ended, so I sat in one of the chairs and let her look at the lump on my skull.

"Ooh," she said. I heard a wince in her voice. "The knob's about an inch across, and it's pretty ugly, but it's scabbing over already. Maybe we can get some ice from someone, try to keep the swelling down."

"No. Let's just get to the bottom of what's going on here."

She stepped back and looked down into my eyes. "Do you feel disoriented or anything?"

"No. My heads hurts, but I think I'm okay. My mental processes seem normal."

I could tell she felt sorry for me, because she bypassed the opportunity to remark about my mental processes—or my lack thereof. She fell into the chair opposite me and met my eyes, her tired face blank and bleary-eyed. Finally she said, "How could Robert have gotten hold of a knife?"

"How could someone have gotten hanged in the middle of a busy ward? There's something seriously wrong here."

She nodded. "And what about the Phantom, whatever that is?"

I looked out the window at the grounds again. In the dark, the scene was very nearly idyllic, with paved streets, new redbrick buildings, bright streetlamps. It was the picture of a modern hospital. How did something like this happen? The window acted as a prism, creating red, blue, and green arcs around the streetlights. When I glanced back at

Elizabeth, I could see she had followed my eyes and was looking at the same thing.

Sighing, she said, "This place scares the hell out of me."

A soft knock sounded against the door, and one of the men who'd been with Dr. Beckwith walked into the room. He wore a gray suit that looked to have been thrown on, not surprising given that it was well after midnight. He was a slight, balding man of no more than thirty, with a rounded nose and bright blue eyes. "We need to clear up a few things. My name is Dr. Davis. I'm one of the psychiatrists here. And you are?" He had the patrician tone of East Coast old money.

"I'm Robert's cousin, Elizabeth Hume," she said, "and this is my friend Will."

I was surprised she didn't introduce me with my full name, though I thought perhaps it was because I was an infamous "murderer"—even though I had been cleared both times I was brought to trial. My name would probably dredge up suspicion and slow us down.

Dr. Davis hesitated, then reached out to shake my hand. He looked curiously, as most people did, at my right hand when I offered him my left, though all he could see was my glove.

Appraising Elizabeth with his intense blue eyes, Dr. Davis asked, "Are you Mr. Clarke's legal guardian?"

"No. My mother is."

I could see that she wanted to take those words back, but I didn't think it would matter anyway. Surely they had records. Mrs. Hume had been acting strangely, though, and I wondered if she would be up to the task of dealing with this situation. While Elizabeth hadn't said anything to me about her mother's lapses, I was sure she felt the same way.

"All right." He drew a small notebook from his inside coat pocket. "Could you give me her address and telephone number?"

"Don't you have them?" she asked. "Surely you have records of your patients' next of kin."

"I'm sure we do." Dr. Davis folded his arms across his chest. "I just thought we might expedite things a bit."

I stood up. "This is nonsense. We want to talk to the warden."

"This is a hospital," Dr. Davis said. "We don't have a warden."

"I don't care what you call him. We want to see him. Now."

"I'm not sure that will be possible."

Elizabeth shot up out of the chair. "Perhaps you'd prefer we go to the newspapers. I'm sure they'd be interested in how a patient here got hanged and another had a knife."

The doctor glared at her. "Give me a few minutes." He left the room, closing the door quietly behind him.

"This is ridiculous," I muttered. "Dead men lying about, patients with weapons. How do they run this place?"

She shrugged and sat down, and I looked over the contents of the doctor's library. Freud's *The Interpretation of Dreams* caught my eye. I picked it up and began paging through it, and soon came across this remarkable passage:

"The dream is not meaningless, not absurd, does not presuppose that one part of our store of ideas is dormant while another part begins to awake. It is a perfectly valid psychic phenomenon, actually a wish fulfillment . . ."

I read farther down the page. According to Freud, dreams—all dreams—were a form of wish fulfillment. I didn't want to think of the implications right now.

The office door opened. I turned around and saw a young man slip into the room. He closed the door and stood staring at us from behind wire-rimmed eyeglasses.

"Can we help you?" I asked.

He hurried over toward us, his legs gliding rapidly, with none of the normal accompanying motion in his upper body. His arms were tight to his sides, one holding a book, the other with fist clenched. He appeared to have no physical handicap, but his movements were completely un-natural, as if he were trying to walk without touching the ground while bracing for an impact. He wore a shirt and trousers, rather than a nightshirt, but I still thought he might be a patient. He scurried around behind the chair on the other side of the desk, putting the furniture and ten feet between us and him. He was a good-sized boy, perhaps five ten and 170 pounds, and around twenty years old, with fine features and dark hair. His face looked normal enough.

"I'm Will," I said. "What's your name?"

"Francis. Francis Beckwith."

Elizabeth sat up straight. Something had put her on alert. "Hello, Francis," she said. "I'm Elizabeth."

"Robert Clarke did not kill Patrick Cook," he said. His voice struck me as that of an automaton. Now I understood Elizabeth's reaction. He sounded like he could be the caller she had described.

She stood but didn't move any closer to him. "Do you know that for a fact?"

"Yes."

"How do you know, Francis?" she asked.

"The Opera Ghost killed Patrick."

"Pardon?" was all Elizabeth could muster.

"The Opera Ghost," he repeated, "who is also known as the Phantom."

"Oh. I see." She tried to keep her voice even, but I could hear the disappointment.

Francis's mouth tightened. He also saw that she didn't believe him. "The Phantom killed Patrick with the Punjab lasso. That is how he kills everyone." He held up the book. "See. Here's proof." The corners of his mouth turned up in what looked like an attempt at a smile, as if he thought one would be appropriate at the moment, but there was no humor behind it.

I squinted at the title. *The Phantom of the Opera*. He thought some ghost story was real. Still, I thought I'd humor him, to see if anything might come of it. "What is the Punjab lasso?"

"It is a length of rope used as a garrote. Its use was popularized by the Punjabi *Hashashins* in the Middle Ages. The Opera Ghost uses a Punjab lasso made of catgut." He rattled off these details like Gatling-gun fire.

"So you're saying the man wasn't hanged," I said. "He was strangled."

"That is correct," Francis said.

Elizabeth took a step toward him but stopped when he flinched. "Did you see the murder take place?"

"No. But I saw the body. It was the same."

"The same?" I said.

"As the others."

"Oh." I thought I understood. "The murders in the book."

"Yes," he said. "But I was not talking about them."

"No?"

"No. I was talking about the three others *here* who have been killed."

I stared at the young man across the desk from me for a moment. "You're saying four men here have been murdered?"

"Yes." Reaching into his pocket, he pulled out a folded piece of paper and carefully opened it. It was a hand-drawn map, perhaps two feet square. It looked incredibly detailed. "Victor was killed here," he pointed to a spot, "and Albert was—"

The office door opened, and Dr. Davis walked back in. "Francis." He put his hands on his hips and cocked his head. "What are you doing here?"

Francis quickly folded the map and returned it to his pocket. His eyes dropped to the floor. "Nothing."

"Nothing?" Davis asked.

"No." Now the young man's voice was sullen.

"You're supposed to be home. In bed."

"You are not my father."

"No, I'm not. And it's a good thing for you he's not in this room. Now go."

"You are not my father," Francis repeated, louder.

"If you don't go home now, I'm going to talk to him about it."

Francis stared at him defiantly for a moment before scurrying around the desk and out into the hall.

"Thank you, Francis." Davis looked at me and rolled his eyes before closing the door.

"Who is he?" Elizabeth asked.

"Francis is Dr. Beckwith's son," Davis replied.

Elizabeth glanced at me. "He reminds me of Robert."

"Yes, well, that would make sense," Davis said, "since they are both schizophrenic."

"I thought Robert was diagnosed as having dementia praecox."

Davis nodded. "Yes, but a few years ago the diagnoses were fine-tuned a bit. He's now classified schizophrenic with autistic symptoms."

"Whatever that means," I muttered.

Davis cleared his throat. "It's a complicated syndrome, really more a classification than a particular disease." He sat behind the desk and gestured for Elizabeth to take a seat. When she did, he said, "Dr. Beckwith is unable to join us. He is understandably busy dealing with the events of the evening. He wished me to relay to you his concern, and said he would resolve this matter."

"That is not satisfactory," Elizabeth said.

"Miss Hume, really," Dr. Davis said. "A man just died. Don't you think the administrator of the hospital may have a few responsibilities beyond you?"

"Then he had better be prepared to speak with me tomorrow."

Dr. Davis nodded. "I'm sure he will as soon as he is able." He picked up a piece of paper on his desk—the statement the policeman had taken from us—and perused it for a moment before rubbing his chin and looking at Elizabeth. "How did you happen to come here this evening?" He asked the question casually, as if the thought had just occurred to him and was of no import.

"I received a telephone call," she said.

"From whom?"

"I . . . don't know."

"What did the caller say?"

"That Robert had been accused of killing a man and was threatening to kill himself."

"Was it a man or woman?"

"A man."

"He didn't tell you his name?"

"No."

"You didn't recognize his voice?"

I leaned forward. "Why are you so interested in the caller?"

Dr. Davis turned his attention to me. "He may have information about the murder, of course."

From the way he was asking, I thought his concern might well be something else. Perhaps plugging a leak at the hospital?

"I don't know who phoned me," Elizabeth said. "Now you can answer a few questions for me. How would a patient be able to strangle a man? How would one get hold of a knife?"

"Miss Hume." Dr. Davis tried to smile, but it looked like he had a touch of dyspepsia. "We are just beginning to investigate, but you need to understand that unless this matter remains confidential, your cousin will likely spend the rest of his life in the state prison at Jackson. I don't think I need to tell you that that would destroy him. Our concern is for the good of the patient. Unless we are forced to do otherwise, Dr. Beckwith and the Eloise Hospital police will conduct the investigation and deal with the matter privately."

"Why are you so certain Robert is the killer?"

He squinted at her. "Are you jesting?"

She simply stared at him.

He shook his head, incredulous. "He was found holding the rope, standing over the dead man."

"Perhaps Robert was just the first to find him."

"He should have been sleeping in his ward. Why else would he have been there?"

"I don't know," she said. "Why don't we ask him?"

He sat back in his chair and scowled at her. "It sounds like you'd prefer us to report this to the authorities. I'm sure that can be arranged."

"No. That's not what I'm—"

"No? Then perhaps you could listen to what I'm saying. If Robert remains here, we can help him. If he is tried, he will go to prison and then we won't be able to help him. *If he remains here,* we can take the proper precautions to ensure he doesn't kill again and that no one hurts him. Do you understand now?"

Elizabeth glowered at him. Her face was turning red. I thought I'd better jump in before she said something she'd regret. "Dr. Davis, how can you deal with this privately? Not that I expect anything like honesty from the police, but they'll just forget about a murdered man?"

"Of course not, but you have to understand. In an enlightened society, the insane are not subject to the same rules as the rest of us. The policemen here are specially trained in the . . . peculiarities of enforcing the law in a place such as this."

"What about the dead man?" I asked. "What about his family?"

"He had no family. He will receive a funeral and be buried here, just as many other people who died of natural causes have been."

Elizabeth jumped in. "I'm sure you could get into a lot of trouble—

legal trouble—for not reporting a murder on your premises. Why would you be willing to do that? And I'm afraid," she added, "that 'the good of the patient' is not a reason I find sufficient."

"You would prefer that your cousin goes to prison."

"No." After thinking for a moment, she said, "Robert will be treated well?"

"Of course." He flashed a smile, in the way one does when concluding a discussion, and began to stand.

We did not. "You are the alienist in Robert's ward," Elizabeth said. "Is that correct?"

"We prefer the more modern term of 'psychiatrist.' But yes. One of them."

"Did you work with him?"

"Yes," Davis said. "I've known Mr. Clarke for some years."

"Do you think he would murder someone?"

He gave her a cold smile. "You'd be surprised at what people will do."

"What can you tell us about the man who was killed?"

"I don't suppose I should tell you anything. He was a patient here. Would you like me telling everyone about your cousin?"

Elizabeth ignored his question. "Were he and Robert acquainted, or was this a random act?"

"I don't know," Davis said. "I seldom see patients except for treatment."

I could see Elizabeth was getting irritated with his obfuscation, so I cut in. "If you can't discuss the patients, perhaps you can discuss the Opera Ghost, otherwise known as the Phantom."

He rolled his eyes again. "Ravings," he muttered. "It's all I hear now. The Phantom this and the Opera Ghost that."

"I don't understand," I said.

"The Phantom is a character in some ridiculous book the advanced patients read," Davis said. "Where Morgan gets his ideas for books from, I don't know. Stirring up the patients like this . . ."

"Morgan?"

"Our English teacher. Now, if you will excuse me." He stood. "I still have a great deal to do tonight."

I pushed myself to my feet and was reminded of the lump on my head. Elizabeth stayed where she was. Davis walked around the desk to the door. Opening it, he turned back to us. "Please, follow me."

Still seated, Elizabeth said, "I'd like to see Robert."

"I'm afraid that won't be possible."

"Please, Dr. Davis."

"I'm sorry, Miss Hume. He is in no condition to accept visitors."

I looked down at Elizabeth and nodded toward the door. There was nothing else to be gained by our remaining here. She sighed and stood, and we followed Dr. Davis out of the room and into the hallway. A Negro man in crisp white trousers and shirt carried a stack of bedding past us. The place was very subdued now, with only a few staff members visible.

Davis led us down the hallway in silence, guiding us through the building to the main entry, where he unlocked and opened one of the heavy wooden doors. We descended the stairs and headed up the sidewalk toward the gate. My head throbbed, which held my attention, but not so much that I couldn't see Elizabeth shivering. I wrapped my good arm around her, and she snuggled in closer. The night seemed very different than when we came here—colder and more frightening.

"Tell me, Dr. Davis," I said. "What will happen to Robert?"

"He will receive treatment," Davis said over his shoulder, "humane treatment—and will be isolated until he is able to commune with the other patients." Picking up his pace, he added, "Should that day come."

"You're saying he may have to spend the rest of his life in solitary confinement?" I asked.

"I'm sure that won't be necessary. Mr. Clarke should respond to treatment."

"I'm coming back tomorrow to see him," Elizabeth said.

Davis made no comment, just continued on toward the gate. He clearly wanted to be rid of us.

"Tell me this, Dr. Davis," I said. "Why would people here say this was the fourth man killed? That number didn't come out of thin air."

"Over time, men are released. The paranoids, who are numerous, are always certain they've been murdered."

"*You're* certain they were released?"

He stopped and turned back to me. "Are you one of the paranoids?"

I laughed at him. "I don't think it takes a paranoid to find this entire situation disturbing."

Dr. Davis continued on to the gate in silence. The guard who'd let us in unlocked and opened it, and we walked out.

"Good night," Davis said. Out of courtesy we wished him the same before continuing to my car, which was parked at the curb across the road, in front of the little lake.

I got the car started, and we climbed in. After negotiating a U-turn, I headed east on Michigan Avenue. "So." I glanced over at Elizabeth. "What do you think?"

She was looking at the lake, glowing in the moonlight. "Dr. Davis was very interested in discovering who had phoned me," she said. "I think they're more interested in their security breach than really investigating the murder."

"I don't understand how the administration can overlook a murder, no matter how Davis defended it."

She shrugged and shook her head. "They seem to have no doubt that Robert is the killer. Yet they want to keep him from a life sentence in the state prison . . ." Looking down at her hands folded in her lap, she said, "I just can't see how they could keep this from going to court."

"Have you ever heard of that book?"

"*The Phantom of the Opera*?" Elizabeth asked. "No."

"Neither had I. We'll have to look into it." I glanced over at her. "Do you think Robert could have killed four people?"

"I can't believe he would kill anyone. But I've never really known him. He's been stuck in that place for more than twenty-five years. That could drive anyone to murder."

I nodded, remembering what I'd wanted to ask her. "Was Francis the one who phoned you?"

"Yes!" she exclaimed. "I meant to tell you. I'm nearly positive."

"He must be a friend of Robert's."

"And being Beckwith's son, he would likely have had access to a telephone," she said.

"So you're going back tomorrow?"

"Yes." She looked away, pursing her lips, then met my eyes again. "Would you come with me?"

"Of course I will."

"Your father won't mind if you miss work?"

"I doubt it," I said. "I don't think he's used to me being back at the factory yet. He still wants me to spend a couple of months in New York taking the rest cure for my supposed neurasthenia."

"Glen Springs does sound lovely," Elizabeth said. "Perhaps one of these days . . ."

I reached over and took her hand. "It would be nice to get away together sometime. Far away."

She nodded.

"In many ways," I said, "this has been the worst year of my life. I began it in jail, and since then, I've been threatened by gangsters, tricked by a con man, seen men murdered, and, Lord, even killed two more people. Even with all that horror, it's been a good year. I got you back." I raised her hand to my lips and kissed the back of it.

She was quiet for a long while. I looked over at her and saw she was crying.

"Are you all right?" I asked.

"We can't escape," she said in a miserable voice.

"One day we will, honey. We'll be able to get away for a nice—"

"That's not what I mean, Will. It's the goddamned tragedy. Every day. Everywhere we go. Everything that has happened to us since I can remember. It's all been tragedy." She looked at me, tears trickling down her cheeks. "What did I do to deserve this?"

*That's easy,* I thought. *You loved me.*

# CHAPTER TWO

*Wednesday, August 7, 1912*

## Elizabeth

My mother was becoming increasingly worrisome. Since I'd won her release from Eloise Hospital last year, I'd seen more merit to my Uncle Peter's claims regarding her mental state. She was not, as he had said, out of her mind, but her forgetfulness had progressed from the occasional loss of a house key to the loss of hours, sometimes days.

I had been trying to keep this from Will. What with the Gianollas, Adamos, and Bernsteins, he'd been plenty busy with gangsters, though, to be fair, so had I. My plan had been to let him in on the secret slowly.

Very frankly, my concern was for more than my mother. I didn't know if I wanted to marry Will, or anyone, and I didn't know his feelings on the subject at the moment either. If we did stay together, I didn't want Will to consider the possibility that his golden years would be spent as my caretaker. My mother's problem was hereditary, unless it was a terrible coincidence that she suffered from exactly the same malady her mother had.

Besides, my own mental state was already far from stable.

No matter how I wanted to introduce Will to the subject of the

Hume women's insanity, the option was wrested from me when he entered our kitchen that morning.

My mother and I were having breakfast, sitting across from each other at the kitchen table. Her hair was still a rich auburn like mine, but her face gave away her secret. In the morning light she looked pale and drawn, with deep furrows on her forehead, at the sides of her eyes, and around her nose and mouth. I remembered her skin as pink and healthy, not the pale yellow I saw before me. Her eyes had been a rich chocolate brown, not the flat brown of a mud puddle. I wasn't sure whether it was my imagination or she really was fading away. These days, on the few occasions she went out, I'd noticed she'd taken to wearing makeup. This morning her face was naked. She was fifty-seven going on eighty.

The bell rang, and I heard Will at the door, discussing his facial hair with Alberts.

Lord. With his scraggly beard and mustache, Will looked like a hobo; a handsome hobo, I must admit, but a hobo nonetheless. Of course, I would never bruise his ego by sharing that opinion with him. I would stick it out until he decided it wasn't working. He would reach that point. Eventually.

When he walked into the kitchen, his eyes focused on my coffee cup. I pushed my chair back to get him one.

"Sit," he said, gesturing for me to stay where I was. "I'll get it."

Mother turned and saw him, and her face lit up. "Why, there you are, Reginald. It's about time you woke up."

Will stared at her in confusion, then glanced at me. I took her hand. "It's Will, Mother."

She frowned at me. "Don't you think I know my own husband? Why, I . . ." She looked at Will again, and her jaw dropped. Finally she turned away and muttered, "It must be the light." She stood and swept out of the room without another word.

My father had been dead for almost two years. Will's eyes followed her from the room.

"I'm trying to get her to see a doctor," I said, "but she's too embarrassed."

He poured himself a cup of coffee and sat down next to me. "Will she be okay without you today?"

"I'll ask Alberts to watch her closely while I'm gone. We need to go back to Eloise."

He yawned and rubbed the sleep from his eyes. "And I need a nap. That was a late night."

"I'll speak with Alberts. Take a nap while you wait."

"If it's all the same to you, I'll drink all your coffee instead."

I patted his shoulder. "You do that. I'll be right back."

Alberts was polishing the china in the dining room. I told him what had happened. His mouth tightened, but he just nodded and said he would keep a close eye on Mother today. A few weeks ago she had wandered out of the house while she was in one of her states. We hadn't even known she was gone until a boy rang the bell and said the fishmonger two blocks down had recognized my mother and was entertaining her until we could get there.

I ran up to my bedroom and searched through my closet for the green wide-brimmed hat that matched my dress. When I found it, I settled it onto my much-too-short hair and pinned it in place. I wasn't happy about leaving my mother to her own devices today, but no one else would speak for Robert.

We drove off toward Eloise Hospital again in the brilliant light of a new morning. "The more I think about last night," I told Will, "the more I wonder about Dr. Davis. He gave me the impression he would say anything to get us to leave and drop this matter."

Will glanced over at me. "What we don't know is if he was doing Beckwith's bidding, or if it was on his own."

I shook my head. "I can understand Dr. Beckwith wanting to save his job, but wouldn't any decent person contact the authorities?"

"I don't know, Elizabeth. Men have done frightful things to protect their careers."

"What if Robert didn't kill that man? All we know for certain is that the police had him cornered in that office."

"And that he had a knife."

I turned in the seat to look at him. "But it wasn't the murder weapon, which also makes me wonder. If he had a knife, wouldn't it have been easier to stab the man than to strangle him?"

"Seems that way. Then again, we're not crazy." Will pulled up to a line of vehicles trying to turn left onto Michigan Avenue. Smoke from exhaust pipes filled the air with its wretched odor. "Maybe he can't stand the sight of blood."

I could barely hear him over the sound of car horns. "Yes, it's possible," I said, perhaps a bit too testily. Will didn't normally play devil's advocate with me. "But did you even see a rope?"

He raised his eyebrows and shrugged. "No, but it could have been in the room with the murdered man, or anywhere else, really. The cops might have taken it before we got there."

"Perhaps. But what if someone else strangled the man and framed Robert? The killer could have given him the knife and set the authorities on him."

"At least we already know who the killer is," he said.

Sarcasm. Now we were back on familiar ground. "The Phantom?"

He nodded. The wagon ahead of us moved twenty feet, and he nudged the car forward. We were sixth in line for a left turn onto Michigan Avenue. I hoped we had "courageous" (in Detroit, that means suicidal) drivers in front of us. The honking went on unabated. It was the only sound one could count on in the city these days.

"One of us needs to read that book," I said.

"Sounds like a good project for you," he shot back.

I looked at him from under a raised eyebrow. "Afraid if you read something other than *The Horseless Age* you might expand your mind?"

He gingerly placed his hand on top of his head. "I'm not sure how much expanding it can take at this time."

I didn't deliver the sympathy he'd been fishing for. "Yes, I'd hate for you to fill up all that empty space."

"Kind of you," he muttered.

The first car in line, a sturdy Hudson roadster, shot out into the intersection, cutting off a Model T trying to go straight through on Michigan. I nearly cheered.

Getting back to the subject at hand, I said, "If Francis Beckwith was correct, three other men were murdered the same way. If that's true, his father isn't covering up because he's afraid for his job. He's covering up because he's involved somehow."

"It could be," Will replied, "but it certainly seems unlikely."

"Let's see what Robert has to say about it."

The car at the front of the line, an elderly curved-dash Olds, puttered forward about two feet before the driver slammed on his brakes, letting a stream of cars pass by on Michigan.

This time Will joined the honkers.


In my mind, Eloise Hospital was a house of horrors, and nothing I'd seen last night changed my opinion. It had been a very long time since I'd come here with my mother, but my memories were of gibbering men and women being led around like animals, and children holding on to the bars of the fence near Michigan Avenue, shouting at the carriages traveling past.

And by my own memories of insanity.

I was surprised at my impression as we drove up. The asylum didn't look nearly so frightening in the light of day, other than the fence that surrounded the complex, made of heavy wire bound together in squares, topped with four rows of barbed wire. Behind it, three huge redbrick structures dominated my view.

I pointed out the first one, a rather ordinary three-story, to Will as we drove past. "That's the Administration Building. That's where we'll likely find the good Dr. Beckwith."

Just past it, also in front, sat the main asylum, known here as Building B, where we'd spent two horrifying hours the night before. It was a sprawling structure with twin cupolas and a grand entry. In front along with them, but farther ahead, was the County House, the residence of Wayne County's indigent.

"This place is gigantic," Will said. "I can't believe the scope."

I nodded. Perhaps twenty individual structures stood inside the fence: off in the distance, a farm with pigs, cows, and fowl, and then closer, a smaller building I thought to be a bakery, and another that looked like an electrical dynamo, with black smoke billowing out the smokestack. To the left and right were warehouses and redbrick buildings ranging from house sized to huge three-story structures. In the back corner of the grounds stood a long, low building painted white.

It all looked empty. "It's like a ghost town," I said.

An ice truck rolled down one of the streets, and steam leaked from a freight train parked by what I assumed to be the food stores, but other than a few men working at the farm, only two people were in sight. It seemed odd. On a beautiful morning such as this, what could be more rejuvenating than the outdoors?

Contrasting with the grounds was an area farther up Michigan Avenue, with men, women, and children moving about a variety of businesses, including a restaurant and an inn.

When Will and I walked up to the gate, I felt a bit of hope that we would be able to clear Robert of this murder. Will had proven himself to be skilled, or at least effective due to his doggedness, at solving these sorts of puzzles. I have to admit, however, that I was concerned about bringing him into another mess. After all his troubles the past two years, he deserved a respite. Not only that, he tends, as they say of unskilled boxers, to "lead with his chin." He'd almost gotten himself killed many times over while sorting out his own troubles. He didn't need any help from me. All that said, I had to help Robert, and I didn't think I could do it by myself.

A guard who looked sixteen years old and couldn't have been more than twenty stood on the other side of the gate. He wore a green wool uniform and cap.

"We're here to see Robert Clarke," Will said.

"And you are?" the guard replied.

Will gave him our names. After the guard eyed us for a moment, he said, "Wait here," and walked over to the end of the gate, where a small guardhouse stood. He went inside and picked up a telephone.

"Where did he think we'd wait?" Will muttered. "In the lake?"

"You've been doing a great deal of muttering lately, you know," I said.

He frowned at me. "I'm sorry, Mother."

"You should watch that," I said. "Mumblers are generally overlooked by the ladies." *As are men with facial hair that makes them look like tramps,* I thought.

"Wait," Will said. "Am I a mumbler or a mutterer?"

Not having a sufficiently witty rejoinder, I didn't answer. Instead, I sneaked a glance at him. When we first met, he had been a little gawky, all legs, and handsome in a young-boy way, but now he was a man. He had grown into his body, and his face was strong and intelligent. I was surprised to see how often other men were intimidated by Will. I didn't think he saw it at all. To me, his eyes, large and brown, were always the giveaway. When he looked at me, I saw the love in them and caught a glimpse into his soul, into his innate strength of character. When he was hurt, which was often, I saw the pain. I always, even at his worst, saw his decency and his desire to do right.

The guard finally ambled back to the gate and said, "Mr. Clarke is to have no visitors today."

I could see Will readying a retort, so I put my hand on his shoulder to get his attention, then took a half step closer to the gate. "Please, sir," I said, giving the young man my best smile. I'm not usually one to use my "feminine wiles," but I'm willing to make exceptions for good causes. "He's my cousin. Could we just pop in for a minute?"

He looked a little dazed but did nothing other than shake his head.

I kept the honey in my voice. "Could we please speak with Dr. Beckwith, then?"

The guard eyed me in a way that was much too familiar. I wanted to slap him, but not only was I trying to wheedle a favor, the wrought-iron bars of the gate were in the way. Finally he said, "Do you have an appointment?"

I can't believe I actually did this, but I batted my eyes. "We don't, but we only need five minutes. I promise."

He nervously cleared his throat but didn't bend. "You have to make an appointment."

"Then we'll see Dr. Davis."

"Do you have an appointment?"

*Of course we don't, you idiot,* I wanted to say. *He is the third person we've asked for.* Instead, I said, "He told me he would be available today."

"You need an appointment."

"Could you check? Please?"

He smiled, showing us a mouthful of crooked teeth. "I'd like to help you out, sweetheart. Say you lose this guy"—he nodded toward Will—"and come back around five."

Will took hold of the gate with his good hand. "Hey," he said, then called the boy a name that I will leave to the imagination.

The guard stiffened and slowly shifted his attention to Will.

"Didn't anyone ever teach you how to talk to a lady?"

"Will, please," I said. "Don't. I'll make an appointment. Come on."

I tugged at his arm, but he was still staring at the guard, who just stood there, watching Will with an insolent smile. He was on that side, and we were on this side, and, as far as he was concerned, all was right with the world. Eventually Will let me pull him away from the gate.

Glancing over his shoulder at the guard, Will called him another name. The guard gave him a hearty wave.

"What do you say we go see your attorney for some advice?" I asked.

"An excellent idea," Will muttered.

The time commitment to this problem was beginning to worry me. Only a week before I'd told Clara Arthur, the president of the Michigan Equal Suffrage Association, that I would serve as the interim president of the Detroit Suffrage Club. A constitutional amendment was on the ballot this November to legalize woman suffrage in the state, and Detroit was a key component of that. My predecessor had been forced to quit unexpectedly when her husband decided they were moving to, of all places, Alaska.

However, work was one thing, and family was quite another. I would phone Mrs. Arthur with the bad news as soon as I got a chance.

Will turned right from Michigan onto Woodward and rolled down the street at five miles per hour looking for a parking space near the Hammond Building. Now midday, it had warmed into the eighties, and I wished I had worn a cooler outfit: a skirt and shirtwaist, perhaps, rather than the heavy cotton day dress I'd chosen. Will was more appropriately clothed for the day in a lightweight brown suit. I still couldn't get over how fit he looked. He had maintained his exercise regimen and built up a great deal of muscle, and since he quit drinking he had lost the bloating and discoloration caused by his heavy alcohol use. Probably as beneficial to his psyche was all the stretching and exercise he did with his right hand, which had recovered to the extent that he could pull a glove on his left. He was much less self-conscious about it now that he could wear a pair of gloves, rather than only one.

A wagon pulled out from a spot across the street, and Will swung his Model T Torpedo around in a wide U-turn, setting off the blaring of half a dozen automobile horns. He executed a perfect parallel park between a gray Model T and a black Packard.

"Nicely done, sir," I said.

He tipped his derby. I climbed out onto the sidewalk next to Campus Martius Park, and he followed me. We walked around to the front of the automobile and began looking for an opening in the traffic. Will glanced at the Torpedo, and he smiled, just a little.

"You love this automobile, don't you?" I said.

He shrugged. "It's fun to drive."

I arched my eyebrows. "I just don't like to think I'm competing with a pile of metal for your attention."

He leaned in close to me. "Nothing could compete with you."

I'd been joking with him, of course, and I didn't doubt his love for me. Still, the words combined with the look in his eyes made me flush. "Thank you." He leaned closer still and kissed me on the cheek.

A small gap appeared in the traffic. I lifted my dress, and we darted out into the road. The unfashionably low heels of my shoes let me stay ahead of Will. We made it, though just barely. The number of vehicles on the roads was staggering. Automobiles, trucks, wagons, coaches, horses, and streetcars fought each other for the right-of-way. The streetcars were the only sure winners, with bicyclists and pedestrians dodging between and around them. It was no surprise that numerous traffic accidents were reported in the newspapers every day.

The elevator man took us to the tenth floor. Though the Hammond had been eclipsed by many larger buildings, it was still one of Detroit's finest, with marble floors and wainscoting, and oak trim throughout. The door opened on the penthouse directly in front of a polished mahogany desk, behind which a young woman sat. She was pretty enough but awfully skinny. On the wall a sign in some exotic striped wood read PETERSON, VANVLIET, AND SUTTON. The young woman called a secretary, who, after a short wait, escorted us to Mr. Sutton's office, which was at the front of the building on a corner.

I greeted Mr. Sutton, a vital man with dark hair and piercing brown eyes, and stepped aside for Will to speak with him. Mr. Sutton immediately commented on Will's beard and mustache, and, as men are wont to do, they leapt into a discussion about the relative merits of various types of facial hair. (One more reason to hope Will shaved soon.) I tried not to listen.

A large set of windows behind Mr. Sutton's desk looked out over

Campus Martius Park, and I walked to the window and looked out at the lovely view. In the park were the Merrill Fountain and the Soldiers and Sailors Monument. Beyond them loomed the sturdy Detroit Opera House and the Pontchartrain Hotel, one of the city's finest. All around them were businesses: billiard halls, shops, vaudeville and moving picture houses, restaurants, and saloons. Scuttling past were the standard array of motor and horse-drawn vehicles, along with the Baker and Woodward Line streetcars.

Behind me, Will and Mr. Sutton continued discussing facial hair. When I first met Will's attorney a couple of years ago, he had long, fuzzy muttonchop whiskers that aged him at least ten years beyond the forty I guessed him to be. Now he wore economical sideburns and a trim mustache.

The men joined me at the window. "Impressive view, isn't it?" Mr. Sutton asked. "Although I have to say that, for me, the bloom is off the rose. All that changes nowadays are the billboards. I already get enough advertising thrown at me."

He was certainly right about that. Above the buildings soared the electric billboards for Goodyear and Diamond Tires, and Kellogg's Breakfast Biscuits. Every side wall that could be seen from the road or a building was covered in advertisements, among them Occident Flour, Benedictine Cordial, Sim Ko and RaJah Coffee, and Chalmers automobiles.

He rubbed his hands together. "So, what can I do for you today?" He gestured toward a pair of red leather club chairs in front of his desk, which was devoid of any objects other than a telephone and a family photograph: Mr. Sutton some years back with his wife and two small children.

We sat, and I explained to him what had happened with Robert. Will filled in, and then we answered Sutton's questions as best we could. Once he understood the situation, he began pacing the room. "First of all, let's talk about access to the patient. They don't have to let anyone see Mr. Clarke, not even his guardian. They can deem it too dangerous for the other person or the patient. If they do let the guardian in, they don't have to let anyone else see him."

"Can we get him out?" I asked.

He stopped and put a finger to his chin. "Unlikely. Even if your mother asked for his release or transfer, the hospital doesn't have to allow it, and under the circumstances you've described almost certainly won't. If Mr. Clarke has been deemed legally insane, the hospital essentially can do with him as they like."

"What if we got the police involved?" I asked.

He raised his eyebrows. "I thought you said they were."

"Yes, but it's Eloise's police force. I'm talking about going to Detective Riordan."

Mr. Sutton looked down at the carpet, then back at me. "You may be able to get Robert moved, although it seems to me the likely place he'll end up is the state prison. What you've described to me is first degree murder, and it doesn't sound like the police are interested in looking for any other suspects."

I took a deep breath. It all seemed so hopeless. "What can we do for him?"

Mr. Sutton sat on the edge of his desk. "Do you believe he's guilty?"

Will and I glanced at each other. "I . . . I don't know," I said. "Based on what they said at Eloise, yes. But from what I know of Robert, no. He's no killer."

"From a legal perspective," Mr. Sutton said, "we can ask a judge to release or transfer him, but it will certainly invite the administration of the hospital to turn him over to the authorities. My advice would be to have your mother ask, quietly, for Robert's release. If they refuse, your options are limited."

I blew out an exasperated breath. "You believe that anything we do is likely to get him thrown into jail and eventually prison?"

"If they won't let your mother take custody."

"Which they won't."

Mr. Sutton shrugged. "Wish I had better news for you."

When we got back to my house, I phoned the Michigan Equal Suffrage Association and broke the news to Mrs. Arthur. She was surprisingly sympathetic, even though I told her only that I was having a family problem, the specifics of which I could not discuss. She said they had interviewed another satisfactory candidate prior to "hiring" me. (Is starting a volunteer job the same as being hired?) She was disappointed but asked me to let her know if my situation changed. I assured her I would.

I left Will in the kitchen, climbed the stairs, and walked down the hall to my mother's bedroom. The door was cracked open. I knocked. When she didn't reply, I peeked in to see that she was sitting in the rocker in the corner. The lights were off and the curtains drawn, making the room, normally bright and cheerful, into a murky gray cell. My heart went out to her.

I remembered sitting on her lap in that very chair when I was a child. She would tell me stories, stories she made up on the spot, about ship captains sailing to China or explorers crossing the deserts of Africa. I would sit with my arms around her neck and nuzzle into her, breathing in her smell, a soothing blend of wool and Narcissus toilet water. The stories always seemed to end with a moral of persistence: If you never give up, you will prevail.

I walked in and stood near her. "Mother, would you join Will and me for lunch? We need to discuss something."

Her eyes cut to me, suspicious. "What?"

"Robert. He's in some trouble."

"At Eloise?"

"Yes."

"And you want to talk to me about him?" she asked.

"Yes." I understood her suspicions. When my mother had been released after her monthlong stay in Eloise, she refused to discuss the hospital or anything that had happened to her. With her current confusion, I was sure she suspected a return was in her future.

"Mother." I knelt down in front of her and took her hand. "I want you to know that you have nothing to worry about. No matter what happens, I would never send you away. I'll live with you for as long as you'll let me."

Her face softened. "You can't give up your life for me."

"I won't be giving up anything. You're my mother, and I'm going to take care of you."

She stood and hugged me. "Thank you. I'm just so . . . frightened. The world is starting to slip away."

I squeezed her tight but had nothing to say in return. My concern was the same: How long would the person I knew as my mother continue to exist?

Arm in arm, we padded down the stairs and into the kitchen, where Will had put a kettle on and was now sitting at the table. The sunlight pouring in through the windows was amplified by the white cabinets, walls, and countertops to a level that, after being in my mother's darkened bedroom, seemed somehow obscene, baring every detail.

Will stood. "Good afternoon, Mrs. Hume."

"Hello, Will," my mother said with a jaunty air that she clearly forced.

"Please, Mother," I said. "Sit. Will is involved in this as well."

Mother's eyes cut to me. "Why? He isn't Will's concern."

"Mrs. Hume," Will said, "any problem of Elizabeth's is a problem of mine as well. I want to help."

"You don't understand." She settled into a chair. "This is a family matter."

"Then help me understand."

The kettle started to whistle, and I lifted it off the burner and poured the water into the pot while Will walked over to my mother and set his hand on her shoulder. "I want to help," he said. I took three teaspoons from the cutlery drawer.

"Oh, my goodness." Mother drew a deep breath and sighed. Glancing at me, she said, "And I suppose you want *me* to tell him?"

"What?" I was so startled I dropped the teaspoons, and they clattered onto the counter. "No, no. We just need you to help us with something."

I could feel Will looking at me. I didn't meet his eyes. Instead, I hurried to say, "Here, let me get the soup and bread, and we can have a nice lunch first."

He let it drop, but I knew as soon as we were alone I would have to tell him.

Will and my mother made small talk while I heated the chicken noodle soup I had made the previous day, cut three thick slices of bread and buttered them, and poured us all glasses of milk. While we ate, Will and I explained the situation and what Mr. Sutton had told us to do. My mother was reticent, I believe from her lack of confidence in her abilities, but agreed to speak with Dr. Beckwith and try to win Robert's release.

After lunch, she sat at my father's old desk and phoned the hospital. I stood next to her, and Will sat in one of the chairs opposite the desk. She asked the operator for the number and waited while she was connected and the phone was answered.

"Yes, I'd like to speak with Dr. Beckwith, please," she said.

After a short pause, "Regarding Robert Clarke."

A few seconds later, I heard a muffled voice through the phone's receiver, and her eyebrows knit in concentration. "Rebecca Hume," she said. "Is this Dr. Beckwith?"

She bit her lip as she listened to the man speak. "When, exactly, do you think he will be available?"

A moment later, she put her hand over the mouthpiece and looked up at me. "He says Dr. Beckwith will be out of the office for a few days."

I glanced at Will, who was frowning, then said, "All right. Just leave a message for him to return the call."

She did and hung up before looking at me again. "Was that all right?"

Giving her shoulder a gentle squeeze, I said, "Perfect."

"Sounded like a dodge to me," Will said. "What next?"

"I think we should go see our old friend Detective Riordan," I replied.

We sat with my mother for a time before leaving. Her spirits were higher, and she seemed to be in full control of her faculties. I reminded her that I'd promised Will's parents I'd have dinner with them that evening and asked if she wanted me to cancel. She said no, thank you; she would be just fine without me. I assured her that I would come home immediately after dinner and, feeling some trepidation, informed Alberts about our plan for the rest of the day. I asked him to phone Will's parents if he needed to get a message to me.

That finished, we headed out to the automobile. Will started it and climbed in, and I followed him onto the seat. Before he had a chance to bring it up, I said, "I know. I owe you an explanation . . . but . . . I don't . . ." My eyes welled up.

He took my hand. "What is it, honey? You know you can tell me anything."

"I know." Tears spilled out and ran down my cheeks. I looked back toward the house and saw my mother peering at us around one of the parlor curtains. "Drive," I said. "Let's go."

He pulled out onto Jefferson heading east, away from downtown, and said, "Why don't we stop somewhere before we see Detective Riordan?"

Unsure of my voice, I nodded.

At Grand Boulevard, he turned right, past Electric Park and across the Belle Isle Bridge. He continued past the casino's jammed parking lot to a wooded spot along the river to our right and little Lake Tacoma to our left. I could see in Will's face how shaken he was. He knew something between us was going to change. Pulling onto the shoulder, he shut off the ignition and nudged me. "Let's go down to the river."

He got a blanket from the backseat and took my hand. On the lake, men paddled canoes. On the banks, lovers sat close together or lay on their backs watching clouds go by. We went the other way.

My head was heavy as Will led me down a thin animal trail to the shore. After he laid out the blanket, we sat and looked at the water and, beyond, the city of Windsor. I didn't want to say anything, but he was silent, waiting for me to speak.

"Robert is two years older than me," I finally said. "When I was little, my mother and I would take the train to Eloise once a month. In the days before we went, I could feel the tension build in the house. My father didn't want us to go. My mother got more and more nervous as the time got closer. When we were there, she tried to make the best of it. We'd often take Robert on walks around the grounds. One Sunday afternoon they had a concert, and we took him to that."

"So what happened?"

I coughed out a little laugh. *My life had been turned upside down.* "Well, among other things," I said, "I learned that Robert wasn't my cousin."

Will scooted closer and put his arm around me. "Do you want to talk about it?"

I picked a long blade of grass and began twirling the stem between my fingers. "It was a beautiful day. I remember that. Sunny, brilliant blue sky. We were at the amusement hall, watching a brass band play onstage."

"How old were you?"

"Eight." I didn't even have to think about it. "I was eight. Robert hated the music. It was too loud for him. He hates loud noises. He covered his ears and hunched down in his seat for the entire concert. I stopped paying attention to him. Especially when the band played their last number." I smiled as I remembered. "They introduced a new song by John Philip Sousa: 'Stars and Stripes Forever.' I can still see it. Shifting my head from side to side to see the band around all the hats. There had to be two hundred people there. When the band finished, we all stood and clapped. Then my mother leaned down to me and said, 'Where is Robert?' I glanced to my right and saw an empty seat."

I turned to Will. "He had been right there. Mother asked me again where he was. Her voice sounded funny, tight and nervous. Even though everyone around me was standing and applauding, I had the sensation of being the center of attention." I dropped the piece of grass and brought my hands up to my cheeks. "My face got so hot. I didn't know where he'd gone. Mother shouted at me that she'd told me to watch him. I told her that I had been watching him—and I was. Somehow he slipped away."

I paused. "We started searching for him. She told me to go around to the right, and she went to the left. I felt absolute panic. But . . . I didn't really want to find him. I knew if Robert didn't turn up, I wouldn't have to go back to that dreadful place."

I looked down at my lap, and a tear dripped onto my dress, leaving a dark circle. Will held his handkerchief out to me. I took it, crumpled it in my hand, and looked out at the water. I didn't see the river, though. I saw Eloise.

"I walked to the back of the hall and down the stairs. When I reached the bottom, I thought I heard a door close below me, but I didn't think anything of it. I was sure Robert would have run out of the building, maybe toward the lake. I hurried outside to look for him."

I shivered and fell silent. Will waited for me to continue. Finally I did. "He wasn't down by the lake. I started crying with frustration. I thought he'd drowned, and I knew it was my fault."

Another tear slipped down my cheek. "A few minutes later, Mother ran across the pavement and shouted at me. 'Elizabeth! What are you doing?'

"'I'm looking for him,' I said.

"'Oh, my God,' Mother moaned. She spun around in a circle, looking in every direction but not seeming to really see anything. She grabbed hold of my shoulders and bent down into my face. She was hurting me. 'Elizabeth,' she said. 'We can't lose your brother.'"

"Oh, my Lord," Will whispered.

"I stared at her, too stunned to say anything." I was crying hard now and choked down a sob. "I told her Robert was my cousin. Mother looked back at me, as if surprised I was still there. 'No, he's not,' she said and told me to wait there while she got the police. I watched her run off toward the asylum buildings, and then I walked down the shoreline, looking into the water, thinking about Robert."

"He's really your brother?" Will asked.

"Yes. My father wouldn't hear of keeping a 'defective' child, of course, so they packed him away and told me he was Aunt Theodora's son. I wondered, did that mean Aunt Theodora was my mother? But even then I knew. Mother looked at Robert the same way she looked at me: with the love of a mother toward her child." I let out a long sigh.

I must have been quiet for a while, because Will prompted me. "What happened after your mother went for the police?"

"I thought about hearing the door close. I walked back up to the amusement hall and went downstairs."

I stopped.

I couldn't tell Will what had happened in that basement. Ever.

"Was Robert there?" Will finally asked.

"Yes." I looked away from him. "We got out together."

"How did you find him?"

"He found me and brought *me* out." I brushed off my hands and started to stand. "We should be going."

"Elizabeth." Will took my hand and kept me there. "What aren't you telling me?"

"Nothing," I said, annoyance creeping into my voice. "He found me, and we left."

"All right. But just know that I'll listen whenever you want to talk about it."

I climbed to my feet and started back to the automobile. "There's nothing to tell. He was in the basement. The reason I'm so emotional is because Robbie is my goddamned brother, not my cousin. My parents lied to me, and I lied to you."

I couldn't help myself from bursting into tears again. Damn this being a woman.

Will drove over the bridge and continued up Grand Boulevard, bound for the Bethune Street police station. I had tried so long to forget this, but now I couldn't get the image out of my mind. I had been only eight years old. I was only eight when I discovered I was insane, certainly crazier than Robert. That knowledge had been with me every day. Every day I tried to hide my thoughts, never completely certain what was real and what was imagined. I'd never had a doubt that, as soon as it was discovered, I would be sent to live at Eloise, the most frightening place on earth.

When my mother ran off that day to get the police, I returned to the amusement hall and walked into the little lobby. Everyone was gone. Though the lights were all off now, the room was lit well enough by the windows that I had no problem seeing. The sign over the double doors straight ahead read STOREROOM. I tried the doors: locked. I turned and looked back. My options were to climb the stairs to the amusement hall or try the basement. He hadn't been upstairs, and I doubted he had returned.

The door to the basement was just inside the entrance. I tiptoed to it and turned the knob. It opened with a creak, so high-pitched as to be almost silent. I peered down the steps. They were unlit, but somewhere down there a light was on. The last few stairs and landing were yellow-tinged black, foggy outlines in the gloom.

I was so frightened. I called his name, but it just echoed back to me. I took a hesitant step onto the first stair and then the second. The leather soles of my shoes made no more than a little scraping sound against the cement, but each step sounded like the drumming of a snare. Another step and another, and finally I was on the landing.

A single gas lamp on the wall near the stairs provided the only light in the cavernous room, barely enough for me to see silhouettes of musical instruments and dozens of old theatrical set pieces strewn across the floor.

"R-Robert?"

Nothing.

I leaned over the railing and looked below me. The stairs went down another level, also dimly lit. I bucked up my courage and started down the stairs again, creeping from step to step. At the bottom, I peered into the blackness, trying to listen while my heart thundered in my ears. A faint glimmer, like the moon on a cloudy night, glowed at the other end of the room.

Something creaked, and I started. Someone was here.

"Robert?" I said again.

Still nothing.

I swallowed hard. Stretching as high as I could reach, I turned the valve on the gas lamp to light it fully. The room was still dim, but now I saw old wagons and horse tack, a battered tin trough, piles of fence posts . . . and on the other side of the room, where the light came from, a series of doors. The floor of the room was dirt, the wooden ceiling much lower than in the room above.

I stepped down from the cement landing onto the dirt floor and skulked across the room. The glow came from behind one of the doors. I crept up to it, my heart in my throat. It was cracked open, a stone caught between the door and the jamb.

Standing at the door, I said, "Rob—?" My voice caught in my throat.

No reply.

My mouth was so dry. I pushed the door open an inch and peeked in. The room was brightly lit. I saw nothing other than a wooden floor and the wall opposite me, perhaps twenty feet away. I opened the door a little farther and whispered Robert's name. No one answered.

I took a step inside and looked around the door.

What I saw took my breath away.

Hundreds, perhaps thousands, of trees stood before me, going on for miles. Every tree was perfect, tall and green-leafed.

I took a step into the room. The door swung shut with a bang, startling me. I spun around, frightened, but no one was there.

When I turned back to the forest, a girl looked at me from behind a tree. Another stared back at me from behind the next one. They looked frightened and angry. Behind every tree, a girl stood—hundreds of them, thousands.

I screamed.

They all screamed back.

I spun and grabbed the doorknob, twisting and pulling, but the door wouldn't open. Still screaming, I threw myself at it, battering my shoulder, my fists. Jerking on the knob, I looked back at the forest. The girls had disappeared, yet still they screamed in my ears.

The room swam before me, spinning in drunken circles. Then darkness.

Blessed darkness.


When I came to, I was lying on a bench in the gazebo near the amusement hall, my mother leaning over me, tears streaming down her face. She told me Robert had carried me out. I started to tell her what had happened, but even at eight years old I knew it was crazy. If I told her, she would leave me here with Robert. I kept my mouth shut. Though the doubt and fear stayed with me as my constant companions, I never told anyone.

And, to my everlasting shame, I never returned to visit my brother.

"Elizabeth?"

I turned and looked at Will.

"We're here."

Startled, I looked across the street at the Bethune Street police station and was brought back to the present.

It wasn't much to look at: a squat redbrick cube with a short marble stairway and a pair of white doors covered with scuff marks. Most of them looked to have been made by heels of shoes, and I could imagine men in custody who were not eager to enter the building. My ears roared with the sounds of Detroit: automobile horns and engines, people laughing and shouting, a piano, a curse.

I wiped my eyes one last time with Will's handkerchief, put on a smile, and started to climb out of the automobile.

Will took my hand and stopped me. "Lizzie?"

I glanced at him.

"We're going to get Robert out of this."

I looked down at my lap. "I can't tell you how guilty I feel. I've let him rot in that place. I don't know what I'll do if I can't help him."

"Listen to me." He lifted my chin and turned my face until I was looking into his eyes. "We'll get him out, Lizzie. I promise."

## Will

We climbed the station's steps and headed straight for the desk sergeant, who looked down from his throne behind the narrow desk separating him from the rabble. He was a florid Irishman, a type so common among police officers as to be a stereotype, with a bulbous nose and heavy ginger brows over a pockmarked face.

He smiled at Elizabeth as we approached. "Yes, miss? What can I do for you today?" Glancing behind her, he saw me and his face soured. He looked back to her and said hopefully, "Are you turning him in, then? Another murder, perhaps?"

She smiled back and replied, "No. That's in my plans for later this week, but I need a strong back today."

"I could supply that back for you, miss, and we could get him out of the way for a few years. Say, ten to twenty?"

"So kind of you." Out of sight of the desk sergeant, she reached back and patted my arm, surely to keep me from saying something stupid. "Thanks, but no. I would appreciate it, though, if you would ask Detective Riordan if we could have a moment of his time."

"Certainly, miss. Your wish is my command." He picked up his telephone's receiver and winked at her. "And I mean that."

I swallowed all the comments that occurred to me. We needed to speak with Detective Riordan, and this idiot stood between us and him.

We waited in the lobby among fifteen or so unfortunates, some mothers and wives waiting to speak with their imprisoned sons or husbands, others obviously waiting to report crimes, such as the old man with a three-inch cut leaking blood down the side of his head. Elizabeth was watching him. He didn't notice the droplets until they'd fallen behind his ear. Then he would scour that area with his handkerchief and sit, wincing, until the next one dribbled down.

She walked over to him and pulled out her handkerchief. "May I?"

After he'd appraised her for a moment, he nodded, and she laid her handkerchief along the cut line and then placed his hand over it and pressed it against the wound. "There. Keep pressure on it, and it will stop bleeding soon."

"Thank you, miss," he said. I thought for the hundredth time that Elizabeth would be a wonderful nurse. She'd volunteered for years at the McGregor Mission and had relayed to me stories of bandaging, splinting, and even of a few times stitching up wounds.

I stood when I saw Detective Riordan walk out of the back hallway and move toward her. "Good afternoon, Miss Hume," he said to her back.

She turned around with a smile. She'd recognized his voice. "Good afternoon, Detective."

He wore a dark suit but was without the fedora that normally hung low over his brow. His ever-present cigar smoldered in the left side of his mouth. I wondered if he had smoked cigars prior to his face being slashed, or if he had picked up the habit simply to try to mask the scar that ran from the side of his mouth to his ear.

I joined them, and we greeted each other. Even though we had come to terms earlier this year, Detective Riordan eyed me as warily as I did him. I suppose it was to be expected, given that I had nearly gotten him fired and he had come within a cat's whisker of getting me convicted of first degree murder.

"What can I do for you today?" he asked.

"We need some advice—and maybe some help," I said.

"With buying a razor?"

I put on a smile and rubbed the sparse whiskers on my cheek. "You're jealous. I can see that already." The chill between us was thawing rapidly.

Detective Riordan shook his head, muttered something about my sanity, and said, "Come on back." He led us down a hallway to a conference room about twelve feet square with a single chair on either side of an oak table. The room smelled sour. He asked us to sit and left to get a chair for himself. When he returned, he said, "I'd invite you into my office, but then one of you would have to sit on my lap, and that might be embarrassing for Will." He winked at Elizabeth. "Now, what do you need?"

She explained the situation to him. I noticed she went back to calling Robert her cousin. I suppose that was the more comfortable explanation. When she finished, he sat back and thought. Every few seconds the tip of his cigar would glow a little brighter. Finally he said, "There's not much I can do. They have their own police department, so it's out of our jurisdiction. They've never been cooperative in investigations that I know about. I could call or go there, but I'm afraid that once they find out the Detroit police know about the murder, they'll immediately arrest Robert. At that point, they won't take any chances, regardless of the situation."

"But he's not a killer," Elizabeth said. "We can't let him suffer for someone else's crimes, not to mention that, if I'm right, it also means leaving a killer on the loose inside the asylum."

"The Phantom," Detective Riordan said with a wry smile. He placed the cigar in his mouth again. "It seems to me you have a dilemma. We can alert the state police and see if they would be willing to investigate. If they do, the likelihood is that Robert will end up in prison. Or maybe they could find the real killer. It's a long shot. Are you willing to take the chance?"

"I don't know." Elizabeth looked down at her shoes. "Dr. Beckwith won't let Robert out, and we can't force him to without getting Robert prosecuted." She shook her head and looked up at me. "There's nothing we can do."

I exchanged a glance with Detective Riordan. All he did was shrug, but I understood. This was Elizabeth's decision. Neither he nor I could put Robert at risk.

It seemed there was no solution to the problem. I didn't know what else to try. Having discovered how important this was to Elizabeth—saving her *brother*—I felt entirely inadequate.

Just then an idea rushed to the surface, one of those that seem to rise unbidden from some great depth. I touched Elizabeth's arm. "I know how we'll do this."

Looking at Detective Riordan, I said, "Commit me."

It seemed like a solid idea. "I can go into the asylum as a patient and poke around, find out what's really going on." I was short on details at the moment, but it seemed to make sense, assuming I could be assured of being released. "They take indigent people, right?" I asked. "Not just lunatics and imbeciles?"

"Yes, that's true," Detective Riordan said, "but the poorhouse is a separate building." He gave me a sardonic smile. "As is the tubercular sanatorium, so I wouldn't advise going there either. You need to be in the asylum if you want to investigate."

"Wait," I said. "Sana*tor*ium?"

"For tuberculosis," he said. "Sani*tar*ium for mental problems."

I shook my head. "Are they just trying to confuse people?"

Detective Riordan smirked at me. "You'd probably notice the difference pretty quickly."

"Hmm." I thought for a moment. "Could my family have me committed—to the sanitarium?"

"Not to Eloise," Riordan said. "Rich folks go somewhere they pay for. The county won't foot the bill for you."

I looked at Elizabeth. "Then why is Robert there?"

She glanced away. "My aunt and uncle weren't well-to-do."

I nodded, reading between the lines. Judge Hume wouldn't pay for a private facility.

"Will, you can't do this," Elizabeth said. "It's insane."

"Exactly." I stuck my tongue out to the side of my mouth, mugged at her, and rolled my eyes in circles. She didn't smile, nor did Detective Riordan when I looked back at him. I gave up on the attempt to lighten the mood. "So what if I go in as someone other than Will Anderson?"

"In order to be committed," Riordan said, "a judge has to declare you incompetent, and there's not a judge in Wayne County who doesn't know your ugly mug. They might happily declare you incompetent, but that won't get you into Eloise."

I sat back and thought. "What if I wore a disguise and got picked up on the street for acting loony?"

Elizabeth broke in. "You won't be able to wear a disguise once you get there. You'll be recognized. And what about your hand?"

"Dr. Davis and Francis Beckwith are the only people who I think would remember my face, and I was wearing gloves when they saw me.

They'd have no reason to know my hand was burned. All I have to do is stay away from them."

Riordan looked at Elizabeth and shrugged. "It might work."

"If I got committed," I said to him, "you could have me uncommitted, or whatever they call it, right?"

Riordan smiled. "Let me savor the image of you in a straitjacket for a few minutes before I answer."

"I'm serious," I said. "You can get me out, right?"

"If the doctors agree to release you."

"And if they don't?"

"A court order would be required."

"Could you arrange for one?"

"No guarantees. But if you went in with amnesia, your parents would likely be able to get you out once they discovered you were there."

"So you're saying there's a way in, disguise myself as a tramp with amnesia, and a way out, my parents come and get me."

Riordan rubbed his chin. "You might be able to get in and out again. But I think the question is more, is this a good idea? If you somehow get committed, you'll be under the complete control of the asylum. The police and guards will be able to do what they want, and I'll have no power to help you."

"I'm willing to risk that."

He shook his head slowly and took a pull on the cigar. "You're going to need a story."

"What?"

"Remember, you're a lunatic. You have to be believable." He seemed to be warming to the idea, or at least to the challenge. "I'd keep it simple. Amnesia is a good one, and you can be out looking for your dog or something like that. You have no idea who you are, where you live, et cetera. That mess on your face will help your disguise, but you need to stink and have clothing that befits a man who's lived outdoors for a while."

Elizabeth started shaking her head halfway through Riordan's soliloquy. "I forbid it. You'll get yourself killed. If anyone ought to go in, it's me."

"You wouldn't even be able to get close to the men's buildings," I said. "Listen, give me some credit. I'll figure out what happened, and if Robert is innocent we can get him out."

"No," she said. "It's too—"

"Elizabeth, someone in that asylum is killing patients. If I can do something about it, don't you think I should?"

"Well . . ." She turned to Riordan. "How safe do you think it will be?"

He shrugged. "Most people who go in come out alive. Will's shown he can handle himself." He looked at me. "I'd say it would all depend on your ability to stay out of trouble." Laughing, he shook his head. "Forget it. You're a dead man."

"You're really rolling today, Detective," I said. "I think I liked you better when you hated me."

His ice blue eyes stared into mine. "This will be dangerous."

I shrugged. "Somebody's got to figure out what's going on there."

"What about communication?" Elizabeth asked. "He's got to be able to get hold of us if there's a problem."

I liked the way the conversation had turned. Not "*Should* I go?" anymore.

"There's no easy way," Riordan said. "He won't be able to get to a telephone."

"Elizabeth," I said, "what if you volunteered at Eloise? With your experience at the mission, I'm sure you could get in. We could talk."

"But they know me now. I doubt they would let me volunteer."

"You could disguise yourself, too."

Riordan looked thoughtful. "If all else fails, I could probably get you out to interview you as a person of interest in some crime. I think if you try this—and I would recommend against it—we ought to put a time limit on your stay."

"How long?" I asked.

"I don't know. Two weeks?"

"No longer than two weeks," Elizabeth said. "If you can't figure this out by then, we'll pull you out anyway."

"It sounds like you're on board," I said.

She looked down at the table for a moment before meeting my eyes. "If you really want to do this, I won't stop you."

"This is all on the assumption you can get in," Riordan said. "I'm betting that doesn't happen."

"It's settled, then," I said. "I'm going to need a few days to get ready and arrange my affairs." *And build up enough courage,* I thought.

"As much as I think this is a bad idea," Riordan said, "if you're going in, then the sooner the better. People and clues have a way of disappearing, and memories become foggier by the day. If you take too long you'll never figure it out."

"It's probably for the best," I said. "If I think about this too much, I'll never do it."

Elizabeth and I strode up the steps to my parents' gray shingle-style Victorian home, one of many mansions along this stretch of Rowena. The street was lined with elm trees, every one fifteen feet tall, and I imagined a corps of arborists measuring and trimming the trees so as to maintain that uniformity.

"You're really going to try this?" Elizabeth asked.

"Yes. And you heard Riordan. The sooner the better."

She sighed. "You should tell your parents."

"No. You know them. They'll try to stop me."

"Which is probably a good idea."

"Undoubtedly it's a good idea from the perspective of keeping me safe, but that's not why we're doing this." I took hold of her hands. "Elizabeth, we're doing this for Robert—but I owe you everything. I want to do this for you."

After a moment, she raised a hand and cupped the side of my face. Looking into my eyes, she sighed and nodded. "Thank you. I won't bring it up again."

I kissed her and then rang the doorbell. My mother answered the door and stared at me for a moment before a smile creased her face. "I'm sorry, sir, but tramps have to go 'round back to the kitchen door for scraps."

"Just give it a couple of weeks," I said, stroking my beard. "I'll look like a lumberjack."

My mother and Elizabeth exchanged a significant look but didn't comment as they walked arm in arm toward the parlor. I followed.

"William!" my mother called to my father. "The children are here!"

Turning back to Elizabeth, she said, "I'm just going to check on the dinner." She bustled toward the kitchen, bellowing, "William!"

"I'm coming, I'm coming," my father replied in an exasperated tone from the back of the house, probably his den.

Elizabeth and I sat on the sofa. My father joined us a minute later. We stood, and he hugged Elizabeth and shook my left hand. "Here, sit, sit," he said. We returned to the sofa, and he sat in one of the burgundy upholstered chairs opposite us and leaned in close. "Have you heard anything else from the Gianollas?"

"Not a word," I said.

Earlier in the year, we had been drawn into the middle of a Black Hand war, which ended only a month ago in a very gruesome manner. The Gianolla brothers' gang had emerged victorious over the Adamo gang and had taken over the Detroit rackets. The wheels had been set in motion when the Gianollas demanded we allow the Teamsters Union into my father's company, Detroit Electric. Tony Gianolla, the gang leader, told me at our final meeting that we had done what he wanted and he was going to let us alone. Elizabeth and I doubted that, but thus far he had not contacted us. I hadn't shared with my parents the story of our experience at the final encounter with the Gianolla brothers. There was no sense doing so at this point, and they wouldn't have believed me anyway.

"Good," my father said. "Perhaps he was telling the truth."

"I'm sure it would have been the first time," Elizabeth said.

My father sat back in the chair. "We will have to remain vigilant. They could come back at us at any time."

I nodded. "True, but I think he meant it. I don't want to sound naive, but Tony Gianolla wanted Adamo's death more than anything. I think he's satisfied."

"Dinner!" my mother called from the kitchen.

We headed into the dining room, where the cook had set out a roasted chicken, mashed potatoes, gravy, Brussels sprouts, and French bread.

We were eating when I said as casually as I could, "I'm going on vacation for a couple of weeks."

"Oh?" My father looked at me from under his brow, his knife and fork held on either side of his plate. "Where are you going?"

My parents believed I suffered from neurasthenia, the nervousness that ailed so many Americans, and had been trying to get me to take the rest cure at the Glen Springs Resort in New York, renowned for its healing radioactive waters. I didn't want to lie to them but didn't think a little misdirection was dishonest. "I thought I would go to a hospital . . . you know . . ."

"Ah," he said. "Taking the rest cure. Well, that will take more than two weeks."

"I'm going to try two and then decide what to do from there."

He nodded. "Good, good. Where are you going?"

"I thought I'd stay in Michigan. I don't want to be too far away."

"Have you made a reservation?"

"No, not yet."

"Then Battle Creek is the place to go. Dr. Kellogg's sanitarium is the best in the state."

"I'll look into it," I said.

At that, Elizabeth changed the subject, asking my mother where she had gotten her dress, which Elizabeth thought was absolutely lovely. That ended the discussion of my sanitarium stay.


I pulled the Torpedo to the curb a block past Elizabeth's house. Jefferson Avenue was lined with cars now, a sight that would have been unthinkable only a few years ago. The automobile had become the overwhelming choice of the well-to-do.

Elizabeth turned to me. "Would you like to sit out on the porch? It's a beautiful night."

"I'd love to."

"Good. We can try to work up a plan that will keep you alive at Eloise."

We climbed out of the car and walked, arm in arm, down the sidewalk past the other grand Victorian homes that dominated this stretch of the road. Cars whizzed past. I'd gotten in the habit of counting electrics, to see how we were holding up against the dreaded internal combustion automobile. Of the twenty-two cars that passed before we turned up Elizabeth's walk, exactly none were electric. Fourteen were Model Ts, three were Packards, two were Hudsons, one a Chalmers, one a

REO, and the last was some unidentifiable vehicle that looked home-made. My father had certainly made the right decision in transitioning his business from horse-drawn carriages to automobiles, but I was increasingly concerned that he was backing the wrong horse in that race.

Elizabeth went inside to check on her mother and get us some lemonade. I sat on the swing and looked out over the wide expanse of the Detroit River and the town of Windsor, Ontario, on the other side, more than half a mile away. It was a peaceful night, and the porch, elevated about eight feet above ground level, let me look over the tops of the cars and pretend they weren't constantly puttering past.

I'd been waiting for the better part of ten minutes when I decided I'd better see what was keeping Elizabeth. I gave a tentative knock on the front door, opened it, and peered inside. Quiet voices were just audible on the second floor. I stood at the base of the stairway and said, "Elizabeth?" No response. I tried again, a little louder.

I heard a door open. "I'm going to be a minute, Will. Would you be a dear and get us the lemonade?"

"Certainly, my darling. Would your mother like some?"

"No," she said quickly. "Please, just pour a couple of glasses. I'll meet you out on the porch in a few minutes."

"All right, but can I help with anything?"

"No. Thank you." The door shut again.

I poured two glasses of lemonade and sat again on the swing. I had been hoping for a little romance. While I try to be levelheaded about such things, I am a young man, after all, so I try to forgive myself my machinations to bed Elizabeth. Seldom had I had better leverage. Here I was only days—hours?—from voluntarily incarcerating myself with a herd of lunatics for no reason other than to help her brother. Dare I say it, a noble cause for a change, and, damn it, one that ought to earn me at least one night of bliss. Given our exchange inside, I tried to forget about it but couldn't. The previous night we'd been heading toward a wonderful conclusion, and now I wanted her so badly I was practically shaking with desire.

At least ten more minutes passed before Elizabeth opened the door and stepped out. "I'm sorry, Will, I need to be with my mother."

I tried, unsuccessfully, I'm sure, to wipe the disappointment off my face. "Is she all right?"

"No. She's disoriented again."

"Do you think she'll sleep soon?" I wasn't giving up without a fight.

"Probably, but . . ."

"I could wait here for you until she does. I've got nowhere to be."

Elizabeth gave me a faint smile. "I'm sorry, Will. She needs my attention right now. Perhaps we can . . . spend some time together tomorrow night." She leaned down, rested her hand on my knee, and kissed me. The swing swayed back, pulling her off balance, and I swept her into my arms and set her on my lap. "I miss you, too," she said. "You know, that way."

"Sexually," I said, waggling my eyebrows.

She playfully slapped my chest. "Yes." With a grin, she whispered, *"Sexually."*

She hopped off my lap, and we stood in front of the swing. She placed her hands on either side of my face and drew it down to hers. We kissed for a minute, a preview of things to come—soon, I hoped.

When she pulled back, I said, "Tomorrow night. If I'm still around."

Smiling, she nodded. "Tomorrow night."

"I'm going to hold you to that," I said.

"I'm going to hold *you* to that, pal. So I guess you better not go anywhere."

"Ah, that's your plan," I said with a grin. "Keeping me here with the promise of sex."

She kissed me again. "Call me in the morning. We'll put that plan together."

"Sure. Good night." I headed down the steps, damning my luck—but I thought my chances for the next night were good.

Contrary to the popular wisdom, I'd never found cold showers to be helpful. Tonight, though, it might be worth a try.

# CHAPTER THREE

*Thursday, August 8, 1912*

## Elizabeth

It was a particularly difficult night for my mother, and first thing in the morning I phoned an employment agency, asking them to send over candidates for nursing care. I had to have some assistance. Our current servants would not be up to the task. Helga, our maid, had recently had a number of arguments with my mother. Even if they had been getting along, Helga was a cleaner, not a companion. Alberts was not the nurturing type my mother needed, and, had I asked him, his male ego would have been stung. I needed someone who would appreciate her many good qualities, someone to watch over her and protect her whenever I was unable.

The agency said they had three women with impeccable references that they would send over shortly. I had a few minutes, so I thought to sneak a smoke. I grabbed a cigarette and lighter from my purse and walked out the kitchen door into the backyard and then through the grape arbor into the garden. Even though the rest of the yard was colored the deep green of summer, the garden looked like something out of Dante. Last year's beans, long and stringy and full of insect holes, drooped off of gnarled brown vines; stumps of empty cornstalks poked out of the dry dirt; and sunflowers, their yellow petals gone, brown faces pockmarked and empty, littered the garden floor. My mother and

I both enjoyed gardening and took pleasure in eating food we had grown. No one had planted this year. I used my foot to smooth out the only sign of recent activity: half-buried cigarette butts.

I leaned against the fence and smoked. I forced Will to quit after he'd been shot, and I thought I had quit as well. After two days, I was going berserk and started up again. I was down to half a dozen cigarettes a day and only smoked when I was out of Will's sight. I didn't enjoy being a hypocrite, but it wasn't the first time, and I was certain it wouldn't be the last.

After the cigarette, I went back inside and phoned Will, but he didn't answer. Probably still asleep, I thought. I'd try him later. When my mother woke, I fixed her oatmeal and coffee and sat down with her at the table.

I took a sip of coffee. "Mother, you know I have been concerned about you lately." She started to say something, but I held up a hand. "Please, let me finish."

Her eyes dropped to the table.

"As I said, I will never send you away. But you know as well as I that there are times of confusion for you now. I will be with you as much as possible, but I can't always be there for you. As you said, I need to live my life as well." I took a deep breath. "I'm having some nurses come around this morning for us to speak with."

"No," my mother said immediately. "I don't need a nurse."

"You're right," I said, reaching across the table to her. I laid my hand on her arm. "You don't need a nurse, but you need an assistant, a companion, someone to help keep you on track. We will decide together who it shall be. I won't force anyone on you."

She pushed back her chair and stood. "I'm getting dressed. I'd hate for the nurses to think I'm a lunatic."

"Mother," I said to her back as she swept out of the kitchen, her breakfast uneaten. I cursed and headed to my purse for another cigarette.

Alberts showed the women into the living room to wait and, one by one, brought them into the den so my mother and I could speak with them privately. They all seemed competent and nice enough to me, but my mother was having none of it.

The first nurse was Italian. "Obviously a gangster's woman," my mother said.

The second was Russian. "Jew," my mother whispered. "They steal."

The third nurse was a second-generation Irish girl. "Drinkers," my mother said with a knowing nod.

I was mortified by her appalling lack of manners but didn't think it was necessarily a bad interviewing technique. After all, the nurse we chose would be required to contend with difficult behavior. The first two were not fluent in English and seemed a bit timid for the assignment, but I thought the Irish girl, Bridget Kelly, was perfect. She was sturdy and tall, perhaps thirty years old, and seemed to have a sunny personality. Yet for some reason she struck me as a Celtic warrior. I could picture her in a leather skirt with helmet and club.

I thought she would be able to hold her own with my mother. It didn't hurt that she was a pretty girl, hazel-eyed with a blaze of faint freckles across her cheeks, which would hold her in better stead with my mother than had she been plain. Her brown hair was swirled atop her head underneath a small-brimmed robin's-egg blue hat, and she wore a conservative blue day dress, a shade or two darker than the hat.

For a younger woman, Mrs. Kelly had an impressive résumé. She worked at Harper Hospital from 1902 until 1907, moving from nurse's assistant to a supervisory position. Later that year, she began working with private patients, which she continued until 1910, when she hired on at Eloise Hospital for two months. She said she immensely preferred working as a private nurse and quit the job at Eloise when she was offered another of those positions, as caretaker for a Mrs. Whitney, who had recently passed away.

Mrs. Kelly's husband had also recently died, so she was again living with her parents. Her father worked for the Michigan Coal Company as a driver, and her mother took in washing. Mrs. Kelly said she'd been working since she was a babe and enjoyed the labor. Nothing to do, she said, made her nervous.

I asked her to wait for me in the living room before apologizing to the other two women for my mother's behavior, pressing five-dollar bills into their hands, and sending them on their way. I then went back to the den to speak with my mother, but she was gone. I climbed the stairs and found her sitting in the rocker in her bedroom, gazing at her wedding photograph, which she held in her lap.

I knelt down next to her and rested one hand on the arm of the chair. "Mother, I know you don't want to do this, but I think Bridget Kelly would be perfect."

She said nothing. Her eyes didn't leave the photograph, which trembled, just a bit, in her hands.

"What if we hired her on a trial? Say, a week? If you approve of her after a week, we'll keep her on. If not, we'll find someone else."

Finally she looked at me, her eyes pooling with tears. "Perhaps you should just send me back to the crazy hospital. It's where people like me belong, isn't it?"

"Mother." I gently took hold of her arm. "You're not crazy. You're just getting forgetful."

She shook her head slowly.

"Would you like to talk with Dr. Miller?" I said. "Or perhaps another doctor? I could—"

"No. There's nothing to be done for what's wrong with me. I will just slip into dementia like my mother did." Tears rolled down her cheeks.

"But you're so young," I protested.

"This began with my mother when she was fifty-two. By sixty, she didn't know who I was. I don't think I need to remind you I'm fifty-seven."

My eyes welling, I squeezed her arm. "Then let me help you, Mother. No matter what happens, I'll be there for you. I just need some assistance. I can't be with you every minute, and I want you to be able to live normally."

She took a deep breath and sighed. "I know you're right. I just . . . I just don't want to admit it's happening to me. I . . ." After another sigh, she looked down at the photograph in her hands and went silent.

"Do you think we can try Mrs. Kelly?" I asked.

She gave me a hesitant nod.

"All right." I stood and patted her shoulder. "I'll go see about making the arrangements with her." I turned and walked to the door.

I had just reached it when she said, "Elizabeth?"

With a hand on the doorjamb, I turned back to her. "Yes, Mother?"

"I love you."

It was nearly enough to cause me to break down. "I love you too, dear," I replied. On the way down the stairs I dried my face with my handkerchief and tried to make myself presentable.

Bridget Kelly awaited me on the yellow sofa in the living room, holding her purse primly on her lap. I sat next to her. "Mrs. Kelly," I said, "my mother is a kind woman, and generous, but she is so frightened by this forgetfulness overtaking her that at times she will be rude, perhaps cruel, to her caretaker. If I offer you this position, you must agree to turn the other cheek and return her only kindness. I love her dearly, and want her remaining years to be as peaceful and enjoyable as possible. Can you do this?"

"Yes, miss," she said with a confident nod.

"You worked at Eloise Hospital for a very brief time. Do you have an aversion to insanity?"

"No, miss. All my private patients have had dementia, and I've loved them like my mum. When I was at Eloise I worked in the County House, with the poor. I just like working private."

I nodded. "Tell me about yourself. Do you have a beau?"

"No, miss. Since Mr. Kelly passed on from the influenza, I haven't found the interest again."

"I'm sorry."

"Don't you worry, miss." Allowing herself a little smile, she said, "Mr. Kelly's the reason I haven't found the interest again. Being married is no bargain."

I laughed. "I've never had the pleasure, but I can imagine."

"Pretty lady like you," she said, "it's a wonder nobody's snagged you yet. Bet they've tried."

"Well, a couple have. No one's got me to the altar yet."

"Just watch out for them, miss. Always scheming, they are."

"That's a fact. Tell me, Mrs. Kelly. Do you have any children?"

"No, miss. The Lord never blessed us with a child."

I nodded. I couldn't imagine finding someone more perfect to be with my mother. *If she can't get along with this woman*, I thought, *she can't get along with anyone.*

I decided. "I would like to hire you on a trial basis. My understanding is that we directly pay the agency the sum of eight dollars and forty cents per week, provide you with room and board, and give you Sundays off. I will also allow you two additional evenings to yourself, though the schedule will vary. Is that acceptable?"

She beamed. "Yes, miss." She must have really needed the job.

"The trial will be for one week and will commence as soon as you are ready. How does that sound?"

She stood and said, "I can start tomorrow."

"Fine. Eight A.M.?"

"Yes, miss," she replied.

"Would you like me to send for your things, or will you arrange that yourself?"

She laughed. "I have but a few things, miss. Not so much I can't haul it over myself. I'll bring it tomorrow morning if that's all right."

I told her it would be fine. When she left, I phoned Will again but still got no answer. Just before noon, while I was setting up a room in the servants' quarters for Mrs. Kelly, Alberts called me to the telephone to speak with Detective Riordan.

I picked up the phone and put the receiver to my ear. "Yes, Detective?"

"I tried Will, but he didn't answer. I hope you don't mind that I called you."

"Not at all. What can I do for you?"

"I've given your situation a lot of thought. It's too dangerous for Will to go inside Eloise. It sounds like the administrator is involved somehow. There's too strong a chance that Will would be discovered."

"But what will we do?"

"I'm not sure," Detective Riordan replied, "but there has to be a better way to go about this."

"I'm sure you're right." And I was. Will had too strong a predilection for getting himself in trouble to come out of this unscathed. "I'll try to talk him out of it. I may need to bring you in for reinforcements."

"I'd be happy to run him over the coals."

"You may need to. Literally." These days, when Will committed to something, he followed through.

I told Detective Riordan I would let him know Will's response to the change in plans. He said he was working until six o'clock and gave me his home telephone number in case I couldn't reach him at the station.

I phoned Will again and again got no answer, so I went back to my duties. When I took breaks from cleaning and organizing, I tried to cheer up my mother, but it was to no avail. She talked to me in monosyllables, and doled those out like precious gems. I tried Will's apartment again at three and let the telephone ring for at least two minutes. There was still no answer.

He had said he would call in the morning. Not everyone saw him as reliable, but he had always been so for me. In the back of my mind, I wondered if it had anything to do with my refusing his affections last night. No, that was silly. He understood the circumstances. Still, he was a man. Men enjoy the idea of being under the control of their nature, as if they are nothing more than animals. Sometimes I agree with the sentiment, but . . . Will? He loved me. I had no doubt of that. I tried to forget the thought.

Unfortunately, the alternative looked even worse. I phoned the Detroit Electric factory; as I expected, Mr. Wilkinson, Will's father's secretary, said that Will had not been there all day, and his father had not heard from him. Nor had his mother, I discovered when I phoned her at home. I tried the Ford factory to see if Edsel knew anything. It was a long shot at best, as Will was still trying to repair their relationship, but Edsel wasn't available anyway. I sat back, my fingers tapping on the desk, while I tried to reason out what Will was up to.

Perhaps he had decided not to commit himself to Eloise after all and was afraid to tell me. Or was there a more sinister explanation?

I tried not to think about the Gianolla brothers.

I left Alberts with my mother and drove our Baker Electric to Will's apartment, where I let myself in with the key he had given me. As I closed the door behind me, it struck me that I had never been here alone.

"Hello?" I called. "Will?"

I stood for a minute and listened. I heard the buzz of quiet voices in the apartment below, the jingle of a streetcar bell from down the block, a hum that seemed to be all around me: electricity? There was no sign of life in Will's apartment, though. I walked from room to room, eying the contents and sniffing the air. It was as I'd last seen it, no ashtrays, or traces of cigarette smoke or perfume.

I stopped in the parlor to think. He had finally had the holes in his wall fixed. Where they had been, he had hung a round piece of oak, about two feet in diameter and two inches thick, for his knife throwing. A pile of automobile magazines lay scattered on the coffee table. A single glass sat on an end table, a ring of sticky liquid on the bottom. I picked it up. No sign of lipstick. I sniffed it. Ginger ale.

His bed was made. There were no signs he'd left quickly. He'd turn up.

I just hoped he did it soon.

I crossed the hall and knocked on the door of the apartment opposite Will's. The shrew-faced woman who answered slammed the door in my face when I asked if she had seen him. Apparently they were not chummy neighbors.

I didn't want to leave Alberts alone with my mother any longer, so I got back in the automobile and headed home. On the way, I remembered that Will had decided I was the one who was supposed to read *The Phantom of the Opera*. I have to admit my curiosity had been piqued, though I don't normally read "popular" novels, by which I mean fluff intended for nothing more than entertainment. But now I thought some light reading might take my mind off Will, so I stopped by Baker's Books on Woodward to pick up a copy. They didn't have it, in fact had never heard of it, but the man said he would order it for me. I left my number and address, and he said they would deliver the book when it arrived.

Finally I returned to our house. After checking on my mother, I went into the den, sat at the desk, and called the Bethune Street police station. Detective Riordan was not available.

I put my elbows on the desk and massaged my temples. I had run out of ideas. There was no next step.

Will had disappeared.

Time passed slowly. My mother and I were both in a sort of suspended animation, trapped in amber: I dreaded the arrival of news about Will, while my mother dreaded every new minute, believing that each tick of the clock brought her closer to losing her mind.

I phoned Will's parents' house and spoke with his mother. My second call of the day brought more questions from her, which I tried to deflect. I was simply trying to find him, as we'd had plans, though they were loose. She hadn't heard from him. I thanked her and asked her to have Will phone me if she did speak with him.

We rang off, and I tried Mr. Wilkinson at the Detroit Electric factory again. He had still heard nothing from Will. From time to time I tried Will's apartment but did not get an answer.

Detective Riordan phoned me just after five o'clock. When I answered the telephone, he said, "Good afternoon, Miss Hume."

"Have you had any luck?" I asked.

"No—and based on your question, it doesn't sound like you've got any better news."

"No."

"It's not all bad news, though," he said. "I checked with every police station, morgue, and hospital, including psychiatric hospitals, in the county, and gave them his name and description. Near as I can tell, he hasn't been arrested, killed, or admitted. He's out there somewhere."

"Perhaps with the Gianollas." Finally putting my fears into words made a chill run up my spine.

"I don't think you want to consider that right now. Will's pretty smart for a rich kid. Give him time."

"I know you're right," I said, "but . . . I'm worried about him."

He was quiet for a moment, and I heard agreement in his silence. "You know," he finally said, "if he doesn't show by tomorrow, you might run a missing person ad."

"That's a good idea." These sorts of advertisements were in the papers all the time: pictures of a husband or wife gone missing or a child that had disappeared. Every one was a heartbreaking last-gasp attempt by desperate people.

"Don't offer a reward," he added. "It will only bring crooks out of the woodwork who'll try to trick you out of the money. If you want to reward someone, that's your business. Just don't put it in the paper."

I agreed to leave it out.

"Have you alerted his parents yet?" he asked.

"No, though I've asked if they know where he is. They've probably got their antennae up."

"You'll need to warn them before you run the ad. In the meantime, maybe you should start on your plans. Did you decide to volunteer at Eloise?"

"I suppose . . . yes. I have to help Robert."

"They'll take a few days to confirm you," he said. "Why don't you get the process started?"

"I will." I would, too, though I was hesitant. Spending my time at Eloise seemed to require abandoning Will, and I was unsure how I could leave my mother on her first day with Mrs. Kelly. Nevertheless, Robert needed my help. Now.

We agreed to contact each other if we located Will and wished each other a good night. After supper, I sat with my mother in the living room. We both read, as we often did together at night, but I doubted she had any more success than I at digesting the words. I thought her mind would be occupied as mine was: with a fear of the future and a longing for the past.

# Will

I woke myself with a scream. *The trunk.*

I lay in bed, rubbing my face, drenched in sweat. My head was heavy, brain sluggish, like I hadn't slept at all. I certainly knew I wouldn't be sleeping any longer. When I glanced at the clock, I saw it wasn't yet six—too early to phone Elizabeth, but not too early to work on my plans. It was time to prepare for being committed to an insane asylum. Now that I'd slept on it, I wasn't so sure it was a good idea. What did I know about crazy people? For that matter, what did I know about investigating a murder? Other than a knack for getting people to want to kill me, I had no abilities when it came to crime.

Still . . . Robert was Elizabeth's brother, and I told her I'd do this.

So, step one: Procure some clothing that would be believable on a crazy tramp. I knew just the place, in fact had spent the better part of a night there a few months ago, before I was awakened by a policeman's nightstick to my kidney.

I pulled on a pair of black leather gloves and dressed in a plain outfit that I didn't think would look too out of place near the mission, a simple gray suit with black button-top boots and a black derby. I decided against a tie. When I was satisfied with my look, I dug into my wardrobe for an outfit I wouldn't miss too much, wishing I still had some of the clothing I'd given Elizabeth for the mission. I decided on a white shirt, a pair of brown tweed trousers that were loose in the waist, and a pair of brown oxfords that I hated—they had heels that were almost two inches high. They were fashionable, but I felt like I was on stilts. How women managed on heels like that, I couldn't say.

I stuffed the clothing into a burlap bag and headed out the door. On the way to the streetcar stop on the corner, I found a nickel on the sidewalk and pocketed it. Better yet, I had only a short wait before a trolley came along. Unbelievably, a seat was even open, so after stuffing my newly found nickel in the coin box, I enjoyed the luxury of sitting, rather than standing. It seemed that this was going to be a lucky day.

At Randolph and Larned I hopped off the trolley. I was only a block away from the McGregor Mission. The men had been booted out for the day at six, but many of them never made it farther than a block or two, cadging pennies and nickels from the few swells who came by this part of town. The air smelled of horseshit, sewage, and moldering garbage, with undertones of rancid cooking oil. The streets were full of wagons and bicycles, the occasional car or truck, and men and women rushing pell-mell in all directions. The street corners were likewise occupied, though these by beggars—men, women, and, worst of all, individual children. There was no way to know if the children were sent out by enterprising parents, as we so often heard, or if they were really on their own and my coins might be all that stood between them and death. They were all filthy, pathetic, skinny creatures who would be better off living almost anywhere else.

On the corner of Brush Street, I noticed a group of men on the next block who looked like possibilities for a clothing swap. While I waited for a wagon to pass, however, I saw the cutest little girl, no more than four years old, standing in front of me. Her hands were cupped together in front of her, and her big brown eyes beseeched me. As surreptitiously as I could, I fished a quarter out of my pocket and pressed it into her palm. I was immediately set upon by a mob, people of all ages, begging, shouting, pawing at me.

"Stop!" I shouted. "I'll give you all—"

Instead, they began punching me, and then someone hit me on the head with a pipe. I saw stars and staggered. Hands slithered into my pockets, inside my coat. I tried to fight them off. A fist slammed into my face, then my stomach, doubling me over. They pulled my coat over my head, pinning my arms, and ran me backward into an alley before throwing me against a wall. The stink of their breath, clothing, and desperation was all I could smell. My jacket was torn off, and one man held me down while another ripped the glove off my left hand and then my right, bending my fingers back. Pain surged up my arm, and I cried out.

In a minute it was over, and they melted away. I lay on the ground panting for breath like a fish out of water, my head pounding, body aching.

The smell of horseshit seemed to be everywhere. I pushed myself up and sat against the wall of the building behind me. Now I saw the twenty-foot-high pile of dung that blocked the alley only a few feet away. Automobiles had made these eye-and-nose-sores less prevalent throughout the city, but in Detroit one was never far from a gigantic pile of horseshit.

I started to laugh. Why, I don't know. My hand and head were killing me, my right eye was swelling, and I hurt everywhere else. What's more, the bag of clothing I'd meant to trade was gone, as well as my coat and wallet.

A shadow fell across the alleyway. A fat cop leaned in to see me in the shadows. I stopped laughing. He moseyed toward me, flipping his nightstick in circles. His wool uniform was too tight, the fabric separating around the buttons on his belly, showing little diamond-shaped patches of white shirt.

"What you doin', boy?"

He had a dark two-day stubble on his face and red eyes that showed a night of no sleep, heavy drinking, or both. He did not look like a man who would brook any nonsense.

"Nothing," I said. "I'm . . . all right."

He grinned, amused at my response. "Shit. You look like you got run over by the five-fifteen."

Waving out toward the street, I said, "I got beat up by . . . a bunch of them." I tasted blood in my mouth. Behind him, vehicles zoomed by the alley's entrance, and people walked past on both sides of the street.

"What's your name?"

"What?"

"Your name, shithead. What's a matter, you Chinee?"

Even though I wasn't thinking entirely clearly, I realized this was an opportunity. Detective Riordan had been afraid the judge would recognize me. The way I looked right now, no one other than perhaps Elizabeth and my family would know me. If I could convince the police I was insane they would likely want to dump me in Eloise Hospital.

I looked up at the cop wide-eyed. "I . . . I don't know."

After a few more questions regarding my identity, to all of which I feigned ignorance, the cop led me down the street, his hand clamped on my arm. I received plenty of stares but just looked straight ahead and went where he told me, which, ultimately, led to the corner of Bates and Randolph—police headquarters. The lobby was high-ceilinged, probably three thousand square feet, likely as large as Detective Riordan's entire station. Fifty people, give or take, mostly civilians milled about. Over the buzz of conversation, I heard a woman wailing, but I didn't see her, which was disconcerting. The room smelled less than the Bethune Street station, though body odor was the prevalent scent. A Greek family walked behind us, arguing loudly in their language. The noise made my head pound harder, but I closed my eyes, trying unsuccessfully to block it out.

The fat cop pushed me past the people in line in front of the desk sergeant, who sat behind the tall oak podium. A man was reporting the theft of his automobile, a Packard, but the fat cop shouldered him aside. He looked up at the sergeant and said, "John Doe. Loony."

The desk sergeant nodded toward the back of the station, and the fat cop shoved me in that direction. Only now did it occur to me that no one would know I was inside Eloise, and I wavered on continuing. I would need a great deal of luck, not only to accomplish my mission, but now to get out of Eloise when I was done. I wondered again if I should just end this here—tell them who I was, that this was a mistake—but I couldn't. I had to see this through, regardless of the consequences. Maybe, I thought, I could move the odds a little more in my favor.

I'd been quiet since the cop gave up on getting my name out of me, but now I said, "You know, the name Detective Riordan rings a bell."

The fat cop opened the door to the jail and pushed me inside. Sneering, he said, "What? You think you're Riordan?"

"No, no, that's not what I mean. But maybe I could talk to him? Do you have a Detective Riordan?"

He gave me a big push down the hallway. "I'll get right on that."

I hoped his answer was less sarcastic than it sounded, but I wasn't going to count on it. We walked down a corridor with a concrete floor, a red brick wall on one side, plaster on the other. A guard sat next to the metal door at the end. As we approached, he pushed himself to his feet and unlocked the door. The policeman handed me over to him and simply said, "Nut."

The guard eyed me. I looked back at him with no expression. I knew what these men were capable of. I'd had one beating today and had no intention of provoking another. He pushed me through the door and down the hall to a holding cell about twenty feet square. Behind the iron bars were a dozen men. Other than one old man rolling around on the floor, hugging himself, all the prisoners sat quietly on the benches that lined the perimeter. The guard unlocked the door and shoved me in. I took a seat on an open piece of bench between a couple of men who looked pretty harmless. From farther down the corridor I heard men shouting, cursing mostly, back and forth between cells. Their voices echoed through the jail.

As the afternoon progressed, I spoke with two other prisoners, one accused of automobile theft, another of assault. They were both completely innocent, they said. I nodded and agreed that they must be. Hours later, the guards brought us supper, such as it was—bread, beans, and coffee. I'd gotten used to eating this slop but had never acquired a taste for it. I ate the bread and beans, but skipped the coffee after a small sip. True to form, it tasted closer to piss. As urine may well have been an ingredient, I decided thirst was less a concern than I had thought.

Another man was brought in after supper, but he was quiet. The man rolling on the floor began grunting but eventually fell asleep. Down the hall the other prisoners kept up their shouting for quite a while, but at some point, late at night, I fell asleep leaning against the cell bars.

# CHAPTER FOUR

*Friday, August 9, 1912*

## Will

No dreams. Breakfast—some sort of sticky paste and coffee—came just after the guards changed shifts. I ate the paste and choked down the coffee. I was tired, dirty, and hungry, my right eye was swollen shut, and the knot on my head hadn't stopped throbbing. I hoped I was put in front of a judge today. I couldn't have been in more perfect condition.

The man on the floor ate his breakfast and went back to his rolling. A few of the other men struck up conversations, but I stayed to myself. I leaned back against the bars and considered my effort to this point. So far, so good. I needed to fool the judge, and I'd be on my way to Eloise Hospital. There I would find Robert Clarke and discover who was murdering the patients.

It seemed simple enough, but I tend to think everything seems simple, and I'm nearly always wrong. Elizabeth had pointed this out to me before. Many times.

I would be under surveillance, but I didn't think they would lock me up. I was nonviolent, merely the victim of amnesia. If Robert had been able to wander the grounds on the night of the murder, I ought to be able to skulk around a bit. Best laid plans and all that, but I thought I would be given enough freedom to really search the place.

A few hours later, a man brought us our lunch. I didn't even look at it. The light never changed. With no window and no watch, I had no idea how much time was passing. It made me realize how regimented my life had become based simply on the time of day. I didn't listen to my body but instead relied on a clock to tell me what I should be doing. I'd have to change that.

The guards were unable, or unwilling, to give me any information regarding my fate. I was worried that, if my court appearance was delayed too long, my face would return to normal, which would almost certainly result in me being identified. As it happened, I had nothing to worry about. Half an hour later, a guard carrying a set of shackles unlocked the cell door and barked, "Doe!"

I stood. "Could you tell me what's going on?"

"Doc's gonna look at you."

Pointing at the shackles, I said, "Are those really necessary? My problem is that I don't remember who I am. I'm not violent."

He didn't answer. Instead, he swung the door open and advanced on me. Eyes wary, he locked my wrists and ankles into the shackles. The other prisoners watched in silence. When the guard finished, he jerked me to my feet and dragged me out of the cell. The ankle shackles didn't allow me more than a shuffle, and I couldn't get my balance.

"If you'd stop for a—"

"Shut up." He shot me a warning glance and kept dragging.

Eventually, I was able to catch up and shuffled along, double-time, at his side. He brought me to an interrogation room where two men already stood. Shoving me inside, he slammed the door shut. My new companions were shackled the same as me. The man closest to me was bald and overweight, perhaps fifty years old, the other a young man in his midtwenties, who looked like anybody one might see on the street. We all eyed each other suspiciously but eventually came to the conclusion that we weren't going to kill one another.

"So, what's wrong with you two?" I asked.

The younger man gestured toward the older one. "This one don't speak English. Kraut, I think."

I nodded.

"Ain't nothing wrong with me, though," the younger man said.

I appraised him. "Then why are you in here?"

"Oh, it's my wife."

"What did she do?"

He gave me a sage nod. "She wouldn't pass the potatoes."

"So . . . what did you do?"

A key jangled in the lock, and the door swung open. The guard who'd dragged me down here stepped into the room, nightstick at the ready. "Doe. Let's go."

He grabbed my arm and pulled me to another room, where an older man in a suit stood behind a table, on top of which sat a black valise. A young woman in a long white nurse's dress stood next to him with a notepad. The guard stopped me in front of the man and stood at my side, nightstick tapping against his thigh.

The doctor—I assumed he was a doctor, as he didn't identify himself— asked me to put out my tongue. I wondered what the tongue of a crazy person looked like but complied. Next, he took my pulse and listened to my chest, stomach, and back with a stethoscope. Finished, he looked me in the eye. "Who are you?"

"These gentleman have been calling me John Doe."

"Is that your real name?"

"That's what they tell me."

He leaned down to look into my eyes. "Where are you from?"

I pretended to think about it. Finally I looked back at him and said, "Cuba?"

"Cuba, eh?"

"*Sí, señor.*"

"Hmm." He clucked his tongue. "You don't sound like you're from Cuba."

"Oh." I put a puzzled look on my face. "Do people from Cuba get these headaches that don't go away?"

"How long have you had it?"

"I don't remember a time I didn't."

He glanced at the guard. "Did he look like this when he came in here?"

The guard shrugged.

The doctor tilted his head and gave him a baleful stare. "Yes or no?"

"Prob'ly."

"Where'd they find him?"

The guard shrugged again. He didn't care.

The doctor sighed and looked back to me. "How long have you been in Detroit?"

"Detroit?" I laughed. "Why would I want to go to Detroit?"

"You're in Detroit now."

"No."

"Where do you think you are?"

"I'm . . . uh . . . I . . ." was all I could manage.

"Where were you yesterday?"

I screwed up my face like I was trying to remember. Again I said, "Cuba?"

"What town?"

"I don't know," I said. "I remember trying to find my dog."

The doctor stared into my eyes, and I could see him thinking—was I faking? A second later, he turned to the nurse. "He's got a lump on his head, but his pupils look normal. I don't think he has a concussion. Amnesia's the only thing that makes sense to me." Now he shrugged. "Either way they'll sort it out." He turned to the guard. "Send him in."

"Send me in?" I asked. "Where?"

"Court. They're going to get you in front of a judge. If he believes you're incompetent, he'll send you out to Eloise."

"Oh, yes, please," I said. "I've heard nice things about her."

The doctor and nurse exchanged a significant glance before the doctor told the guard, "Get to it."

The guard pushed me down the corridor into another cell, again by myself, for which I was thankful. I sat on the cot, pushed myself back against the wall, and stared at the other brick wall in front of me. When I thought about what I was doing, a chill ran up my spine. Only a few months ago I'd been locked up in this place, waiting for the trial that seemed destined to put me in the state prison for the rest of my life. I'd been lucky then, though not as lucky as it seemed at the time.

Now I was going into court again—voluntarily. Sometimes I wonder how big a goddamned idiot I am.

About an hour later, a pair of guards came for me. They put me in shackles, dragged me out of the cell, and brought me to the back of the station, where a Black Maria—a battered horse-drawn wagon, barred windows in the back—stood just outside the door.

"Up," one of them grunted and shoved me toward the short steps. I climbed into the empty wagon, finding that the ankle shackles allowed me just enough slack to climb from one stair to the next. I sat in the far back, near the window, to filter some of the sour stink of body odor that emanated from the padded sides of the wagon. The guard closed and locked the door, the driver snapped the reins, and the wagon began moving.

*Talk about service,* I thought. *A solo limousine ride to court.*

The wagon stopped thirty seconds later, and the door swung open again. A line of men wearing shackles climbed in, shoving me toward the front until I was jammed against the wall, one of eight men on each side crowded into a space made for perhaps five. No one spoke. A guard closed and locked the door again, and the wagon started out for the courthouse. Fortunately, it was only a five-minute ride. They unloaded us again and locked everyone into a single large cell.

One by one the men were led into court. None of them returned. After perhaps an hour, when they'd gone through about half the men in the cell, the guard called for John Doe. I stood and, still manacled, followed him down a corridor to a side entrance of the courtroom, where a judge I didn't recognize, Judge VanderVeen, if the nameplate was right, sat behind the bench.

I glanced at the prosecutor and gulped. Behind the table sat District Attorney Higgins, a man who knew me well, who had in fact twice unsuccessfully prosecuted me for murder, most recently earlier this year.

My plan was finished before it even started.


The guard brought me to the defense table, which was occupied by a young man in a cheap blue suit and a bow tie. I kept my head turned away from Higgins and hid my mangled hand in my lap. There was nothing to do but bluff this out.

Almost immediately, the judge banged the gavel, and my hearing began. Higgins called for the doctor who had examined me, if you could call what he did in the hallway of the police station an examination. He took the stand and gave a brief recounting of our discussion. The judge stared at him as placidly as a cow in a pasture while he explained that I needed to be sent to Eloise Hospital for long-term evaluation.

The judge turned to me. "Stand up."

Trying to keep my hand hidden and my face tilted away from Higgins, I stood, as did the young man next to me.

"What's your name?" the judge asked.

I lowered my voice as much as I could and still hope to have it sound like I wasn't disguising it. "John Doe, sir." In my peripheral vision, I could see that Higgins was looking at me. My right side, which he was seeing, was considerably more beat up than my left. I shifted my stance a bit to give him less profile.

The judge blinked. "Is that your real name?"

"I think so. That's what these gentlemen have been calling me."

"Yes, well, are you crazy?"

I laughed. "Crazy? No." The craziest people I'd met all denied they were crazy. It seemed a good bet. "I just can't find my dog."

He ignored the comment about the dog and asked, "How long have you been in Detroit?"

"Detroit?" I laughed again. "I've never been to Detroit."

"Then where are we?"

I turned left and looked behind me before leaning in toward the judge. In a confidential way, I said, "In a courtroom, sir."

The judge was apparently a good-humored man, because he just gave me a grin and turned to Higgins. "What say you, Mr. District Attorney?"

I held my breath.

He barely looked up. "We suggest Mr. Doe be remanded to the custody of Eloise Hospital for an evaluation period of ninety days."

It was that easy. The beating had been a blessing. The judge agreed with Higgins, and in no time a guard brought me to an individual cell in the back of the courthouse, where I waited, and waited, and waited. I was subjected to all the normal noises of a large jail—shouting, laughing, hooting, crying, and plenty of cursing—but hours passed before I saw another human being. It was a trustee—another prisoner—bringing me a tin plate with beans, a piece of stale bread, and a cup of watered-down coffee that, remarkably, did not taste of urine. This time I cleaned my plate and finished the coffee.

# Elizabeth

I slept restlessly, unable to stop fretting about Will. Advice I'd given him, *Worry about the things you can control, not the things you can't,* went through my mind, but it didn't help. I phoned his apartment at 3:00 A.M. and, as expected, got no answer. I finally climbed out of bed at six and tried again, with the same result.

Mrs. Kelly arrived at our home at eight o'clock sharp. I pushed thoughts of Will to the back of my mind. I had to get her off to a good start. My mother hadn't come down from her bedroom yet, which was fine as it would give me a little time to orient the nurse prior to setting Mother loose on her.

First we brought her belongings up to the servants' quarters. The third floor of our home has four bedrooms and a small bath. Alberts long ago had laid claim to the largest room, a spacious bedroom originally designed for a couple. The other rooms are quite small, and as Helga occupies one, I let Mrs. Kelly choose from the other two. She decided on the room at the front of the house, which gave her a lovely view of the river. Helga had chosen a room in back, which was quieter but looked out only on the backyard and garden.

I asked Mrs. Kelly to meet me in the den when she'd finished with her belongings. She returned in only a few minutes and stood at attention in front of the desk. "Reporting for duty, miss."

I wondered how it would feel to pick up and live with a family you hadn't known the day before. Domestics most often spent six days a week, day and night, with people who treated them as fixtures. To us, Alberts was part of our family, and I know he felt the same way, particularly after my father was murdered. Helga had been with us for only a few months and was shy and withdrawn. She seldom joined in conversations, even when I tried to draw her out. It wasn't her duty to converse with us, so I tried to respect her desires and didn't force her. It just seemed to me an awfully lonely existence.

I thought Mrs. Kelly would be different. "Please," I said, "sit."

She eased herself down onto one of the burgundy club chairs opposite the desk and perched on the edge, as if thinking I was testing her somehow.

"I told you a bit about my mother yesterday. I'd like to fill in as much of her story as I can. Over time, you will need to learn enough about her to help supply what she loses. Unfortunately, it's likely this dementia will escalate, and she will forget more and more, and be fully with us less and less."

"I'll do my best, miss."

"I know you will," I said with a smile, then proceeded to tell her an abbreviated version of my mother's history: She grew up in comfortable surroundings in the city. Her father was an ice magnate; her mother, a member of high society who had died of complications from dementia long ago, when I was still a child. Her father, my grandfather, passed on in 1905 from consumption. She had one sister, Theodora, who had recently passed away. I warned Mrs. Kelly about my uncle Peter, whom I did not expect she would meet, and told her a little about my father, emphasizing his good points. I did not tell her about myself.

I heard some clattering in the kitchen and thought my mother must be up. "Now, I suppose we should discuss strategy. My thought is for you to simply be there to help my mother. Ask if you can get her a cup of tea, a warm blanket, listen to her, try to get her to converse with you. It will take some time for you to break through. She is angry and suspicious, and most of all afraid."

Mrs. Kelly nodded.

"Be kind to her, and she will learn to appreciate you. She is a good and kind woman herself. She will see that you are only trying to help, and eventually she will trust you." I smiled. "It's just the 'eventually' that we have to get to."

"I'm a patient woman, miss."

"I believe you are, Mrs. Kelly."

"Call me Bridie, please." She gave me a lopsided grin. "I'd like not to be reminded of Mr. Kelly any more than necessary."

I returned her smile. "All right. Bridie it is." I pushed back my chair and stood. "What do you say we begin the period that will lead us to 'eventually'?"

When we entered the kitchen, my mother was standing at the counter with her back to us, sorting silverware.

"Good morning, Mother," I said with enthusiasm.

"Good morning, Mrs. Hume." Bridie's voice was a bit tentative.

Mother didn't turn around. "I told you I don't need a nurse." Her voice was cold. "And I certainly don't need you to buy me a companion."

"Mother, we talked about this last night. You agreed."

"I don't need her help." Her voice trembled.

I put a hand on Bridie's arm and whispered, "Perhaps you should wait in the living room."

With no expression, she nodded and left the kitchen.

I walked up to my mother and stood next to her. "I understand that you're angry with me, but that's no excuse to be rude. Didn't you teach me to behave like a lady during the most adverse circumstances?"

"That was before you were a traitor," she spat.

My head jerked back as if I had been slapped. After a long moment, during which neither of us moved, she began slamming the cutlery into the drawer's wooden compartments. Stunned, I retreated from the kitchen and stood in the hallway trying not to cry while silverware banged with loud metallic clashes.

*So unfair,* I thought, as tears trickled down my cheeks. It was so unfair. I was supposed to be everyone's rock, the one who keeps her head while everyone else falls apart. I was doing my best, trying to be the best daughter I could, and she hurled it back into my face. I had to be there for my mother and for Will and for Robert, but how could I? Robert was locked into solitary confinement for life, Will was missing, and my mother was losing her mind.

Spinning on my heel, I marched to the den, taking one deep breath after another, and pressed the door closed behind me. I collapsed into the chair at the desk and wondered where I would find the strength. They all needed me—but I needed them. I needed someone. Something.

I thought about heroin, how it had made all my dark places light, all my sorrows joys. I thought I would like a little bottle to sip from, to get me through these trials. For better or worse, I couldn't convince myself that I would sip, or that I would stop at a little bottle. I knew where it would lead, and I'd rather slit my wrists than endure that again.

Someone had to be the rock. It would never again be my mother. She needed time. Even in her state, sooner or later she would see that I was only trying to help her.

A light knock sounded against the door.

Wiping my eyes, I said, "Yes?"

"Excuse me, miss." Bridie pushed the door open and slipped inside the room.

"Did you hear?" I asked.

With a sympathetic look, she nodded.

I sat up in the chair and clasped my hands together on the desktop. "Do you have any ideas?"

"If you don't mind me saying, miss, it might be better if you was to leave me with your mother today. She's got to get used to me being here, and it won't happen quickly if she can just keep swiping at you."

"Perhaps . . . perhaps you're right."

"I'll be gentle with her, miss," Bridie said.

I hesitated. "Bridie, could I ask you about Eloise Hospital?"

"Yes, miss."

"You said you left because you preferred private care. Was that the only reason?"

She glanced away, and her mouth tightened. I could see her internal struggle.

"You can tell me," I said. "I certainly won't hold it against you. I'm no fan of that place."

"I just . . . It gave me the shivers, miss. I couldn't get used to being there."

"What did you think of Dr. Beckwith?"

She shrugged. "Never met the man. He didn't consort with the help. I did my job, and I went home. I left as soon as I found another job, and I've never been back."

"All right. Thank you. And I will leave today." It would let me move forward with my plan to volunteer at Eloise. I had to do something.

"Don't you worry, miss. Your mum and I will become fast friends, you'll see." She gave me an encouraging smile and left the room, closing the door behind her.

I gathered myself and phoned the hospital, asking them the procedure for becoming a volunteer. I was told I needed to apply in person at the Administration Building inside Eloise with at least two references from people of good standing in the community. They were in desperate need of volunteers, being out in an area with little population. If I checked out, they could have me working in a matter of days.

The woman asked my name. I hesitated. Since my name was likely to be recognized by some of Eloise's staff, I gave her the first name that came to mind: Esther James, the pseudonym Will had spontaneously chosen for me when checking in at the Cosmopolitan Hotel earlier in the year. She asked when she might expect me, and I promised to be in the following afternoon. I needed time to prepare.

"Before five?" she asked.

"Yes, ma'am," I replied like a good volunteer.

"Good. We don't stay one minute later."

I couldn't blame them. "I'll be there."

The next thing I did was check a Michigan Central train schedule. I thought about driving our Baker Electric, but we seldom took it more than ten miles. The round trip to Eloise and back would be more than thirty miles, and there were no charging stations outside of downtown. The automobile was supposed to average fifty miles on a charge, but I'd never tested it. I didn't fancy the idea of being stranded out in the hinterlands. Or worse, at Eloise Hospital.

I was surprised to find no mention of Eloise on the Michigan Central schedule or, for that matter, any stops near Nankin Township. I knew there was train service, so I phoned the ticket office, only to find that they had sold the route to Detroit United Railway. Apparently, a monopoly in the city wasn't enough for the DUR. They were expanding their stranglehold over the area.

Indeed, on a DUR interurban schedule sheet I did find Eloise. Trains left the DUR downtown station for that destination throughout the day, beginning at 7:40 A.M. The last train returning to Detroit left Eloise at 8:35 P.M. That would give me some flexibility.

Next, I thought about my recommendation letters. I had one from Clara Arthur, but of course that was for Elizabeth Hume, not Esther James. Anyway, given the politics involved, I didn't know if the hospital administration would consider the president of the Michigan Equal Suffrage Association to be a person "of good standing." I had on hand some stationery from the McGregor Mission from a fund-raising effort a few months back, and I knew Father McGregor believed I did a fine job with the men there. I decided he wouldn't mind telepathically dictating me a letter of reference. He didn't have a telephone, so in order to check the reference someone from Eloise would have to travel to the mission. I didn't think they'd take the time to do that.

After typing Esther a glowing recommendation from Father McGregor, I phoned Edsel Ford at work, as it is in his nature to help, and asked if he would mind serving as my reference. Even though he was our friend, I didn't explain the situation to Edsel. He would almost certainly want to become personally involved, and this was not his fight. I told him I was playing a practical joke on a doctor I knew at Eloise and wondered if he would write a letter of recommendation for my pseudonymous character. He told me he'd have it typed up on Ford Motor Company stationery and signed by his father.

"What if they call him, though?" I asked.

"He'll never talk to them," Edsel said with a laugh. "No one can get him on the telephone. A secretary will have a copy of the letter and will confirm that he wrote it. He's in the office this morning. I can have it ready within the hour."

"Wonderful, Edsel. I'll stop by before noon, if that's all right. Thank you."

Finished with my telephone calls, I sat back in the chair and thought. Not only did I need a new name, I needed a new look. I phoned my hairdresser, asking for an emergency appointment. She said she could squeeze me in at one thirty.

Walking down the hallway, I passed the kitchen and saw it was empty. Alberts was standing in the foyer and simply pointed up the stairs toward the bedrooms. I nodded to him and continued to the living room. I told Bridie I'd be gone most of the day, and while she waited for my mother to come out of her room, she could read a magazine, or knit, or do whatever she did with her leisure time. At that, she gave me a curious look. I silently chastised myself. I took it for granted, but leisure time was a foreign concept to the working class.

I knocked on my mother's door and told her I was leaving and would be gone until that evening. Should she need anything, she only had to ask Mrs. Kelly, who would gladly help her. Mother did not reply. I pulled Alberts aside and asked him to keep an eye on the two of them while I was gone. I thought Bridie was a gem, but one never knew in these situations. Most people can put on the personality they think is expected of them while they are under supervision. Their true nature only comes out when they want to reveal it. We would be watchful.

Nearly ready to go, I dug a photograph album out from the bottom of a closet. The pictures were from a few years back, when Will and I were engaged. Rather than doing what I had intended, finding pictures of Will for the newspapers, I found myself paging through the album, stopping on a picture of the two of us wearing sailing whites, standing on the front of a sailboat at the Detroit Yacht Club. The boat belonged to friends, and we were by no means sailors, but we both wore devil-may-care grins, adventurers out for a voyage on the river.

That had been a fairy-tale time for us. We were still children, well-to-do, attractive, blessed, in love. In my naïveté, I thought I knew what pain was, and what it meant to lose something. I had lost so much since. Perhaps Will had already been added to that list.

I bent again to my task and found three pictures that were reasonable facsimiles of Will's current appearance, other than the beard. It was unfortunate, for identification purposes only, that he'd never sported a beard before. I returned to the den and typed out three advertisements asking for information as to the whereabouts of Will Anderson, with a description including his height and weight. As Detective Riordan had suggested, I left out any mention of reward.

Before I left the house, I tried phoning Will one more time. As I expected, no one answered. I caught a streetcar and rode from Jefferson to Woodward and then all the way up to the Ford factory in Highland Park. Edsel, as promised, had had the letter typed out and signed by his father. I picked it up, told Edsel I would have Will phone him, and headed back down Woodward Avenue to Madame Michelle's.

She had her chair open for me when I arrived. I placed my hat on the rack and sat. She ran her fingers through my hair, still so short although it felt like a long time since I'd cut it. "Your hair looks fine to me, Elizabeth," Madame Michelle said with her lovely French accent. "What is the emergency? I cannot make it grow faster."

I looked up at her and said, "Break out the hydrogen peroxide."

I shook out my hair, looked in the mirror, and laughed out loud. Blond? Me? The effect was startling. It was as if I had been transformed into another person. My skin color was light enough, I thought, to make it work, but I couldn't get over the person I saw in the mirror. The thing that surprised me was that I couldn't decide if I looked better as a blonde. I thought it might draw attention away from my eyes, which seemed to me to have grown sadder, heavier somehow, over the past few years.

There was no one at Eloise who knew me well, though I thought it likely that at least Dr. Davis and the guard we ran into yesterday would still recognize me. I would have to avoid them.

I paid Michelle and added a generous tip before finding a pay telephone and trying Will's apartment one more time. It rang for more than two minutes, and I had the feeling it would continue forever without an answer, so I hung up and phoned Alberts. Will hadn't contacted them. I spoke briefly with Bridie, who cheerfully told me that things were progressing as well as could be expected and not to worry.

Taking a deep breath, I put another nickel into the coin slot and phoned Will's mother. She still hadn't heard from him. This time I made no attempt to disguise the concern in my voice but simply asked her again to phone me if he contacted them. She said Will's father was at the factory, so I phoned Mr. Wilkinson, who hadn't heard from Will either. He connected me with Mr. Anderson, and I broke the news to him that Will had disappeared and that I would be placing missing person advertisements in the newspapers. He quizzed me but gave up quickly when he realized I knew little more than he. We each tried to reassure the other, but I could tell his concern was no more assuaged than mine. He said he would also begin a search for Will. After promising to phone one another if we discovered anything, we rang off.

I walked to the offices of the three major newspapers in town, the *Free Press*, *News*, and *Journal*, and placed the advertisements. They all claimed they couldn't run the ads until Wednesday because of press setup time or some such thing. Each was adamant about it until I offered the salesman an extra five dollars in cash to get the ad in the Sunday paper. They all said they would see to it.

It was nearly five o'clock when I wearily stepped up onto a trolley for the ride home. I'd done what I could. My quiver held no more arrows. Now I simply had to hope that one of them would find its target.

On the trolley ride home, I was overcome with melancholy. I couldn't shake the sense of foreboding that filled me. Robert was locked up for murder. It was incredibly unlikely that, by myself, I would find evidence to clear him.

Will was missing. As Detective Riordan said, Will had extricated himself from some incredibly difficult situations, and had shown a great deal of physical and mental fortitude. He had never just disappeared, though. I knew that, no matter what was keeping him away, he would have contacted me by now if he could.

As for my mother: I thought it likely that as her dementia progressed, she would become even less accepting of her circumstances or of Bridie, assuming Bridie put up with her long enough for it to even be a consideration. This was the critical time in their relationship. I needed to help my mother accept Bridie, as well as to find some degree of peace with the changes in her life.

I didn't see how I would successfully resolve any one of these problems, much less all three.

I got off the trolley half a mile from our house so I could compose myself before getting home. By the time I flung open the door, I had a smile plastered on my face. Alberts greeted me. I waited for him to comment on my change in hair color, but, being a man, he didn't seem to notice. He told me that Mother had been hiding out in her room most of the day (and was at this moment as well), but Bridie checked in with her regularly to see if she could help with anything. He was highly complimentary of our new nurse, which I took as a very good sign. Alberts generally reserved judgment about people until they had proven themselves. I asked him to have Bridie meet me in the den in fifteen minutes, as I needed a little time to wash up.

Perhaps five minutes later, I walked down the hall to the den and saw that the door was closed, which was unusual. I opened it to see Bridie in front of the bookcase, her fingers running up and down the molding that triggered the door to the secret room. She jerked her hand away and ran it back and forth on the front of a shelf, in a manner so as to appear inconsequential.

"Would you like to see it?" I asked.

Turning toward me, she said, "See . . . what?"

That made me angry. "We're not going to get along very well if you can't be honest with me."

"I'm . . . sorry, miss." She hung her head. "Helga told me about the room. I just thought I would look for the door. I'm sorry. I'm not normally—"

"Enough said. Now, would you like to see it?"

After a moment, she quietly answered, "Please."

I walked over and pressed the trigger to the door, which popped open an inch. I pushed it all the way open. "See for yourself."

Her smile was that of a little child, but it vanished and she looked back at me, her face full of worry. "You won't shut me in there, will you?"

"Oh, Bridie," I said with a laugh. "Why would I do that? You have to trust me as well."

"Yes, miss." She looked through the door, then back at me. "Shall I go now?"

I nodded. "Take your time."

She disappeared down the passageway. I took a seat at the desk and waited a few minutes for her return. When she popped out the door, she said, "I've never seen anything like it."

"It's not so special. It's just a little room."

"Yes, miss," she said, "but it's a *hidden* little room."

I nodded my acknowledgment.

"Would've come in handy with Mr. Kelly around," she added.

I laughed again and asked her to sit. She perched on a chair across the desk from me and said, "Your hair is very pretty, miss."

I thanked her and asked about her day.

"Oh, I suppose I could say it was a bit tedious. Though the last time Mrs. Hume came downstairs, she didn't turn her back when she saw me. She didn't speak to me, but she didn't turn away." Bridie gave me a warm smile. "Don't worry yourself, she'll see the light."

"I'm sorry to burden you with this, but you must understand. I'm involved in some very difficult situations. My beau has disappeared, and my . . . cousin has been accused of murder."

"Murder?"

"Yes." I explained my worries regarding Robert and Will. As I did, her mouth tightened, and she grimaced in sympathy. I could see genuine concern written in her eyes.

When I finished, she said, "Well, miss, don't worry about your mother. I'll watch over her, and Mr. Alberts helps out a great deal. He's a good man, I know that already."

"Yes, he is," I said. "I'm very thankful for him."

She yawned, and I thought about how stressful her day must have been. "You run along now, dear," I said. "Take some time for yourself."

"Thank you, miss." She studied me for a second and gave me a gentle smile. "You take care of your other problems. I'll mind your mum." She stood and walked to the door.

Just before she reached it, I said, "Bridie?"

She turned around.

"I don't need to worry about you, do I?"

"No, miss. Cross my heart and hope to die." She crossed her heart with a forefinger. "I'll never lie to you again."

She left the room, quietly closing the door behind her. She had shaken my confidence a bit, but I still had a good feeling about her. I decided to keep trusting my instincts. I had startled her when I walked in. Her reaction was what any servant's would have been. She had owned up to it. Anyway, what did she have to gain by accessing an empty room?

I phoned Will's apartment. No answer. I looked at the wall clock and saw that it was after six, so I tried Detective Riordan at home. His wife answered. Her accent was British and very proper, which surprised me, particularly the British part. She sounded like a pleasant woman and quickly called her husband to the telephone. He came on the line a few moments later. After we established that neither of us had heard from Will, I filled him in on my day.

He said he had been making quiet inquiries into the reputation of the Eloise Hospital Police Department and had found nothing out of the ordinary. "Get into the asylum and see what you can find out," he said. "I'll put out a missing person report for Will in the morning. But, Elizabeth?"

"Yes?"

"Don't worry. I'm sure he's safe and sound."

# CHAPTER FIVE

*Saturday, August 10, 1912*

## Will

The dream woke me hours before a guard unlocked my door, hauled me out of the building, and loaded me into a Black Maria for transport. The two men I'd seen in the interrogation room at the police station already sat inside.

"Gentlemen," I said.

They nodded their greetings.

Once we were under way, I asked the younger man again what he had done when his wife wouldn't pass the potatoes.

"Same thing anyone else woulda done."

"Which was?"

"I threw my fork at her."

"That's why you're here?" I asked.

"Yeah." He paused, thinking. "Well, I didn't so much throw it. It was more like—" He raised his hand a few inches, which was as far as the shackles would allow, and thrust his fist forward several times.

"So you stabbed her."

"Well, sure, but it was a fork."

I nodded and made a mental note to avoid him at mealtimes. The older man was looking out the window, watching the city pass by. *"Mein Herr?"* I said. *"Sprechen Sie* English?"

"*Nein*." With a glimmer of hope in his eye, he pointed at me. "*Deutsch?*"

"*Nein,*" I said. Though there were dozens of German men with little to no English at the Detroit Electric factory, I'd never gotten past "Hello" and "How are you?"

He went back to looking out the window, seemingly accepting his fate.

We rode for the next hour or so in silence. The clop of the horse hoofs was hypnotizing, and the wagon swayed back and forth in motion with the horses' gait. It would have been a pleasant hour, had I not been heading to an insane asylum to which I had been committed for three months.

I spent the hour thinking about strategy. Once I was inside, I needed to find Robert and make sure he was all right, as well as determine who was killing the patients and how many he had dispatched thus far. Oh, and try to keep him from killing anyone else. And then get myself out of there in one piece.

Unfortunately . . . I didn't know if I would have enough freedom at the asylum to investigate anything. I didn't know how painful—or damaging—the treatments for amnesia would be. I didn't know if I would even have access to other patients. With no information, I couldn't formulate a plan. Worst of all, neither Elizabeth nor Detective Riordan would know I was at Eloise Hospital.

By the time the wagon stopped and the doors opened, I was no longer wondering how big an idiot I was.

It was crystal clear.

Stepping down from the wagon, I glanced up to see a water tower, the words ELOISE HOSPITAL written across it in white letters.

"Let's go," one of the policemen said.

We shuffled to the gate in our shackles, a policeman marching on either side of us. A guard swung the gate open. A pair of policemen stood inside waiting for us.

*Shit.* One of them was the older cop who had whacked me with his nightstick less than a week ago. I ducked my head and let my hair fall into my eyes, trying not to be obvious about it, but keeping him from getting a good look at me. I thought I might appear crazier looking out from under my brow anyway.

The Detroit cops handed us over along with a sheaf of papers, then removed our shackles and headed back toward the gate.

The older Eloise cop said, "Listen here." Tapping his nightstick against his palm, he waited until everyone looked at him. "We'll all get along fine if you do as you're told. You don't, you're gonna get this"—he brandished his nightstick—"or worse. And believe me, we've got worse." He glanced at me. I kept my face blank. He showed no sign of recognition.

He looked through the papers, stopping to call out, "Srugis?" The younger man grunted. "Zimmermann?" The older man raised his hand. The cop looked at me. "You must be Doe, then."

I nodded.

He led us up the long walk to the Administration Building. The other cop followed along behind. Both had their nightsticks at the ready. A dozen women in nightshirts were shambling along a path on the side of the building, walking behind an orderly like a row of baby ducks following their mother. One of them wandered off onto the grass. An orderly ran, shouting, up to the woman and dragged her by the arm back onto the path.

We continued past the main entrance to another doorway, under a sign reading ELOISE HOSPITAL POLICE. The older cop opened the door, and they shoved us inside. A long wooden counter separated the front of the room from the back, where a large barred cage held perhaps a dozen men.

From somewhere nearby, but out of sight, a man howled and then grunted like an ape. All three of us flinched, but the policemen didn't seem to even notice. Most of the prisoners sat quietly, though one stood staring out through the bars mumbling a Hail Mary, and another was marching back and forth at the front of the cell with military precision. When the guard unlocked the door, the man saluted him and waited until the three of us were in the cell and the door was locked to begin marching again. Here the sour stench of body odor was sharp. Srugis, Zimmermann, and I took seats together on an open piece of bench on the side. The man nearest us scooted away and then adjusted his location until he was precisely as far away from us as he was from the man on the other side. I scrutinized the other prisoners, looking for threats.

A few of them looked mad, no question about it—drooling, eyes focused somewhere other than reality—but most looked no different than the thousands of people one might meet on the outside, in a restaurant or at a park. I tried to picture Henry Ford sitting here with us and thought he might well look the maddest of all. The Hail Mary man and the "guard" continued at their tasks, but everyone else sat still and quiet, occasionally sneaking glances at the cops.

They had enough of their faculties intact to have at least some idea of what was happening to them, and they were afraid.

Guards pulled men from the cell in groups of three until Srugis, Zimmermann, and I were the only ones left. All the while, the cops in the front of the room ignored us, going about their business. Srugis muttered vague threats under his breath, though he quieted whenever one of the policemen glared at him. Zimmermann just sat quietly, waiting for his fate to unfold.

Later that afternoon, the sound of clanking metal came from up the hall; then someone was slammed against a wall with a cry of pain. A man let loose a terrible roar. The sound of the struggle continued toward us—the crack of a stick on a skull, shackles rattling as they flailed about, fists hitting flesh.

Three policemen dragged a man down the hallway. Two guards followed, their truncheons out, arms cocked. The man was half a head taller than any of the policemen, perhaps six-five, and although he may not have outweighed them all, the cops' weight tended to fat, while he looked lean and muscular. He had flaming red hair and freckles and big hazel eyes that bulged from his head. His gaze bounced around the room, not settling on anything, and he strained against the chains and the guards like a wild animal. "Let me go!" he bellowed.

I blanched at his roar, as did Srugis and Zimmermann. I was certain that even Srugis was thinking the same thing I was: *Don't put him in here.*

The cops stopped just outside the cell. "Watch out, boys," one of them said. "This here's Tyrus Raymond Cobb of the Detroit Tigers."

This clearly was not Ty Cobb, who, although a big red-haired man, was not nearly this big, nor was his hair nearly this red. But I wasn't going to be the one to break that to the giant.

One of the guards opened the cell door, and the cops pushed and shoved against him. After a savage chop to the kidney with a nightstick, the red-haired giant fell into the cell. He immediately jumped to his feet and looked around him, fixing us all with a glare. At least they had left him shackled. It might even the odds if he decided to take us all on.

"Hey, Peach," one of the cops called with a smile. "Don't kill none a them or you're gonna miss the next season or two."

The giant, veins bulging at his temples, leveled a deadly stare at him.

"Ain'tcha got a game today, Cobb?" another cop asked, taking a step toward the cell.

The giant sneered at him. "Yeah. And I'ma kick all y'all's asses if you don't let me outta here. Why 'ontcha come on over here where we can talk about it?" His massive arms shot toward the cop between the bars until the chain clanked against the metal. The cop started and took a step back.

"What?" the big man said, a cold smile on his face. "Y'all 'fraida me?" He turned and looked around the cell, his eyes finally lighting on me. There seemed to be something missing from his countenance. After meeting his eyes for a second, I realized the missing component was reserve. His face was that of a ferocious predator, the top of the food chain. In here, I reckoned, he was. He looked at me as a lion might at a helpless gazelle fawn. By the time I had looked away, he was stalking toward me.

He leaned down within inches of my face. "Do I look like a nigger to you?"

My face flushed. I slowly drew my head back far enough for my eyes to focus on him. "What did you say?"

He leaned in farther. "You lookin' at me like you own me. Do you own me, boy?"

I ducked around his head and stood up. If I backed down, I'd be a marked man. He might rip me apart, but it seemed likely he would do that anyway. I thought about Wesley and gave the giant my best dead-eyed stare. In a low growl, I said, "I don't own anyone. Now back the hell up."

The man who believed he was Ty Cobb stared at me for a long moment before one side of his lip began to quiver. He inhaled, and I tensed. I wasn't going to let him kill me without a fight. Because of his size, I thought I'd be quicker, but I needed to strike fast and move outside his range. If he got me wrapped up I was a goner. Having my right eye swollen shut, I wouldn't see his left hand until it was too late. I hoped he was right-handed.

*Knee to the groin,* I thought, *step left, side kick to the fulcrum of the knee. When—if—he goes down, left hook to the side of the jaw, reassess.* I wished I had a knife.

Everything slowed down. The giant's eyes narrowed. *Watch the eyes,* I thought. The cell was deathly quiet, as if everyone were holding his breath. *As soon as he moves . . .*

A key turned in the lock, and the cell door swung open behind the giant. "Doe! Srugis! Zimmermann!" a man called.

"Yep," I said, my eyes never leaving Ty's.

A second later, the giant swayed forward. His attention shifted to the man behind him, though he didn't turn around.

"Yeah, that's a gun in your back, shithead," the guard said. Another stood next to him, his gun also leveled at Ty. "Let him be," the first man said, "or I'm gonna put a hole in ya."

I started walking around the giant.

"Nobody threatens me, cop," he said.

"Ah, fuck ya," the guard said, though the tone of his voice didn't match the brave words.

I walked out of the cell with the other men. The guard backed away from Ty and locked the door behind him. I shot a glance at the giant before we left the room. His eyes tracked me to the door. I couldn't stop a long sigh of relief from escaping my lips.

I just hoped that would be the last I saw of Ty. Someone that violent would surely be locked away from the other patients. If I encountered him again I'd run. If I couldn't run, I'd try to kill him—somehow. The devil is always in the details, isn't he?

The guards brought us down the hall to a room labeled INTAKE, where a bespectacled red-faced nurse sat behind a desk near the door. Four large orderlies sprang from their seats and stood in front of us, trying, and largely succeeding, to look menacing. One of the guards leaned over the desk and handed the sheaf of papers to the nurse. They talked in low voices for a few moments before he and his partner left the room.

One of the orderlies spoke with the nurse and took a set of documents. Turning to us, he barked out, "Zimmermann!" and waved toward a door on the side of the room.

Zimmermann jumped in his seat, startled, before standing and walking to the door. Another orderly joined them. He opened the door, and they all disappeared inside. Srugis started grumbling about alphabetical order and shot angry looks at the staff members.

The first orderly returned, got another set of documents from the nurse, and said, "Your turn, Srugis."

Srugis didn't move. One of the other orderlies jerked him up from the chair and shoved him toward the door. Rounding on him, Srugis shouted, "Why, you son of a bitch!" He threw a looping hook at the orderly, who blocked it and delivered a straight right to Srugis's nose. Blood spurted, but he kept swinging, screaming incoherently. The first orderly got him in a chokehold and started dragging him to the other room.

"Hey!" I shouted, jumping up from my chair. "Take it easy. He's just scared."

The orderly who punched Srugis turned on me and shoved me down into my seat. "Shut your goddamn mouth, or you're gonna be next!"

I stayed in my chair. There was nothing I could do for Srugis.

After a few minutes, the first orderly returned and got my paperwork. He eyed me and said, "Let's go." The last orderly took hold of my arm, and we followed the other man through the side door. The room was small and all white, one wall lined with clothing hooks, about half of them full of shirts and trousers. In the back, a pair of double doors led to another room.

Behind those doors, a man shouted, "No! Let go—" *Srugis.*

I winced.

"You goddamn sons a whores! Get off—" I heard a sharp *crack!* and didn't hear anything further from him.

The orderly let go of my arm and said, "Strip."

"What?"

"Shower. Strip."

I glanced at him and then back at the other orderly before I began removing my clothing. In short order I was standing naked in front of them, suddenly feeling very cold.

"Take your shoes," the first man said, pointing toward the double doors. His eyes kept cutting to my hand and then to the round burgundy scar on my shoulder. He obviously hadn't noticed them before. I was actually getting used to people staring at my deformity. I picked up my shoes and followed him through a different set of doors to a large shower room with rows of nozzles poking from the wall. A scowling orderly, his shirt and trousers soaked, waited inside for us. Two others were dragging Srugis out the door by the arms. He was naked. His eyes were open, but he looked dazed. Dark blood ran from his nose, turning pink as it mixed with the water on his chest and stomach. A red-stained towel slipped off his legs and fell to the floor.

The orderly in the wet clothing said, "Put your shoes down there."

I complied.

"You ain't gonna make any trouble, right?"

"No." I just wanted to get through this.

He and the orderly who had brought me in marched me to the nearest shower. One of them twisted on the faucet, and a blast of freezing water doused me.

I jumped out of the spray, shouting, "Shit!"

They grabbed me by the arms and jerked me back into the cold water, holding me under. The spray felt like needles on my skin. Finally they pulled me out, and one of them threw me a towel. "Dry yourself off."

As soon as I was dry, one of the orderlies began searching me—hair, underarms, groin—for vermin. Without complaint, I let him do it. When he finished, another of them threw me a nightshirt. Stenciled on the front was EH – B6. I slipped it on and, when the orderlies refused to let me retrieve my stockings, put on my shoes without them. They grabbed my arms again. "I can walk," I said. "I'll go where you want."

Neither of them said anything. They just dragged me back to the other room, where a man in a dark pinstriped suit waited. I was startled to see that it was Dr. Beckwith. As far as I knew, he hadn't really looked at me the night Elizabeth and I came here, but I watched him for signs of recognition. The orderlies stood off to the side, within pouncing distance should I prove to be a danger to the doctor. Beckwith introduced himself and asked me my name, where I was from, what I was doing in

Detroit, and so on. I told him about my headache but on every other subject had no information to give him, other than I thought I had come from Cuba.

"Amnesia?" he asked.

"That's what they tell me."

"I am the administrator of this hospital, but I like to keep my hand in. I've been having promising results with amnesiacs, so you and I will be spending some time together. Speaking of hands, what happened to yours?"

I looked down at my left hand and then my right. I stared at it for a while. "I don't know," I murmured, holding it up near my face and looking at it, front and back.

"I understand you have a bullet wound in your shoulder."

"I do?"

He studied me for a long moment. "Have we met before?"

I leaned in toward him and spoke excitedly. "Have you been to Cuba?"

After staring at me another few seconds, he said, "I've never been to Cuba. Nor, do I think, have you."

"Oh, *señor*," I said. "I could tell you about the crocodiles and the sugar and such. And don't get me started on the rum—"

"That will be all, Mr. Doe." He turned to the orderlies. "I'll be by later for a full exam."

He seemed to have bought my act. The orderlies marched me to the front door, unlocked it, and led me to Building B. Now I'd need to keep an eye out for Dr. Davis. Our first stop was a barber, who shaved off my beard and mustache and buzzed my hair down to stubble. When he finished with that, the orderlies dragged me out to the hall again and turned right down the main corridor—the opposite direction from Dr. Davis's office—and right again at the end of the hall. Noises, not quite animal but not human either, filtered out of the rooms around us—grunts, shouts, and moans from the tormented, the mad, the miserable.

After another few twists and turns, they stopped, and one of them spun the cap off the end of a pipe that ran down the wall from the ceiling to about four and a half feet off the floor. Putting his mouth up to the opening, he barked, "Doe! B6!"

A moment later, a muffled voice replied, "Sixteen-twelve."

They moved me past half a dozen doors before opening one that led into a small room, a cell really, eight feet wide by seven feet deep. Its contents consisted of nothing more than a chamber pot and a metal-frame bed screwed to the floor next to the back wall. An army blanket and, wonder of wonders, a pillow, lay atop the bed. The window was blocked by vertical iron bars spaced about three inches apart.

One of the orderlies pushed me inside. The door closed, and a key turned in the lock.

I sat on the bed and tried to slow my heart. I'd made it this far. I was inside Eloise, and fortunately, Dr. Davis's office was about as far away as was possible in this building.

Perhaps five minutes later, someone unlocked the door. Dr. Beckwith walked in with an orderly and a nurse, a huge woman, nearly six feet tall and extremely overweight. They left the door open, and I noticed someone behind them in the hall.

There, peering in at me with intense concentration, stood Dr. Beckwith's son, Francis.

Francis eyed me, his body stock-still. I had no choice but to ignore him. If he recognized me and identified me as Elizabeth's companion, I was sunk. I half-listened as Dr. Beckwith explained that I would be examined over the next few days. Once they determined what was wrong with me, they would begin a regimen that might cure me.

I nodded, just wanting them to leave before Francis opened his mouth.

"I say 'might' because there are no guarantees with insanity," Dr. Beckwith pronounced, writing something on his pad.

I glanced at Francis again. His face was blank, his attention focused on me. He remained quiet. "Will I have to stay in this . . . room?" I almost said "cell."

"At night, yes. For now, anyway."

"How about during the day?"

"It depends." He turned to the nurse. She handed the doctor a large medicine bottle and an eyedropper.

"I have some medicine for your headache," he said.

"What is it?" I knew I should keep my mouth shut—go along to get along—but the possibility of another addiction petrified me. Likewise, if they kept me drugged, I might never discover the murderer.

"Just headache medicine," he said. "Nothing to worry about."

Nothing worries me more than a doctor telling me I have nothing to worry about. "What kind of headache medicine?"

He opened the bottle, and I smelled the pungent odor of chloral hydrate. They wanted me to sleep.

"I'm feeling better," I said. "I don't need any medicine." From the corner of my eye, I caught a movement in the hallway. I looked. Francis was gone.

Dr. Beckwith opened the bottle and extracted a dropper-full of liquid. He glanced at the orderly, who took a step closer to me. Beckwith said, "You don't want to cause any trouble, now, do you?"

"No, but I don't—"

The orderly grabbed my left arm. I spun away from him.

"Bessie," Dr. Beckwith said, sounding alarmed.

The nurse grabbed my burned hand and twisted it behind my back. Pain blazed through my hand and shoulder. I grunted and arched upward, trying to relieve the pressure. As I did, the orderly pinioned me to the bed.

"God damn it!" I said. "I'm not—"

Beckwith nodded to the nurse, who took hold of my nose and squeezed my nostrils shut. The doctor stood just to the side with the eyedropper poised near my mouth. I struggled against the people holding me, but they were both very strong. Eventually I had to breathe, and Beckwith slipped the dropper into my mouth and squirted the chloral down my throat. I tried to cough it up, but it was already gone. He pulled another dropper-full from the bottle and repeated the action. This time I didn't struggle much. I was already fading.

"I'll check in with you tomorrow," Beckwith said. The orderly took hold of my legs and tossed them onto the bed.

I lay there helpless, my vision blurring. From some great depth, darkness rushed up at me and stole away the light.

# Elizabeth

It was a long night. My mother wouldn't speak with me, and I had a difficult time sleeping. I was not unhappy to see the sun finally peek up from the horizon. After breakfast and three cups of strong coffee, I began to dress for my trek to Eloise Hospital.

In my normal life, I dress comfortably, or as comfortably as women's clothing allows, so I decided the opposite approach would be the course to take for my disguise. I dug a corset out from the bottom of a dresser drawer and strapped myself in. It had been months since I'd worn one, and I nearly suffocated. Even wearing the blasted thing as loosely as possible, my waist was compressed by at least two inches, and the effort to breathe was so great I felt like an elephant was sitting on my chest.

I put on an old-fashioned white high-collared dress, very stiff and Victorian, with high button-top boots and a wide-brimmed white hat with a spray of peacock feathers. Among the playthings my mother had saved in her planning for grandchildren were dress-up clothes, which included a pair of wire-rimmed spectacles with clear lenses. I donned those and eyed myself in the mirror. It was a fairly good disguise.

I put the glasses in my purse and went downstairs to see Bridie and Alberts. I told them I'd be gone most of the day. They eyed my costume but said nothing. I didn't have to worry about my mother's reaction to my clothing, as she didn't look at me when I said good-bye. I left the house a little after seven, walking down to the trolley stop amid radiant sunshine. It was warm for as early as it was, in the high seventies, I judged. It was perfectly comfortable, even in the outfit I wore, although every breath made me more thankful I had forsaken the corset in my everyday life.

I made it to the Detroit United Railway central station at seven thirty, ten minutes before the train was to leave, bought a first-class ticket, and climbed onboard the first of four passenger cars, where I found a seat in an empty row. The train chugged out of the station and down the shoreline before cutting first through Corktown, then Dearborn, and out into the country, stopping regularly to pick up and drop off passengers.

We traveled past the occasional cluster of homes near intersections, generally small farmhouses, uniformly white, dense-looking somehow, as if they were solid cubes stacked together rather than hollow wooden structures. I couldn't decide what made them seem so. Perhaps because they had only a few small windows, and those were higher on the walls than the large windows in the homes to which I was accustomed.

I worried about Will. I worried about what I would find at Eloise, and about Robert. I worried about my mother and hoped that Bridie was the person I thought she was. I worried so much that I was shocked to see the grounds of Eloise Hospital coming up on my right.

The train pulled into the Eloise DUR station with a chuff and a wheeze, and I climbed out, making it a point to look at the fields on this side of the road, tall with corn and wheat, rather than up ahead at the little lake, the gazebo, and the amusement hall. No fence stood on this side of Michigan Avenue, which surprised me, but I imagined it was unnecessary when only the best-behaved patients were allowed to see shows or walk near the lake.

I wondered if I would be able to get past the guard. If he was the same man with whom Will and I had argued on Wednesday, the odds were good he would recognize me. I walked along the road, away from the hospital's entrance, trying to think of a strategy. It was ridiculous to have come so far and have no plan for getting inside, but I suppose that was an indication of my state of mind. I stopped about two blocks away from the gate, pondering my predicament.

Coming toward me was an open-bodied carriage pulled by a pair of horses, clip-clopping down the road. As it got closer, I could see that the carriage was a little two-wheeled cabriolet, the top folded back. A man wearing a gray suit with a matching riding cap was at the reins. He stopped and tipped his cap to me. He was a compact man of perhaps thirty, with a wide mouth and very red lips, a prominent nose, and small eyes such a light brown as to appear almost crystalline. His countenance was somewhat rodentlike, though more in line with a cute little field mouse than its less attractive relatives.

"Can I offer you a ride, miss?" he asked.

"No, thank you," I replied and began walking toward the gate again.

"Are you perhaps going to the hospital?"

I stopped. "Yes, I am."

"As am I, miss. I would be happy to convey you."

"But I don't know you, sir."

"Allow me to introduce myself," he said, rising from the seat and leaping to the road in front of me. He gave me a deep sweeping bow. His movements were sure and practiced. "Clarence Morgan, at your service."

I've read books, not books I would normally admit to reading, in which the hero used those words, but no one had ever said them to me. Somehow he made them sound natural.

"Pleased to meet you, Mr. Morgan. My name is . . ." I almost introduced myself as Elizabeth Hume. "Esther James."

He rose from the bow. "The pleasure is all mine, Miss James, let me assure you. Now that we are acquainted, may I offer you a ride? I promise to have no motive other than to assist a lady."

He didn't seem threatening in the least, and I thought he might give me some cover. "All right, Mr. Morgan. I would be happy to accept."

He held out his hand and helped me into the carriage, then hopped up and snapped the reins. "Where can I take you, Miss James?"

"Just inside is fine, Mr. Morgan. I can find my way from there." The entrance to the Administration Building was perhaps two hundred yards from the gate.

"Don't be silly. Are you here to visit someone, perhaps?"

"No, I am a new volunteer."

"New, as in new today?"

"Yes."

"The Administration Building, then."

I saw no reason to apprise him that I knew where to go. Men love to help a damsel in distress.

When he stopped in front of the gate, he handed me the reins. "Would you hold these for me?"

"Certainly." I took them.

He hopped down from the carriage and, producing a key from his pocket, walked up to a small wooden door in the brick wall to the right of the main gate. He unlocked it, looked back to me and held up an index finger, then quickly opened the door and closed it behind him. A second later, he appeared at the gate and worked some apparatus to open it. "Would you like to pull her through?" he called.

Well, a man entrusting his rig to a woman. This Mr. Morgan was not of the ordinary sort. "I would, thank you."

He stood at the side of the gate while I drove the carriage inside the hospital grounds. The guard never even came out of the guardhouse. Mr. Morgan closed the gate, climbed on again, and started the horses walking toward the Administration Building.

"What is your business here, Mr. Morgan?"

"I'm a teacher. The guard overlooks it, but don't tell anyone I have the key." He looked at me with a twinkle in his eye. "Or that I borrowed Dr. Beckwith's carriage without asking him."

"It's not wise to tell your secrets to a complete stranger, Mr. Morgan."

He laughed. "Oh, but now that we're acquainted, I feel I can lay myself bare to you. Strictly in a metaphorical sense, of course," he quickly added. "Now, what was I saying? Oh, yes, the key. Constantly checking in and out is a ridiculous waste of time. I've been working here a couple of years now, but I'm still not used to the supervision." He shrugged. "I grew up on a ranch. I like open air and freedom."

"Quite understandable, Mr. Morgan. Living here must feel like living with a set of domineering parents."

"Exactly. You do understand." He nodded. "I just think human beings should be free."

"Are you an anarchist, Mr. Morgan? Not that I mind if you are."

"No, Miss James. Order is necessary." He grinned at me and admitted, "I just don't care for people imposing order on *me*."

I smiled back. "I agree completely, Mr. Morgan. Tell me, what do you teach?"

"English. Two of the R's, as they say."

"Do you teach the insane or indigent?"

"I suppose the best answer to that is yes. I teach the most capable of the patients, regardless of their classification."

"Do you enjoy working with them?"

"I'm not sure 'enjoy' is the right word, Miss James. The patients here can be difficult. I know I'm opening their minds to new worlds and new forms of expression, and I do take satisfaction from that."

He pulled up in front of the main entrance and hopped down from the carriage. As he walked around to my side, he said, "This is Building A, otherwise known as the Administration Building. Ask at the desk in the lobby. They'll direct you to one of the offices on the second floor, I don't remember which." He offered me his hand, and I let him help me down. He was careful to keep his distance and even averted his eyes when I dismounted.

"Thank you, Mr. Morgan. I appreciate your help."

"Pleased to have been of assistance, Miss James. Good luck to you."

He climbed back into the carriage and began turning the horses around. As he pulled away, back in the direction from which we'd come, he said, "If you need a ride in the future, you can call on me. Assuming Dr. Beckwith isn't out."

I laughed, again thanked him, and started up the walk to the Administration Building. I thought I had found an ally, should I need to call on him.

At the end of the walk, atop a short flight of stairs, was a pair of wooden doors that would lead me into my undercover assignment. I hoped it would be a successful one.

After I waited more than an hour to see the volunteer supervisor, the approval process took ten minutes. I expected to have to maneuver through a rigorous screening, but once she saw that I was a respectable woman, she stamped my application and attached the reference letters, saying little more than "My, Henry Ford" under her breath. I told her I would be available to start immediately and would prefer to work with dementia praecox patients, male if possible. In a stiff voice, she told me that volunteers were needed throughout the hospital and must be prepared for duty of all sorts.

"Of course," I replied. "I thought you might like to know my preference, should there be any flexibility."

"Are you going to be one of those *occasional* volunteers," she asked with a touch of scorn, "or are you willing to work a full schedule?"

"I'd like to work full-time. Six days a week."

The corners of her mouth rose in a brief and humorless smile. "Can you start Monday?"

Given that it was Saturday, this surprised me immensely, but I supposed the Henry Ford reference had given me blue-ribbon status. I hesitated. My mother had to be eased into Bridie's new role, but as Detective Riordan said, the trail grows cold very quickly in a murder investigation. "Yes, ma'am," I said. "That would be fine."

She pulled a train schedule from her desk and ran an index finger down and then across it. "If you leave from the central station at seven forty, you will arrive here at five past nine. Would that be acceptable?"

I said it would. In another situation, I might have commented on the fact that she assumed I'd be taking the train rather than driving. Not here. The less attention I drew to myself, the better.

She told me where to report and stood, indicating our interview had concluded.

"Excuse me, but where would I find information on a patient's location?"

"Administration."

"Thank you. I'll stop by there on the way out." I turned for the door.

"They're closed to the public on weekends. Internal assignments only."

"Oh. Thank you. I'll check Monday, then." I left the office, walked down the hall to the lobby, and pushed on the door. It didn't budge. I looked back at the guard, who ambled over, eyeing me all the way, and pulled a large ring of keys from his pocket. He unlocked the door and opened it, standing so that he partially blocked the doorway.

"Excuse me," I said. I was not rubbing up against him to get through the door.

After a few seconds, his mouth turned sour. He let go of the door and stepped back. I caught it before it closed, and with a curt "Thank you" I left the building and started for the gate.

When I got to the train station, it was nearly devoid of passengers, which I thought a bad sign. That was confirmed by the rail agent, who informed me that I had just missed the eleven-fifteen train and the next one wasn't due for more than three hours. I phoned home and asked Alberts how my mother was faring. He said she had ignored Bridie all day but not to worry, that my mother would soon thaw to the younger woman's friendliness.

"I hope you're right," I replied. "I just phoned to let you know I missed the train, so I won't be getting into the station until four thirty."

"Would you like me to bring the automobile, miss?" he asked.

"You're a dear, Alberts, but no. I'll have a bite to eat and catch the next train back."

We arranged for Alberts to pick me up at the downtown Detroit station when I arrived and then rang off. I headed toward the restaurant in the cluster of businesses just down from the station. Most of the traffic was male and on the way to the inn, a narrow two-story clapboard building. Of course, I wouldn't think of going into a saloon by myself, so I kept my course steady and walked farther down the dusty road.

I had a bounce in my step. While my problems had not yet diminished, I had gotten inside, as Esther James, hospital volunteer. I would need to cultivate allies so as to gain every possible advantage. Clarence Morgan might be part of the solution. He seemed to be the right kind of person to talk to: the classic "outsider," an intelligent man who hadn't buckled to the demands of conformity that weighed down every large institution. As a member of the staff, he would be in the middle of the goings-on, and I was sure that the rumors and gossip at Eloise were as pervasive as anywhere else I'd been.

I stopped at the restaurant, a squat gray building a hundred yards down the street from the inn. The sign over the doorway read WEXLER's. I opened the door and walked into the small dining room. The walls and floor were covered with dark wood, which gave the place a cavelike feel. Perhaps fifteen people occupied the place, mostly couples, although two middle-aged women in nurses' white dresses and caps sat by themselves at a table in the front.

I walked over by them and stood, looking around the restaurant for a place to sit, hoping they'd ask me to join them. They didn't. Finally I glanced down, as if I'd just noticed them, and spoke in a timid fashion, not quite meeting their eyes. "Hello, my name is Esther James, and I'm a new volunteer at the hospital. Would you mind horribly if I sat with you?"

"Go ahead, sit," one of them, a very large brunette, said. "I'm Bessie, and this is Alice."

"Thank you." I slid down into the seat next to Alice, a striking woman with pale blond hair and skin so white it was nearly translucent. She nodded at me and quietly said hello.

Bessie turned in her seat, raised her hand, and waved to the waitress. "Hey, menu here." She looked at me again. "First day?"

"I just got my application in."

"You from the city?"

I nodded.

"Scared?"

I hesitated but said, "Yes."

She gave me a dismissive wave. "Just stay away from them unless you got an orderly around. Especially the women." With her hand shaped into a claw, she swiped the air in front of her. "Watch out for the nails. And the teeth."

The waitress brought me a menu. Without asking what it was, I told her I'd have the special and a cup of coffee. Esther James's motto was "Live dangerously." We made small talk about the weather and the hospital for a few minutes before I asked them, "How long have you worked here?"

"Me, seventeen years," Bessie said. "Alice, what, about two?"

The other woman nodded.

"That's impressive, Bessie," I said. "You must really enjoy your work."

She bellowed out a laugh. "Needing a job and enjoying yourself are two different things, missy."

"What don't you like?"

"Patients, mostly," Bessie said. "In case you haven't noticed, most of them are crazy."

"Well, yes, I imagine so," I replied.

With a disapproving glance at Bessie, Alice shook her head. "The patients need us. They are poor wretches with nothing to do and nothing to look forward to."

"Blah, blah, blah," Bessie said.

"Don't listen to her, Esther. She cares for the patients as much as anyone. Bessie just hates the thought of someone finding out she has a heart."

"Pah," Bessie scoffed.

"You can't imagine how sad it all is, Esther," Alice said. "So many of these poor folks are just dropped here and forgotten."

I could imagine it just fine.

Bessie appraised me. "You'll have to watch out for the doctors."

"What do you mean?"

"You're going to have the same problem with the old lechers as Alice here."

There was the opening I was looking for. "I haven't met many of them so far. Just Dr. Beckwith and Dr. Davis."

"Oh ho, you've met the boss." Bessie shook her head. "Of course you did. Just look at you." She glanced at my left hand and said, "Well, if you're looking for a husband, Beckwith is single."

Alice nodded, pushing around the remains of her dinner with her fork.

"No, I'm not looking for a man." *Well, that's not entirely true,* I thought. *There are two I'd like to find.* "What happened to his wife?"

"You mean, did he kill her?" Bessie asked.

I turned to her. She burst out laughing. "Just joking. She died in childbirth."

A shocking subject for a joke. "I don't need to look out for him, do I?"

The waitress brought me a plate of meat loaf, mashed potatoes, and green beans. Alice leaned forward so I could see her and shook her head, mouthing, *No.*

Bessie was quiet until the waitress left, and then she leaned in over the table, eyes narrowed. "Tell the truth. You're not spying for Beckwith, are you?"

"What? Of course not. Do you think he would do something like that?" I stabbed a bean and ate it.

"No," she said, but her eyes were wary. She shrugged. "Anyway, he's all right."

Not exactly forthcoming. I thought I'd change gears. "You said his wife died. Did the child survive?"

"Hah!" Bessie barked out a laugh. "Francis. There's one for you. Every time I turn around, that little sneak is two inches away, eying me."

Alice recoiled. "Bessie!"

"Well, he is," Bessie said, taking a bite of pie.

"Oh, gosh," I said. "Is something wrong with Francis?"

"Really, Esther," Alice said to me. "His father runs the hospital."

I wasn't sure if she meant they shouldn't talk about Francis because his father ran the hospital or that there couldn't be anything wrong with him because his father ran the hospital. Either way, I didn't think I should pry further. "You're right. I'm sorry. But, if you don't mind, is Dr. Davis all right?"

They exchanged a glance. Finally Bessie said, "Don't trust him."

"Why?"

I saw Alice give Bessie a little shake of her head. "Just don't," Bessie said.

I looked from her to Alice. "Well, now you're really scaring me."

"If they don't assign you to Building B, you probably won't even run into him," Bessie said. "And if they do, that's where we work. If you have any trouble, just give me a shout. I'll straighten him out for you."

"Thank you." They must have worked with Robert, I thought. "Building B is the insane asylum, right?"

"That's where they keep the men," Bessie said. "So long as they behave. Otherwise, they dump them in the Hole."

"The Hole?"

Giving her friend a disapproving look, Alice said, "That's just what some people call it. It's solitary confinement. The most dangerous and the suicidal are housed in cells, just like a prison."

"Really?" I grimaced. "That sounds like a place I want to stay away from. Is the Hole in Building B, too?"

"No, and don't worry," Bessie said. "They don't put volunteers anywhere near the place."

I took a bite of mashed potatoes and nodded. I couldn't think of another way to ask where it was without causing suspicion. I'd wait. The waitress brought over their checks, and I took them. "My treat, ladies. I appreciate you filling me in on the place."

They both thanked me. "Well, we'd better be getting back," Bessie said.

"Back to work?"

"No, we've got the rest of the weekend off. Need to do laundry."

"Oh, really? Do you live on the grounds?"

"Yeah," Bessie said. "The job don't pay much, but we get free rooms in the dormitory."

"That's nice. Are there things to do around here that keep you occupied?"

She laughed. "Not unless you consider lunatics to be high entertainment. But sometimes they have concerts or shows at the amusement hall."

The mention of the amusement hall sent a chill through me, but I merely nodded.

"It's pretty down there in the summer," Alice said. "Quiet, too."

It occurred to me that they would also know Mr. Morgan and might provide a character reference. It would be good to know if I could trust him. "Say, do you know Clarence Morgan?"

Bessie nodded. A cloud seemed to pass over Alice's face, but it was gone as quickly as it appeared, and she nodded as well.

"He gave me a ride into the hospital this morning," I said. "He seemed like a nice man."

Bessie shrugged. "He's okay. Kind of snooty, if you ask me."

"He's all right," Alice said.

From the look I thought I'd seen, I wondered if she disliked Morgan or was smitten with him and was angry at me for mentioning him. I plowed on anyway. I didn't see a segue into my other topic, so I just leaned in toward Bessie. "I heard a rumor today that someone was murdered here earlier this week."

Bessie's mouth tightened. "Come on, Alice." She pushed back her chair and got to her feet. Alice stood as well and stepped around the table. Though she was taller than average, she was dwarfed by Bessie, who leaned down toward me and said, "Ain't nobody getting murdered. And some people should learn to keep their mouths shut."

My mother was sitting by herself in the living room when I returned home, reading a *Woman's Home Companion*. I wondered if her choice of magazine was for illustrative purposes. Whether it was or not, she quickly made it clear to me how she was feeling.

"Hello, Mother," I said.

She looked up and gave me a baleful stare. "I've given her the night off."

"That's fine," I replied. I was not looking for an argument. Truth be told, I wanted to have a bite to eat and go to bed. "Did anyone phone for me today?"

Her eyes had already returned to the magazine. "Not that I know of. But you shouldn't rely on me, now, should you?"

I sighed and left the room. Alberts was just coming down the back stairs when I entered the kitchen. "Detective Riordan called this afternoon," he said. "He wanted you to phone him as soon as you got home."

"Thank you." I hurried to the den and asked the operator for Detective Riordan's number. He was the one to answer the telephone.

"Hello, Detective, it's Elizabeth Hume. Do you have news?"

"Yes—and I think it's good."

"I could use some good news."

"I managed to track down Tony Gianolla today. He seemed honestly surprised when I asked what he'd done to Will. I don't think they're involved."

"How certain are you?"

"He doesn't seem like much of an actor. I'd bet they're innocent. Of this."

"That's a relief. Then what do you think happened to Will?"

"I've been giving that a lot of thought," he said. "There's no one else you think would harm him?"

I thought about the Adamos. The brothers were dead, and what remained of the gang had scattered to the wind. The Bernsteins had told Will he owed them a favor, but they had left us in peace. "No. Say, do you think there's any chance he jumped the gun and is already at Eloise?"

"The same thought occurred to me. I checked. According to the hospital's admissions department, no one fitting Will's description has been recently admitted. By the way, I put in the missing person report this morning. It's going out all over the area. Did you place the advertisement?"

"It will be in the papers tomorrow."

"Good," he said. "That may generate a lead or two. Keep your spirits up, Miss Hume. I'll keep looking, and you do the same."

"Thank you, Detective. I appreciate your help. Would you do me a favor? Could you call me Elizabeth?"

"Only if you call me Thomas."

"I'm not sure I can do that."

"I'll tell you what. When we have official business, you can call me Detective Riordan. This is not official business, so call me Thomas."

"Well . . . all right."

"Good night, Elizabeth."

"Good night, Thomas." It felt wrong to call him by his Christian name. I hoped I could get used to it, but I didn't think I would.

When I rang off, I saw Alberts standing in the doorway, his hands on his hips. He looked peeved. "Miss, with all due respect, would you mind telling me what you are up to?"

"Will has gone missing. He and I are trying to discover . . . well, it's complicated, and I don't need to worry you with it."

He sat in one of the chairs on the other side of the desk. "If Mr. Anderson is missing, why did you spend the day at Eloise Hospital?"

Alberts deserved to know. I spent the next ten minutes explaining the situation to him.

When I finished, he said, "How can I help?"

"Really, I just need you to run the household while letting . . ."

"While letting your mother think she's running it," he finished.

"Yes."

"I will do my best."

"I know you will." I reached across the desk and squeezed his hand. "Thank you. I really can't tell you how much I appreciate what you do for us."

"No more than I appreciate your kindnesses over the years."

We looked into one another's eyes. His had faded to a powder blue and were surrounded by wrinkles. His working years would soon be over. I squeezed his hand again and stood. "Did Bridie go out?"

He was on his feet before I was. "No, miss. She's in her room."

"Judging from Mother's reaction, today wasn't a good day for either of them."

He bit the inside of his cheek, and I prepared myself for a painful answer. Instead he said, "Your mother will realize soon enough that Bridie's only trying to help."

"Thank you, Alberts. I'm going to speak with her." I took the back stairs up to the third floor and knocked on Bridie's door.

When she opened it, her expression was guarded. "Evening, Miss Hume. I was dismissed. I thought I oughtn't press her."

"No, that's fine. Was she any better today?"

Bridie dropped her eyes and took a deep breath. "Well, truthfully, she was not. She's very unhappy with me."

"No, Bridie. she's very unhappy with me and is taking it out on you."

"Perhaps."

"Are you willing to continue?"

"Yes, miss." She smiled, and it didn't look entirely forced. "I like me a challenge."

# CHAPTER SIX

*Sunday, August 11, 1912*

## Will

The door slammed against the wall, and the light was flipped on. "Doe!" a man barked. "Up!"

I opened my eyes to beaming bright lights. My head felt like it had been filled with concrete. Who was yelling at me? I squinted at the man in my room, and the memories flooded in. I was inside Eloise Hospital. My name was John Doe.

I looked out the window. Still dark. Rubbing my eyes, I asked, "What time is it?"

"Six. Now get up." This orderly was a brawny youngster, a farm boy from the look of him.

I threw off the blanket and swung my legs over the side of the bed. The chloral hydrate had left me with a dull mind and a sharp headache. The one positive factor was that I hadn't had the dream.

The orderly stood watching me, arms at his side, ready to pounce. Taking a deep breath, I stood and wobbled toward the door. There I joined a line of patients in nightshirts stumbling along toward the center of the building. Each shirt carried the same legend as mine: EH – B6. Only the footwear differed. Some of the men wore white cotton slippers, but most wore what I assumed to be the shoes they were wearing when admitted. The conversation in the hallway was minimal, muttered, combining to make a low moan. It was like the march of the dead. This was my first sight of the bulk of my companions on this journey. They looked tired, most of them thin and listless, some obviously drugged. Srugis passed me staring straight ahead. Farther back, I saw the German, Zimmermann. I decided to fall in with him, rather than Srugis, who would be armed and dangerous at breakfast.

Zimmermann recognized me and nodded hello.

"Good morning," I said.

He gave me a nervous look. I think it had finally dawned on him that he was locked in an insane asylum.

A pair of men in suits strode up the hall toward us. One was Dr. Davis. I faded off to the side and kept a tall patient between us until he passed. He didn't see me.

I followed those in front of me to the dining hall, a cavernous room with four long rows of connected tables. The patients lined up and sat at the tables in the order they entered. One after another plunked down next to the previous man on the benches. Half a dozen orderlies stood around the perimeter, eyes scanning the patients. Eight women stood against the walls next to wheeled racks of tin plates.

I sat next to Zimmermann and waited with some curiosity for my food. I hoped it would be palatable, so I could maintain my strength, but there was no smell of food whatsoever, just a hint of coffee. A bug-eyed old man sat across the table from me. He wore a towel wrapped around his head like a turban. I nodded to him, and he quickly looked away.

As soon as all the patients were seated, the women began wheeling the racks around the room and dropping plates in front of the patients. I could see nothing but a brown amorphous pile on the plates, which, I saw when one began serving my table, held a piece of bread with a brown substance slathered over it and a mess of sticky slime in a slightly lighter color. When every patient had his food, the women followed with cups of coffee for everyone.

I sniffed the fare in front of me. The butter, if that's what it was, was rancid, the bread stale. I tried a small bite of the—oatmeal? It was tasteless, which, under the circumstances, I thought to be a good thing, so I ate a bit more, alternating with sips of tepid coffee.

The bug-eyed man leaned in from across the table and whispered, "You gonna eat that?" He was pointing at my bread.

"Be my guest."

Eyes darting side to side, he slipped the disgusting hunk of bread off my plate, slid it along the tabletop, and set it in his lap before finishing his own piece. When he did, he raised my bread and wolfed it down, seemingly afraid I would demand its return.

When he finished it, he said in a hushed voice, "Did he get anybody last night?"

His bug eyes were staring at me. "Who?" I asked.

"The Phantom. Did he get anybody?"

Hoping to draw out more information, I said, "I don't know what you're talking about. I just got here yesterday." I looked at Zimmermann, who had scraped off as much of the butter from his bread as he could but still was trying to eat only the unbuttered side, nibbling small bites from the back.

The left side of the old man's mouth raised in a crooked grin. "Don't go out at night. That's when he hunts. If you do, keep your gun up near your eyes."

It took a second to digest that nugget. "I'll remember that. Have you seen him?"

He nodded.

"Really?"

He nodded harder, as if I just needed to see a more emphatic nod to believe him.

"My name is John," I said. "What's yours?"

"You may call me Daroga. Or the Persian."

He certainly didn't look Persian, but I nodded. "All right, Daroga. What's the Phantom look like?"

"Wears a mask, so nobody knows."

"How big is he?"

"Oh, reg'lar," he replied.

"What does he wear besides a mask?"

"Black. All black."

"When did you see him?"

His face contorted, and he looked up and to the left. "Tuesday," he finally said.

"Last Tuesday?"

This time he hesitated too long for me to believe his nod. "Where was he?"

"Comin' outta his tunnel."

"Where's that?"

"Not tellin'."

"Where's the tunnel come from?"

"Beneath the opera house, near an underground lake."

"The opera house?"

Opening his eyes wide, he nodded.

I couldn't imagine there was an opera house here or anywhere around here. "Do you mean the amusement hall?"

"No. The Paris Opera."

"But . . . that's in France."

Daroga stuck his index finger in his mouth, curled it over the back of his bottom front teeth, and began snapping it forward, clicking the nail insistently. He didn't reply.

"That would be an awfully long tunnel," I said, hoping to revive the conversation. "Why would he come here?"

He pulled his finger from his mouth and gave me a knowing nod. "Wants us in his torture chamber."

"You're serious."

He nodded. "Oh—and watch out for Beatrice."

"And just who is she?"

His forehead wrinkled, and he squinted at me. Had I been anywhere else, I'd have sworn he was putting me on. "I'm not sure if she's a ghost or a person. Still digging into that. But she helps the Phantom. Somehow." Daroga gave me a significant look and raised an index finger to his lips. That was the last he would speak of it.

It was difficult to sort the nonsense from the truth in this place. The Phantom of the Opera, assisted by a ghost or woman named Beatrice, was killing patients—according to one lunatic. Difficult to believe under any circumstances. Then again, I knew for certain that at least one man had been murdered, which made it more likely there was some truth in Daroga's scuttlebutt.

So—I needed to discover the identity of the Phantom and the

mysterious Beatrice, and expose them before someone else got killed. It seemed a tall order.

The patients all ate quickly, but even so, the orderlies rousted us before most finished their meals. They trundled us off to the dayroom, a large space, perhaps forty feet by eighty. Square tables filled the center; the exterior was set with wooden chairs. The door at the back of the room was closed. Speaking tubes, like the ones I'd seen in the hallway, were screwed into each wall.

Zimmermann and I took a seat at one of the tables and watched the rest of the patients filter in. Srugis came over and sat next to me. I tried to engage him in conversation, but he kept his mouth shut, only throwing wary glances toward the doorway.

A few minutes later a nurse marched in with a pair of hulking orderlies, her eyes scanning the men until they lit on us. "Srugis, Doe, Zimmermann. Come with us."

Zimmermann and I got up. Srugis didn't move. I reached down and nudged him. "Come on."

"Ain't your business," he snapped at me.

"Mr. Srugis?" the nurse said, louder.

He stared straight ahead, a little smirk playing on his face. One of the orderlies grabbed him by the front of his nightshirt and yanked him out of the chair. Srugis's hand flashed in a movement toward the other man's midsection. The orderly froze, gasping, and stared down at the red stain on his stomach. Srugis jerked a bloody butter knife out of it and drew back his arm to stab the man again. I leaped up and grabbed him in a bear hug. Srugis struggled against me, and the other orderly dove on us, knocking us to the floor. I rolled clear, and the orderly hammered Srugis with three punches to the face, bouncing his head off the tile. I think he was unconscious with the first blow.

The men in the room screamed, shouted, pumped their fists in the air. The nurse hurried the man who'd been stabbed into the hall, and the second orderly stood, butter knife in hand, and stared down the room. The shouting decreased and then died as a half dozen other orderlies poured in with a guard, who had his gun drawn. He waved it around the room. "Sit down! Everybody! Now!"

Most of the patients heeded his order and sat, some in chairs, others on the floor. Probably a dozen men remained on their feet, continuing whatever they'd been doing—until they were thrown down by an orderly. Eventually, we were all seated or lying on the floor.

After a short conference, a pair of orderlies took hold of Srugis's ankles and dragged him, still unconscious, out of the room. His nightshirt bunched up under his armpits, and he wore nothing underneath.

A few of the patients began talking. "Shut it!" the guard shouted. They did.

We all sat silently under the watchful eyes of the staff members for perhaps fifteen minutes until the nurse returned to the room with two more orderlies, one of them a Negro, and said, "Doe. Zimmermann. Come with me."

She led us to a little waiting room, and then she and the white orderly escorted me into an office where I was interviewed by three men. They didn't identify themselves, but I assumed they were doctors. The nurse and the other orderly stood nearby, eyeing me while I continued with my impersonation of an amnesiac. The doctors seemed to buy it, because they sent me out after ten minutes without any indication they were onto me. When they finished, the nurse brought me to the waiting room, instructed me to sit, and then brought Zimmermann into the office. The Negro orderly leaned against the wall and waited with me. He looked like a nice enough fellow that I ventured to ask, "What are they going to do with Srugis?"

"He the guy with the knife?"

I nodded.

"Already took him to the Hole."

"The Hole? What's that?"

"Somewheres you don't wanna go."

"Why?"

"That's where they put the real crazies. The dangerous ones. So you watch yourself. Stay out of fights. You don't wanna go there," he repeated.

After a few minutes, Zimmermann and the nurse returned. Looking at me, she said, "You don't speak German, do you?"

I shook my head. "Hasn't anyone been able to communicate with this man?"

She ignored my question and told the orderlies to bring us back to the dayroom. We started off down the hallway and turned the corner. Three people were walking toward us, but they were silhouetted by the big window at the end of the hall. I could make them out just well enough to see that the two men on the sides were orderlies and that the man in the middle was huge. I got an uneasy feeling. We walked down the hall, and they continued toward us. They were almost upon us when I first saw the big man clearly.

It was Ty. He walked freely, no shackles or even handcuffs, and the orderlies looked to be no more concerned with him than they were with me. We moved farther to the side to let them pass. When Ty and his escorts were about ten feet away, the corners of his mouth rose in an amused smile that seemed to say, *I've found you,* and he gave me a short nod that said, *We'll be seeing each other again soon.*

The dayroom was crowded. Every seat at the tables was taken by men playing cards, chess, or checkers. Zimmermann and I sat in chairs near a window. I alternated between watching the door for Ty and looking out at the lawn and the buildings past it. A few wagons traveled by, but there was little activity. Inside wasn't much different. Even the men playing games moved slowly. Two orderlies watched us, one from an open door that led into the hallway while the other wandered the room.

I decided to wander as well. Along the way, I tried, unsuccessfully, to engage men in conversation while simultaneously watching the doors for Ty and Dr. Davis. Then I spotted Daroga, the old man in the turban-esque towel who had told me about the Phantom. He was sitting across a table from a younger man, playing chess. Unlike the others I'd seen, they were actually playing chess, not tasting the pieces or playing some variation of checkers with them. I stopped and watched them for a moment.

Daroga glanced up at me and moved his arm protectively around the chessboard. "You need something?"

"No, Daroga," I said. "Just watching."

A laugh burbled out of the throat of the young man across the table from him. "Daroga," he muttered.

"You got a problem, Chuckie?" Daroga demanded.

The younger man kept smiling, his eyes on the board in front of him. He was a good-looking boy with short but exceptionally thick brown hair. "Daroga," he repeated, chuckling.

The old man stared at him a moment longer before looking at me again. "Or the Persian."

The young man glanced up at me and muttered, "His name's Papa Dill."

Daroga slammed his fist on the table. "Daroga. Or the Persian."

"Fine," I said.

The young man glanced up at me and mouthed, *Dill. Papa Dill.*

I glanced at Daroga, but he hadn't noticed it. I nodded back at the young man and said, "There's not much to do around here, is there, Daroga?"

A satisfied expression settled onto Daroga's face, only mildly counteracted by his bugging eyes. He had a flat, upturned nose, a wide mouth, and an unusually round head. "Why?"

"I'm bored."

Daroga squinted up at me. "What'd you say your name was?"

"John Doe," I said.

He gave me a sidelong glance, and the right corner of his mouth collapsed in what looked like a smile. "You got a lot of relatives in here." Chuck advanced a knight on the board.

I shrugged and looked around the room. Everyone seemed to be in a torpor. "Daroga, do you spend all your time in this place sitting around?"

He looked at me from the corner of his eye. "Did Mama Hand-me-down send you?"

I wasn't sure whether Mama Hand-me-down was a "What?" or a "Who?" so I just said, "No."

Squinting at me again, he nodded. "You from the government?"

"What?"

Glaring at me, he said, "You heard me."

"No, of course not."

"Who's the president?"

"Of the United States?"

He nodded.

"William Howard Taft."

"Who's the governor?"

"Chase Osborn."

He appraised me for a few seconds, then nodded and smiled at Chuck. "The son of a bitch don't even know who's running the country." He gave me a sly smile and leaned back, moving his arm away from the board. Squinting up at me, he said, "What'd you ask me?"

"I asked if you do anything besides sit around in here."

"Oh yeah. But they give us Sundays off." He felt around the edges of the towel on his head, straightening his turban.

I nodded. "Say, maybe you could help me find someone."

He countered Chuck's knight with a bishop. "Who's that?"

"Robert Clarke."

His eyes narrowed. "What do you want him for?"

"Someone told me to look him up here. They said he'd be helpful."

"Helpful? Hmm." He carefully watched Chuck make his next move. "Him and Patrick got transferred."

"Patrick . . . Cook?"

He nodded. "They're both in our reading group. They got transferred out. I think the Feds're doing experiments on 'em."

"Are you sure they're gone?"

"Well, I didn't see them get loaded in the truck, but they're gone, ain't they, Chuck?" He looked over at his friend, who nodded.

"Did they get sent to another asylum?"

"Dunno. Sometimes when the government wants experiments done, the sons a bitches lock us up." He put his hands up near his temples and waved his fingers around. "They tinker in our heads. You ain't the same when they're done, let me tell you."

"No, I imagine you aren't." I was ready to ask him about the Phantom when, out of the corner of my eye, I saw the door at the back of the room open a few inches. I glanced up and saw someone standing just outside, peeking in.

Francis Beckwith.

I turned my back to the door and watched Daroga and Chuck make a few more moves. When I turned around again, Francis was gone. I breathed a sigh of relief. After another couple of minutes, I checked the door again. It was still closed. I moved away from the chess players and tried to engage a few other patients in conversation. Some didn't seem able to talk. Others told me strange things such as the story a bird had told one man, but most, with hopeful smiles, just talked about their families—the last time they visited or, even more heartbreaking, memories of "before."

Francis Beckwith stepped in front of me. I hadn't even noticed he'd gotten into the room.

"You were here Tuesday night," he said in his strange voice that somehow made me think of a duck. "After Patrick was killed."

I didn't respond, just glanced around to see if anyone had heard. No one seemed to be paying us any notice.

"You came with Elizabeth Hume, Robert's cousin." He wore a white shirt tucked into a pair of dark trousers, a black belt tightly cinched around his waist. His brown hair was long, neatly combed except on top where the curls made it unruly. "You asked me questions."

"All right, all right," I whispered. "Can we talk somewhere else?"

"Why?"

"Because I don't want everyone to hear us."

He raised his voice a bit. "I don't like secrets."

"That's fine." I turned and took only a single step away from the table. Francis mirrored me. "Why are you here?"

"Because I'm insane, or so they tell me."

"You are not." His face was strangely expressionless, even when he spoke, like a still pond disturbed by only the smallest ripple when his lips moved.

I glanced around us. No one seemed to be paying particular attention, although Daroga was looking this way. I took another step back. "Why do you say that?"

"You are investigating."

"Would it bother you if I was?"

"Yes."

I waited for him to explain himself, but he didn't.

I held up my right hand. "Francis, I have been very nervous ever since I got this burn." That was certainly true. "I need some time to think and relax. When I came here the other night, I thought it might be a good idea to be committed, to spend some time away from home."

"But my father's notes say you have amnesia."

"Yes, I know, but please, Francis, don't tell anyone. I really need the time here."

He studied me, clearly conflicted.

"Please?" I said again.

A hint of an expression, anxiety or exhilaration, I couldn't tell, passed across his face. "Are you afraid of the Phantom?"

"Of course I am. How could I not be? But that's how important being here is for me. I'm willing to risk my life."

"The Phantom doesn't like your kind." He put on a smile. It was clearly an expression with no organic basis but was rather something he taught himself to do.

"Why do you say that?"

"You will see." He turned and hurried away with that strange stiff gait, negotiating the turns through the other men so that he didn't touch any of them. In seconds he was out of the room, leaving me to ponder the meaning of his warning.

Or was it a threat?


I sat next to Zimmermann for the next hour, speaking only once, to ask an orderly the real name of the old man with the towel turban on his head. He told me the man's name was Dill. So Chuck had been right. When they called us for lunch, I hurried to line up behind him and Dill, whom I still wanted to ask about the Phantom. We sat, again in the order that we entered, and waited for our food. It smelled awful, like the scum that sits on top of a pot of boiling meat.

I nudged Dill. "Daroga, what do you know about these murders?"

He made a show of looking around before ducking in toward me. "He ain't the Phantom in the book, you know. That one's horse pucky—just a character. The one here's a real killer." He touched a spot under his right eye with a forefinger. "I watch out for him. He's after *me*, you know."

"Why is he after you?"

"Roosevelt. That son of a bitch." He shook his head disgustedly.

"Teddy?"

He nodded. "And I'll tell you something else. He lives down in the Hole."

"Roosevelt?"

"No, you idiot. The Phantom."

"What *is* the Hole?" I asked.

"It's solitary. I spent some time there a while back."

"Isn't that guarded? How would he get out?"

"There's ways. I been in and out of the place. I know it like the back of my hand."

"Where is it?"

"Under the police station."

"In the Administration Building?"

"Yep. They pretend it's just a basement." He gave me a dark look. "But it ain't."

"Then what is it?"

"It's a dungeon."

I had no idea how much of this was fantasy, but I figured it couldn't hurt to get as much information as possible. "Could Robert Clarke be the Phantom?"

He laughed. "That son of a bitch can barely tie his shoes. How's he gonna strangle all them guys?"

"All what guys?"

He gave a furtive look to each side. "Paul Robinson, Albert Bell, and Victor Foerster."

I committed the names to memory. "The Phantom killed all of them?"

He raised his eyebrows and nodded again.

"When?"

He didn't hesitate. "Robinson was September, almost two years ago, Bell got it last July, Foerster, this last March."

"So the frequency of the murders is increasing."

"Yep. But it sure as hell ain't Robert Clarke."

"That's not what Dr. Beckwith says."

"Beckwith," he said scornfully. "He's another one."

"What would you say if I told you I saw Patrick Cook's body the other night?"

"What?"

"He'd been strangled. He had a big purple welt around here." With an index finger, I drew a line across my throat.

"Son of a bitch. The Punjab lasso." He shook his head. "Tell you what, though. Keep your gun up around your eyes."

"What?"

One of the servers was getting close, so he just shook his head and stopped talking. She set plates in front of us that held a chunk of boiled meat—beef, I'd guess—with another piece of "buttered" bread.

"Come on," I muttered. Turning to Dill, I said, "Is this as good as it gets?"

"The Waldorf it ain't," he replied, stabbing his meat with his fork. He lifted it from his plate and began to gnaw off a piece. I did the same. The meat clearly had never been acquainted with salt or pepper. It was a boiled, tough, gristle-filled lump of inedible garbage.

"I can't eat this," I said.

"You better. There ain't nothing else."

A jowly man across the table from me grunted and got a funny look on his face. He gingerly chewed a couple of times before reaching into his mouth and pulling out a long piece of vein, like a big gray earthworm. Holding it up in front of him, he stared at it for a few seconds, shaking it back and forth, then tilted his head back and dropped the vein in, slurping it down like spaghetti. Fighting the urge to vomit, I pushed away my plate.

One set of doors opened, and patients began streaming in, herded along by orderlies. I stopped paying attention after a dozen or so, as they were sitting on the other side of the cafeteria, but just as I was turning back to Dill, I caught a glimpse of a large man from the corner of my eye.

I turned and looked.

It was Ty.

Ty looked even more ridiculous than everyone else in the too-small nightshirt that ended at his knees, but the sight didn't amuse me. His eyes were scanning the room. I ducked my head and hoped he didn't pick me out from the hundreds of others here. The orderlies sat the men at the farthest table from us, and Ty went along with his orders willingly, placidly even, acting the perfect patient. I wondered what his game was.

I arranged myself on the bench so as to hide behind other men and kept my head down. He didn't seem to have noticed me. When they filed us out of the cafeteria, I kept my face turned away from him. The longer he didn't know where I was, the better. I needed to find a weapon. If he was going to be at meals, one of these days he was going to recognize me. I didn't like my chances if he did.

After lunch, I was taken to my room and locked in. It occurred to me that a fire would kill just about everyone in this building. I couldn't believe the orderlies or guards would risk their lives unlocking every door and escorting the patients to safety. I sat on the bed and looked through the bars on the window while I thought. Hundreds of patients walked the grounds, all in tightly packed bunches led and followed by orderlies.

I needed to get out of this room and do some reconnaissance. It seemed unlikely that Beckwith had really transferred Robert out of here, but he certainly had moved him. If I were to have any chance of clearing Robert, I had to find out what happened that night. For that, I needed to speak with him.

Over the course of the afternoon, I was visited twice by orderlies for no apparent reason, but they both locked the door securely after them. They let me out for supper (another hunk of gristle and a piece of bread), but I never got out of an orderly's sight. As much as I disliked the idea, I knew I had to bide my time to try to escape the building. They were watching me too carefully now. I could do nothing but continue to ask questions of as many people as possible. Somehow I needed to get the names of the murdered men to Detective Riordan, but at this point I had no conduit.

The big nurse, Bessie, came by to check on me once, but Dr. Beckwith didn't visit that night to feed me chloral hydrate, nor did anyone else. I was left to lie on the bed, nothing to read, nothing to do except think. I hoped Elizabeth or Detective Riordan would figure out I was here, since I could think of no way to alert either of them. I wondered what would happen to me the next day. I lay awake a long time, thinking about why I'd come here. Yes, Robert was Elizabeth's brother, and it was a grand gesture on my part to try to save him—but I wondered if there was more to it than that. I had been throwing myself into danger after danger, risking death time and again.

Was it merely that I was trying to be a good man? Or was the reason more complicated, with perhaps a dash of self-destruction in the mix? Either way, one thing was certain.

Coming here *was* lunacy.

# Elizabeth

Bridie spent Sunday at her parents' house, which seemed to put my mother in a better frame of mind, and she allowed me a détente of sorts. Her situation had created such a dilemma for me. I refused to consider institutionalizing her, regardless of her condition, yet I couldn't take care of her by myself. She had always been a reasonable woman, but her equanimity was leaving with her memory.

This day, however, seemed almost a return to the past. After church, she and I sat side by side on the porch swing, swaying gently back and forth while the traffic streamed east: families in automobiles, carriages, and wagons, heading for Electric Park and Belle Isle. The children leaned out the windows, their hair flowing in the wind, smiles of outrageous anticipation on their faces.

At first, it warmed me to see those children. After a while, though, I began to wonder what had happened to my capacity to feel such hope and joy, to be able to look forward to something with such immense enthusiasm and wonder. My circumstances had certainly been more difficult over the past three or four years, yet it seemed there was a bottomless chasm between who I used to be and who I was now. I didn't know if heroin in and of itself was to blame, but since I'd given it up, my ability to feel joy was blunted, as if the ecstasy of the drug had used up my allotment. I still felt pleasure and happiness and satisfaction, but the palette had been diluted. My happy emotions, once painted in rich oils, were now the product of watercolors.

Later, we made a picnic lunch and took a walk along the river. Mother was lucid most of the day, with only occasional lapses, after which she would become uncharacteristically quiet and withdrawn, though her anger didn't reappear.

Of course, Will was in the back of my mind all day. Three men replied to the advertisement in the newspaper, all of whom Alberts queried. He reported that they were all put off by the news of no reward, and he assured me they were frauds. I phoned Will's apartment in the morning and again in the late afternoon, though now I had no expectations he would answer.

My hopes were dimming.

# CHAPTER SEVEN

### Monday, August 12, 1912

## Will

No dream. No dreams at all, that I remember. I woke feeling refreshed.

Then it was the same routine—door thrust open, light switched on, "Doe! Up!" The food was the same unappetizing slop as the day before. Again, I ate the tasteless oatmeal. It was far superior to what I'd be served for lunch or supper, and I had to eat something.

After breakfast, when the other patients were sent out to their jobs, one of the orderlies led me to another room, this one in the basement. I kept an eye out for Dr. Davis, but he didn't turn up on the way. When the orderly opened the door, I saw a long line of metal bathtubs, much longer and taller than is usual, perhaps seven feet long by four feet high. Two patients sat in the tubs on the far end. They looked comfortable enough.

Dr. Beckwith stood near the door, conversing with two nurses. One was Bessie, the large woman I'd seen before, the other another tall woman, though this one had a medium build and hair so blond as to be almost white. "Good morning, Mr. Doe," Beckwith said. "It is still Doe, isn't it?" Three burly orderlies stood nearby.

"What's this about?" I asked.

"Hydrotherapy. It's the latest thing."

"What are you going to do to me?"

"Simply immerse you in water, alternating warm and cool. We've found the shock to be stimulating to the brain."

"Warm and cool doesn't sound like it would cause any shock." I wasn't too worried about it, however, as the other patients looked to be enjoying a soak. I have to admit the idea of a bath sounded good to me. It had been a while, and I smelled like a goat.

He nodded to the orderlies, two of whom took my arms and led me to the nearest tub. It was filled to within a foot of the top. "Strip," one of them said. I knew better than to fight about it, so, turning away from the nurses, I pulled the nightshirt over my head and dropped it to the floor. "In." The orderly nodded to the tub.

I raised a leg over the side, dipped a toe in the water, and immediately pulled it out. The water was freezing cold. I looked back at Beckwith. "I thought you said cool."

"Do you need these gentlemen to assist you?" he asked.

"No." I stepped into the tub, first one foot, then the other. I stood there a second, trying to find the courage to sit.

"Down," the orderly said.

Holding the side of the tub with my hands, I began to squat. The water was so cold it felt like it was burning me. When my nether regions hit the water, the shock caused me to stand abruptly. The orderlies put their hands on my shoulders and shoved me down into the tub. My legs slipped out from under me, and my back hit the bottom. The pain arcing from my injured shoulder forced the breath out of me in a whoosh of bubbles. The orderlies' hands held me under. I fought against them, kicking and struggling, but had no leverage.

They jerked me out of the water and dragged me to the next tub. Steam was rising from this one. They picked me up and shoved me down into the water, immersing me all the way under. I screamed. After the cold tub, this water felt like liquid magma. I fought them all the more, but to no avail. They were stronger and had all the leverage. After half a minute they pulled me out and dunked me back into the cold tub. It was worse this time. Then back into the hot water.

After a few seconds of agony, they pulled me out and laid me on the concrete floor. Dr. Beckwith stood over me. "Who are you?" he asked, a pen poised over his pad.

"I . . . I don't know," I gasped through the shivers racking my body.

"What is your name?"

"I . . . don't . . . know," I replied.

He looked up at the orderlies on the other side of me. "Gentlemen, let's try that again, if you please."

"No," I said. "It won't help."

"How do you know that, Mr. Doe?" Dr. Beckwith asked. "Are you a doctor?"

"No. But it—"

"Again," Beckwith said to the orderlies.

After another four rounds of the torture Dr. Beckwith euphemistically called hydrotherapy, the orderlies grabbed me and started to encase my hands in what they called a cuff, a white canvas contraption like a small tube with straps on both ends. I suppose the shock had unhinged me a bit, because I fought them and called Dr. Beckwith a few choice names before they secured the cuff on me, completely disabling my hands, and dragged me from the room. All the while, Beckwith stood silent, watching the proceedings with a clinical detachment.

The orderlies brought me upstairs to my room and threw me on my bed, where I lay shivering for hours. At one point, I heard the patients shuffle down the hall to lunch, though no one unlocked my door. It was just as well.

Hours after that, an orderly opened the door and Dr. Beckwith strolled in. He folded his arms across his chest and looked at me through narrowed eyes. "So, Mr. Doe. You have a problem with authority, it seems."

I kept my mouth shut.

Beckwith watched me patiently. "Do you understand that I am one of the most qualified psychiatric doctors in the country?"

"That may be, but torture is not a modern psychological technique. Perhaps you should try psychotherapy." I didn't know much about it, but I was pretty sure psychotherapy didn't cause *physical* pain.

"Hmm." Looking out the window, he chuckled, clearly amused by my stupidity. "So you think patients should decide their own treatment?"

Again, I decided keeping my mouth shut was my best course of action.

He was quiet for a moment before nodding to himself. "Perhaps we can find you a cure, Mr. Doe. Would that make you happy?"

"Of course it would. I don't want to be here any longer than I have to."

"You've made that clear enough. I think perhaps we should try another therapy on you."

I sat up. "What do you mean to do to me?"

"Nothing to be alarmed about. I'll go prepare." He spun on his heel and marched out of the room. The orderly followed and locked the door behind him.

*Now what have I gotten myself into?* I stood and walked around the room, loosening my tight muscles as best I could with my hands bound in front of me. I had no idea what to expect, other than having no doubt it would be unpleasant.

About thirty minutes later, the orderly and another returned and brought me down to a wagon. One drove, and the other stayed in back with me. We crossed the river, and the driver continued on, veering left until he was at the back of the grounds, where he stopped at the rear of a white two-story building with long, low wings that ran for hundreds of feet on both sides. I heard coughing and wheezing and made the assumption we were at the tubercular sanatorium, which was confirmed when we went inside. Coughing men and women, all wearing nightshirts like me, walked from one place to another, led by orderlies and nurses.

We entered through a back door. My orderlies gave the inmates a wide berth and brought me to a toilet. "Doc said for you to piss before we start," one of them said. I had no pressing need, but I went to the restroom just the same, figuring, why give up the opportunity? After a few contortions, I managed to raise my nightshirt with my cuffed hands and was able to go. When I finished, they led me to a room with a white metal door.

Dr. Beckwith waited inside, rolling a pair of metal tubes between his palms. The blond nurse from the hydrotherapy room stood next to him. A number of iceboxes, or at least iceboxlike cabinets, stood at the back of the room. Half a dozen folding wooden chairs sat against the wall next to them. Two beds were placed in the middle, each with re-straining straps hanging from the sides.

Beckwith nodded toward the closest bed. The orderlies pulled me on top of it and began strapping me in.

The image of the trunk flashed in my mind. "What are you going to do?"

"We've been working on a little experiment." He held up one of the tubes so I could see it. It was made from shiny silver metal and was about three-quarters of an inch wide by four inches long. "Radium has been found to be an effective treatment against a wide order of mala-dies, tuberculosis among them. The restorative power of radiation is really most fascinating. We've just begun some experiments with ra-dium therapy in curing insanity."

"You've just begun?"

One of the orderlies cinched the strap across my chest, pinning my cuffed hands to my stomach.

"Well, yes, but it's very promising, and it might help you find your memory." He smiled. "Of course, no treatment is one hundred percent effective. Don't worry about the side effects. They aren't all that prob-lematic."

"What sort of side effects?"

"It all depends on how long we continue the treatment," Beckwith replied. "You will probably lose a little hair. Your scalp may be slightly irritated. It's possible that you will feel a bit disoriented. We'll just have to see."

I reckoned it couldn't do too much harm. Everyone knew about the healing effects of radiation. Mr. McFarland at the Detroit Electric fac-tory had been bragging about his new revigator, essentially a cooler that uses uranium to treat the water. Spinthariscopes had been hits at par-ties for years; I didn't know anyone who hadn't watched radium burst into beautiful blue flashes of light, magnified in the little tube one held to one's eye. Of course, there was the healing water of Glen Springs that had been beckoning Elizabeth and me for years.

I'd give it a go—even though there was nothing wrong with me. "There's no sense restraining me like this. I'll submit to the treatment."

Beckwith smiled again. "It's not just a case of submission. The placement of the radium tubes is critical to the experiment. If they move, we won't achieve the maximum benefit."

It wasn't like they were giving me a choice anyway, so I decided to wait to fight a battle I had a chance of winning. The orderlies finished strapping me in, and Beckwith taped the tubes to the sides of my head, using a ruler to measure the placement. "We'll just leave you here for a while. Someone will check on you in an hour or so."

They all filed out of the room and locked the door behind them. I closed my eyes, trying to ignore all the little itches that arise as soon as one is unable to scratch them. Soon enough, I fell asleep.

The sound of a key turning in the lock awakened me. I tried to raise my head, but the strap across my forehead made that impossible. The door creaked open and was pressed shut. Quiet footsteps padded toward me.

Above me, a face loomed.

Francis Beckwith.

Francis looked down on me, his face impassive. His wire-rimmed eyeglasses sat slightly askew, the right side higher than the left.

No one else had followed him into the room. My heart leaped in my chest.

I struggled to keep my voice calm. "What can I do for you, Francis?"

He didn't answer, just stood there looking at me, as if he were memorizing me. The seconds passed. His left eye twitched, and twitched again.

"Francis?" I whispered. "Are you all right?"

His mouth tightened. "I don't want to be bad," he said, his eyes lowering to my throat.

The shock of that statement coursed through me. I was completely at his mercy. "Of course you don't." I kept my voice down, speaking as soothingly as I could. "Everyone knows you're a good man."

"I am not. I am bad." His face contorted. "They all know that. My father says I cannot help myself." His agitation was increasing.

Had I thought anyone was in earshot, I would have been screaming my head off. Instead, I kept my voice down. "Whatever you've been doing, Francis, you can stop. You just have to want to."

"No. You should not be here." His hands rose above the table.

My heart was in my throat. "Francis, you don't want to disappoint your father, do you?"

His hands froze. "My . . . father?"

"I'm sure he's disappointed when you hurt people." I couldn't stop the tremors in my voice.

"I don't hurt anyone." His eyes darted toward the door.

Now I heard someone talking out in the hall. Francis ran toward the door. It was quiet for a moment; then the door clicked open and swiftly closed. I held my breath, listening for him.

He was gone.

Perhaps a minute later, a key rattled in the door and someone twisted the knob, but the door remained shut. The key turned again, and the door opened. Dr. Beckwith said, "Alice, I thought you locked it."

"I . . . did," the nurse said. "I thought I did."

"It was your son," I said. "He was just in here. He's not supposed to be wandering the hospital, is he?"

Their faces appeared above me, Dr. Beckwith's creased in a smile, though it looked like he was forcing it. "Now, now. You've been sleeping, haven't you? I'm sure it was just a dream."

"No, I'm telling you. It was him."

"How do you know my son?"

"He's all over the hospital. How could I not know him?"

He glanced over at the nurse, then back to me. "Well, we'll make sure he doesn't come back. Now, let's talk about your temples. How do they feel?"

"Warm."

"Not hot?"

"No."

"Good. What's your name?"

I pretended to think about it. "I don't know."

He nodded. "We'll give it another hour and see how you do."

"If you're going to do that, would you let me out of this bed or at least leave someone here with me?"

"We'll have an orderly right outside. You won't have anything to worry about."

"No. I need someone in here."

Beckwith gave me a reassuring smile and patted my arm. "Now, now. There's nothing to—"

"I'll stay with him if you'd like," the nurse said. "I'm off duty now anyway."

"You are?" Beckwith asked. "Why didn't you say something?"

She looked away from him. "I don't mind. I didn't have any plans."

"It looks like you've got a volunteer." Glancing at the nurse, he said, "Thank you, Alice. I'll be back in an hour."

"You're welcome," she murmured as he strode to the door.

When he closed the door behind him, I said, "Thank you, ma'am. I appreciate it. I believe Francis meant me harm."

"Well, I'll stay here. You don't need to worry. Do you need anything for pain?"

"No, thank you. Say, I'm curious. Do you suppose Francis is why Dr. Beckwith chose this profession?"

Her eyes cut to the door and then back to me. When she spoke, her voice was a whisper. "You could get yourself in a lot of trouble asking questions like that."

"I don't mean anything by it. It would be understandable that he would want to cure his son."

After another glance at the door, she leaned in a little and spoke quietly. "I suppose Francis is the reason. Dr. Beckwith had been the head of surgery at the hospital in Kalamazoo before he became the administrator at the state hospital there."

"Interesting," I said, marveling that someone here was giving me answers. I would fish for whatever I could discover. "But . . ."

"What?" she asked.

"Well, a state hospital would have the best facilities and funding. It just seems odd that he would have left such a high-profile job to come to a county facility."

"This is one of the most progressive asylums in the country," she said.

"Still, Dr. Beckwith seems like an ambitious man. I don't think he would give up a job like that without a really good reason. Doesn't that make sense?"

"I heard that Francis . . ." She trailed off. "No, I don't gossip."

"So there's a story, isn't there?"

She didn't answer.

"Alice? Can I call you Alice?"

"It's Nurse Jensen. And I don't gossip."

Subject closed. "I'm sorry. I understand. If you don't mind me asking, what do you think about this Phantom business?"

"I don't think anything about it," she said.

"What about the patients who disappeared? Robinson, Bell, Foerster, and Cook. From what I hear, they all were murdered."

"Who did you hear that from?"

"A man named Dill."

"Oh, I hope you don't call him that," she said with a laugh. "Since he read some book in Mr. Morgan's class, he only answers to 'Daroga.'"

"Or 'the Persian,'" I said.

"Right. It was the same book that got them all worked up about patients being killed."

*The Phantom of the Opera.*

"That's the one." Shaking her head, she said, "He's a paranoid, you know. And delusional."

"You really don't think anyone has been murdered?"

"Of course not."

"What if I told you I saw Cook's body? He was strangled."

She frowned. "Of course he wasn't. Patrick was transferred last Wednesday."

"I saw his body Tuesday night. And I'm not crazy. I just can't remember who I am."

"Pshaw," she said, turning away and disappearing from my view. "You weren't even here then." I heard her settle into a chair.

I couldn't very well tell her why I was here that night. "My mind is obviously not working well at the moment. I'm sure you know a lot more about what's happening here than Dill would. I'm sorry for doubting you."

"That's all right."

"Could I ask you something?"

After a pause, she said, "I suppose so."

"Do you know any employees or patients here named Beatrice?"

"Beatrice? Can't say I do." She sounded amused. "Why?"

I felt stupid continuing to use Dill as my source, but I admitted to her what I'd heard from him.

"More nonsense," she said.

"Do you know Robert Clarke?"

"You don't think he was murdered as well, do you?"

"No, not at all. I heard they put him in the Hole."

The chair gave a little creak, and a few seconds later she appeared above me again. "Why are you interested in Robert?"

I didn't have a good answer to this question, but I had to say something. "I think I have some connection to him. If I could speak with him, maybe I could figure out who I am. One of the patients mentioned him, and the name felt so familiar I asked what he looked like. I don't know why or how, but I think I know him."

She studied me for a moment but didn't reply.

"Do you think you could find out if he's there? In the Hole?"

"No. Since I'm not part of the staff there, they wouldn't let me in."

Another dead end. I thought for a second. "Do you know anyone who could see if Robert's there?"

Her face screwed up in concentration. "I wonder . . ."

"What?"

"I could ask Mr. Morgan, the reading teacher. I suppose he might have some excuse for going there."

"Do you think you could arrange for me to speak with him?"

"I suppose it couldn't do any harm to ask."

"Thank you, Nurse Jensen."

"Oh, call me Alice," she said.


# Elizabeth

At nine fifteen, I stood in room 112 of Building F, waiting for my job assignment. I only half-hoped my request would be honored, which was good, because it made the inevitable letdown more palatable.

"Tubercular sanatorium," the woman said. "See Nurse Kowalski."

"Really? The sanatorium?" I'd worked with consumptives at the mission, but that was only one or two at a time, not the hundreds of patients I knew to be here. It made me a bit nervous. Tuberculosis is a very contagious disease.

She nodded and handed me a form detailing my assignment. I was to bring the form to the front desk, which was also where I would be working. My duties included answering the telephone, helping visitors, and assisting the nurses as needed. There was nothing on the sheet regarding working with patients, which made me feel a little better. Even though the sanatorium was not where I wanted to be, I accepted the assignment without complaint. I was inside the grounds now. I would experiment to see how much freedom of movement I would be allowed.

The guard did not impede my passage on my way out the door this time. The walk to the sanatorium took about ten minutes, as it was the most isolated section of the hospital. When I got off the train that morning, I had seen at least a hundred men working in the field on the other side of Michigan Avenue, and now, as I walked toward the back of the complex, I passed dozens more working in the barns and the piggery. They were dressed as the men in the field had been, in denim trousers and white shirts. I was close enough to see the letters EH and then other letters and numbers stenciled on the shirts. I thought these men must be patients.

The center of the building was a nearly square two-story clapboard structure that looked like a guardhouse. The sidewalk passed alongside one of the long single-story wings that angled away from it. Through the open windows I could hear inmates coughing and wheezing. It seemed strange to me that these people would be housed at the same hospital as mental patients. My heart went out to the poor souls, isolated from loved ones, left here to die so that no one else would be infected.

Inside the center structure, the receptionist summoned Nurse Kowalski, a tiny woman who explained my duties and sat me at the front desk. The woman who had greeted me departed. I spent the morning there with no one to speak with and little to do. Mostly, I considered my course of action. As Detective Riordan . . . Thomas . . . had said, every passing day made it less likely we'd find the killer. I needed to learn about the murders, assuming there really had been more than one, and determine if there was any evidence supporting the idea that the Phantom existed. When I was relieved for a lunch break at one o'clock, I decided to search out Clarence Morgan and see if he could shed any light on the matter.

I was disappointed to learn that he was teaching English to indigent patients in the old school building from one o'clock until two but thought to go there nonetheless and see if I could get a few minutes of his time later in the day.

When I peered into the classroom, he was standing at the chalkboard, upon which was written, *Hello, I am a monkey*. He used his piece of chalk to point at each word, and the class, about twenty men, recited the sentence in broken English.

"And what does a monkey do?" he asked.

They all scratched their underarms and the tops of their heads, and broke into monkey hoots and gibbers until everyone was laughing. Mr. Morgan jumped up on the desk and, holding his arms away from his body, capered about like a chimpanzee, pointing first at one man, who repeated the phrase, and then others. Each said, "I am a monkey," with a heavy accent while the other men continued to hoot and scratch.

Mr. Morgan glanced my way, looked back, and then his head snapped around to me again. He hopped off the desk and said in an embarrassed tone, "Miss James, I apologize for that little display."

One of the men in the class whistled at me. Morgan's head whipped around, and he barked, "Leon!"

The man who had whistled quickly turned away. Morgan eyed him for another second before meeting me at the door with a cool smile. "How may I help you?"

"I was wondering, would you have a few minutes for me later today? I have some questions about the hospital."

"Certainly. I'm finished at four. Would you be available then?"

"That's perfect. Where would you like to meet?"

He thought for a moment. "Would you perhaps like to get a cup of coffee in the cafeteria?"

I didn't want to create any complications with Alice, on the chance she was sweet on him. "I was hoping to speak with you somewhere a bit more private." I thought about how that sounded and quickly added, "It's nothing indecent. I just have some questions that I'd prefer not be overheard."

"There's a gazebo by the amusement hall on the other side of the lake. It's nearly always deserted in the late afternoon. Perhaps four fifteen?"

The memories of that Sunday afternoon flooded back.

"Esther?" Mr. Morgan said. "Would that be acceptable?"

"Oh." I forced myself back to the present. "Could we make it a little later?" I had to stop by the Administration Building first.

"Four thirty? Five?"

"Is five too late?"

"No, that's fine," he said. "I've got plenty to keep me busy."

We said good-bye, and I started back for the sanatorium, suppressing the thought of the forest and the girls . . . of my madness. The rest of the day dragged by. I sorted some papers and answered the telephone twice, but other than that there was nothing to do but sit and think. I didn't know Clarence Morgan well enough to trust him, but I had to start somewhere.

At four o'clock I was dismissed from my post and, after being let out of the sanatorium, walked up to the Administration Building. I asked the guard in the lobby where I could find the admitting office. He directed me farther down the center corridor. I walked the short distance to the office, where I waited fifteen minutes to speak with the woman at the counter, a thick matron with gray streaks in her red hair.

"Excuse me, can you tell me where I would find a patient named Robert Clarke?"

She eyed my badge before picking up a ledger book and paging through it. "Clarke, Robert. Building B."

"Really? I was told by staff there that he had been transferred out of the hospital."

She pointed to a two-foot-high stack of papers on a desk in the back. "Could be, honey," she said with an air of indifference. "All's I know is I've got a month of paperwork to file, and they won't give me any help."

"Do you think I could . . . that is, could I see the files?"

She took a closer look at my badge and met my eyes again. "Unless you are assigned to administration, you can't look at anything."

"I promise I won't—"

"Nope." She slammed the ledger book shut and took it with her to the back desk.

I tried to keep a meek expression on my face through all of this, though it was quite an effort. "One other thing, ma'am?"

She rolled her eyes conspicuously.

"A neighbor of mine, about twenty-five years old, a man with dark hair and a burned hand, is missing. His parents think he might have amnesia. Have you seen anyone like that come through lately?"

"Nope." She reached up and snatched the top piece of paper from the stack in front of her. "Now, if you'll excuse me."

"You know, there's no reason to be so rude. Do you really hate your job that much?"

She just started humming, staring down at the paper in her hands.

Brimming with sarcasm, I thanked her and looked at my watch. I still had time to make my meeting with Clarence.

I left again through one of the main doors, which the guard unlocked for me. He stood back while I walked out, and I thanked him before leaving. Perhaps gratitude for his forced decency would help him learn some manners. The guard at the gate opened it for me, and I crossed Michigan Avenue to the lake, which was really more a largish pond. I could see the small white gazebo in front of the amusement hall on the other side and their reflection on the glassy water. I averted my eyes.

Clarence was waiting for me, standing with his arms straight, palms flat against the rail, staring out at the lake. He'd undoubtedly seen me coming but seemed to be transfixed by the water in front of him. I had just put my foot on the step when he said, "I wonder how much truth there is in reflection."

I walked around the wicker chairs in the center, my heels ringing on the hollow wood floor. "How do you mean?"

He turned to me, sheepish. "Oh, it's silly, I know, but since I was a child I've thought there was another universe that existed in mirror image to our own. When I was young it was the only way I could make sense of seeing myself in a mirror. Later, when I began to understand the nature of evil, I convinced myself that the injustices here are balanced out in the mirror world. The bad here are good there." He grinned, but he didn't look amused. "I know, it's stupid."

"I don't think it's stupid at all," I said. "I hope there is somewhere that the bad pay for their sins. Maybe your mirror world is the afterlife, and the pain people have inflicted on others comes back to them, and those who suffered in this world are given an equal amount of pleasure. Everything would balance out. It's a nice thought."

He turned and sat on the rail. "It would be comforting to know the bad could that easily be turned to good. It doesn't seem to work that way here."

"Then here's to the mirror world."

He nodded and smiled, though again it looked pained.

"It's pretty here," I said, gesturing toward the lake.

"Yes, I like it. It's quiet. So." He glanced at me. "What did you want to ask me about?"

I brushed some leaves from one of the wicker chairs and sat. I hoped to draw him out, get to know his character a bit without raising his suspicions. "Your teaching style is a little unorthodox."

He laughed. "I suppose there is still a little thespian in me."

"Oh, you were an actor?"

"For a while." He hooked an arm around one of the posts holding up the roof. "My dream was to be a Shakespearean actor, which wasn't a popular idea with my parents: good, clean farm folk. When I was sixteen I moved from Seattle to San Francisco and apprenticed with an acting troupe for two years. That didn't work out so well, so I decided to become a teacher. I taught in secondary schools for a number of years before I came to Eloise a couple of years ago."

"After all those years of wanting to be an actor, why did you give it up?"

"Oh, it's a bit embarrassing, really. The star took a liking to me. A little more of a liking than I was comfortable with, to tell you the truth." He tipped his head to the side. "I suppose I should have said he was a man."

"Ah."

"Nothing happened," he added quickly. "It was just that I discovered acting troupes were loaded with fairies, and for some reason, they were drawn to me. I tired of fighting them off and gave up the theater."

I wondered if he would use that term had he known Wesley McRae. I left it, though. "Why teaching?"

With a grin, he said, "I suppose you could see why this afternoon. It's still acting, just a different kind."

I nodded. "Is your family still in Seattle?"

He looked out at the water again. "They've all passed."

A gust of wind rippled the surface. "I'm sorry," I said.

"Don't be. We weren't close."

"It must be lonely."

His eyes dropped to the railing in front of him.

"I'm sorry," I blurted, realizing I had crossed a line. "I'm sure you have friends, companions. I shouldn't assume. I don't even know if you're married."

He tried to smile but failed miserably. "Oh. I was, but my honeybee is gone now."

Seeing the anguish in his eyes, I decided to drop the topic. I thought this must have been a recent development, though some people hold on to their pain as determinedly as they would the love. My gut feeling was that Clarence was an honest man, but I would proceed cautiously. "I'm here because I'm looking for someone."

Eyes wary, he cocked his head. "Are you with the police?"

"No. I'm looking for my cousin, Robert Clarke. Do you know him?"

"Robert, yes, he was in my reading class. He was transferred recently. Stephen, that is, Dr. Beckwith, said he had been sent to a state facility."

"Do you know where?"

He shook his head. "No, but there aren't that many of them. I'd guess it's either Pontiac or Kalamazoo."

"How sure are you that Robert was transferred?"

"Why would Stephen lie to me?"

"I'm sure he wouldn't. I'm just afraid for Robert. How had he been doing?"

"He seemed all right to me," Clarence said. "Why the cloak and dagger? You can just ask administration. They'll tell you where he is."

"They don't seem to be able to give me an answer."

"Would you like me to try to find out?"

"Could you do it on the sly? I think they're withholding the information because they don't want us to know."

"Us?"

"My mother and I. My mother is Robert's guardian."

A little smile played on his lips. "If it's important to you, Esther, I'll do it."

"It is. Thank you, Clarence. Oh, say." I tried to be as casual as I could. "Have you seen a young man here with a badly burned right hand?"

He thought for a moment. "No, not that I recall."

I hadn't expected anything different, but still his words hit me like a sledgehammer. I knew Will wouldn't leave me. If he wasn't here, he wasn't likely to turn up anywhere . . . alive.

My fears must have shown on my face. Clarence leaned in toward me. When he spoke, his voice was quiet and concerned. "What's your connection to him?"

"He's a friend who's turned up missing."

"From Detroit?"

I nodded.

"I'll keep my eyes open. I'll let you know if I do see him. But, Esther?"

"Yes?"

"Do you know how easily someone can disappear off the streets of that city?"

When I got home, Alberts told me he'd spoken with four men and three women today in response to the missing person advertisement. All of them, he said, were out-and-out frauds, just looking to cadge a reward.

I sat in the kitchen and had a bowl of leftover soup. My heart ached. After all we'd gone through, Will and I had finally gotten to where we should have years ago. We knew each other's faults and foibles and loved one another just the same. Now he'd been gone for four days. The fire of hope that burned inside me had ebbed to a mere spark.

A thought tickled at my mind. What if Will had run? With all he'd been through over the past couple of years, what if the pressure was too much for him to handle? I tried to push the doubts away, but they kept insinuating themselves into my thoughts. Will was a man and had all the weaknesses of a man. He'd fought them, but it was a harder battle for him than for most. Perhaps he couldn't fight them anymore. Still. A telephone call? A note? Would he have gone off somewhere, anywhere, without the decency to let me know?

Of course he wouldn't.

I spoke with Bridie for a few minutes. She'd made no progress with my mother but told me not to worry; she wasn't one to give up. I thanked her and walked down to the den. Sitting at my father's desk, I switched on the lamp and thought.

Bridie wasn't giving up. Which was precisely what I was doing. Will was intelligent, and he was nothing if not resourceful. Just because Clarence hadn't seen him, I couldn't assume Will wasn't at Eloise. There had to be well over a thousand patients, and a new one wouldn't be in a reading class; he would be undergoing an evaluation.

Still, assuming he *was* there, how would I find him?

I had an idea. I phoned the Baker Electric garage, asking them to deliver our automobile at 6:00 A.M., and to be absolutely certain the batteries were fully charged. Fortunately the garage was open twenty-four hours a day. Without spending the night at Eloise, which I had no intention of doing, I had no other way to get there early enough to start my search for Will and Robert before I had to work.

Finished with that, I phoned Detective Riordan and asked him to see if Robert had been transferred to the Pontiac or Kalamazoo asylum. He said he'd do it the next day.

I climbed into bed and lay awake, staring at the ceiling. At some point, I finally fell asleep.

# CHAPTER EIGHT

*Tuesday, August 13, 1912*

## Will

The tingling in my temples was still there when I woke the next morning. I wasn't sure if that was good or bad. My mind seemed to work normally, so I disregarded it. I ate with Dill and told him about the radium treatment, which he was certain was some sort of governmental plot, though he couldn't answer me as to exactly what the government would gain by having tubes of radium attached to my head.

"But it's Roosevelt," he said knowingly. "Don't doubt it for a minute."

It was only then that I realized it had been two nights since I'd had the dream. I wondered what that meant. Was this place doing me good?

An orderly brought me to the barber, who shaved my face and head again, and then led me back to my room, where I expected to hear that Dr. Beckwith would be seeing me for treatment of some sort. Instead, the orderly threw me a pair of dungarees and a white shirt with EH – B6 stenciled on the front. "Put them on," he said. "It's time for work."

"What am I going to be doing?"

"You'll see soon enough. Now get dressed. You've got one minute." He left the room. I dressed, and as promised, he walked in while I was still tying my shoes.

"Let's go." He led me to the building's rear entrance, which he unlocked before taking me down the road toward the back of the complex. It was sunny, and I was perspiring just from the walk. We crossed the river and passed the stock barns to the single barn set behind them, in front of which stood a long row of empty pigpens, surrounded by wooden fences. The grunts and snorts of pigs came from the other side of the barn.

I hoped he would keep walking, but he stopped there and turned me over to the wizened pig farmer, Mr. Jones, who handed me a shovel.

"Wait," I said. "I'm no expert, but aren't you supposed to do this with a pitchfork?"

"I ain't handing pitchforks to a buncha loonies," he replied and led me to a pen. A big—tall and fat—man about my age joined us from a few pens over. His forehead and cheeks were sunburned bright red. His face was vaguely piggish, and his belly slopped over his belt. His arms were huge. I thought there was probably a lot of muscle hiding under the fat. He also wore a pair of dungarees and a white shirt, but his shirt had no letters or numbers on the front, which I assumed meant he was an employee. He listened while the farmer instructed me how to muck out the pens.

The stink was so distracting I couldn't concentrate on what he was saying, though I saw how simple the task was from watching the dozen or so other men up to their ankles in pig shit mixed with straw. They scooped up the muck with their shovels, dumped it into a wheelbarrow, and, when the barrow was full, wheeled it to a wagon and shoveled the filth onto an extremely foul-smelling mountain of shit.

It was a simple matter, but he might as well have been asking me to move a literal mountain. Between my injured shoulder and burned hand, I couldn't use a shovel or move a wheelbarrow. I tried to explain that to the farmer. He wouldn't listen. I offered to do some other sort of work, but he was insistent that I muck out the pens. His final words to me were that I was to do everything George—the fat man—told me to do. When the farmer turned and walked away, George thrust the shovel into my chest. "Shovel."

I took it from him, turned around, and muttered, "Yes, that's what it's called."

"What'd you say?"

"Nothing." I stabbed the shovel into the straw-filled muck and tried to raise it into the wheelbarrow. In order to do so, I had to rest the handle on my right forearm, which made the pig shit very difficult to balance. I ended up shoveling the same muck over and over.

George yelled at another patient, who was lying down in the pen he was supposed to be cleaning, and stalked over to him, shouting warnings. I forgot about him and shoveled. When I got the wheelbarrow loaded, I grasped a handle with my left hand and tried to do the same with my right. A bolt of pain shot up my arm, and I let go. I stretched out my fingers and tried again. With the barest of grips, I lifted the wheelbarrow and made it one step out of the pen before the handle slipped out of my hand. The wheelbarrow tipped over, dumping my load to the side of the pen door. "God damn it!" I couldn't do this. I put my left hand on my hip and looked up at the sky, blue and featureless.

"Hey, pinhead." George stared at me from the side of the pen. "What are ya, a moron? Ya can't even work a wheelbarrel?"

I glared at him. "It's my hand." I held my right hand up in front of me.

He wasn't any more impressed than the farmer had been. "Shovel that shit back up or you're gonna be eatin' it."

Righting the wheelbarrow, I muttered, "Wouldn't be much different from what they feed us anyway."

He walked around to the door of the pen. "What'd you say?"

"Nothing."

"Bullshit." He shoved me, almost knocking me over backward into the pen. "What did you say?"

I got my balance and gave him a level stare. "I said it wouldn't be much different than the shit they feed us here."

"Is that what you think?" He grabbed hold of my shirt and jerked me to the ground. Holding me there with one hand, he jumped on top of me and forced my face down into the pig shit. "Eat it!" I struggled, but he was too heavy and strong for me to gain any headway. I screwed my eyes shut and kept my mouth tightly closed. He just kept grinding me into the sticky filth. Finally he grabbed the collar of my shirt and pulled my head out. "How was it?"

I refused to give in to the fat son of a bitch. Looking up at his pig face, I said, "Needs salt."

"Too bad I ain't got none." He jammed my face back into the shit.

This time he didn't grind, but instead was content to just hold me there. Again I struggled, but he was sitting on my back, bearing down on my head with both hands. It was useless. I forced myself to relax, hoping he would let me up if he thought I was suffocating. At last he picked up my head and bent down to look in my face. "You're gonna eat it, or you ain't gonna make it back to Building B." He pinched my jaws open, reached down and grabbed a chunk of shit, and jammed it into my mouth. Working my jaws up and down with his hands, he grinned in my face. "How do ya like it?" He threw my head back down into the shit. I spit out as much as I could, but the nasty stuff coated the inside of my mouth.

"And that's just the start if you don't get to work." He kicked me in the side.

"All right!" I shouted. "I'll do it." I shoved a forefinger into my mouth and tried to clean out the shit before getting to my feet and going back to work. I picked up the wheelbarrow and filled it, then wheeled it over to the wagon, all under the watchful eye of the grinning fat asshole. I wanted to cleave his face with the blade of the shovel.

I must have been glaring at him, because he walked over to me and shoved me once, not hard enough to knock me over, just enough to establish his dominance. "Whatcha looking at?" he growled.

I kept my eyes down. "Nothing."

"Nothing, *sir*."

I could feel my face turning red, felt the shame running through me. "Nothing, sir," I mumbled. *God damn it,* I thought. *I hate this place.*

## Elizabeth

Five A.M. seemed to come only moments later. I dragged myself out of bed and got ready for the day, trying to believe that Will was all right, that he had gotten himself into Eloise and had begun his investigation. Today I would start the search for him. First I would see if I could get into Building B. I would keep my eyes open for Robert as well. Perhaps the matron in administration was right, and he was still in that building. If I didn't find either of them there, I would discover the location of the "Hole." If Robert hadn't been transferred to another facility, he was likely in one or the other. Will would be looking for Robert and would be close to him.

I would believe in Will.

After strapping on the corset, I dressed in my second most stodgy outfit, a high-necked yellow day dress with a matching wide-brimmed hat, and walked outside to a beautiful morning. It was cool this early, but very pleasant, with the sun already peeking over Windsor's skyline across the river. The Baker Electric sat against the curb in front of our house as promised. It was a beauty, like a tall opera coach with a rich lacquered black finish, brass lamps and trim, and a fine European broadcloth interior. I thought it as nice as any Detroit Electric, though I would never have admitted that to Will.

After I unlocked the door, I climbed onto the bench seat in back, where I switched on the automobile and checked the meters. They showed a full charge. The Baker had had a complete going-over by the garage only a few months before and had come through with a report of complete health, including the batteries. If I got the average of fifty miles on a charge I would have no problem, but there is a difference between *average* mileage and *actual* mileage. I needed somewhere between thirty-five and forty miles to make it through my day without being stranded.

I opened all the windows, pulled the steering tiller down in front of me, and pushed the shifter to first speed. Pulling the tiller toward me slightly, I eased out onto Jefferson Avenue at four miles per hour, though I quickly shifted to second, then third, which got me up to fourteen, four over the city speed limit. I didn't worry about that, as I wasn't even keeping up with traffic. It didn't take long before I was out of the city, bouncing down from the pavement onto the dirt road. It was relatively smooth, so I shifted all the way up to fifth gear and sped along at twenty-four miles per hour. I pulled off my hat and let the wind blow back my hair.

It seemed to me that breakfast in Building B's cafeteria would be my best chance to find Robert . . . and Will, if he was at Eloise. It was not yet seven when I arrived. I peeked at the guard but couldn't see him well enough to determine if he was the lad who had been so obstinate with Will and me, so when I pulled up to the gate I looked away and held my badge out the window. He opened the gate, and I drove through with my hand up near my face, as if I were shading my eyes from the sun. I parked in the lot in front of the Administration Building, pinned my badge to my dress, and walked down the sidewalk to Building B. Together the structures made an impressive, or should I say repressive, edifice. Blocky, solid-looking, like a massive brick wall barring the patients from the world. Or perhaps vice versa.

I walked up the stairs with a bounce in my step. Confidence is ninety percent of pulling off any bluff. If challenged, I could feign ignorance. I was simply looking around the facility before work. I strengthened my resolve, threw open the door, and stepped up onto the polished marble floor. Seeing my badge as I marched toward him, the guard acknowledged me with a nod. His eyes followed me as I passed, but it wasn't a suspicious look. Rather, it was a man's hungry gaze, one to which I had become too well accustomed. I swept on to the main hallway.

When I used to come here with my mother, we passed the cafeteria many times. I was hoping breakfast would be served at seven. The patients didn't begin their labors until eight, so I doubted it would be earlier. Sure enough, I heard a buzzing down the hall and continued on, hope beginning to rise that I would find them.

The hallway was nearly deserted, only a few orderlies and nurses scurrying from one place to another. The first two cafeteria doors were closed. Glancing ahead, I saw that the other pair were also shut, so I stopped at the first door and tried to twist the knob. It was locked. The door to its left was locked as well.

I looked into the small window in the door and scanned the sea of patients, easily three hundred men packed together eating. Not seeing Will or Robert in my first quick look, I started over from the row of tables nearest me.

Behind me, a man said, "Miss Hume?"

I turned to see Dr. Davis standing before me, his eyes wide with astonishment.


Dr. Davis put his hands on his hips. "What are you doing here?"

I glanced at the man next to him, then met the doctor's eyes. My first thought was to try to bluff my way out of the situation, but my

"Esther James" disguise was not nearly good enough. "I'm volunteering." I scratched my throat, using my arm to block his view of my name badge.

He appraised me for a moment. "You hadn't been prior to Robert Clarke's, um . . ." He searched for a word, finally settling on ". . . situation, correct?"

I stopped scratching but cupped my chin, leaving my forearm where it was. "No. Being here again made me realize how difficult these patients' lives are. I thought I should try to help."

He looked at the other man. "Will you excuse us for a moment?"

The man glanced at me before backing away, telling Dr. Davis he'd see him on rounds.

The doctor turned back to me. "You're here to help." It was a statement, not a question, but it was clear he didn't believe it.

"Yes, I am. Now, if you will excuse me, I need to get to work."

"Volunteers don't start until nine," Dr. Davis said, glancing at his pocket watch. "I think you have a few minutes to spare."

"Yes, well . . . I really am busy, so—"

"Perhaps you'd prefer I speak with Dr. Beckwith about this."

"Obviously that's your prerogative, if you really think it necessary," I said, my hearbeat pounding in my ears.

"Wouldn't it be easier for us to talk?"

"Oh, I suppose I can spare a few minutes," I said, as breezily as possible. The last thing I wanted was a public argument with Dr. Davis. My cover story was already being shredded.

He took my right elbow and led me down the hall. With him at my side, I didn't need to hide my badge, but it would be only seconds until I was facing him again. As we walked, I turned away just a bit, hoping he didn't notice, and reached up with my left hand, sliding the badge off my collar. I palmed it as we passed the lobby and continued down to his office. He unlocked the door, opened it, and ushered me in. I slipped the badge into my purse. He followed, closing the door behind him, and stepped up close to me, too close. I held my ground, determined not to let him intimidate me.

He made a point of staring at my hair before cocking his head. "Would you like to amend your story?"

I took an involuntary step backward but maintained eye contact.

"Dr. Davis, I can understand why you would be suspicious of me, but I am here simply to help."

"Please. You told me you believed your cousin to be innocent. You're here to perform some sort of amateur investigation."

"I won't disagree that it had crossed my mind, but I'm here to help the patients. If I do that, perhaps another person would help Robert."

"Your attitude has had a serious adjustment since the other night," he said, looking me up and down, "and I don't think arrogant is too strong a term for how you acted then. I wonder why you're displaying such perfect manners today?"

"I was awakened to come here in the middle of the night because my cousin had supposedly killed someone. How would you have acted?"

Studying my face, he said, "So you are truly here to help the patients?"

"Yes."

"But you'd like to clear Mr. Clarke of the murder."

"Well . . . of course, I'd like to see him get the care he deserves."

He thought for a moment. "Perhaps I can be of some assistance with your cousin." He pulled out his pocket watch and consulted it again. "I have an appointment. You and I will need to discuss this further."

"I don't really see the—"

"Do you think you can get him out of here by yourself?"

His words sent a tremor through me. Robert *was* here. There was no question Dr. Davis could grease the skids and make this easier. "No, I don't."

"Does your shift end at four o'clock?"

"Yes."

"Then you will meet me here immediately after. No later than four fifteen." The corners of his mouth rose in a humorless smile. "As I said, I may be able to help your cousin."


Dr. Davis escorted me to the exit, unlocked the door for me, and watched me leave. I would have liked to get another look at the cafeteria, but I couldn't risk running into him again.

I spent the morning at the desk in the sanatorium. I could think of little but Dr. Davis, but I didn't know what to do about him. I couldn't be too cavalier with my actions. Robert was at the mercy of this institution, a mercy none too freely given.

The morning passed by at a glacial pace, other than a nurse nearly biting off my head for calling a man with tuberculosis a patient. They were "inmates." The only patients around here were the lunatics, she said.

That sorted, I filled out the entry paperwork for two new inmates, a white man and a Negro woman, both of whom were brokenhearted to have been forced to leave their families. I was surprised to find that Negroes and whites were housed together, although the few colored women here were relegated to the far end of the ward.

Just before noon, Bessie walked in the door. "Hi, Esther," she said. "How would you like to have lunch with Alice and me?"

"Well, I thought . . ." I didn't really have an excuse. I couldn't very well tell her that I wanted to search the hospital. "I'm not really feeling too well," I finally said.

"Ah." She gave me a dismissive wave. "It's just being around all these sickies. Come on. It'll do you good to spend some time with healthy people."

She wasn't taking no for an answer. "Sounds like just the thing," I said. I wouldn't let it be a total loss. They could help me narrow my search. If I had to sort through all of the thousands of patients and inmates here, I would be forever in finding Will and Robert.

She unlocked one of the front doors, and we walked down the sidewalk toward the barns. "Do you mind if I have a cigarette?" I said. "I'm not proud of my smoking, but I find it relaxing."

"I will if you don't share."

I laughed and fished two cigarettes from my purse. "Modern women," I said. "The privileges of men aren't enough. We need their vices as well."

I lit our cigarettes and put my lighter away. It was a pleasant day. The sky was blue, and the sun shone directly overhead. The temperature was still rising. By midafternoon it would be hot, but now it was perfect. A truck passed us. I hid my cigarette at my side, but Bessie apparently didn't care if she was seen. She took a drag just as the truck drove by.

"Alice thought you might be mad at me," Bessie said.

"Mad? Why?"

"She said I came on a little strong about the supposed murders the patients have been jabbering about. I just get sick of that crap."

"No, that's fine. I understand."

"Good." Bessie took another drag from her cigarette.

We passed the barns and crossed the little bridge over the river, where we finished our cigarettes before continuing to the Administration Building. On the way we made chitchat, keeping the discussion light.

Alice was waiting for us inside, at the entrance to the staff cafeteria on the first floor. "Hello, Esther. It's nice to see you."

I told her it was nice to see her as well, and we walked into the cafeteria, a large room with servers behind counters at the near end. The walls and marble floors were white, as were the tables and chairs. The room looked to seat about a hundred people, although only a third that many were here now. I walked to the counter behind Bessie and Alice and followed their lead, choosing the beef over the mutton to go with the mashed potatoes, corn, and pears. They were not required to pay, but, as I was a lowly volunteer, I paid thirty cents for the meal. I hoped the quality lived up to the price.

They had already found a table by the time I'd finished paying, and I wended my way through the hospital staff, mostly orderlies and nurses. I sat next to Alice. "Ladies, you told me before to be careful around Dr. Davis. He requested that I meet with him later today. How worried should I be?"

"He's no different than any other man," Alice said. "I wouldn't be worried. That new doctor, though, Meyer. Now there's one for you." She and Bessie blathered on with gossip about the newest staff member, a man I had yet to meet.

I glanced at my watch and began eating in earnest. I was due back at the sanatorium in thirty minutes, and I had a stop to make first. We discussed the weather, and Bessie complained about the Detroit Tigers for a while. It appeared that Alice and I were of one mind on the subject: complete disinterest.

When Bessie wound down, I said, "I've been all over this place and haven't seen the Hole yet. Where is it?"

"It's in the basement," Bessie said.

"Here?"

She nodded. "Other end of the building. The police station's on the main floor, and they keep the real crazies down in solitary."

"Ah. No wonder I haven't seen it."

"Be thankful you never will," Alice said.

We finished eating, and I said that I'd better return to duty, as I didn't want to be late on my second day. I thanked Bessie and Alice for the lunch invitation and agreed we must do it again soon. We returned our trays to a window in front, said our good-byes, and parted after Alice unlocked the rear door. They turned left down the road that led to Building B, and I continued straight, beginning the trek back to the sanatorium.

I realized Dr. Davis could be pivotal in resolving this mess. If I could convince him to help me, this could all end quickly and satisfactorily. If not, after our meeting, perhaps I would be able to visit Building B and continue my search for Will and Robert.

Marching up the sidewalk to the barns, I pulled another cigarette from my purse and lit it, drawing the smoke deep into my lungs. Inside one of the open stalls at the piggery, an old man in overalls was admonishing the only worker in sight, a man who looked like he had been rolling around in the mud. They were perhaps a hundred feet away, so I didn't catch the words, only the farmer's tone, which was angry. I tried to watch out of the corner of my eye as I passed them. Shoveling muck into wheelbarrows seemed a simple enough task, one that anyone could do with a minimum of instruction. I reminded myself that not everyone had been blessed with a fully functional brain, and the farmer and I both needed to remember that.

I was almost to the end of the block and had to turn my head to see them. The farmer stopped talking and held out the shovel to the man, who took the handle, stabbed the blade down into the muck, and held his other hand up in front of him. Now he was saying something. He held his hand in front of the farmer's face.

His right hand.

I stopped and stared.

It was Will.

# Will

Fortunately, the farmer called for a water break only fifteen minutes after George tried to make me eat the pig shit. I rinsed out my mouth as best I could and got a little water in me before George herded us all back to work. I filled the barrow and wheeled it over to the truck, dumping it twice along the way. He hovered around, eyeing me.

I stayed at it, and eventually thought I had the pen done, but when I called George over, he declared it nowhere near clean and told me to work harder. Exactly how he could determine if a muddy pen of pig shit was "clean" was beyond me.

Even though my progress was slow, I eventually made my way to the next pen. Sweat poured off me, soaking my shirt and trousers. Sunburn scorched my face. My right shoulder and hand burned with pain, and I tried balancing the barrow with my wrist, but it was difficult to do and slowed me down even more. The other patients cleared easily three times as many pens as I could, and at lunchtime George told me I wouldn't be getting a break until I caught up.

He left with the other men, heading down the road toward the front of the complex. The farmer, carrying a bucket of water and a dipper, came over to speak with me. While I drank and washed the filth from my face and head, I tried again to convince him that I was better suited for another form of labor, but, in an angry tone, he lectured me about the value of hard work.

I lost my temper, thrust the shovel into the muck, and shook my hand in his face. Again, I tried to explain to him that I could not do this. He was not impressed. He simply said that if my pens weren't in order by four o'clock, he would be turning in a poor report to the doctors, which I would be very sorry about. Motivational speech completed, he turned and headed back toward the barn.

I picked up the shovel with my left hand, steadied it with my right palm, and drove it into the muck.

"Will?"

I froze.

"Will."

I turned to see the most welcome sight of my life. Elizabeth, radiant in a yellow day dress and a matching wide-brimmed hat, stood near the fence. She wore wire-rimmed eyeglasses and had dyed her hair blond, but the changes did little to alter her appearance.

I looked over my shoulder for the farmer, but he was out of sight. Hurrying to Elizabeth, I reached over the fence to hug her, only just remembering in time that I was coated in pig feces and mud. She leaned in toward me, and we shared a brief kiss—my mouth tightly closed— before we both realized we would be in serious trouble if we were seen.

"Thank God," she said. "I was so worried . . ." She touched the top of my head, and a little frown snuck onto her face. "Oh, your hair." Her hand brushed my cheek. "And a black eye. Are you all right?"

"I'm fine," I said.

She looked around. "Can you get away?"

"I don't know how. The farmer will be back any second."

"How about the barn?"

I was game to try. "All right. Go on over there. If you can get inside, I'll join you in a minute."

I headed back to my pen, eyes darting between the back of the barn, where I had last seen the farmer, and Elizabeth marching up to one of the barn doors. Now, down the road, I saw the other muckers heading back to the piggery. They crossed the bridge, an orderly pushing them along. They would be here in no more than a minute. The only good news was that George wasn't with them.

Elizabeth disappeared inside. As soon as she closed the door, I followed, hurrying over and slipping into the dark interior of the barn. The heat was stifling.

"Over here," she called from the nearest stall.

It was all I could do not to take her in my arms. We settled for another kiss. "I can't tell you how happy I am to see you," I said. I noticed she tasted like cigarette smoke but didn't remark on it, as she didn't comment on my stench.

"Oh, my God, Will. I was so worried." She gripped my arms. "Are you sure you're all right?"

"Yes. I'm fine, really. I've got some names for Detective Riordan to investigate. I believe they were killed by the man they call the Phantom."

She dug into her purse for a pencil and scrap of paper.

"Patrick Cook was killed the night we came here," I said. "The others are Paul Robinson, who was murdered two years ago, Albert Bell, killed last summer, and Victor Foerster, who was killed in March. Oh, and according to one patient, the Phantom is being assisted by a woman named Beatrice." I didn't think it would be productive to mention that he also thought Beatrice might be a ghost.

She scribbled down the names and stuck the paper back into her purse.

"And I think Francis Beckwith is the Phantom," I said.

"Do you? He seemed like a very mild-mannered boy."

"Trust me, he's not. I think Francis did something in Kalamazoo that was bad enough for his father to give up his ambitions and run."

"Really?"

"Have Riordan dig into it. I'll bet he finds something."

She nodded. "I will. Right away. Have you spoken with Robert?"

"No, but I think he's in solitary confinement in a place they call the Hole. It's in the basement of—"

"—of the Administration Building," she finished. "Let me investigate. I can move around here easier than you."

"I might have a lead on getting in there. Let's both try."

She wasn't enthusiastic but agreed. "If you get in a bind here," she added, "Clarence Morgan, the English teacher, might be able to help. He's been sympathetic."

I nodded. "One of the nurses is trying to get me in touch with him."

"Be careful, but I think he's trustworthy."

"Okay. By the way, how did you get in here? Are you volunteering?"

She explained that she was working at the sanatorium and then said, "Has anyone recognized you?"

"Francis Beckwith, but near as I can tell he hasn't said anything." I didn't tell her about my close call. I just needed to stay away from Francis long enough to find Robert.

Her features darkened. "You haven't seen Dr. Davis?"

"No."

"Good. He recognized me. If he sees you, we're really going to be in trouble." She took a deep breath. "Do you think you and I could meet tomorrow?"

"It's hard to say. This morning there was a man here who just about . . . well, let's say he kept a close eye on me. If he's not here tomorrow, we've got a chance." I smiled. "I'd guess I'll be on pig duty until they've broken me, which is going to take a while."

She gripped my shoulders. I tried not to wince. "We should get you out of here before something awful happens. I can work on finding Robert."

"No. I haven't accomplished anything yet. I need to do this."

"It's . . . it's too dangerous, Will."

There seemed to be something she wasn't telling me. "What is it, Elizabeth? What's wrong?"

"Nothing. It's just this . . . I'm afraid you're going to be hurt. Or worse."

I lifted her right hand from my shoulder and kissed the back of it. "We knew I'd be taking a chance coming here, but I did it to help Robert." I thought I'd show a little unfelt bravado. "Besides, what could they do to me that I haven't already been through?"

She gave a quiet laugh. "That's true. You've pretty well been through the wringer. I just don't want it to happen again."

"I'll be fine. Keep your eyes and ears open. We can try to meet here every day at—"

The door swung open, brightening the barn. We both ducked. "Doe?" the farmer shouted. "Where the hell are you?"

The hinges on one of the stall doors creaked. Then another. He would be on us in seconds.

I gestured for Elizabeth to stay back and walked out of the stall. "Mr. Jones?"

He put his hands on his hips. "Where is she?"

If Elizabeth were caught here with me, they'd never let her back inside the hospital grounds. "Who?"

"The woman you come in here with."

"What? No. I had to go to the bathroom."

"Other nitwit said you come in here with a girl."

"And you believed him?"

"Don't know why he'da made it up." He leaned into the stall and gave it a quick look. I held my breath. He scrutinized me again. "You didn't take a shit in there, did you?"

Trying to keep my sigh of relief inaudible, I said, "No."

"So for some reason you had to come in here to piss?"

"Well . . . I'm kind of shy."

"Get back to work."

"Yes, sir." With Mr. Jones shadowing me, I walked out of the barn and away from Elizabeth, which was difficult, but I did it with a new-found sense of optimism. She knew where I was, which was the most important thought I could have. It was suddenly much less likely I would languish here.

I returned to my duty, watching out of the corner of my eye for Elizabeth. She walked down the street toward the sanatorium a few minutes later. I set to clearing the muck. Mr. Jones checked on me a few times, but less often as the afternoon progressed. I cleaned five more stalls, in the process getting a sore back to go along with blisters on my left hand, an aching shoulder, and a deep bone pain, like a toothache, in my mutilated right hand. I was more than relieved when, still in the full heat of the day, a pair of orderlies brought me and my six companions-in-shit back to Building B, where I happily submitted to a freezing shower. I opened my mouth and let the jets of water inside, and I cleared my nose as best I could, having no handkerchief. Still, all I could smell was pig shit.

Those of us who had returned from our jobs were herded into the dayroom by orderlies. It was a much smaller gathering than I'd experienced before—perhaps fifty men where there had been four times that many. None of my acquaintances were here, so I sat on one of the chairs and looked out the window. It would keep me out of Dr. Davis's sight, should he pass by. I looked outside at the closely mown grass, large trees bursting with leaves, and tidy rows of redbrick buildings. A train chugged away east, toward Detroit, its smokestack billowing oily gray smoke into the blue sky.

An observer might look at all this and assume that the hospital was as it appeared—a well-kept institution employing only the most modern techniques, with nothing more than the best interests of the patients in mind. In reality it was so much less than that. As with all human institutions, a rot had crept in. I saw it in the grounds—dead patches of brown grass, blighted gray trees stripped of their leaves, neglected buildings with peeling wood trim and rotting foundations. I saw it in the people as well. What I might have otherwise ascribed to professionalism in Dr. Beckwith or some of the nurses, I thought more likely to be indifference, or even an abhorrence of their charges.

"Get off!" a man commanded from behind me, near the door.

The room went silent. I cringed and slid down farther in my chair. I knew that voice.

"Get in there," another man growled.

I half-turned to see Ty standing just inside the doorway to the room, a pair of huge—though not quite Ty-sized—orderlies to either side of him, and George from the piggery behind. All three of them held nightsticks at the ready.

I couldn't believe this. If anyone belonged in the Hole it was Ty. They were going to turn this lunatic loose on us?

I turned and faced the window again, though I saw nothing in front of me. My senses were fully attuned to the giant. I heard him turn and strut into the room, moving first to the right, behind me, though still near the back wall. He strolled around the perimeter and then began making his way to the front. No one else moved. It seemed the breeze even held its breath while the big man moved about the room, establishing his dominance.

He stopped, perhaps thirty feet right of me. I could see him standing over a table with his hands on his hips, a man seated on either side of it, both with eyes cast down at the tabletop. After perhaps thirty seconds and no other movement in the room, he resumed his stalk, continuing to move closer to me. I kept my eyes pointed straight ahead, praying he wouldn't notice I was in the room.

The back of my neck tingled. I wondered how often prey knows that it's prey.

Ty stopped. A chair scraped against the floor, and it creaked as he settled into it. He was perhaps ten feet to my right and five feet behind me. I didn't know if he was facing toward me or away. I couldn't look without him noticing.

I angled myself to the left to make it more difficult for him to see my face, while preparing to leap from the chair at his slightest movement. Seconds passed, then minutes. A bead of sweat slid down my face just in front of my right temple. Ty didn't move. No one else spoke, moved about the room, or even seemed to breathe.

Gradually, tentatively, the patients began to lower their guard. Two of the men across the room began a quiet conversation in Italian. Another man, who was seated at the window two chairs over from me, directly in front of Ty, stood and padded behind me to the other side of the room. Half a dozen more men walked in and took seats. Their presence, coupled with Ty's inactivity, spurred even more conversation and movement.

Yet I was rooted in my chair, feeling his eyes on me.

Behind me, a man moved heavily across the floor, and the legs of Ty's chair shrieked. I jumped out of my seat just in time to see Ty, hazel eyes bulging, swing a heavy wooden chair at my head.

## Elizabeth

When Will started speaking with the farmer, I climbed over into the next stall as quietly as I could and was fortunate the man didn't hear me. I waited a few minutes to sneak out of the barn and return to the sidewalk, continuing my trip back to the sanatorium.

Speaking with Will had lifted a huge weight from my shoulders, but a second weight, that of the meeting with Dr. Davis, still pressed down on me. He didn't strike me as a man with much character. I thought to put off the meeting until I could be armed, but all he had to do was tell Dr. Beckwith I was here, and I would be unceremoniously tossed out on my backside.

I wanted to phone Detective Riordan immediately and let him know I'd found Will, but I was already late. Unfortunately, my clothing was permeated with the odor of pig excrement when I returned to the sanatorium. The scent was remarked upon by the woman I replaced—fifteen minutes later than I was supposed to. After giving me a mild upbraiding, she left to get her own lunch.

Shortly after she'd gone, Clarence Morgan walked in the door, wearing a crisp white linen suit. "Good afternoon, Miss James," he said, removing his straw boater.

"Good afternoon, Mr. Morgan."

He looked around the lobby, which was quiet, not even the occasional patient or staff member moving from one place to another. "Have you a quick moment?"

"I can't leave the desk, but I can talk for a minute. What can I do for you?"

"Just curious. Have you found out anything about your cousin or the other man?"

"Yes, in fact. The other man is here, which his parents will be happy to know. I have reason to believe that Robert is still here as well, being held in solitary confinement."

"Hmm." He cupped his chin in his hand and thought. "Beckwith may have sent him there."

"How can I get in to see him?"

"You can't. They're watched twenty-four hours a day by armed guards. They almost killed a patient who came sneaking in there last year. He was lucky to pull through. Nobody up there has a sense of humor—and that's the guards. Those patients would just as soon slit your throat as say hello."

Will said he was going to find a way to get inside. I had to warn him off. "It's impossible?"

"There aren't any volunteers in solitary. They don't allow visitors. You can't do it." Looking up at me again, he said, "Anyway, why would Stephen have lied to me about Robert? If he was in the Hole, I don't know why he wouldn't have just said so."

"You're probably right. Still, I have to know where he is."

He smiled. "I'll see what I can find out."

"Thank you."

"If you want to brace the administration to get some facts, I could help you. Perhaps this afternoon, when you finish work. I don't have any classes the rest of the day."

"No," I said in a small voice, remembering my appointment with Dr. Davis. "Thank you, though."

His forehead furrowed. "Esther, is something wrong?"

"No. I just . . . I have to meet with Dr. Davis this afternoon."

Eyebrows raised, he said, "Business?"

"Yes," I said quickly. "Of course."

"Sorry. I didn't mean to imply . . . I have no doubts about your character, Esther. That's not what I meant."

"No offense taken. Thank you."

We said our good-byes. As he was walking toward the door, I said, "Say, Clarence?"

He stopped and turned around.

"Would you mind keeping an eye on the desk for a few minutes while I make a telephone call?"

"Not at all." He came around behind the desk and took my place.

I walked down to the bank of pay telephones near the entrance and phoned the Bethune Street police station. Luckily for me, Detective Riordan was in his office. I barely let him get out a greeting before I said, "I found Will today. He's here. At Eloise."

"Oh, good." He sounded genuinely relieved. "Is he all right?"

"So far, yes. He doesn't seem to be too much the worse for wear. He gave me some names of men he suspects have been murdered." I waited a moment while he got a piece of paper and a pencil, and then I recited the names Will had given me.

"I'll check into them and see if I can find out anything, Elizabeth."

I suppressed a smile. "It's Esther. While I'm here, anyway. Will believes these men were killed by Francis Beckwith, the son of the administrator. He also thinks Francis may have committed a crime at Dr. Beckwith's last posting at the Kalamazoo State Hospital. Something bad enough that Beckwith quit his job and left town."

"Why does Will believe Beckwith's son is the killer?"

"He didn't give me a specific reason, but he seems convinced. He asked me to have you look into it."

"Interesting. Listen, Elizab . . . Esther?"

"Yes?"

"I think we ought to consider getting Will out of there. If Dr. Beckwith is involved in covering up these murders, he could be in serious danger."

"I told him the same, but he's determined to finish this."

"Stubborn fool." A match flared, and I heard him puff at a cigar while he thought. "All right. You be careful. I'll call you when I have news."

We rang off, and I returned to the desk, thanked Clarence for his help, and got back to work. I tried not to worry about Dr. Davis, but he kept creeping into my mind. Just after three o'clock, one of the doctors, a small man named Dr. McPherson, asked me to accompany him on his rounds. Having had no instruction to the contrary (or realistically, any instruction at all), I agreed and walked with him, first through the women's "shack," as he called it, and then through the men's. In both, the inmates either lay on their beds or sat on the rocking chairs opposite them, most in front of windows. Of course, many of the inmates were coughing and wheezing, and the overwhelming suffering brought tears to my eyes. I steeled myself and gave smiles to all, for these poor folk were due more than sympathy. As I had the chance, I glanced at my watch, the meeting with Dr. Davis still foremost in my mind. Four o'clock passed, then four-fifteen, the time I was supposed to meet with him, and finally at four twenty-five I asked Dr. McPherson if I could please be excused. Looking at his watch, he apologized and immediately agreed.

The guard let me out, and I hurried down the sidewalk over the bridge and down to Building B. Dr. Davis's door was closed. I knocked. No one answered. I wondered if he had decided I wasn't coming. I knocked again, and again got no response. My heart sank. He would be going to Dr. Beckwith for certain.

"Finally." Dr. Davis sauntered up the hall and stopped next to me. "Come in." He opened the door.

He was making me nervous. I looked into his office and glanced back at him. "What did you want to speak with me about?"

Dr. Davis gave me a satisfied little smile. "I can help you with your cousin." He paused. "Or not. Your choice."

Now, I am not one to leave my fate in the hands of others, but I suppose I underestimated Dr. Davis. He was not an imposing man, nor did he radiate that aura of menace that seems to precede some people into a room. I found him vaguely repulsive, but certainly not dangerous.

That is why I took a deep breath and followed him into his office.

Dr. Davis closed the door and smiled at me. The murmur of the hallway was replaced by the whir of a lawn mower outside the open window. "Here." He moved to the sitting area and gestured toward the sofa. "Sit."

"I'll stand, thank you."

"So be it." He crossed the room and stood about a foot and a half away from me, close but within acceptable social margins. "Now tell me. What is your scheme?"

"Scheme?"

"There is no coincidence in your appearance at Eloise."

"I admitted to you this morning that I came here, in part, to help Robert."

"Is that so?" His breathing had quickened, but he regarded me with amusement.

My stomach was clenching. Now he was between me and the door. "I don't think this—"

He plucked the eyeglasses off my face and peered through them. "You put on spectacles that do nothing and dyed your hair."

"I . . . I didn't . . ."

He huffed a breath onto one of the eyeglass lenses and began polishing it with his tie. "Miss Hume"—he looked back to me—"you came here disguised, using another name. And yes, I looked in the volunteer records, Esther."

"I didn't think Dr. Beckwith would let me volunteer otherwise."

He held out the glasses. I reached for them, and he took me by the wrist, stepping closer still. He leaned in, so that his face was only an inch from the side of my neck, and breathed in deeply before pulling back with a confused look. "I have to question your choice of perfume, Miss Hume."

I had stopped noticing my stink, but now I was pleased to smell of pig feces.

His bright blue eyes met mine. "Your cousin is locked away right now . . . on these grounds. Dr. Beckwith is trying to decide what to do with him. The easiest solution would be to turn him over to the police. The solution with the fewest complications would be for him to disappear. The third, and riskiest, option is to offer him treatment and hope he doesn't mention a word of this murder to anyone."

I took a step back, and my heel ran into the wall. His fingers tightened around my wrist, and he closed the gap.

I tried to brave it out. "Why is that the riskiest? Let me take him away. I guarantee he won't say anything."

"I wish it were that simple, Miss Hume." He raised his other hand and traced the line of my dress around my throat. "You see," he spoke more intimately, "Dr. Beckwith is afraid for his career. A murdered patient would cost him his job." He licked his lips. "Fortunately, I hold a great deal of sway with our administrator. He listens to me. That's influence your cousin needs."

I shuddered. "What do you want?"

"Nothing." While he looked into my eyes, his index finger ran down the front of my dress, over the buttons, between my breasts. "Well, perhaps just a little kindness on your part."

I was so terrified I was frozen in place. All the self-defense training I'd had in Paris disappeared. Fright rooted me to the floor.

His finger and then his knuckles brushed up and down over the front of my dress in a rhythmic motion. "Perhaps you and I could get to know one another," he whispered in my ear.

I was thankful for the heavy corset that stood between his fingers and my body.

"You do me a favor, I'll do you a favor." His breathing quickened still more.

"N-no, please," I said, my voice trembling. "Please—"

"Just relax, my dear," he said and nibbled my ear. He put both hands on my shoulders and began to push me to the floor.

A knock sounded against the door, three loud raps. "Ignore it," Dr. Davis whispered. He pressed harder, and my legs began to give way.

The door opened a foot. "Hello?" A man's voice. "Dr. Davis?"

Startled, the doctor let go of me and took a step back.

A straw boater and then a man's face peeked around the door: Clarence Morgan. "Dr. Davis, I wondered if . . ." When he saw Davis and me, he stopped short. "Oh, sorry if I'm interrupting anything."

"No, not at all," Dr. Davis said. "We were just . . . discussing new treatments." He caught my eye and gave me a hard look.

"Yes," I said.

Clarence stepped into the room. "That is exactly what I wanted to discuss with you, doctor. I've been hearing promising things about psychotherapy."

Davis's mouth soured. "Yes, well. I think we were finished here. Weren't we, Miss *James*?"

"Yes."

"Fine." He handed me my eyeglasses before taking hold of the bottom of his waistcoat with both hands and jerking it down, straightening it. "I look forward to continuing our discussion." He looked at his pocket watch. "I don't have time to speak with you now. I have an appointment. Please see yourselves out." He turned and strode out the door.

I just stood there, too stunned to think. Clarence watched Dr. Davis leave before turning back to me. "I thought I ought to check in on you."

"Th-thank you." I felt cold and wanted nothing more than to flee. "I . . . should go."

"Esther," he said. "What did he do?"

My fingers were numb. My mind was enveloped in a fog. "Nothing, Clarence. I'm not feeling well."

"Would you like to see a doctor?"

An involuntary laugh burbled out of my throat, and I found I couldn't stop. "No, no, thank you."

"Here," he said. "Let's get you a warm drink."

"No. I have to go."

"All right. I'll walk you."

I looked through the window at the lawn and the trees while my thoughts scattered about in an incoherent jumble. Clarence held the door open for me, and I walked into the hall, doing everything I could not to run. Stopping, I turned back to him and laid a hand on his wrist. "Thank you, Clarence."

Smiling, he tipped his straw boater. He turned to escort me up the hall and stopped dead in his tracks. I looked up at his face. His mouth was tight with tension.

I turned. Bessie and Alice were standing in the next doorway, watching us.

I had to pass them to get out of here. I realized how bad it looked for the two of us to walk out of the office by ourselves, not to mention share an intimate gesture, but I was too shaken to care. Bessie arched her eyebrows at me while Alice leveled her gaze at Clarence.

"Listen," he said, walking up to them. "It's not what it looked like, honeybee."

I hurried around them with a "Good day, ladies" and marched down the hallway toward the front entrance. I kept my eyes on the floor all the way out, not even looking at the guard who unlocked the door for me, and stared at the pavement all the way to my automobile. When I reached it, I jumped in and drove away as fast as I could. My hands were shaking so hard I could barely change speeds. Once I was well away from Eloise, I pulled the automobile to the side of the road and shut it off.

I clasped my hands to my chest, trying to stop the shaking, while my mind raced. I had nearly been raped. I couldn't do this anymore.

*I'll identify Will and get him out,* I thought. *I can't do this.* Robert had likely killed that man. Even if he hadn't, he was still going to spend the rest of his life here. What difference could it possibly make if I were to discover that someone else did it? How was it my business anyway? Wasn't this why we had police? My mother needed me. The Detroit Suffrage Club wanted me to run the group. I had to get out the vote for the election, which was barely three months away. It was important. It would take all my time.

And, if I returned to Eloise . . .

I couldn't stop my hands from trembling. I balled them up into fists and screwed my eyes shut, trying to block the tears that ran down my face.

If I returned to Eloise . . .

I would again have to face Dr. Davis. I choked back a sob. He had nearly, my God, he had nearly *raped* me. And he would have had it not been for Clarence. And I would have lain there like a coward and let him do it. What had I become?

A black knot of anger began to form in my stomach. How dare he? I thought I was a modern woman, able to put men in their place, safe in the world in which I lived. But I wasn't. Because I was a woman, *because I was a woman,* I would always be vulnerable.

I pulled a cigarette from my purse, lit it with shaking hands, and sucked the smoke hungrily into my lungs. I held it in, and when I finished that cigarette, I lit another with the burning end and smoked that one.

I shook, but now I shook with anger. When I got home I would take the Colt .32 and the Mauser .22 from their boxes in the closet of my bedroom. I would load them. I would put the Colt in my purse. Tomorrow morning I would strap the Mauser to my thigh.

I would return to Eloise.

And if that son of a bitch Davis even looked at me sideways, it would be the last thing he'd ever do.

Bridie and Alberts were talking in the kitchen when I got home. They quieted as soon as they heard me. I stopped in the doorway and asked them how the day had gone with my mother. Bridie said it was a little better, to which Alberts gave a tentative nod, and she continued with a brief recounting of my mother's activities, such as they were. She had spent most of the day in her room and was there now after having her supper alone.

"Thank you," I said, turning away and striding down the hallway. "I will not be dining tonight."

Alberts stopped me at the base of the stairs. Detective Riordan had phoned. His message was that Robert had not been admitted to any of the state asylums. I thanked him, climbed the stairs, and, at the top, saw a band of light under my mother's door. I stopped and looked at the door for a moment before shaking my head and continuing on to my room.

First I pulled off my shoes and stockings and then stripped off my dress and the suffocating corset. Dressed in only my undergarments, I took the guns from the closet and cleaned and oiled them as I had learned in Paris. When I was satisfied with that task, I loaded both guns and flicked on the safeties, then stuck the little Mauser into its holster and set that on the shelf in the closet again. I picked up the Colt pistol and lay on the bed, thinking about the man I'd killed with it only a few months before.

He was a member of the Gianolla gang, in fact was one of the men who had kidnapped Will. I was standing in the doorway of a restaurant with my gun trained on him when he pulled a huge pistol from a shoulder holster. He had been about to shoot Will. It took me at least five seconds to pull the trigger. During that time, he could easily have fired the gun. My hesitation could have gotten Will murdered.

I had killed the man. That thought seemed ridiculous. Me, Elizabeth

Hume, society girl, had shot a man to death . . . but it was to save Will. I wondered—would I pull the trigger to keep from being raped?

I wet my lips and looked at the pistol. Cool black steel, designed for nothing other than shooting men, a perfect tool for the job. With my index finger alongside the trigger guard, I aimed toward the center crystal in the chandelier above me, sighting it in the middle of the little raised metal V at the end of the gun. I pictured Dr. Davis's face.

I'd warn him off—but I had little doubt about my reaction to him should he try anything further.

# Will

I had no time to duck. The chair arced toward me in a blur. I braced myself for the impact and heard a sickening smack of wood on a skull and the sound of wood splintering. A second later, a man fell into me and collapsed on the floor, a gash in his dented temple pumping blood.

I looked back to Ty. Holding the remains of the chair overhead, poised to strike again, he glared at the man on the floor, who I now saw was George—the big man from the farm.

An orderly barked into the speaking tube, "Emergency! All hands! Dayroom Two!"

The alarm rang out. One of the huge orderlies who'd come in with Ty rushed over and cracked him on the head with his nightstick. Ty gave a little stumble but righted himself and turned on the orderly, who hit him in the head a second time. The chair legs slipped from Ty's hands, and the broken chair thudded to the floor behind him. He stood there, dazed. The other big orderly hit him in the back of the knees with his nightstick, and Ty collapsed, his legs cut out from under him. The first man cracked him over the head again, and Ty stopped moving altogether.

More orderlies and guards rushed into the room, shoving the patients back against the walls. It all happened so quickly I was still trying to catch up. I looked at George, who lay at my feet. A pool of blood spread around his head in a circle, like a saint's halo in a Renaissance painting. His legs were twitching, and a little moan, the sound almost like a car engine, spilled from his mouth.

An orderly shoved me back. Two men grabbed Ty by the ankles and began dragging him out of the room, while others got a stretcher for George.

It could have—should have—been me. It had been my luck that George got in Ty's way.

The other orderlies began barking at all of us to get up, go back to our rooms. One of them grabbed my arm and shoved me toward the door. I did as they said and wandered back to my room, my head spinning. An orderly locked my door behind me, and I sat on the bed. Ty had meant to kill me. He'd nearly succeeded. George was severely injured, although frankly, that seemed to be justice. He deserved a chair to the head.

Surely now they would lock Ty in the Hole and throw away the key. Logically, it was the last I should see of him. I knew differently. Ty and I were going to meet again. I had escaped him twice. I didn't expect to be so lucky the third time.

I had supper, such as it was, with Dill and Chuck. This time I was hungry enough to eat the gristly meat, though only after carefully looking it over for veins. Ty wasn't present, which I hoped meant he was now a resident of the Hole.

After I'd been sent back to my room, an orderly came in and told me it was time to go to the reading class. I stared at him for a second before remembering Alice's promise to talk to Mr. Morgan, the reading teacher. The orderly brought me to the rear exit of the building, where a handful of men, including Dill and Chuck, already stood. He unlocked the door, and we left for the schoolhouse, the other students with *The Complete Poetical Works of John Keats* under their arms. I am no fan of poetry and had paid as little attention to it as possible during my schooldays. Still, I thought a reading class with this bunch was bound to be interesting and potentially illuminating.

We took a road that led past a copse of elm trees to a wooden building, a one-room schoolhouse that was neglected compared to the other buildings at Eloise, with faded whitewash and warped doors.

Mr. Morgan, a narrow-hipped man with a good physique and an easy smile, waited for us at the desk in front and stood when we entered. He wore brown tweed trousers and a white shirt with rolled-up sleeves. When he introduced himself, he held out his right hand to shake.

I returned it with my left hand, and he looked at my right for a moment before he met my gaze again. "Hello, John. It's a pleasure to meet you."

"You as well, Mr. Morgan."

He handed me a copy of the book and sat on the corner of his desk. "All right, gentlemen, take your seats. We will start tonight on page 354—'La Belle Dame sans Merci.' John, would you like to read, please?"

I looked around, hoping he was talking to another John, but the five other patients in the room just looked back at me. I found the passage.

"'La Belle Dame sans Merci,'" I read.

> *"Ah, what can ail thee, wretched wight,*
> *Alone and palely loitering;*
> *The sedge is wither'd from the lake,*
> *And no birds sing.*

> *"Ah, what can ail thee, wretched wight,*
> *So haggard and so woe-begone?*
> *The squirrel's granary is full,*
> *And the harvest's done.*

> *"I see a lily on thy brow,*
> *With anguish moist and fever dew;*
> *And on thy cheeks a fading rose*
> *Fast withereth too.*

> *"I met a lady in the meads*
> *Full beautiful, a faery's child;*
> *Her hair was long, her foot was light,*
> *And her eyes were wild.*

> *"I set her on my pacing steed,*
> *And nothing else saw all day long;*
> *For sideways would she lean, and sing*
> *A faery's song.*

> *"I made a garland for her head,*
> *And bracelets too, and fragrant zone;*

*She look'd at me as she did love,*
*And made sweet moan.*

*"She found me roots of relish sweet,*
*And honey wild, and manna dew;*
*And sure in language strange she said,*
*I love thee true.*

*"She took me to her elfin grot,*
*And there she gaz'd and sighed deep,*
*And there I shut her wild sad eyes—*
*So kiss'd to sleep.*

*"And there we slumber'd on the moss,*
*And there I dream'd, ah, woe betide,*
*The latest dream I ever dream'd*
*On the cold hill side.*

*"I saw pale kings, and princes too,*
*Pale warriors, death-pale were they all;*
*Who cried—"La belle Dame sans merci*
*Hath thee in thrall!"*

*"I saw their starv'd lips in the gloom,*
*With horrid warning gaped wide;*
*And I awoke, and found me here*
*On the cold hill side.*

*"And this is why I sojourn here*
*Alone and palely loitering,*
*Though the sedge is wither'd from the lake,*
*And no birds sing."*

Morgan pushed himself up off his desk and took a few steps toward the window. Gazing outside, he said, "What do you think this poem is about, John?"

"I . . . don't really know," I said. "I'm not much for poetry."

His head swiveled back toward me. "Do you know what *la belle dame sans merci* means?"

"The pretty woman without . . . thank you?"

"Same word," he said, "but no. In this case, it means 'mercy.' And who is your *belle dame sans merci*?"

"What do you mean?"

"What mistress holds you in thrall? For many of the men in here, drink is the *belle dame*." He held one arm out in front of him and recited, "'She found me roots of relish sweet, and honey wild, and manna dew/And sure in language strange she said, I love thee true.'" He walked back from the window and stopped in front of me. "We all have a *belle dame sans merci*, John. What is yours?"

It's good that I had no intention of baring my soul to Morgan, because I wouldn't have known where to start. "I don't really remember," I said. "It's all just a blur."

Looking at the floor, he slowly shook his head. Finally he sighed and looked up at me. "I'm disappointed in you, John. I thought you would understand."

I shrugged. "Sorry." I realized I had been so caught up in the poem that I'd read with all the emphasis and emotion I would put into any reading, yet he didn't seem to think it strange. I was finding that the more normal I acted, the crazier everyone seemed to think I was.

Morgan settled again on the desk and had another patient read. The class continued for an hour or so before he wrapped it up. The orderly was preparing to escort us back to the ward when Morgan told him to leave me behind. He wanted to speak with me.

"I'm supposed to bring them all back," the orderly said.

"I'll be responsible for John," Morgan said. Glancing at the other men, the orderly grimaced. "It's all right," Morgan said in a soothing tone. He walked up to the orderly and turned him toward the door. "I'll take full responsibility."

"Well . . . all right." The orderly rounded up the rest of the men and marched them out of the building.

"Sit," Morgan said, waving toward the chairs. He returned to his desk and sat on the edge again. "As you might suspect, Alice talked to me about your situation."

Nodding, I sat in the same chair I had previously.

"You are looking for Robert Clarke."

I nodded again.

"Why?"

I started telling him the story I'd told Alice. "I think he can help me discover who I . . ." Seeing a look of extreme skepticism on his face, I trailed off.

"If you want my help," he said, "you must tell me the truth."

"I . . ." I squirmed in my seat. He was not going to buy the cock-and-bull story I'd told Alice, and it was useless to try to convince him. Right now, he was my only chance to get to Robert. I'd level with him. "Robert Clarke has been accused of killing Patrick Cook, of essentially being this Phantom that all the patients are frightened of. I don't believe he's the killer."

"Who is Robert to you?"

"He's my . . . friend's cousin."

"Does your friend happen to be a beautiful young lady who is volunteering here?"

He knew. "Yes."

He picked up a red rubber ball from his desk and began tossing it in the air and catching it. "I don't know that anyone has been killed."

"Trust me," I said. "I can't vouch for the other men who were allegedly murdered, but I saw Patrick Cook's body."

He picked up another ball, threw it in the air, and began juggling them both with one hand. Shaking his head, he said, "I'd like to help you, but I can't get into solitary confinement. They don't allow visitors."

"Oh. That's . . . unfortunate."

"How important is it to you to find out if he's there?"

I cocked my head at him. "I'm here, aren't I?"

"Good point." He thought for a moment. "There might be a way . . ."

"Tell me."

"The guards and policemen all get together and play poker at the station at least once a week. It rotates depending on their schedules. They all get drunk—totally, completely, and astoundingly drunk. If you want to try it, I could check into when the next one is."

"Try what? I can't even get out of my room at night."

"Perhaps I could help you with that." He slipped a hand into his pocket and extracted a key. "I've got a master key that will unlock your door."

"Will that also get me out of Building B and into the police station?"

"No." His eyes narrowed, and the corner of his mouth turned up in a little smile. "Talk to Mr. Dill about that. I don't know how he does it, but he gets out of the building."

"Really?"

"I've seen him outside at night. Twice now."

I couldn't understand why Morgan was so eager to help. "Mr. Morgan, I'm sorry, but I don't understand your motive for helping me."

His forehead furrowed. Still looking up at the balls, he said, "I told Esther I would help her. By helping you . . ."

I studied him. I saw no artifice, no cunning. It was my best chance, maybe my only chance. This could all be over. "I'll do it."


"One more thing," I said.

Morgan glanced at me. "Yes?"

"Why did you choose *The Phantom of the Opera*?"

One of the balls struck the top of his fingers and bounced across the floor. He caught the other one and scowled at the first as it caromed off a desk. "Francis loves the book. A surprising choice for him, I must admit. He's normally not the most romantic of types."

"Romantic?"

His eyes cut over to me. "I take it you haven't read it?"

"No."

"The Opera Ghost—the Phantom—loves Christine Daaé so much that he gives everything for her. She is his *belle dame*. It's all very romantic."

"And Francis suggested it?"

"Yes."

I'd be careful. "What do you think of him?"

"Well," Morgan said, "compared to the patients, I'd say he's pretty normal. At least Stephen is getting him some help."

"Stephen?"

"Dr. Beckwith," he said. "He's a good man."

I had my own thoughts on that topic, but I kept them to myself. "Why do you suppose Francis suggested the book?"

"Why does anyone enjoy a book? The story? The writing? The characters? There are as many reasons as there are readers."

"Still, he chose *The Phantom*, while these murders—alleged murders—are taking place."

"You're suggesting Francis is the killer?" Morgan laughed. "First of all, I'm not conceding there is a Phantom. But Francis? I can't imagine. All he does is draw maps."

"Why are you so certain?"

"Well, he's . . . *Francis.* He's an odd one, but . . ." Looking down at the floor, he trailed off.

"What?"

"No." He shook his head. "It can't be."

"What?"

"I saw him practicing with a length of rope, using it like a . . ."

"A lasso?" I finished.

He glanced up at me sharply. "Yes. The Punjab lasso?"

"Patrick Cook was strangled or hanged with a rope. I saw the marks around his neck. From what I understand, it would be consistent with the Phantom's modus operandi."

He shook his head again. "Stephen will be devastated. Assuming it's true."

"Were Albert Bell, Paul Robinson, and Victor Foerster members of the reading group?" I asked.

"They were," he replied. "Why?"

"I believe they were also murdered by the Phantom."

"But they were trans—" He looked stupefied. "Stephen said they were transferred."

"I don't believe they were."

"This is all just so difficult to believe," he said. "If it weren't for Esther . . ."

"Esther?"

He looked at me from the corner of his eye. "Your friend?"

"Oh, Esther, right." Of course Elizabeth was using a pseudonym.

"I guess my reality over the past few days has driven my real life from my head."

He stood and straightened his trousers. "We'd better get you back to Building B. If you're too late it will attract attention."

"Just one last thing," I said. "I was told that a woman named Beatrice was helping the Phantom."

He gave me an enigmatic smile. "Let me guess. Mr. Dill told you that."

I nodded.

"Look, John. Let me make this clear. Dill is a paranoid with a capital *P*. Prior to his becoming the Persian from *The Phantom*, he got the notion that his wife, 'Mama Hand-me-down'"—Morgan made quotation marks in the air—"and his children were part of Roosevelt's conspiracy. He chased them around their house with a club. He was just lucky he didn't catch anyone. If you take the word of numbskulls like him, you're going to be looking for a conspiracy in every peach basket. Now, come on. We'd better get you back."

He unlocked the door, and we headed out of the schoolhouse. On the way, we talked about the poem I'd read. He said it was his favorite and that I had done a wonderful job reciting it. If they actually gave patients a grade, he said, I would receive an "Outstanding." I thanked him.

Just before we got to the building, he said, "I'll give you a heads-up when I hear about the poker game."

"I very much appreciate what you're doing for me." Holding my left hand out to him, I said, "The name's Will Anderson."

He took my hand with his left. "Clarence." Holding onto my hand, he said quietly, "Will, I think your *belle dame* is Esther."

I started to protest, but he said, "You wouldn't be here against your own best interest unless you were in the power of another. Keats wasn't talking about a literal pretty woman taking one in thrall, but sometimes poetry does work that way. The knight in the poem was ruined by his *belle dame*, and I fear yours will do the same for you."

"If she does," I said, "then so be it."

He studied my face for a moment before putting one hand on his breast. Gesturing theatrically, he recited, "'The die is cast, come weal, come woe; two lives are joined together./ For better or for worse, the link which naught but death can sever.'"

"My," I said, "you're a cheery one, aren't you?"

He burst out laughing and clapped me on the back. "That one's about marriage anyway. I remind myself of the last line whenever I think about it."

He walked me back to my ward, where Bessie was waiting at the desk. When she saw us, her jaw tightened, and she stood, stepping around the desk.

Morgan stopped in front of her. "Bessie, I know what you think you saw, but it wasn't what it looked like."

Her mouth twisted up like she'd sucked on a lemon.

"I'm not lying," he said. "I was protecting her from Davis. That's all."

That perked my interest. *Dr. Davis?*

"You're not allowed here after visiting hours. Beat it."

Anger flashed across Morgan's face. He rounded on her. "Bessie, this is none of your business."

The big nurse took a step toward Morgan and stared into his eyes. "I don't know what Alice sees in you."

"It's not like we're courting," he said.

"No, I don't know what you're doing. All I know is she's upset."

He started to say something but thought better of it. Instead, he walked past me and Bessie out to the hallway. She suddenly seemed to realize I had been witnessing all this. "What are you doing here?"

"Morgan brought me back from his reading group. Should I go back to my room?"

She shoved me down the hall and followed behind. Without a word, she pushed me into the room and closed and locked the door behind me.

I stood in front of the window, trying to catch a bit of the breeze wafting through the blinds. The sun hadn't yet gone down. Bands of rose-colored light leaked in through the bars, striping my nightshirt. It's strange where one can find beauty.

Seeing Elizabeth had lifted such a burden. Since I'd gotten here, doubt constantly nagged at me—*Would I ever leave this place?* Now Lizzie knew I was here. She would get me out when necessary.

That worry gone, I could focus even more on the murders. The reading group was the key to this. Robert had been a member. My only suspect, Francis Beckwith, had suggested the book *The Phantom of the*

*Opera*. I had to find out more about him. Tomorrow morning I would get with Dill, come up with a plan to break into the police station.

Through the window I heard men snoring and muttering in their sleep, rolling over with squeaks of bedsprings, coughing, and passing gas. The sound of a train rolled past; horses nickered; an occasional shout or scream cut through the night. I hadn't expected all the noise. I'd always been persnickety when it came to sleeping, and it didn't take much to throw me off.

Finally, long after the night had cooled and frogs settled in for a night of chirping, I fell asleep.

# CHAPTER NINE

*Wednesday, August 14, 1912*

## Elizabeth

When Helga woke me at 6:00 A.M., I had a headache, a sore mouth, and the remnant of a dream causing a severe case of melancholy. When I am under stress I clench my teeth in sleep, and the cause of the current stress was quite obvious. That cause was also the trigger for the dream: the first time Will and I (pardon me, but no euphemism will do here) had intercourse.

The dream was accurate. Will was drunk, and I had been drinking as well, though I was by no means in my cups. We had been kissing and started getting carried away. He reached up under my skirt, and I took hold of his hand and gently moved it. Normally, that would have been enough. This night the hand returned, more insistent now, touching me clumsily.

"Will," I whispered. "No. I don't want—"

He covered my mouth in kisses and he worked his fingers against me, into me. The feeling, a mixture of pleasure and pain, caused me to gasp. He must have taken that as permission, because he climbed on top of me and began thrusting himself against me, too drunk to know what he was doing.

I wanted him, too, but not now. We were only six months away from marriage. And not this way, with him too drunk to remember the act.

"No, Will," I gasped. "Please." I looked into his eyes, and I saw he was not himself. His mouth was slack, and he rutted against me like an animal.

I tried to squirm out from under him, but he pinned me in place, took hold of himself, and entered me. It was over in a few minutes. It took me months to admit to myself that I could have stopped him. Back then, he wasn't much stronger than I and even then I knew a few tricks that would stop any man in his tracks (mostly involving the testicles).

I wanted him to stop. I would never have initiated the act. Yet somewhere in the back of my mind I knew if I didn't submit, he would find someone who would. Oh, we'd still get married, and the floozy would probably remain nothing but a guilty memory, but I would know—and I didn't know if I could live with that. So I submitted.

Little did I know that that night would not only end our relationship, it would trigger a chain of events leading directly to the deaths of four men: my father, Frank Van Dam, Wesley McRae, and my new fiancé, John Cooper. I went crazy long before those men were killed. What else could explain me aborting my child . . . our child? I love children and had wanted them all my life. I so looked forward to having them with Will. Yet I ended the life of that baby. Nothing I had ever done had filled me with such self-loathing. I would never forgive myself. I didn't want to.

Some people might say the scandal of my pregnancy would have been too great. I couldn't have the baby. We were unmarried. My parents would have been horrified. The Humes don't do these things. I believed every option would ruin me.

If I could change the course of history, would I have stopped him? Certainly, but that is not a privilege we are afforded in this life. We make our decisions, and we live with the consequences. My consequences: the inability ever to have children, everlasting guilt, endless remorse, and an eternal responsibility for those deaths to have meaning. I would never fulfill my responsibility nor escape the guilt and remorse. I would never have children.

I had no one else to blame. Not even Will.

I took a gram of aspirin powder before I fixed my mother breakfast and brought it to her bedroom. Knocking lightly, I called, "Mother?"

"Yes, dear?" Her voice was muffled, sleepy.

"Breakfast," I said, pushing the door open. I carried the tray in to her and waited at the side of the bed until she sat up and arranged the pillows behind her.

She smiled. "What a nice surprise."

I set the tray over her lap. "Bacon, eggs, toast, and coffee." I leaned down and kissed her cheek. There was a chance that by the end of the day I would be in jail. I wanted our last meal together, if that's what this was, to be pleasant.

"Thank you, dear." She picked up the coffee cup and took a sip while I plucked a piece of toast from the rack and took a bite.

Things were going so well I even dared to ask, "How are you this morning, Mother?"

A dark cloud passed over her features as a thought occurred to her. Whether it was the shame she felt at the loss of her senses or her anger with me I couldn't say. Either way, it made me wish I could take back those words.

"I'm fine," she said, though neither her face nor her voice conveyed that fact.

Ignoring her tone, I said, "That's wonderful."

She stared straight ahead.

"I'm sorry I can't be here today, but I'll be done soon, and we'll be able to spend more time together."

She gave me the stingiest of shrugs, an almost imperceptible raising of her shoulders.

"All right, then, fine," I said, in a tone much cheerier than I felt. I kissed her cheek again and turned for the door. "I'll see you this evening."

She didn't reply.

I returned to my bedroom, strapped the Mauser's holster to my thigh, and prepared to leave, only just now remembering that I had forgotten to call the Baker Electric garage last night to pick up the automobile and charge the batteries. It still stood at the curb where I'd parked it, its batteries much too low to risk another drive to Eloise. I swore at myself and, with a cigarette dangling from my lips, walked down to the trolley stop in a light rain, umbrella unfurled. I supposed that if I shot Dr. Davis it would do me no good to go on the run, and, if I were caught, Clarence's testimony as to the doctor's indiscretions of the day before would land me a chance of being acquitted.

Besides, automobile be damned, I wasn't letting Dr. Davis think he had scared me off.

I just made the seven-forty train, not even getting into my seat before it started chugging out of the station. The trip seemed to take forever. The sky was a solid gray, no delineations of clouds, just a heavy wet blanket over the bleak landscape. Rivulets of water washed down the window next to me, and a damp chill cut through to my bones. It was August, but this morning felt like October.

On the way I decided to plead with Will to leave. A hospital that brooked murder and rape was no place for him, or anyone, to be.

The train reached the station just after nine, and I made my way in through the gate and down the streets, the raindrops splatting against my umbrella. I felt the outside of my purse, tracing the outline of the .32, and then reached inside and took hold of the grip. It felt warmer than the air around me now and gave me confidence, the way my blanket had when I was a child. A "security gun" made more sense than a "security blanket" anyway.

I passed the piggery and looked for Will, but only a few men toiled there feeding the hogs. He was not among them. I guessed he would be sent out when the rain stopped, but, having no idea how farm work was scheduled, I figured I would just check every chance I got. At the sanatorium I took my place at the desk and did my normal tasks: a little paperwork, an orientation of a new inmate, and a lot of time with nothing to do but fret.

Just after eleven a policeman strolled through the door and stopped at the desk. He was an older man with bloodshot and red-rimmed eyes, an untrimmed beard and mustache, a potbelly that strained the buttons of his blue wool uniform, and a distinct scent of cabbage. He cocked a hip and said, "Dr. Beckwith wants to see you."

A chill ran up my spine. "Well," I replied, "I have my lunch break in about an hour. I could go then."

"Now, he said.

"All right." I picked up my purse and umbrella. "Then I'll go now."

He smirked. "Good girl."

I frowned at him. "You don't have to be rude. I told you I would go."

He put both palms on the desk and leaned down to within inches of my face. "And I told you to get moving. So get moving."

"You made your point about three comments ago. You don't need to continue to be so obnoxious."

He squinched up his face and talked in a high, whiny voice like a petulant child. "You don't need to continue to be so obnoxious," he parroted.

Now, I don't like being told what to do (a trait I share with Will). I don't suppose that excuses what I did next, but the emotions of the last couple of days were boiling over in me.

I walked around the desk and poked my umbrella into his fat stomach. He took a step back. "I told you I would go," I said and jabbed him again. He stumbled back another step, his right hand fumbling for his sidearm.

I spun and stalked toward the door, realizing even in my charged emotional condition that an armed confrontation with this man would be a bad idea. He hurried after me. I tried to throw open the door, but of course it was locked. He caught up to me and grabbed my arm, spinning me around. His expression softened when he saw my face, and I only realized then that I was crying. The anger had burst so intensely in me that it needed an outlet.

Looking away, he said, "You . . . go, then." He released me and unlocked the door.

I turned and marched out of the building, popped open my umbrella, and hurried down the sidewalk, my face hot with anger and shame. The rain hadn't let up, and now no one was in sight at the piggery. My head pounded like it was going to explode, with that feeling of unreleased emotion that I so often get after a confrontation that ends before it really begins.

Footsteps continued behind me. I didn't need to glance back to know that the policeman was shadowing me. At least he had the decency to stay back and let me walk to the Administration Building alone. I felt ashamed of myself for provoking him. He might be an idiot, but I am a lady.

I hated this place. It was obvious that my assignment was over. Dr. Davis must have gone to Dr. Beckwith and told him I was here. This would be humiliating, but I was determined to accept my fate with dignity.

At the Administration Building, I climbed the stairs to the third floor and marched down the hall. By this point, the policeman had tightened the space between us and followed directly behind me into Dr. Beckwith's office.

A secretary looked up from the paperwork on his desk. "Miss Hume?"

Unsurprised, I nodded.

He picked up the telephone, waited a few seconds, and said, "She's here." He listened and then looked at me again as he hung up the phone. "Go right in." His face and voice were completely neutral, something I didn't expect from his boss.

Dr. Beckwith didn't bother to stand when I entered the room, and instead just sat there behind his desk, eyes tracking me, fingers interlocked behind his head. I stopped in front of him.

"Miss Hume, you have been a naughty girl."

I said nothing.

"You know I could have you arrested."

I remained silent.

He leaned forward in his chair. "I suggest you talk to me. This will go easier on you if you do."

"What would you like me to say?"

"I'd like you to tell me what you've been doing here."

"I've been volunteering. I already explained that to Dr. Davis."

Dr. Beckwith steepled his fingers in front of him. "Yes, and Dr. Davis told me that you were trying to investigate the murder your cousin committed."

"If you're so certain, then why did you even ask?"

"Because I'd like you to tell me what you've uncovered."

Given that his son was the only suspect, and Will remained behind these walls, I decided to keep quiet. "Nothing of consequence."

"Do you believe now that Robert Clarke killed that man?"

"No, I don't."

"But you haven't found any evidence to the contrary?"

"No," I admitted.

"I thought not." He pointed his steepled fingers at me. "You are terminated from your volunteer position. Please do not return. Frankly, I am disgusted with your methods. I would have hoped you had learned from your father's misdeeds, but apparently the apple didn't fall far from the tree."

My anger flared again. "Keep my father out of this," I snapped. "This has nothing to do with him."

He gave me a cold smile. "No, it doesn't. But I'd guess the newspapers would be pleased to hear about the fraud you pulled to get in here, and of course that would resuscitate the stories of your father's crimes. Dredging all of that up again would be a shame, now, wouldn't it?"

I leaned over the desk. "As would the news that four men have been murdered within these walls by someone posing at the Phantom of the Opera, and that you have done absolutely nothing about it." I held an index finger up near his face. "Don't threaten me. You're in no position to hold up anyone else's dirty laundry."

"Perhaps that is true, Miss Hume." He smiled. "But if I go down, it will be in a fireball that will consume your family."

# Will

Dr. Beckwith pointed at the steamer trunk—black leather, with cast-iron hinges and latch, and a huge iron lock—lashed to the back of the automobile. I looked back at him and stared into the bottomless black pools where his eyes should have been.

"Please, please, no." Tears streamed down my face. "Give me another chance."

Again, he pointed at the trunk. I turned to run, but a pair of orderlies grabbed my arms and carried me to the back of the car as easily as they might a baby.

"No! I'll work!" I begged and pleaded, but it was as if he couldn't hear me. He just nodded to the orderlies. One of them opened the trunk, and they lifted me, squeezed me inside, and slammed the lid shut. I heard a key turn in the lock.

"No! No, please, no!"

Screaming, I pushed against the lid and struggled and fought. I couldn't breathe. Black. No light. No air. I gasped and, with the last breath of air in the trunk, let out a blood-curdling scream.

The door banged open. Nurse Jensen stood silhouetted in the doorway.

I tried to blink the horrific vision from my eyes. I realized I was huddled in the corner of the room, slick with sweat, arms around myself.

"Mr. Doe?" she said. "Are you all right?"

"I . . . I . . . yes. I'm fine."

She walked in and stood before me while I tried to gather my wits. "You are tortured," she finally said.

"I'm being tortured, you mean."

"I don't think so. You were having these dreams before you came here, weren't you?"

I sighed and admitted I'd had a few.

"From the start I could tell you were in pain—and not the pain you feel in your hand. It's too much to bear, isn't it?"

I climbed to my feet and walked back to the bed. "No. I'm fine, really. It was just a nightmare."

"We are here to help people like you. You should let us."

I sat on the edge of the bed. "Thank you, Nurse Jensen, but the only thing wrong with me is that I don't know who I am."

She studied me for a long moment, then turned and walked to the door. There, she stopped and glanced back to me. "Think about it. You could have release from the torture." She left the room and locked the door behind her.

I lay awake for hours, listening to the rain patter against the window. When dawn broke, the sky was slate gray. Finally an orderly stuck his head in my room and shouted, "Breakfast!"

I sighed. Another day at Eloise. But, I thought, I might see Elizabeth again today. That cheered me, at least a bit.

When the orderly let me out of my room, I saw Zimmermann in the hallway a little farther back and waited for him to catch up. He was staring straight down at the floor, his face showing no affect whatsoever. Trying to remember the German spoken at the factory, I nudged him and asked, as best I could, how he was. *"Wie geht's?"*

He raised his head as if it required a great deal of effort and looked at me. His eyes were glassy. A line of saliva stretched from the corner of his mouth. A second later, his eyes fell, and he stared at the floor again. He was drugged out of his mind. I doubted anyone in this place had ever figured out how to communicate with him. Maybe he was a lunatic, but I had seen no evidence of it, nor, I believed, had anyone else. The next time I saw Beckwith, he was going to get an earful from me.

On the way to the cafeteria, I kept my eyes open for Ty, but he was gone, hopefully for good. I sat between Chuck and Dill, whose towel turban sat canted to the right.

"What'd Morgan want with you?" Dill asked.

"He wanted to get to know me."

"What'd you talk about?"

I looked around. None of the hospital employees were near. "About the Hole mostly."

"You want to get in?" Dill asked. "The Persian can get you in."

"That's what Morgan said. How do you do it?"

"I'll show you."

"Why don't you just tell me?"

"You ain't goin' without Daroga," he said. The women began dropping plates onto the table, and we quieted, waiting for them to pass. When they had moved on, Dill leaned in close to me. "Can you get out of your room?"

"I think so."

"Well, if you can, listen." He glanced around us. "Give Daroga the high sign at supper. He will meet you in the basement." His lips puckered, and his eyes shot back and forth. "West stairway." Keeping his hand tight to his chest, he pointed his thumb to the right. "End of the building."

"Why are you going to help me?"

"Help *you*? That son of a bitch Phantom wants to kill me. If I can get him first . . ."

"We're not going out to kill anyone," I said.

"If you want into the place, you got no choice but to do what I want."

Chuck muttered something into my ear. I turned to him. "He ain't killin' nobody," Chuck said. "He's just talk."

"What's that?" Dill leaned foward and looked around me at Chuck. "Mumbles over there got somethin' to say?"

"Up your ass," Chuck said.

"Up my ass? Well, up yours, Chuckie." Dill bit into his bread and tore off a chunk. The brown butter smeared across his mouth. "You just come get the Persian," he said, wiping his mouth with the back of his hand. "I'll get you inside, and I'll take care of that sonuvabitchin' Phantom, once and for all."

After breakfast an orderly returned me to my room, where I spent the morning. I was pleased not to be rooting around in pig shit, but the piggery was the only place I would have a chance of seeing Elizabeth. No one bothered to explain why there had been a change in plans. I expected to be dragged out to one of the tortures thinly disguised as treatment or dumped back in a pigpen, but instead they left me to myself. After a long nap, I spent the morning exercising and stretching my right hand, which hadn't stopped hurting since I'd begun my pig-mucking.

They let me out briefly for lunch, then returned me to my room. Shortly after that, a key turned in the lock. The door opened, and Clarence Morgan strode into my room, quickly closing the door behind him. He was nattily dressed in a charcoal gray suit with a matching porkpie hat. "Did you talk to Dill?" he whispered.

I nodded.

"Good. I found out they're having the poker game tonight."

"Will you be able to let me out?"

"I'm going to try. It'll be at least one or two in the morning. By then, the ward will be quiet, and you shouldn't have too much trouble getting out. You don't want to go until the guards and policemen are liquored up, anyway. But listen." He put his hand on my shoulder. "Don't leave your room for at least five minutes after I unlock your door. I don't want to get fired." He turned for the door again but stopped and looked back to me. "Don't forget. Give me five minutes to clear out tonight before you leave."

I nodded. "No problem."

He slipped out and locked the door behind him. I spent the rest of the afternoon in my room, bored to tears. I passed the time watching the road that led to the sanatorium, hoping to at least catch a glimpse of Elizabeth, but I didn't see her. The rain had stopped, and now the sun beamed down on the grounds. The green of the grass and trees seemed to glow as if internally illuminated.

At supper I alerted Dill that I planned to meet him in the basement sometime after 1:00 A.M., as soon as I could get out. With a curl of the lip, he said he'd be ready. I returned to my cell, where I waited alertly for hours, watching out the window. An occasional car, truck, or wagon passed, along with small groups of pedestrians—nurses, orderlies, and other employees heading for the gate. The activity slowed as the hospital settled in for the night. The sun set, and the stars painted a tapestry of pointillism in the clear sky. I wasn't very far from the city, yet here the stars blanketed the heavens, whereas at home I saw only a fraction of them.

Someone cut across the road behind the building, moving toward the rear entrance. Even though all I saw was a black silhouette, I knew it was Francis Beckwith. His walk was unmistakable. He hurried, legs pumping, yet he moved silently, blending into the shadow of a pine tree and flitting out, then disappearing into the building's shadow. I moved to the side of the window to track him, but he was gone. I wondered what Francis was doing, sneaking around in the middle of the night. Once I got out of the room, I'd watch out for him.

I considered whether I truly wanted to bring Dill along. He was likely my only chance for getting inside the police station, but he was a crazy old fool with murder on his mind. Who knew who he'd attack, thinking he was killing the Phantom? Still . . . I had to get in.

Quiet footsteps passed by my room and then returned. A key turned in my lock, and the footsteps stole away. I waited a few minutes before I tried the door. It was indeed unlocked. I opened it and peeked into the hallway. No one was in sight. I crept out, shut the door behind me, and tiptoed to the hall leading to the west end of the building. When I glanced around the corner, I saw that no one stood guard. I ran to the stairway and hurried down to the basement. At the bottom of the stairs was a long hallway with a tile floor, dimly lit by small round ceiling fixtures. One of the lights sparked and faded.

"Psst." The sound came from behind me, underneath the stairs.

I walked around the stairway. Dill, still wearing the turban, stepped out and whispered, "Ready?"

"Yeah." My throat was dry.

"Okay. Let's go. Remember, keep your gun up near your eyes." He turned and, with a hand held up in front of his face, his forefinger extended like the barrel of a gun, began cantering up the hallway.

I followed behind. "I don't have a gun," I whispered, "and neither do you."

"Don't confuse me with facts," he whispered back. It was dead silent down here, other than the padding of Dill's bare feet and the sound of my leather soles on the dusty floor.

We passed a dozen closed doors before he ducked into a dark corridor and felt his way ahead. I heard him turn a doorknob, and a dim light spilled out around us. He nodded me forward. I followed him into another corridor, this one perhaps seven feet tall and five feet wide, concrete all around, with a network of pipes running its length along the ceiling, some red and a foot or more wide, others unpainted lead or iron and three or four inches in diameter. A mechanical hum filled the space. It was cold, perhaps ten degrees cooler than the rest of the building.

I closed the door and whispered, "What is this?"

His eyes bugged out even more. "Tunnel. They run all through the place. They were for gettin' around when there's big snowstorms—and gettin' bodies out so's nobody would see 'em."

Feeling claustrophobic, I stepped into the middle of the corridor. "This goes to the Hole?"

He nodded. "Goes into the cops' storeroom right down the hall. Just gotta make the right turns." His eyes narrowed.

I could see he was concentrating on remembering our route, which did not inspire confidence. "You do know where you're going?"

"Course I do. Now listen. That goddamn Phantom is gonna be in the back, hidin' out in one of the cells. I just gotta figure out which one. You ready?"

"Listen, Daroga," I whispered. "I'm here to find Robert Clarke, not the Phantom."

He squinted at me. "I already told ya. Clarke ain't killin' nobody."

"No, that's not—never mind. Let's go."

"Once we're in the police station," he cautioned me, "we can't talk. There'll be guards with guns. Now listen—the doors around here lock from the inside. They want to keep *us in*, not other people out. Normally no exceptions." He smiled. "Tonight, though—one exception. For poker, they all sneak in and out one of the doors in back. Lazy bastards. Every other door in this goddamned place is locked from the inside. These tunnels will get ya from building to building, but that's the only door that will get ya the hell outta here. So if we get cornered, that's where we're goin'."

He must have seen the nervousness on my face, because he added,

"We oughta be able to get back through the tunnels, but if we have to go outside, I'm goin' back to Building B. You can escape if you want."

"I don't want to, and how would I get over the fence anyway?"

"I don't know. I'd use wire cutters."

"Do you have some?"

His face flashed his annoyance. "Where the hell would I get wire cutters?"

Right.

"Let's go. And for God's sake"—he took hold of my left hand and lifted it in front of my face—"*keep your goddamn gun up.*"

I'd humor him. "Fine."

Settling a hand on top of his turban, he turned and shot away down the corridor like a sprinter, his nightshirt fluttering in his wake. I followed. After a couple of hundred feet, he stopped at an intersecting tunnel and looked both ways. This was an older section, made of red bricks. The concrete floor was covered in water. Bare lightbulbs hung from the ceiling at distant intervals.

"Now, it's . . ." He started to point his finger to the left before, puzzlement writ on his face, he looked right and then left again. His lips pursed. A second later, he splashed off to the right. "This way."

He ran pell-mell down the tunnel, running from dark to light before plunging into darkness again, all the while holding his hand in front of his face. I smelled the sharp chlorine stink of rodent urine and the faded rotting scent of feces. I looked up at the ceiling. Cracks ran in zigzag lines in the cement between the bricks. In my mind, I saw the trunk lid closing. I tried to push away the image.

At the next intersection, he turned right again and stopped. He raised his hand, palm out toward me, and whispered, "Listen."

I stopped. Over the mechanical hum came the sound of faint pounding, vibrating through the pipes.

"What is it?" I asked.

"It's him. The Phantom."

We continued up the tunnel, slower now. My feet were beginning to get wet from the water on the floor soaking through my shoes.

Dill stopped and opened a narrow door. "In here," he whispered.

I looked inside. I saw the beginning of a passageway the height of a ceiling but only perhaps two feet wide, like the corridor that led to

Elizabeth's father's secret room. The walls were studded with pipes and wires. After four or five feet I saw nothing but black. "What is this?"

"It's the wirin' channel that runs between the rooms down here," he said.

"How far would I have to go?"

His face screwed up. While he thought, his tongue stuck out the side of his mouth. "Hundred foot, maybe a little more."

"No. I'm not going in there." Suddenly, I felt chilled.

"You want to find him?"

I nodded.

"Then you're goin' in. Follow me. Keep your mouth shut—and keep your goddamn gun up." He stepped sideways into the narrow corridor and disappeared.

I took a deep breath. I could find my way back. I could go back to my room, go to sleep, pretend this never happened. I couldn't climb in there.

I looked inside. Though the sound was rapidly dissipating, Dill's feet slid across the floor. All I saw was inky blackness. I straightened and took a step back down the tunnel, but stopped. I wasn't here for myself. I was here for Elizabeth. I had to find her brother. I had to save him.

Holding my left hand out to feel ahead, I took another deep breath and stepped sideways into the corridor. A bead of sweat slid down my forehead. A pace left, and another, and another. My lower back slid along a cold metal pipe that bumped out with braces every couple of feet. The opposite wall passed by only inches from my face.

From somewhere in the building came the steady pounding we'd heard in the tunnels. It was a hollow sound—*bang . . . bang . . . bang*. I knew Dill would follow it, expecting to find the Phantom. I looked back. I may have made it only ten feet into the corridor, but the doorway looked to be a football field from me. Dill's steps had faded away. My guts churned. I was freezing. I swallowed hard and slid again to my left, and again, hand reaching out in front of me.

Now I saw a glow perhaps fifty feet ahead, near the floor, and Dill's silhouette framed against it. I swallowed hard and moved faster, trying not to think about the walls constricting, the possibility of someone closing that door, being stuck inside here forever. My eyes stung with sweat; my nightshirt was wet and cold.

Dill passed by the light and faded again into the darkness. I hurried along behind him, trying to shut off my brain.

I was close enough now to see that the light came from a grate near the floor, perhaps a foot tall by two feet wide. Just before I got to it, I heard a door open and slam shut.

"Goddamn Beckwith," a man grumbled, not ten feet from me.

I froze. Dill did, too.

I was back just far enough to be out of the light. On the other side of the grate, a match scraped and flared. I heard one man, and then another, light cigarettes. "How are we supposed to deal with that big bastard if we can't beat him?" the other man said.

It took all my inner strength not to crawl through that grate and join the cops, no matter the consequences.

"Ah." I could hear the disgust in the first man's voice. "He's a idjit."

"Which one? The big bastard or Beckwith?"

"Both," the first man said with a laugh. Tobacco seeds popped.

Ahead of me, Dill started moving again.

"What's that?" the first man asked.

Dill kept scurrying along.

"What?" the other man replied.

"Dunno. Somethin'." A man's shadow passed between the light and the grate, and again as he returned to the other side of the room. They were quiet. The sound of Dill's scrabbling faded away. He was gone, far enough ahead that I couldn't hear him at all.

I held my breath.

"Ah, hell with it," the first man said. "Ghosts, probably." He let out a nervous laugh.

"Don't joke about 'em," the other man said. "They're all over this goddamn place."

Behind me, a light turned on, streaming into the corridor. I looked back. Perhaps ten feet away, light poured in through another grate. I heard a man moving around, the scrape of a chair on the floor, a grunt as he sat.

Cops ahead of me. Cops behind me. Dill was gone. A cockroach skittered over my right ankle. I managed not to shout.

The men by me kept talking. I couldn't wait any longer. I had to get out of this corridor. Cringing, expecting to hear a shout, I slid in front of the grate. Another slide, and I was past it.

"D'ja see that new floozy with the coughers?" the first man asked.

"The blonde?" the other man replied.

I stiffened.

"Yeah. Looks to me like she needs a good fuck."

*Asshole.* I barely kept the whisper from escaping my lips.

The other man barked out a derisive laugh. "You're the one to give it to her?"

"Why not me?"

"Well, let's see," the second man said. "You're old, fat, oh, and let's not forget, married."

*Plus she'd kill you if you tried, you stupid bastard,* I thought.

I stopped listening and started moving. Another twenty feet down the corridor, it was pitch black again. I slid faster, sweat pouring off me, the pounding becoming more distinct. Dill wouldn't stop until he located its source. "Dill?" I whispered.

No reply. A chill went up my spine. I moved forward another ten feet or so and whispered his name again. Silence. My heart pounded. It was getting hard to breathe. I slid back a few feet, trying not to bolt for the door.

*Elizabeth,* I thought. *It's for Elizabeth.*

Another ten feet. Another whisper. "Dill?"

"It's Daroga!" Dill practically shouted. His voice came from near the floor. "Or the—"

"Shh!" I hissed. "The Persian, I know. Now get me out of here."

"Lay down," he said. "The hole is by the floor."

I took hold of the pipe with my left hand and tried to lower myself. I fell most of the way but escaped damage. A ragged hole ran along the floor for about four feet. "Cut myself out a bigger hole," he whispered.

I wriggled inside and ran into his legs. Panting with exhaustion, I pushed myself to my feet. The room smelled of old leather and mothballs. Even in the dark, I could feel that I was in a large space again. "Is this the storeroom?"

"Yeah." Dill took my arm and slipped through the dark room as easily as if it were lit. He quietly clicked a bolt on the door, opened it, and peered out in both directions. We stole into the hallway, turning right and heading down a dim corridor. The floor was white ceramic tile, each piece perhaps an inch square.

Dill turned back, looked at me, and shook the hand he held in front of his face, again mimicking holding up a gun. He waited until I copied his position before moving on.

Huge iron pipes ran down the corridor near the top of the wall, and I heard water running through them. The pounding came from somewhere farther ahead, louder now. Behind us, men laughed. One bellowed out a harsh curse. I flinched and looked back but saw nothing.

A door stood at the end of the hallway. Dill carefully opened it a few inches, peered in, and slipped through. I followed him into another corridor, this one marked along the right side by doors about six feet apart. Each of them had a pair of smaller doors in it—one short and wide, at waist height, for food trays, another perhaps six inches square at eye level.

We hurried in, and I closed the door behind me. The pounding was louder, though it still sounded distant. Someone muttered, low and threatening. The corridor reeked of shit and rot. Dill took hold of my hand again and raised it in front of my face. I walked past him and opened the eye-level door of the first cell. A naked man, as skinny as a scarecrow, lay curled up in the back corner. I didn't know him. I went on to the next, and the next. In all, this passage contained eight cells, all occupied by the most pathetic wretches, either so drugged or so malnourished they didn't move or show the least curiosity to someone looking in at them.

Dill, focused on the noise ahead, kept gesturing at me to move on. At the end of this hallway was another door. I pushed it open a few inches and again saw no one guarding the cells, so we hurried into the next corridor, identical to the first, though there was no door at the end of this one. It was a dead end.

Now the pounding was distinct. The last door in the hallway shuddered with each blow. A mist of dust fell from the ceiling every time the inmate struck the door.

I did not have to use my imagination to guess who was in that cell.

"No!" a man cried. "Stop it, stop it, please, please, that's too much, you have to, you have to . . ." I hurried to the cell second from the end and opened the little door.

Robert stood against the far wall, his hands tight to his chest, head bowed against the plaster. The words streamed from his mouth. "No, no, you can't, you must stop, you must—"

"Robert." I tried the door. As I expected, it was locked. "Dill, how can I get a key?"

He didn't answer.

Robert turned and looked at me. "Make him stop, can you make him stop?"

"I'll try. Now listen to me. Robert, I'm Will Anderson, Elizabeth's friend. I was here the night Patrick Cook was murdered. Are you all right?" He looked much better than the other men I'd seen, though he'd only been in this hellhole a week. I imagined at the end of a month he'd be lying on the floor like a rag doll.

"The . . . pounding. He won't stop, he won't stop, I can't . . . I can't . . ."

"Robert? Who killed Patrick Cook?"

His eyebrows knit in confusion. "I told all of them . . . It was the Phantom."

"But who is the Phantom?"

From the next cell, I heard a roar. I turned to see Dill with his index finger pointed through the little window. "We meet again, O.G.," Dill said. "It's time for you to die."

"Stop it." I grabbed Dill's arm.

Ty started laughing. "Boy, when I get outta here, I'm 'onna reach down your throat and pull you inside out." He resumed smashing his fist against the door.

Dill kept jabbering at him. I tried to tune them out. "Robert?" I said. "Who is the Phantom?"

"He's the Opera Ghost."

"But he's really a person," I said. "Did you see him?"

"Yes . . . but it was dark." He shook his head, bewildered.

"What happened the night Patrick Cook was killed?"

"Patrick had to make number two. He doesn't like the halls at night, so he asked me to go with him. While I waited for him . . . I went to the kitchen . . . to . . . ."

"To get some food," I finished. "That's fine."

"No," he said. "No food after hours." He was quoting someone. "It's against the rules."

"What happened next?"

"I heard someone and hid."

"Was it the Phantom?"

"Yes. And Patrick."

"You grabbed the knife from the kitchen. To protect yourself."

He nodded.

"The Phantom strangled Patrick."

"Yes. But he didn't see me."

"You went to see Patrick. After. That's when they found you."

"Yes."

I turned Dill so that he had to look at me. "How can I get a key?"

"Kill a guard."

"Other than that?"

He shrugged.

I turned back to Robert. "Elizabeth and I are going to get you out of here."

"Just make him stop, please."

I pushed Dill aside and peered in the window at Ty. "You're going to break a bone in your hand. That'll put you on the bench for a month. Where will the Tigers be then?"

He cocked his head at me. "But if I don't bust this door down, I ain't gonna get to kill none a them crackers out there. And you best not be here when this door gives." He raised his leg and kicked the door with the bottom of his bare foot.

I went back to Robert's little window. "Sorry. He'll get tired . . . eventually. I'll get you out of here, though. Just take care of yourself." I closed the little door. "All right, Dill, we'd better get out of here."

"Yeah, you're right. I gotta get a real gun."

After a quick look out, we hurried past the first set of cells. We were nearly to the next door when it began to swing open.

Dill wrapped his arm around me and pulled me behind the door, his hand clamped over my mouth. The door opened, and we flattened ourselves against the wall. A guard sauntered through, a bottle of beer in his hand. Dill waited until the man was about halfway down the hall to nudge me and begin to work his way around the door.

"Hey!" the guard shouted.

Dill shoved me through the door and slammed it shut behind us. He cut in front of me, and we dashed down the hall toward the storeroom. The guard threw open the door, blowing his whistle.

Cops poured into the hallway ahead of us, cutting us off from the storeroom. The one in front had his gun pulled. Dill jerked me left through a door and closed and bolted it behind us. We sprinted to the end of a short hallway, where Dill shoved open a door, and we ran out into the night with the policemen still trying to get the hallway door unlocked.

Then we were in the trees, running parallel to the back of the building. After the constrictive terror of the tunnels, I finally felt free, running through the copse, well lit by moon and stars. Dill stayed to the shadows, and we ran through the trees, hell-bent on survival.

A door banged open behind us. I looked and saw cops fanning out from the Administration Building, but rather than following us, they were running around to the front. I thought they might believe two of their prisoners had escaped and were heading for the fence and freedom, which would have made a hell of a lot more sense than what we were doing.

Dill bolted across the lawn, heading straight for the rear entrance of our building. I started to follow, just as another cop hurried out the door of the station, buckling his belt as he did. I hit the grass. He missed Dill but must have seen me moving, because his eyes scanned over and around me for a good twenty seconds before he started loping around toward the front of the building. I waited until he was out of sight to follow Dill, though I stayed close to the tree line, rather than cutting straight across the lawn.

A movement near the back of Building B caught my eye. The silhouettes of two people moved in sync with one another, almost as if dancing, though one moved gracefully and the other jerked to the side again and again, following the other. Mesmerized, I moved closer to them. Now, in the moonlight, I saw that the man jerking around wore a nightshirt. A piece of fabric fluttered down from his head—the turban. It was Dill. He collapsed to the ground.

The other man was nothing more than a shadow.

"Hey!" I shouted, running toward them.

The other man jerked on something, and Dill's body shook. Now the wraith bent down, and I saw he wore all black—trousers and shirt, cape and fedora. His face was dark other than his mouth and jaw. A mask? He lifted Dill's head and slipped something—a rope—from around his neck.

The Phantom—for it truly was the Phantom—calmly turned and appraised me while coiling the rope. I ran toward him, not sure what I would do if I got close.

"This way!" a man yelled from in front of the Administration Building. Whistles shrieked behind me.

The Phantom's head turned toward the sound, and a second later he melted into the shadow of the building. Policemen shouted as they ran in my direction, though they were still hundreds of yards away.

When I reached Dill, I knelt down and checked his pulse. There was none. I cursed to myself. The policemen were getting closer, their footsteps pounding across the grass. I ran to the rear entrance of Building B, took the steps three at a time, and threw open the door. I ran inside, slowing only at the corner, where I peered down the next empty hallway before sprinting to my room. Pressing the door closed behind me, I fell onto my bed, panting with exhaustion and fear. After about a minute, people began running up and down the hallway shouting, but no one opened my door.

I started sobbing and buried my face in my pillow to stifle the sound. Dill didn't deserve to die. He wouldn't even have been outside if it weren't for me. He might as well have been killed by my hand as by the Phantom's.

Everywhere I went, death followed closely behind—or perhaps it was me who was chasing it. While the dead man inside me had seemed dormant during this short magical time I'd had with Elizabeth, I wondered, had he been working away behind the scenes, gnawing at my edges, wearing me down for the inevitable fall? And it did seem inevitable. I was a cancer, not only to acquaintances like poor Dill, but to the people I cared about. I'd ruined Elizabeth's life and caused the death of her father. I'd gotten Wesley McRae murdered. My parents were still around, no thanks to the danger I'd put them in. One of these days I'd find them dead as well, no doubt due to something I'd done.

I was a cancer . . . but perhaps I could put that power to use.

I tried to picture the Phantom. The face was impossible. Only the mouth had been visible, and it was too dark to really discern anything. My impression was that he was of medium height and not a big man, but quick, graceful, and strong. The image of Dill's strangling crossed my mind. It had appeared to be a dance, and I suppose it was, a *danse macabre*.

Was it possible that Francis had this hidden grace he could summon when using a rope? It seemed unlikely. His movements were jerky, mechanical. Yet I knew he had been outside earlier tonight, and his build was similar to the Phantom's. Francis was nearly as tall as me, perhaps the same size as the man I'd seen.

I cursed. I was really no closer to identifying the Phantom, but one fact was indisputable—he had seen me.

# Elizabeth

Once on the train, I smoked a cigarette, ignoring the two old biddies a few rows behind me who spent fifteen minutes conspicuously clearing their throats and clucking to one another. All the way back to Detroit I seethed. Dr. Beckwith was such a pompous man and was so clearly covering up the murders. I had to expose him. Now I would have to determine how best to do that from the outside.

And what of Will? What would he think when I didn't come again? I had to get him word, to let him know what happened so he wouldn't worry. Clarence would be my best bet for that, but . . . how to get hold of him? As far as I knew, he didn't have a telephone. Unfortunately, I would have to contact him through the hospital, something I thought might be difficult.

By the time I reached the downtown train station, it had stopped raining. I took a streetcar down to Jefferson and then transferred to a Jefferson Line car to take me home. The trolley was full, as most were twenty-four hours a day, so I stood near the doorway and held on to a strap bolted to the ceiling. A young man of perhaps eighteen boarded after I did and squeezed in behind me, tipping his derby to me as he passed. When the trolley started up, everyone swayed back as usual, other than the young man, whose hand cupped the right side of my derriere. There was no doubt it was intentional. I threw my right elbow back as hard as I could into his solar plexus, the nerve center directly below the sternum. I'd learned in France that a proper strike there can paralyze an attacker, and I nearly did so. He groaned, his legs buckled, and just before he would have crumpled to the floor, another man caught hold of him under the arms and supported him long enough that he could regain his footing.

"She's crazy!" the young man blustered when he caught his breath.

I shoved my index finger into his face. "Don't tempt me to show you how crazy I am." I glared at him, eyes narrowed, daring him to make an issue of it, but he looked away and thanked the man for holding him up. Someone offered him a seat and he took it, but at the next stop he pushed through the crowd to exit via the back door. I watched him all the way, wanting to hit him again.

Women were being assaulted like this on streetcars every day, and no one did anything about it. I thought it might be an interesting side-line: Elizabeth Hume, streetcar avenger. Ride around the city and kill any man who dares to grope me. A few dead perverts would probably slow down the rest of them. The thought cheered me.

I got off a couple of blocks from my house. When I walked in the door, I heard Alberts and my mother in the kitchen. They were sitting at the table with Helga.

My mother was shuffling a deck of cards. "Ah, good, Elizabeth, we need a fourth."

"A fourth? For what?"

"Whist."

"Whist?" I laughed. We hadn't played whist since I was a girl. "All right; it sounds like fun."

I sat across from Helga, who gave me a tentative smile. "Miss," she said.

"Hello, Helga."

"You're home early," Mother said. "How was your day?"

"Fine." There was no sense bringing them into my problems. Turning to Alberts, I said, "Where's Bridie?"

"Her mother called and needed her. I don't know what happened, but she ran out of here pretty quickly. She apologized and said she'd be back this evening."

I nodded, hoping it wasn't as ominous as it sounded. "Say, did Baker's deliver a book for me?"

He shook his head. "No, miss. Would you like me to phone them?"

"No, that's all right. I'm sure they'll deliver it when it arrives."

We started playing the game. I tried to be casual about it, but I paid close attention to my mother, who seemed as normal as could be. She was sharp, winning trick after trick, as she'd always done when we played with my father, which was the reason we stopped playing. Helga was a dreadful partner. She didn't understand the rules and had to take back card after card, which only helped Mother and Alberts because they knew her cards better than she did. They continued to pile up the points. I didn't really care. It was so enjoyable to spend time with my mother, her faculties intact, her personality . . . complete. We drank iced tea and played cards for hours. It was obvious that Alberts was taking as much pleasure as I in experiencing my mother at her best.

Late in the afternoon, a knock sounded against the front door. Alberts excused himself and answered it, and a few seconds later I heard Detective Riordan's gentle lilt. I joined them at the door.

"Good afternoon, Miss Hume," he said, tipping his fedora.

"Good afternoon, Detective." I wondered if his use of my surname was due to Alberts's presence or because he had official business with me. I had always thought Detective Riordan was a handsome man, tall and powerful with a rectangular face and fine features. Unfortunately, one's attention was drawn to the scar and his eyes: irises so pale a blue as to almost be invisible, which gave him the predatory look of a wolf.

"I'm pleased to find you at home," he said. "I was out here on a case anyway, so I thought I'd stop by."

"Would you like to come in?"

"Thank you." He walked into the foyer and looked around, his eyes lingering on the little marble table against the paneled mahogany wall, the gilt mirror near the door, the walnut staircase.

I wondered what it looked like from his perspective. A policeman would have little frame of reference for such finery, other than perhaps what he came across in the course of his duties. He would have assumed my home looked something like this, but I wondered if seeing it made him think differently of me.

Alberts took his hat and hung it on the rack.

"Alberts," I said, "would you have Helga bring a glass of iced tea to the den for Detective Riordan?"

"Certainly, miss."

"Detective?" I held my hand toward the hallway that led to the back of the house.

"After you." He followed me in, and I sat on one of the burgundy club chairs in the sitting area. He sat on the sofa across the coffee table from me. "I've discovered something interesting."

"Interesting" most often seemed to be Detective Riordan's euphemism for "criminal." "Really?" I asked. "What?"

"I've been looking into Dr. Beckwith's stint at the state hospital in Kalamazoo. No one at the asylum was talking, but I researched crimes that happened around the time he left."

Helga walked in with a glass of tea and set it on a coaster in front of Detective Riordan. While she did, the detective pulled a cigar from his pocket, arched his eyebrows, and held it up in front of him with the unspoken question, *Do you mind?*

"Please," I said. "Feel free." I am no fan of the stench of his cigars, but it was impossible to think of Detective Riordan without one in his mouth. He would be naked.

Helga pulled an ashtray from a bookcase and set it on the desk in front of him. He lit the cigar and puffed away.

I waited until she had gone to ask, "What did you find?"

"A young man was murdered in Kalamazoo two weeks before Beckwith resigned."

"Do you think his son had something to do with it?"

Taking a long pull on the cigar, Detective Riordan nodded. "The body was found in the woods about a quarter mile from the asylum's grounds." The smoke tumbled from his mouth as he spoke.

A tingling sensation went through me. "How was he killed?"

The detective's expression was grim. "He was strangled."


"It makes sense," I said. "Dr. Beckwith left Kalamazoo after the man was murdered and has been sweeping these murders at Eloise under the rug. He wouldn't have done either without a very strong motive. He doesn't want his son to be prosecuted." I thought for a moment. "How do we prove any of this? You can't investigate on the hospital grounds."

"No." After a pause, he said, "Maybe it's best to go back in time a bit, see if the killer made any mistakes." He picked up the iced tea, then changed his mind and set it back on the coaster. "Unfortunately, we have a problem there. I phoned the Kalamazoo police. They weren't very co-operative."

"Do you think they're hiding something?"

"Hard to say."

"I wonder . . ."

"What?" he asked.

"I wonder if I could get farther with them."

"Elizabeth, no offense, but you're not a policeman. Why would they—" He stopped abruptly, now thinking as I was. "Maybe. But I don't think you'd get anywhere on the telephone."

"Perhaps I could go to Kalamazoo. I was just terminated from Eloise. Dr. Beckwith found out I was there."

"Mmm." A little frown crossed his face. "What does that mean for Will?"

"I'm quite sure that Beckwith still doesn't know anything about him. Even so, I'd like to get him out."

"I'm sure I could get a court order," Detective Riordan said.

"What do you think?"

"How safe do you believe he is right now?"

"Well . . ." I thought for a second. "I talked to him yesterday, and he didn't seem to be too concerned. I don't know. He thinks he's safe enough."

He took a drink. "Professionally speaking, the odds of finding any-thing in Kalamazoo that will prove Francis's guilt aren't in our favor. It's been two years, and even when the case was warm they couldn't come up with a suspect. If you don't think Will is in immediate danger, I'd recommend we leave him there." The detective picked up a pencil from the table and began spinning it around his knuckles, like a drum major with a baton, an activity more in keeping with a nervous man.

"What?" I asked.

"Are you serious about going to Kalamazoo?"

"I . . . think so."

"The more I think about it, the better I like it." He nodded and grinned at me. "Would you mind some company?"

Detective Riordan said he was essentially persona non grata at the police department these days; the brass wouldn't even notice he was gone. I felt a bit nervous about him missing work but decided that was his decision to make, not mine. We consulted the Michigan Central train schedule and made arrangements to meet at the downtown station on Jefferson the next morning at 6:30 A.M. for a 7:00 train. If it ran on schedule, we would be in Kalamazoo at 10:45 A.M. Detective Riordan's opinion, which I thought to be correct, was that between the two of us we ought to be able to wheedle the truth out of the police. Because of the time, we agreed to leave the hotel arrangements until we arrived in the city.

Though Detective Riordan had always proven himself to be a gentleman, I wasn't keen on traveling alone with any man, a problem that was solved for me that evening when Bridie returned.

I was packing for the trip when I heard the doorbell. At that very moment I was thinking about Bridie, as it was after seven and I'd expected news from her earlier.

Alberts let her in and came to get me. "Bridie would like to speak with you, miss."

"Was that her at the door?" I hadn't expected it to be Bridie for two reasons: She would normally enter the house through the back door, and, being a family servant, she needn't ring the bell.

"Yes, miss."

"Why would she ring?"

Alberts looked at the floor. "She asked to speak with you, miss."

He was reminding me it wasn't his place. "I'm sorry, Alberts." I set my hand on his shoulder and leaned in to give him a kiss on the cheek. "You're one of the family. You know that's how I think of you."

One side of his mouth rose in a little smile. "Thank you, Elizabeth."

"All right. Let's see what she needs to talk about." I swept out of the room and down the stairs, hoping everything was all right, but knowing it wasn't the case. There was only one reason she would feel the need to ring the bell.

208 | D. E. Johnson

She was waiting in the parlor, standing at one of the windows looking out at the street, her hands clasped together in front of her, thumbs
pressing back and forth against each other. She turned when I came
into the room.

"Bridie. Is everything all right?"

"No, miss. My dad. He—" She burst out in tears.

"Here." I took her arm, led her to the sofa, and sat her down. Alberts
stood in the doorway. "Alberts, would you have Helga make some coffee, please?"

"Yes, miss." He disappeared.

"Now, Bridie, please tell me. What's wrong with him?"

She wiped her eyes with her handkerchief and sniffled. "He's had a
stroke, miss. He's paralyzed. My mum's off her nut. She can't manage
him and do her work." She started crying again. "They need my help."

Out of the corner of my eye, I saw a movement in the doorway. My
mother stood there, listening.

"That's fine, Bridie," I said. "Has a doctor seen him?"

"Yes, miss."

"A good one?"

"I . . . don't know." Her voice was tiny, so unlike her.

"I'm going to send Dr. Miller over to see him. He's the best." I pulled
open the end table's drawer and took out a pad of paper and a pencil.
"Write down your address. He'll be there tonight. If he can't make it,
one of his colleagues will."

"Thank you, miss—but that's not why I'm here. I need to help my
mum, so I'm going to have to quit my job."

"Nonsense," my mother said, bustling into the room. "You will do no
such thing."

I gaped at her, astonished. She sat on the other side of Bridie and put
her arm around her. "We will continue to pay you while you attend to
your father. When you're able, you'll come back."

I'm sure my mouth was hanging open, but this . . . this was my
mother, back in full form.

Bridie shook her head, wiping tears from her eyes. "It could be
months . . . or longer."

"Yes, it may," my mother said. "And if it is, then so be it."

"She's right," I said. "Your first duty is to your family. We'll welcome you back when you're ready. Until then, we will continue to pay the service. It'll be our little secret."

"Thank you, Mrs. Hume, Miss Hume. I can't tell you . . ." She burst out again.

"You don't have to, dear," my mother said, patting her hand.

We talked for a few minutes until Helga walked in with a tray of coffee, sugar, cream, cups, saucers, and cookies. When she saw the scene, she stopped for a moment but recovered, set the tray on the table, and poured for all three of us.

Over coffee, we consoled Bridie and tried to cheer her up. By the time she left, I thought she was feeling better. Though the task that lay ahead of her was daunting, the continued income and the promise of medical care for her father must have made it seem less so.

Afterward, my mother and I sat on the sofa holding hands. I knew the moment would be fleeting, but I was so happy with her I thought I would burst. Still, I had a decision to make: I had committed to traveling to Kalamazoo with Detective Riordan, and Bridie would not be able to be with my mother. She was fine now. If I had any assurance she would continue in this state, I would have had no qualms about leaving her home with Alberts and Helga, but who knew what the next hour would bring? I could go off to Kalamazoo with the detective and hope she was all right, or I could bring her with us and keep an eye on her.

I decided. "Mother, how would you like to go on a journey to the Wild West for a little detective work?"

"The Wild West?"

"Yes." I smiled. "The wilds of West Michigan. Kalamazoo, to be precise."

# CHAPTER TEN

*Thursday, August 15, 1912*

## Will

When the sun rose the next morning, I was even more determined to catch the Phantom and stop this senseless killing. I would not leave Eloise Hospital until I had done so.

As usual, the orderly came for me early. He didn't notice that the door was already unlocked. I traipsed down to the cafeteria, hoping against hope that I was wrong, that it was some awful dream . . . but Chuck walked alone down the hallway, no Dill at his side. I fell in next to him.

He looked at me and mumbled, "Where is the Persian?"

"I . . ." Finally I just shook my head.

"The Phantom?"

After a short hesitation, I nodded.

"Killed him?"

I nodded again.

His shoulders slumped, but he continued down the hall, the routine drilled into him so sharply that, even in his grief, his feet took him where he was supposed to be.

We ate breakfast in silence, and an orderly escorted me back to my room. On the way, I saw Dr. Davis again, though this time from a distance. He didn't see me. After I'd been back in my room for perhaps an hour, a key turned in the lock, and the door opened. Dr. Beckwith walked in with a pair of orderlies. One of them was carrying a white garment with straps dangling from it—a straitjacket.

I figured I'd better get this out while I could. "There's a man here named Zimmermann. He's German and doesn't speak English. There's nothing wrong with him, but your people are drugging him senseless. I don't think anyone has even communicated with him."

Beckwith put his hands on his hips and smirked at me. "You don't think there's anything wrong with him, Dr. Doe?"

I ignored the sarcasm. "No, I don't. Do you have anyone here who speaks German?"

"I have complete faith in my staff. If he's drugged, it's for good reason."

"Please. Just look into it."

He nodded to the orderlies, who pulled the straitjacket onto my arms and began tying it behind me.

"What's this about?" I asked.

"I'm concerned you will hurt yourself, Mr. Doe," Beckwith replied.

"Why are you doing this?"

He didn't answer.

When the orderlies finished, they pushed me down onto the bed. Beckwith told them to leave. When the door clicked shut, he leaned back against the wall. "I think you were outside last night."

"How could I have gotten out?"

"There's always a way, isn't there? A sympathetic nurse, for example."

"I don't know what you're talking about."

"Two patients broke into solitary confinement last night. I think you were one of them."

"Why would someone break *into* solitary? Seems to me people would be trying to break *out*."

"Yes, that would be more logical, wouldn't it?" He pushed off the wall and walked toward me. "Mr. Dill was killed. You were with him, weren't you? Did you see the Phantom?"

"The Phantom? Now who's crazy?"

"Did you see him?"

"Of course I didn't. I was in here all night."

"You really aren't at all convincing, John. Now tell me. What did the Phantom look like?"

I tried to shrug, but, through the straitjacket, I'm not sure I got the point across.

"I just want to catch him, John. Why won't you help me?"

*Because you ask me about it only when no one else is around,* I thought, but all I said was "If I see him, you'll be the first to know."

His mouth turned grim. "I can make your life very difficult, very painful, by just saying a word. Is that what you want?"

If I told him his son was the Phantom, he would do worse. "I wish I could help you, Dr. Beckwith, I really do. Particularly when you make it so clear I'll regret not identifying someone I've never seen."

He smiled again, the kind of smile a doctor gives a patient just before he breaks the news of a terminal prognosis. "Your case may require stronger measures than I thought, Mr. Doe. I believe I will have to devise a new treatment for you."

They left me in the straitjacket. I sat by the window for the rest of the morning, but again saw no sign of Elizabeth. I did see perhaps a hundred women out for a walk with half a dozen orderlies, who led them down the sidewalk and, after a few minutes, herded them back in the other direction.

I considered Dr. Beckwith and his "new treatment." I thought he would have already dumped me in the Hole if he was certain I had been with Dill. I had to ensure that his uncertainty remained, but if I couldn't get out of this straitjacket it didn't much matter what Beckwith did. I would never find the killer.

I had to get word to Elizabeth that Robert was here. If I could get to Morgan, he would be able to tell her, but I didn't think I'd be allowed to attend any reading classes in the near future.

My chance came at lunch. Alice came into the room with a tray for me. An orderly untied the straps of the jacket and pulled it off so I could eat. He stood in the corner while Alice gave me the tray.

"Nurse Jensen?" I said. "Could you tell Clarence Morgan something for me?"

Her mouth tightened. "What?"

"Could you tell him to pass along a message to the woman we discussed? That the man she's looking for is here?"

Her eyes narrowed. "The woman? Are you talking about the blonde?"

I thought I'd better be honest with her. Or at least as honest as I could be. "Well . . . yes. Esther."

"How do you know her?"

"From . . . earlier." I glanced at the orderly.

She followed my eyes. "You," she said to him. He looked at her, and she nodded toward the door. "Outside."

He shrugged and left the room. She stared back at me, eyebrows arched.

I looked into her eyes. I didn't know whether I could trust her, but at this point, what did I have to lose? "I came here looking for Robert Clarke," I said. "He's in the Hole. I need Esther to know that."

"So you don't have amnesia?"

"No, I don't. I came here to help Esther find Robert. And to find out who is killing patients."

"Patients are really being killed?"

"Yes. Papa Dill got it last night."

Her eyes widened. "Arthur? I wondered . . . What happened?"

"He and I went looking for Robert, and we found him. On the way back, the Phantom caught Dill in his lasso and strangled him."

Her hand went to her mouth. "Oh, my God." A second later, "You got out of the building? How?"

I didn't want to expose Morgan. "Dill got me out of here. We left the building through the tunnel."

"Ahh." Her eyes dropped, and she nodded slowly. "That explains it."

"Explains what?"

"Oh." She glanced up. "Dr. Beckwith. He grilled me this morning. He kept saying I'd better stick to my duties, which is exactly what I've been doing." Her eyes seemed to look inward for a second, and then it was as if a light turned on. "Well, of course I'll tell Clarence. And you had better watch out for yourself. You can never be too careful."

"Would you help me get Robert out of here?"

"No." Her eyes widened. "I could never do that."

"Why not?"

"I don't . . . I'm sorry. I have responsibilities."

"You won't expose me, will you?"

After appraising me for a long moment, she shook her head. "No, I won't. But don't ask me again to help you." She called the orderly back into the room, and he let me pick at the rancid food before putting me back into the straitjacket. I sat on the bed and resumed my vigil of the street behind the building, hoping to catch a glimpse of Elizabeth.

Alice returned later that afternoon. She unlocked the door and stuck her head in the room. "Clarence says to be ready tonight." She closed the door, and the key turned again in the lock.

Morgan said I needed to be ready. I was. Ready to nail the Phantom. Ready to get Robert out of here.

And I was certainly ready to say good-bye to this place once and for all.

Perhaps half an hour after a horrendous supper in my room, a key turned in my door lock. Clarence Morgan, a briefcase under his arm, rushed in and shut the door behind him. After he locked the door again, he turned to me, sweat beaded on his brow. "Alice gave me your message," he whispered. "Esther wasn't in today, and she's apparently not coming back, so I can't tell her about Robert. Or about you."

"What happened to her?"

"I don't know."

"Damn it." I had to get word to her about Robert. At this point, there was no sense keeping up the facade of Elizabeth's identity. "Could you phone her?"

He nodded.

"Her name is actually Elizabeth Hume, and she lives on Jefferson Avenue in Detroit."

"Elizabeth Hume?"

"Yes. I'm sorry. We didn't know whom we could trust here. We have a friend in the Detroit police who will help us."

"What's his name?"

"Thomas Riordan. He's a detective. Elizabeth will contact him."

"I'm sure there's a good story here. I'll expect to hear it when this is over."

"I'll be happy to tell it over a drink back home in Detroit."

"You're buying," he said.

"Deal. Now, could you let me out of this thing?"

"Sure." He started worrying at one of the straps. "What happened last night?"

I told him about our trip to the Hole and Dill's death. While I did, he got me unstrapped, and I threw the straitjacket on the bed.

"So the tunnels were his secret," he said. "Was it Francis? The Phantom?"

I shook my head. "No. I just can't see it. The Phantom was so graceful."

"Hmm." Clarence's forehead furrowed. "Remember, when *I* saw him with the rope he was much smoother, like he was in his element somehow."

I shrugged. "I don't know. I suppose it could be. But perhaps we could talk about this later? Alice said you had a plan for tonight."

"Yes. Dr. Beckwith is taking Francis out for supper"—he pulled a watch from his pocket and glanced at it—"about now. Afterward, he and I are scheduled to play chess. I live next door to them in a double residence. You need to search the house before they get home. I'm willing to bet you'll find Francis's tools of the trade."

"How will I get there?"

"You're going to walk."

"But how—"

He pulled a white uniform from the briefcase and handed it to me. "Orderlies are everywhere. This will give you anonymity." I pulled on the trousers while he talked. "Stephen and Francis will be returning in about an hour. I've made sure their back door is unlocked. You will proceed up the stairs to the bedroom on the far left. I'm willing to bet you'll find Francis's gear there. If not, keep searching, but keep your eye on the time."

I bit my lip. "Assuming I find the disguise, what am I going to do? If I confront him with the evidence, he'll just toss me in the Hole to rot."

"You won't confront him. I just need you to find something—anything—that I can use for leverage with Stephen. With evidence, he will act. You may not believe this, but he's a good man. He's just been blinded by his fear for his son."

He walked to the door, briefcase in hand.

"Why haven't you done this yourself?" I asked.

He stopped but didn't look back. "I haven't the courage."

"Well, you seem to be displaying a great deal of courage right now."

He looked back at me and shrugged as if embarrassed. "I'm going to wait for you by the back doors. When I walk out, catch the door before it closes. Then stay at least fifty yards behind me at all times. Stephen and Francis should have left the grounds by now, but they don't dawdle over their suppers." Grabbing hold of the doorknob, he said, "Give me two minutes." He opened the door, slipped out, and pressed it shut behind him.

I arranged the straitjacket and my pillow under the blanket, hoping to fool someone not taking too close a look at the room. Once I had it ready, I opened my door and sauntered out, trying to look confident.

*My hand.* Anyone who had seen me would know. I stuck my right hand in my trouser pocket, shut the door behind me, and headed down the hallway toward the rear entrance. I passed nurses and orderlies, but none of them gave me a second look. At the main hallway, I turned toward the rear entrance.

Clarence stood by the doors, tapping his toe nervously. When he saw me, he turned and unlocked one. I caught up to him just as he was swinging the door open. Lagging behind, I ambled along, looking at the flowers. When I glanced up, Clarence was already on the sidewalk along the street that led to the back of the complex. I followed, heading toward the river. An ice wagon drove past. The driver nodded at me. I nodded back. Clarence passed the school and headed down a little lane that led to a home, a symmetrical two-story with a front door on either side of the big front porch. Without a look back, he walked in through the front door on the left.

I slipped around behind the house and up the steps to the back door of the Beckwith residence. The white curtains over the window in the door were heavier than the gauzy fabric you most often see for kitchen curtains, but a tiny gap in the center allowed me a peek at a sliver of the hallway. A light burned there, but no one was in sight. I twisted the knob and carefully pushed the door open, straining to listen. It was quiet. I closed it and crept through the kitchen to the hallway. The air was hot, stifling. The stairway was just off the foyer, which would make it difficult for me if they came home. I needed to hurry.

I crept up the stairs and walked heel to toe to the left-most bedroom.

The door was closed but not locked. I opened it and walked in. The furnishings were Spartan—a single bed made military-style, the green wool blanket squared and tucked, a small bureau, a simple desk, covered with hand-drawn maps, and a chair. I first checked the closet. The shelf above the clothes rack was barren. The floor below held only one pair of brown oxfords and a pair of knit slippers, both of which were lined up against the wall with precision. I ran my hand through the clothing but found nothing black and certainly no cape, fedora, or mask.

Next, I looked through the bureau. Again, nothing matched the clothing the Phantom wore. I checked behind it. Nothing. Under the bed—nothing. I looked around the room and was beginning to think I'd need to expand my search when I saw just the tiniest speck of black sticking out from under the mattress. I lifted it to find a black mask made of paper, like one worn at a masquerade ball. Kneeling down on the floor, I pulled the mattress up farther and saw a coiled rope made of fine fibers, like woven violin strings. I pulled that out, leaving the mattress propped up on my shoulder. I ran my fingers across the rope, which was exceptionally smooth and supple, with just enough stiffness to support the shape of the coil.

*The Punjab lasso.*

If Clarence was right about Beckwith, this would be enough to get Robert out of the Hole. Hopefully, out of Eloise. And I'd be joining him.

Seeing nothing further under the mattress, I picked up the mask and rope and stood, trying to decide if I should continue to look for the rest of the costume or if this was enough. A bead of sweat trickled down my temple. It was so hot in here.

I still had time. Glancing around the room, I had a thought. As far as I knew, only Francis and his father lived here, but there was a third bedroom. I crossed the hall and opened one of the doors.

Dr. Beckwith's room. A larger bed, an armoire, and a bureau with a photograph of a youthful, yet stern, Dr. Beckwith with a young woman—his wife? I picked up the frame and looked at the picture. She was a pretty girl, but thin and sickly-looking, smiling weakly. Beckwith's arm was around her, and with the difference in their sizes he seemed to almost envelop her. Was it her death that changed him? I thought perhaps it was. Francis was all he had left of her. To lose him would be to lose her again, this time for good.

I set the photograph back on the bureau, walked down the hall, and glanced into the third bedroom. The walls were covered with photographs of the girl in the picture. Some of them were only of her, others with Beckwith, still others with a family.

A shrine.

I opened the closet door. Dresses, skirts, shirtwaists, and shoes packed the closet. I looked for black, but all I found was a single mourning dress. I opened a drawer in the bureau. Women's underthings. Nothing Francis would wear as part of his Phantom disguise.

*Enough,* I thought. *I really need to leave.* With the mask and rope in hand, I started down the stairs. I happened to glance back, feeling something out of place. Francis's door was still open. I climbed up the steps again, took a quick look at Francis's room, and straightened the blanket before pulling the door shut behind me and descending the stairs. I peered out the picture window but saw no one. It was quiet. I wiped the sweat from my brow, realizing that all the windows were closed. Crazy in August. It had to be ninety-five degrees in here.

I strode down the hallway to the kitchen and crossed to the back door. Reaching down for the doorknob with my left hand, I peeled back one side of the curtains with my right to look out at the yard.

Francis Beckwith stared back at me through the window in the back door.

## Elizabeth

I awoke with great reservations about having my mother come along on the trip to Kalamazoo. She had been wonderful the night before, amazing, in fact. Even though she'd been fighting Bridie tooth and nail, in an emergency she came through with flying colors. That was exactly what I needed today, and it was anyone's guess as to whether she'd be up to the challenge. Regardless, I could not leave her without a qualified nurse, nor could I immediately find a new one in whom I would have the least amount of faith.

Over a cup of coffee, I appraised my mother. She looked wonderful: clear-eyed, clothing perfect, hair just so. "Mother," I said, "are you feeling up to the trip?"

She wiped her mouth with her napkin. "I feel fine, dear. No need to worry about me."

"All right," I said, though of course I lacked confidence. I wanted to give her fair warning, so I said, "I'm afraid it's not going to be what we're used to. We'll probably be spending time in police stations or worse, and will likely have to go to the state hospital."

She said nothing, but her face froze.

"It's strictly for the investigation, Mother. Remember. You will always live with me. Always."

After a moment, she relaxed and reached across the table. Patting my hand, she said, "Tell me what we're doing. I want to help."

I didn't want to risk triggering one of her spells, so, as much as it pains me to admit it, the first thing I did was lie to her. I told her Robert was in no danger. "He's in solitary confinement. No one can get in there." I thought it possible, even probable, that I was telling her the truth, but of course I had no idea where he really was or whether the Phantom would have access to the Hole. That out of the way, I explained that patients were being murdered inside Eloise Hospital, and that we believed the key to solving the case was in Kalamazoo. I studied her as I spoke, watching for signs of agitation.

When I finished, though, she seemed satisfied. "You're sure Robert is in no danger."

"Yes."

"I will help you," she said. "You'll see."

I thought she just might. We finished our coffee, and I made sure I had my Colt .32 and extra ammunition in my purse. Alberts got our luggage strapped on top of the Baker Electric and drove us to the train station, where Detective Riordan was already waiting.

It was a lovely morning: brisk, as mid-August mornings tend to be, and the sun was still struggling to appear above the buildings in Windsor, but the sky was blue and the day held great promise. My mother was behaving just as she had the previous day, and I decided to enjoy myself to the fullest, rather than worry about when she would change back to the confused and angry woman I didn't know.

Detective Riordan was a bit surprised, though not disappointed, I think, to see her. As soon as I could, I pulled him aside, asked him not to mention Robert, and briefly explained my mother's situation.

Mother and I had five bags between us, which I thought was reasonable, even meager, for a two-day trip, though Detective Riordan raised an eyebrow when he saw our luggage. He carried only a small leather valise the color of buckskin, cracked and scuffed from years of use.

After winning an argument with the detective on who was buying the tickets, I purchased first-class passage to Kalamazoo for all three of us. A porter wheeled our bags to Platform Three, where we boarded the train and settled into a private berth. A few minutes later, the train started up with a jerk and pulled away from the station. My mother asked a good number of questions about the investigation and was quite interested to hear about our progress. She was shocked at the lengths to which Will had gone in order to discover the identity of the murderer. "He *has* changed," she said.

I agreed with her, as did Detective Riordan. "He's a very different lad than he was when I first met him," he said with a laugh. "In fact, I wouldn't call him a lad any longer. Will's a man now."

I nodded. "He's a good man."

Detective Riordan, who had beaten Will, diligently attempted to have him convicted of murder, and treated him with total disdain, said, "You're right. I don't know many that good. I was wrong about him."

"Elizabeth," my mother said, "you're lucky to have him."

I had to laugh. "That's not something you would have said a year ago."

"No," she said with a smile. "That's certainly true."

A porter served us coffee and breakfast, and we passed the time pleasantly enough. The only problem I had was being uncomfortable addressing Detective Riordan as "Thomas." I knew he would call me on saying "Detective Riordan," so I compromised by not using his name at all. I quizzed him about his family and background, and learned quite a lot. His wife was from the West Indies. When she was thirteen, her parents died, and she'd traveled to Detroit on her own to live with an aunt and uncle. He met her on his first day as a policeman. He was eighteen, she fifteen. They'd been together ever since, twenty-one years, and had three children: a girl who was eighteen, and boys fifteen and eleven.

"What does your daughter do now?" I asked him.

"She's attending Detroit College. One more year, and she'll be teaching primary school."

"That's wonderful, Thomas," my mother said. "You must be very proud." She seemed much more comfortable than I in using his Christian name.

"Yes." He smiled. "Her mother and I are very proud of her."

Mother reached over and patted my knee. "I'm very proud of my daughter as well. Things haven't always been easy for her, but she's weathered it all and become a better person for it."

A warm feeling flooded through me. I'd taken so much abuse from her that the compliment was unexpected. I was also surprised at the intensity of the feeling. I suppose that somewhere not very far below the surface I was still the same little girl who would play the piano for my mother and father, not because I enjoyed playing, but because I longed to hear their praise. My father was not exactly effusive, but my mother had once been very nurturing, and I missed that.

After a few minutes, Detective Riordan said, "I suppose we ought to put together a plan. Here's what I'm thinking. After we drop off our bags at the hotel, our first stop will be the Kalamazoo police headquarters. Perhaps they will be a little more cooperative in person than on the telephone." He began ticking off points on his fingers. "We need to speak with the detectives who worked the case and, if possible, any of the uniformed officers who were involved. We need to get our hands on the case file. We need to dig up witnesses and speak with them."

"What do you hope to find?" my mother asked.

"Any connection to Dr. Beckwith or his son," he replied. "I can't help but believe there's a thread connecting one of them to the murder. We just have to look carefully enough to find it."

I leaned in. "Do you suppose the police in Kalamazoo are honest? Could they have been in on it with Beckwith?"

Detective Riordan shrugged. "There's no telling. They can't be as bad as the Detroit police, though."

"I hope not," I said with a laugh. "Or we might as well turn around now."

When the train stopped in Battle Creek, the home of Dr. Kellogg's sanitarium, I started worrying about Will again. Now that Dr. Beckwith knew I had infiltrated their ranks, I wondered if he would take a close look at all the new people, though it seemed unlikely that patients would receive any more than the normal amount of scrutiny.

The train ran on time, and we chugged into the downtown Michigan Central station in Kalamazoo a little before eleven. I'd been watching out the window as we entered the city, which was larger than I expected, though obviously not on the scale I was used to. Even though the tracks cut through industrial sections of the city, which are seldom particularly attractive, Kalamazoo seemed more prosperous than most.

A dozen or so people departed the train along with us, and a porter unloaded our suitcases onto a wheeled cart and led us to the taxi stand. The first cab in line was manned by a gangly older man, in a loose black suit that I would guess he had worn for a great many years. He identified himself as Oscar.

He helped the porter load our bags into his motorcar, an odd-looking limousine built by Croxton, a company with which I was not familiar. Even though the automobile was quite large, it was not designed to convey more than three people at a time. Besides the driver's seat, there was only a two-person bench seat in the back under a cabriolet top and a little jump seat in the luggage area in the center.

My mother and I climbed in the back. Detective Riordan squeezed into the jump seat next to the luggage. It looked tight for him, but I knew he would refuse to change places with me.

"What would you say is the best hotel in town?" I asked Oscar.

"The Burdick, ma'am," he said without hesitation.

"Is it nearby?"

"Yes, ma'am."

"Then that's where we shall go."

He started up the automobile, climbed back in, and, after a long look for nonexistent traffic, pulled out onto the road.

"Elizabeth," Detective Riordan whispered, "I don't know that I can afford—"

"It will be our treat," I said. "You are doing this for us."

"No," he protested. "I can pay—"

"Nonsense," my mother said, as she'd done when Bridie told us she was quitting. "I won't hear another word of it."

The Burdick was a new-looking seven-story redbrick that didn't look particularly distinguished on the outside but, once we walked in, proved to be most satisfactory. When we discovered they had vacancies, we asked Oscar to return in an hour and a half. That would allow us time to check in and have a quick lunch. My mother and I took a room on the second floor with a pair of single beds, and we booked a smaller room on the fourth floor for Detective Riordan.

A bellman with a wheeled cart led us to the elevator, where we were joined by the detective, carrying his own valise. We agreed to meet in the lobby for lunch in thirty minutes. My mother and I continued to our room, where the bellman turned us over to a valet, an older man who reminded me of Alberts. He began unpacking for us. The room was spacious and well appointed, with walnut trim and furniture, and fine silk wallpaper with a floral design. Just as important for my mother, it was close to the bathroom (but not so close as to be a nuisance). I tipped the bellman and the valet, and we took the elevator down to the lobby.

Once again, Detective Riordan was already waiting for us, and we ate lunch in the Burdick's dining room before climbing back into Oscar's cab and directing him to the Kalamazoo Police Department. He pulled out onto Main Street and, after waiting for the traffic policeman to wave him through, turned left onto Burdick and continued up only two blocks before stopping again.

I looked out the window. "Are we here?"

Oscar leaned down and pointed up at the building to our right, a large brick structure that had the look of a municipal building. Over the main doors hung a large sign reading MUFFLEY'S, which appeared to be a department store. "The station's on the third floor. The entrance is there." He gestured to an entryway on the side, over which was posted a much smaller sign reading KALAMAZOO POLICE DEPARTMENT.

Detective Riordan climbed out and paid Oscar before I could get to my wallet. I didn't protest. The detective needed his dignity. I asked the cabbie to wait for us, to which he agreed.

We climbed up to the third floor and walked into the police station, a shabby-looking affair with a scuffed counter, behind which sat an unsavory-looking policeman of about forty with a lopsided handlebar mustache and sweat stains under his arms. A few other policemen milled about in the small room, all in essentially the same uniforms worn by the Detroit police: navy blue wool with matching bobby hats and large brass badges in the shape of a star.

The man at the desk looked me over, head cocked, with an amused smile on his face. Pulling out his badge, Detective Riordan cleared his throat. The policeman glanced at it. "Detroit, eh? To what do we owe the pleasure to?" he asked, failing miserably in his attempt at sounding fancy.

"Could I speak with your chief, please?"

"About what?"

Detective Riordan's head tilted just the tiniest bit to the side, and he leveled his gaze at the man. "I'll discuss that with him."

The policeman glared at him for a moment. "What's your name?"

"Detective Thomas Riordan."

"And your companions are?"

"These ladies are my associates," he said.

The policeman stared at Detective Riordan a moment longer before spinning his chair around and strolling back to one of the doors. He knocked and waited a few seconds before opening the door and peeking in. "Chief?" he said in a remarkably polite fashion. "A Detective Riordan from Detroit would like to speak with you."

"Send him in," a man said in a no-nonsense tone.

The policeman waved us around the counter, and we walked to the office. The door had a brass sign on it that read CHARLES W. STRUBLE, CHIEF OF POLICE.

When we entered, the chief was standing behind his desk in the little office. He was surprisingly young and fit, in his early thirties, I judged, with a thick bottlebrush mustache over a protruding lower lip. He stepped out from behind his desk, maneuvered around the trash bin, and held his hand out to Detective Riordan. "Charles Struble."

The detective shook his hand. It looked to be a firm handshake, though without the manly posturing one sees at times. They were both confident men. "Thomas Riordan. Thank you for seeing us." Detective Riordan introduced my mother and me. Chief Struble seemed a bit puzzled as to why we were there but said nothing of it. He excused himself to get another chair from the front.

I didn't know what the office of Detroit's police chief looked like, but I was fairly certain it wasn't a windowless eight-by-eight plaster-walled room with a cracked ceiling and a broken light fixture.

The chief returned with a chair, and we all squeezed around the desk. "Now, Detective," Chief Struble said. "What can I do for you?"

"I have a case that may be related to a murder that took place in Kalamazoo in 1910. A Peter Hamlin was murdered near the state hospital. Do you know the case?"

"Yes, I heard someone had phoned about this—and I do remember it. Not many murder cases in Kalamazoo, thank goodness."

"I wish I could say the same about Detroit," Detective Riordan said with a grim smile.

"I'm sure you do."

"I'd like to look through the case file, if that's acceptable, and speak with the men who investigated."

"Fine by me," Chief Struble said. "We may have a difficult time getting ahold of the detectives. They've both retired and don't have a telephone, at least the last time I checked."

Detective Riordan nodded. "Could you give me their names and addresses, so we could speak to them in person?"

"Sure. Their names are Louis Lindsay and Walter Loeb. When Lindsay's wife died, Loeb moved in with him. As far as I know, they still live together. They're out in Schoolcraft, but it won't take you an hour to get there by automobile." He shrugged. "Maybe they can help you." He pushed back his chair and stood. "I'll get you the file and address. I'll be right back."

He left the room. Detective Riordan nodded to himself. I could see he was impressed with this man.

"This seems to be going well," I said.

"It is indeed," Detective Riordan replied. "You don't normally get this level of cooperation from small towns. From anyone, for that matter. They're usually more worried about protecting themselves than helping solve crimes."

"Protecting themselves?" I asked.

"Who knows what an outside investigation will turn up? Bribery? Incompetence? Most departments don't want to risk it."

"Is it really that big a problem?" I asked.

With a scowl, he nodded. "You can't get away from corruption."

I thought of my father, who had been embroiled in the most public bribery scandal in Detroit history, one that hadn't been exposed until after he'd been murdered. My tobacco cravings reached a fever pitch, so I excused myself and walked to the restroom. There was only one, and it was cramped and smelly. I locked the door, opened the window, and smoked a cigarette as quickly as I could, blowing the smoke outside.

When I returned to the office, Chief Struble was just walking in as well. "Both their pension checks go to this address," he said to Detective Riordan and handed him a piece of paper. Tapping the file against his hand, he glanced at my mother. "Perhaps the ladies would like to excuse themselves. Some of the photographs in here are not for the faint of heart."

Detective Riordan looked at me with his eyebrows arched.

"Mother?" I said.

She didn't seem to hear me. Her gaze was steadied on a citation on the wall with flowery script and a gold seal. I decided to leave well enough alone.

"I would like to see them, please," I said.

Detective Riordan nodded to Chief Struble, who met my eyes for a moment before walking around the desk and standing next to his chair. "I'll defer to you, Detective. Of course I can't let the file leave the office, but you're welcome to look through it. I'll stay, answer any questions you might have." He looked around with an apologetic shrug. "I wish I had better accommodations. They've started a new building for us, but in the meantime . . ."

"This is fine, Chief," Detective Riordan said. "We appreciate your hospitality."

"I hope you find what you're looking for, Detective. I'll help any way I can." He dropped into his seat and set the file on top of the desk. "This is a case that has bothered me for two years now. I'd love to clear it."

We huddled around the desk to look at the file. As soon as I saw the first picture, I asked my mother to leave, but again, she seemed oblivious. The photos of the murdered man nearly made me vomit. The police estimated he had been in the woods for two days before he was found, and scavengers had gotten a good start on him. His eyes were gone, one of his arms had been nearly gnawed off, and something had eaten away at his entrails. I forced myself to concentrate on the neck, which held a deep welt, similar to what I had seen on the man at Eloise Hospital.

I swallowed hard and glanced up at Chief Struble. "Was his neck broken?"

"I don't think so." He pulled a piece of paper from the file. "No, the cause of death was asphyxiation."

"Do you know if the man died there?" I asked. "In the woods?"

"No. I don't remember all the details, but the theory was that the killer moved him after death."

"How far was the body from the state hospital?" I asked.

"The woods begin at the edge of the hospital grounds and extend a mile or so, down to State High School. The body was perhaps a quarter mile from the hospital."

"Close enough that a man could have carried the body?" I asked.

He nodded. "A strong man, sure."

"How about family?" Detective Riordan asked. "Do Hamlin's people live in the area?"

"No," Chief Struble said. "I remember that was one of the biggest frustrations for the detectives. No family ever came forward."

Detective Riordan flipped through the papers and gave him a baffled glance. "There doesn't seem to be much here."

The chief shook his head. "I know. Obviously, it's against regulation, but I wonder if the detectives held on to some of the files."

"What's your take on them? The detectives, I mean."

"They solved their share of cases," Chief Struble replied, "but I can't say I ever trusted them. Both were fixtures long before I started working here, and you know how tight a police station is, Detective. They traded in favors, and everyone owed them for something, so everyone kept their mouths shut." He sat back and thought for a moment. "I remember Lindsay was scheduled to retire, but he hung on to work this case. Then one day, they both up and quit." He shook his head and sighed. "I could get you a court order for them to return the files."

Detective Riordan gave him a wry smile. "Somehow I don't think a court order will mean much to them."

Chief Struble smiled back at him. "Well, I wouldn't mind a bit if you decided to try more persuasive means. Let me give you my telephone number in case you want some help."

# Will

Francis jumped, as startled as I was. Then he howled, "Father!"

"What?" Dr. Beckwith called from the side of the house.

"John Doe!" Francis screamed.

I turned and sprinted for the front. Behind me, Francis threw open the kitchen door and ran in after me. "You do not belong here!" he screeched.

In a flash, I was at the front door. I grabbed the knob, twisted, and pulled. The door rattled in the jamb but didn't budge. I looked for a bolt to throw. Nothing. I needed a key.

Francis was within twenty feet of me now, charging into the foyer. His father was running down the hallway behind him. A fleeting thought of throwing myself through the picture window crossed my mind, but I knew how futile that would be. I might get out of the house, but I'd never get out of Eloise.

Now it was too late. Francis slammed into me, knocking me into the door. We went down together in a heap. I struggled to get to my feet with Francis clawing at me.

*Chuh-chick.* The unmistakable sound of a shotgun shell being racked into the chamber.

I stopped struggling and glanced up at Dr. Beckwith, who stared down at me behind two big barrels, his finger on the triggers.

I fell back to the floor.

Dr. Beckwith thrust the shotgun barrels up under my chin and pushed me against the door. "Breaking into my house," he snarled. "What the hell do you think you're doing?"

"What the hell!" Francis barked behind him, marching back and forth, fists and teeth clenched. "What the hell!"

"Please," I said. "Put down the gun. I won't fight you."

He pushed the barrels upward, forcing my head up as far as it would go.

"What the hell!" Francis said again.

Dr. Beckwith's head whipped around. "Francis! Shut up!"

"What the hell!"

"Your son is the Phantom," I gasped, "and I can prove it."

"Nonsense."

"See for yourself." I pointed down at the mask and lasso I had dropped when Francis hit me. Beckwith lowered the barrels of the shotgun so that they poked into my chest.

"What the hell!" Francis repeated again.

"Call the police, Francis," Beckwith said. "Now."

"What the hell!"

"Call the police. Do it."

"What the—"

"Shut up, Francis! I don't need to listen to you babble right now."

"Saying 'shut up' is rude, Father. We aren't supposed to—"

"Shut your goddamned mouth!" Dr. Beckwith shouted. "Call the police."

Clenching his teeth, Francis glared at his father for a moment before turning and stomping toward the kitchen. "Shut my goddamned mouth," he grumbled. "Shut my goddamned mouth. Shut your goddamned mouth."

"You see it's him, don't you?" I asked.

Beckwith's expression was a mix of sorrow and confusion. For a moment, I thought he was going to cry. Instead, he met my eyes again. "What are you . . . where did you get those?"

"They were under his mattress."

"No. You were going to plant them here."

My throat constricted, but I managed to say, "You know he's the Phantom."

The doorbell rang. Beckwith barely glanced that way before grabbing hold of my shirt and pushing me back into the hallway. He shoved me against the wall and jammed the gun barrel sideways against my neck, choking me. "No" he whispered, an inch from my face. "You were planting them here, weren't you?" He let up on the pressure so I could answer.

"You know better than that," I said.

"I would be well within my rights to kill you. A mad patient breaking into my home? No one would blame me."

"But you're not a killer. You want the murders to stop more than anyone."

He glanced down at my orderly outfit and shoved the cold shotgun barrel hard against my neck again. "Where did you get those clothes?"

"I stole them," I gasped.

The doorbell rang again.

Beckwith glanced that way before taking a step back and pointing the gun at me. "How did you get out of the straitjacket?"

"I'm Harry Houdini. Look, I wouldn't want to admit my son was doing this either—but you must stop him."

His forehead furrowed as he thought. Finally he said, "Who are you really?"

"My name is Will Anderson."

"Will Anderson? You're . . . you're Elizabeth Hume's friend."

"Yes."

"Damn that woman!"

The bell rang one more time. Beckwith pulled me into the parlor and shoved me toward the sofa. "Sit. There."

I did as he said. He unlocked the door, and Clarence hurried in. "What in heaven's name is—" He saw me and froze before turning back to Dr. Beckwith. "What's going on?"

Beckwith glanced at him and then looked back to me with a triumphant smile. "I've caught him. I've caught the Phantom!"


Morgan looked at Dr. Beckwith with a stupefied expression. Francis marched up the hallway, saying, "He was not here when—"

"That's enough," Dr. Beckwith barked.

Francis scowled. "But—"

"Francis!"

"You shut your goddamned mouth, Father! You shut it!"

"Francis," Dr. Beckwith warned. He raised his hand and took a step closer to his son.

Francis stood, quivering, his jaw locked tight, his eyes blazing at his father.

"Did you call the police?" Dr. Beckwith demanded.

Francis said nothing, didn't look capable of anything other than an eruption.

"Clarence, would you phone the police?"

"Certainly." Morgan turned and walked around the two Beckwith men to the hallway. When he was out of Dr. Beckwith's sight, he turned back and gave me a wide-eyed apologetic look.

"Francis, please go with Mr. Morgan and assist him." Dr. Beckwith's voice was back to its usual calm.

A few seconds later, Francis stomped down the hall after Clarence.

"Francis is right," I said, "and you know it. I wasn't here for the first four murders."

Beckwith held the shotgun in the crook of his elbow, though still pointed in my direction. "We had one last night, and you were most certainly here for that. I don't recall any others."

We both listened to Clarence talking to a police officer, reporting a break-in at the administrator's residence.

"Oh, come on," I said to Dr. Beckwith. "Don't you want this to end?"

"It will." His voice was quiet. "It will end."

Morgan returned to the parlor. "They'll be here in a minute." He sidled up to Dr. Beckwith. "Stephen? Are you sure this is the Phantom? John was in my class the other night and didn't seem—"

"His name is Will Anderson. He may or may not be the Phantom, but he came here today to frame my son. He brought the mask and rope with him."

"Mm. I . . . I don't know."

"No, you don't know. So be quiet."

Morgan bit his lip and turned away. An automobile squealed to a stop in front of the house. Seconds later, the door banged open, and two policemen hurried inside, guns drawn.

"Bring this one in," Beckwith said, pointing at me. "Solitary. I'll be over in a bit."

The cops took hold of my arms and pulled me outside, where they searched me, shackled me, and dragged me to an old blue Packard runabout. They squeezed me onto the seat between them, and the driver let out the clutch, squealing away from the curb. He slammed on the brakes, made a herky-jerky three-point U-turn, and drove to the Administration Building as fast as the rattletrap could go.

My hands were shaking. I clenched them into fists, welcoming the pain coursing through my right hand. I'd been in trouble before, but I saw no good end for this.

Would Elizabeth—would anyone—be able to find me now?

The cops dragged me out of the car and down the hallway that I'd been in only the night before. One of them unlocked a cell door, and the other shoved me onto the floor inside. I tucked my shoulder and tried to roll but still landed clumsily, and the manacle on my right wrist dug into the scar tissue there. I gasped from the pain. They slammed the door and locked it. I pushed myself up against the padded fabric on the wall and sat, catching my breath.

The room, about eight feet deep by six wide, reeked of urine and feces and was completely empty, not even a chamber pot. The padded walls appeared to have once been white but now were stained a mottled brown from piss and sweat, including, in a couple of spots, sweat stains in the shape of a man's back, a gap, and then a round spot where the back of his head lay in exactly the same position day after day. In a few spots, the walls were nearly black from what looked like old bloodstains, one back corner spattered as if someone had exploded against the wall. The ceiling was high, perhaps twelve feet, and a single naked lightbulb hung crooked from a pair of wires.

Hours passed. I expected Beckwith to appear at any time to pronounce my fate, but he didn't come. Exhaustion began to overtake me. I curled up on the floor, arms and legs tight to my body, and slept.

I woke to exactly the same scene. The cell—empty; the light—on. The only differences were that now I was freezing and my back and neck were stiff. I leaned against the wall again and thought.

Beckwith was keeping me off balance. He would know I expected to see him shortly after I was brought here. No doubt he wanted my anxiety level as high as possible for whatever came next. The only alternatives were that he couldn't decide what to do with me, or that he was simply going to leave me here, which I had to acknowledge as a possibility. As I told him, I didn't think he was a killer, but he had proven he would go to extraordinary lengths to protect himself and his son. Regardless, I had to take charge of my emotions. I was probably already lost, but I didn't have to give in.

Footsteps passed by my cell at random intervals, but no one stopped. I was getting extraordinarily thirsty. I'd been here for half a day—longer?—with nothing to drink or eat. I'd gotten used to not eating, but I needed water.

I stood near the door, and every time footsteps came near I pounded on it. "Hey! Hey! I need something to drink!"

Another hour or two passed. Still nothing. No one even acknowledged me with a "Shut up!" or a curse. I decided I'd better conserve my strength. I sat with my back against the door.

Some time later, the little eye-level door opened. "Mr. Anderson?" It was Dr. Beckwith.

I took my time standing and moving to where he could see me. "How about something to drink?"

"I'll see if I can arrange for that. First, though, you will need to answer a question. How much does Miss Hume know?"

"Everything."

He smiled. "Come now, Will. I know better than that. In fact, I've talked with her more recently than you have."

"She knows enough to put you and your son in prison for a very long time."

His smile faltered, though only for a second. "No one has proof of anything. I found you with the murder weapon as well as part of the disguise you used while killing Mr. Dill."

I just smiled back at him. "Go ahead. Prosecute me. Just get me something to drink first."

"I'm afraid prosecution isn't in my immediate plans. I'm more concerned at the moment with our problem of overcrowding."

"What?"

"Solitary confinement is getting awfully full." He partially turned away, as if he were having a hard time saying this. "Unfortunately, we're going to have to double up some prisoners."

I knew exactly what he had planned. My guts clenched, and my face flushed, but I was determined to show him nothing. "Look, you need to get your son help, and you need to protect these patients. They're under your care. Doesn't that mean anything to you?"

"Of course it does." He continued in a whisper. "You don't have any children, do you?"

I shook my head.

"Then you don't know what it's like. I love that boy."

"You know what I think?" I asked.

"I don't particularly care."

"If you loved Francis, you wouldn't let him be a murderer. What you love is your career and the power you have over people. A loving father doesn't do what you're doing. Your actions would only be explained by a severe case of narcissism."

He chuckled, seeming to have regained his equilibrium. "Dr. Doe is back to throwing around diagnoses, eh?"

"If you do anything to me, there is a Detroit police detective who will search this place with a fine-toothed comb. You can't save Francis now. Nor can you save your career. Let me go. Turn yourself in. Francis will receive treatment. Treatment he needs."

"I am the foremost expert on schizophrenia in the Midwest, perhaps the entire country."

"That may be, but you can't claim to be effectively treating your son."

After studying me a moment longer, he closed the little door. My stomach churned. Drops of sweat fell from my face onto the floor. I leaned against the wall, trying to prepare myself for what was coming next.

Still, a chill went through me when I heard a key rattle in the door lock. Two policemen stepped into the cell, took hold of my arms, and dragged me out. We started toward the door that led to the second set of cells.

I had no doubt where we were heading. "At least take the shackles off," I said. "Give me a chance."

They exchanged a grim expression but didn't say anything. It looked like they weren't completely on board with their boss's decision.

I tried again. "This is murder. You might as well shoot me yourselves."

One of them opened the door, and they hoisted me along to the end of the hallway.

"So that's it?" I asked. "You're just going to let him kill me? You know Francis Beckwith is the one killing the patients, don't you?"

Still no response from the cops. They stopped at the last cell. One of them peeked in through the eye-level door before twisting the key in the lock and pushing the door open. He and the other man shoved me to the floor inside and slammed the door shut, the key turning immediately.

"Well, looks like they got me a playmate."

I looked up. At the other end of the cell, leaning against the wall with his thick arms folded over his chest, stood the giant who thought he was Ty Cobb.

He grinned at me. "What'sa matter? Cat got your tongue?"

# Elizabeth

My mother remained quiet as we left the police station and got back into the cab. I feared she was on the verge of another of her spells. She sat next to me in the back of the automobile, staring straight ahead, as we drove through Kalamazoo and out into the country.

We were bouncing down a dirt road when Detective Riordan put his elbow on the back of his seat and turned toward us. "I will go in to talk to Lindsay and Loeb. You two will remain in the cab."

"Do you think bullying them will get you anywhere?" I asked. "If these men were police detectives, they presumably understand interrogation techniques, and you know they will be armed. No, your better chance is having us come in." I patted my mother on the knee, and she roused a bit. "Chief Struble said no family ever came forward. We will be Peter Hamlin's grieving mother and sister." I held the back of my hand to my forehead in a dramatic gesture. "We just *have* to discover what happened to our boy."

"Peter Hamlin?" My mother's eyes were wide, puzzled.

"The boy who was murdered," I told her.

"Murdered?" she said. "Oh, my."

I shared a glance with Detective Riordan. Disorientation was always the first sign of my mother's spells. She would soon begin confusing present and past. I only hoped the spell was short and didn't bring the anger that often accompanied her confusion.

"I think I should tell them who I am," he said. "They've probably already heard from one of the stooges at the station."

"That's fine. Do you want to be a family friend?"

He shrugged. "Why not?"

"All right. Mother and I were out of the country on tour with the ballet. I, of course, was the prima ballerina." I was a little large to be a ballerina, but I was daring him to mention it.

A little grin sneaked its way onto Detective Riordan's mouth. "Whatever you say, Elizabeth."

"We only just heard about my brother Peter's murder, and we will beg the detectives for any information they may have."

"All right," he said, "but let me do the talking."

I nodded. We continued on into the village of Schoolcraft. It was a quaint little town, all of about twenty square blocks. Oscar turned right on Cass Street and drove down to a small white one-story house set back from the road. He pulled onto the gravel shoulder and stopped, comparing the numbers on the house to those on the paper Detective Riordan had given him. "Here we are."

"Mother, are you all right to do this?" I asked.

"I'm fine, dear," she murmured.

I glanced at Detective Riordan. "Do you think there is *any* possibility of danger?"

"Elizabeth, these men were detectives. That doesn't mean they're honest or ethical, but what do they have to gain by hurting us? They'll know that all they have to say is they don't remember anything."

After a brief hesitation, I turned back to my mother. "If you would just come with us, dear. You don't have to say anything. Just leave it to us."

She nodded, though it looked like she was a million miles away.

"All right, Oscar," Detective Riordan said as he helped us out of the car. "Don't you get any ideas about leaving. We'll be back. This might take a while."

"Yes, sir," Oscar said with a smile. "I'll be waiting."

It was a strange neighborhood, with beautiful three-story Queen Annes side by side with these little houses that were mostly nice enough, but not what I was used to seeing next to such opulent homes. Lindsay and Loeb's house, however, was not one that was "nice enough."

Paint was peeling off the wooden exterior, and the little porch was crooked, leaning to the left.

The three of us walked up the lawn and climbed the cement steps. I was jittery, instinctively feeling that something was wrong here. Out of sight of the detective and my mother, I reached into my purse and touched my pistol, which gave me a bit of comfort.

Detective Riordan rang the bell. After a short pause, the curtain in the door twitched, and a short man with dark hair appeared behind it, scrutinizing us. His eyes lingered on me.

Finally he opened the door. He was in his fifties, young for retirement. His black hair was still thick and wavy. He wore a tight white undershirt, and his arms and chest bulged with muscles. He couldn't have been more than five feet tall, and he looked top-heavy, like he would tip over. He would have been handsome had it not been for a nose that was flattened and bent to the left. He sneered at us. "Don't want none, gave at the office, and I sure as hell don't talk to Mormons or Seven-Day Adventurers."

Detective Riordan pulled out his badge and introduced himself.

The man didn't look at all surprised to see him, though he said, "What's a Dee-troit cop want with me?"

"Are you Lindsay or Loeb?" Detective Riordan asked.

He said he was Lindsay. Detective Riordan explained to him why we were there before introducing my mother and me as Peter Hamlin's mother and sister.

"Sister, eh?" he asked, cutting his eyes to me.

I smiled and tried not to be visibly disgusted.

"Could we come in for a minute?" Detective Riordan asked.

Lindsay eyed us all before opening the door. "Yeah, why not?"

My mother and I walked into the living room, followed by the men. The house was dark, all the curtains closed. A pair of wooden chairs sat against the wall. A bottle of what looked to be whiskey sat on the end table next to the one upholstered chair, a pink and green floral-patterned disaster. Lindsay sat in it and looked up at us. "Now, what do you want?"

Detective Riordan removed his hat and held it in his hand. He showed my mother and me to the chairs and stood next to us. "Is Detective Loeb here?"

"Nah." Lindsay was nonchalant. "He's visiting his mother."

"Is that right." Riordan didn't say it as a question. He cocked his head at Lindsay. The air between them crackled with tension. "Well, Mr. Lindsay, I was hoping you could help us with some files from the Hamlin murder that have gone missing. I know how it is, with all the paperwork, how some of it can end up on a table somewhere. Have you come across anything like that?"

"Nope."

I put a pleading tone in my voice. "Please, Mr. Lindsay. Even if we can't get to the bottom of this, we'd like to at least have our friend here go through the file. It will help to end my mother's suffering. Please, sir."

My mother gave me a puzzled glance but, fortunately, said nothing.

"I'd like to help you, miss." He leaned forward in his chair. "I really would. But if any files have disappeared, they were taken by someone else. I'd guess it was like your friend here said. Somebody put some of the papers down somewheres, and they ended up getting dumped. Happens all the time."

"Maybe if you just took a quick look," I said. "I would appreciate it so much."

His mouth puckered into a sour expression. He pushed himself to his feet with what looked like a great deal of effort. "I don't have nothing."

Detective Riordan fit his hat onto his head. "Thank you for your time, Mr. Lindsay. I hope you don't mind if we get in touch again. You wouldn't happen to have a telephone, would you?"

"Nah." He smiled. "I talked to way too many people I didn't want to when I was with the cops. I'm what you might call a solitary type."

"Is Mr. Loeb the same?" I asked.

"Yeah. As a matter of fact, he is." He gestured toward the front door. "Now, if you don't mind? I got some stuff to catch up on."

Detective Riordan smiled. "We'll be in touch."

"That's fine," Lindsay said, smiling at me. "Come by anytime."

Detective Riordan directed Oscar to a sweets shop he'd seen in the village. I had a hankering for some chocolate ice cream, but I didn't hold out much hope they would have ice cream in August. Unfortunately, my suspicions were correct.

"December," the man behind the counter said. "Maybe January."

Instead, we had sodas. After bringing a chocolate soda out to Oscar, we sat under a black-and-white-striped umbrella at a small iron table on the sidewalk. It was nearly five o'clock, and the heat hadn't abated. The big thermometer on the wall of the building next to us showed eighty-eight degrees. Detective Riordan slung his suit coat over the back of his chair and sat in front of his strawberry soda. My mother hadn't wanted to order anything, or perhaps wasn't sure what we were doing, but I ordered us both chocolate sodas, for which Detective Riordan insisted on paying.

I used my handkerchief to mop the perspiration from my forehead. "Did you find it odd that he called himself solitary when he lives with another man?"

Detective Riordan nodded. "I don't think he was happy with himself for saying that. I think we should go back and talk to the neighbors, see if Loeb does live there. If Lindsay's just collecting the other man's pension, we'd have tremendous leverage. But I thought we should make ourselves scarce for a little while. I'd bet he's peeking out his windows right now, looking for us."

Picturing him, I laughed. "Good idea. There's something off with Mr. Lindsay, besides the fact that he's an old lecher."

"Elizabeth," my mother said, "I want to go home."

"We will, Mother. Tomorrow, I promise." I put my hand on her arm. "We just have a few more things to take care of here."

"I don't want to wait. I want to go home."

Detective Riordan gave me a sympathetic grimace.

"Just as soon as we can, dear," I said. "I promise."

"I want . . ." Her words just melted away as she looked down at her untouched soda.

I saw this coming, but what was I supposed to do? There was nothing I could do with her, short of getting on a train for Detroit, hoping she didn't explode. I couldn't do that yet. "We'll leave tomorrow, Mother. I need you to be strong for me until then."

She stared down at the bubbly brown liquid in her glass.

I leaned in toward Detective Riordan. "Do you think we could leave her with Oscar while we talk with the neighbors?"

"Maybe. I'll ask him." He pushed back his chair, the metal legs scraping against the cement, and walked over to the cab. A minute later, the detective returned with Oscar's empty glass. "He said he would be happy to watch her."

"Do you think I need to be worried about him?"

Detective Riordan gave me a crooked grin. "Not after what I told him I'd do if she wasn't in perfect form when we come back."

"All right. Thank you." I helped my mother up, and we returned her to the automobile. She went without protest and sat in the back. Oscar climbed into the jump seat. As we walked away, I heard him trying to engage her in conversation. I turned to Detective Riordan. "Let's hurry."

We strode down the block to the home directly behind Lindsay's, a neat frame one-story, a lovely rosebush in front bursting with red flowers. An old slip of a woman enveloped in a flowery housecoat answered the door. She introduced herself as Mrs. Penny and asked us in for tea. She must have been ninety years old. We had only a couple of hours of daylight left, and I wondered if we were wasting our time. She quickly proved me wrong.

She brought the tea into the parlor, where Detective Riordan and I sat on a yellow velvet sofa. The tray shook in her hands. I jumped up and helped her set it on the coffee table, saying, "Here, let me get it, dear." She nodded, and I poured tea for each of us. A cool breeze blew through the side windows, fluttering the curtains.

"Mrs. Penny," Detective Riordan said, "what can you tell us about your neighbor, Mr. Lindsay?"

I handed her a cup and saucer, which trembled in her hand. "Oh, Mr. Lindsay," she said, shaking her head. "He's let that house go." The s-sounds whistled through the gaps in her teeth. She leaned in toward the detective. "You should see his backyard. Disgraceful."

"Does he live alone?" Detective Riordan took a sip from the flowered china cup that looked so out of place in his large callused hands.

"Yes. That other man, Mr. Loeb! Oh, I didn't like him. Rude! Just a mean, mean man."

"How long has he been gone, Mrs. Penny?"

"Hmm." She picked up her teacup with both hands to control the trembling and had a sip. "A year. Maybe longer." She laughed, a breathy whisper. "Yes, longer. Time has gotten away from me a bit, you see. Don't know why I'm still here, tell you the truth."

"Have you noticed anything suspicious about Mr. Lindsay?"

"I thought I did, but our constable told me I was imagining things."

"What did you think you saw?"

"One night, it was in the spring, I remember, this would have been last year. It was a lovely night, the first night I decided to leave my bedroom windows open. Anywho, I heard shoveling in the backyard. It was keeping me awake, but it was one of those nights, you know, after a long winter, that you just want to feel the breeze. I didn't want to close the windows, and anyway, I thought, why in blazes is someone digging up their yard in the middle of the night?" She took another sip of her tea. "I got up out of bed and looked outside. Mr. Lindsay, I'm sure it was him on account of he's such a midget." She cackled again. "He was digging in his backyard, and I would have sworn I saw him roll something big into the hole."

"How big?" Detective Riordan asked.

"I'm sure my eyes were playing tricks on me," she replied.

"How big did you think it was?"

Her eyes widened as she thought about the importance of what she'd seen. Leaning in, she whispered, "About the size of a man."

The next morning, Mrs. Penny had called the constable, who talked to Lindsay and found that he'd just planted a garden in the backyard. The constable told her she was imagining things and to mind her own business.

Detective Riordan asked her if she had seen Mr. Loeb after that, to which she replied, "Not that I remember." Her hand went up to her mouth. "Do you think . . ."

"I don't want to speculate, but you may have been right. Thank you, Mrs. Penny, I appreciate your time." He set the cup and saucer down on the coffee table, looking relieved to no longer have to worry about crushing them. "Could you tell me where we would find the nearest telegraph station?"

She wouldn't hear of us leaving to send a telegraph, and insisted that Detective Riordan use her telephone, even when he cautioned her that his call would be to Kalamazoo.

Carrying the tray, I followed them into the kitchen. The telephone was on the counter, with a large black wire running across the white tile on the wall behind her sink. Detective Riordan pulled out the piece of paper with Chief Struble's telephone number, picked up the telephone, and listened for a second before asking someone to get off the line, telling the caller he had official police business. After a very brief argument, he relayed Chief Struble's number to the operator and waited. Mrs. Penny hovered nearby, hoping, I'm sure, to have a story to tell. Detective Riordan had to repeat the number twice, but finally someone answered the phone. He asked for the chief and then waited a bit longer.

"Chief, this is Thomas Riordan. I have reason to believe that Louis Lindsay killed Walter Loeb and buried him in the backyard of his house."

He listened for a moment before repeating the information we'd gotten from Mrs. Penny. After another short pause, he said, "Yes, I think she's reliable." He winked at the old woman, who ducked her head, smiling. They made arrangements for Chief Struble to meet us in front of the sweets shop, and then we readied ourselves to leave. Detective Riordan and I both thanked Mrs. Penny for her help, and he warned her to stay away from her windows. I slipped a dollar bill onto the tea tray to compensate her for the telephone call, and we walked back to the cab.

Oscar and my mother were sitting quietly in the back. He smiled when he saw us. "Are you ready to go?"

Detective Riordan leaned in the back window. "We're going to be here for a while, Oscar. There'll be a good tip in this, I promise you."

The cabbie nodded his thanks. I climbed in and sat next to my mother. She didn't seem to notice. "Mother?"

Her head turned toward me, but she remained silent. I squeezed her hand. We waited like that until Chief Struble drove up in a new Model T roadster, dark blue with black fenders. He and Detective Riordan conferred for a few minutes, so close together that the brim of the detective's fedora was touching the chief's derby. A minute later, Detective Riordan returned to the cab. "Elizabeth, Chief Struble and I are going to talk to Lindsay. The chief doesn't want to involve the local police, even though he's outside his jurisdiction. We need to go in fast and quiet." He looked out toward Chief Struble and then back to me. "If Mrs. Penny's story is true, the constable might be in cahoots with

Lindsay. You and your mother will stay here with Oscar and wait for us. I'll be back for you within the hour."

I wasn't happy about being left out of the action, but I understood. They were both trained officers of the law. They climbed into the Model T, and Chief Struble swung it around in a U-turn and headed down Cass. We sat and waited.

Oscar and I made small talk. My mother still hadn't said anything, but I could see her hands trembling. She was starting to get agitated. Time passed. I checked my watch. It had been almost fifty minutes since they left. The drive was less than one minute. It seemed to me they were taking a long time, but I decided to wait a bit longer. Not only had Detective Riordan told me it might be an hour, but one of my mother's spells had begun.

She turned to me and said, "Why, Theo, I didn't know you were coming to visit!"

"Theo" was my mother's sister, Theodora, who had passed on.

"Mother," I began.

"Mother? Is Mother here, too? What a nice surprise."

I decided to play along. "Yes, we just need to wait here for a bit. Mother will be joining us. In fact, I'm going to get her right now."

"Should I come along?"

"No, this nice man"—I pointed to Oscar—"needs your help to watch the automobile. I won't be gone long. Just sit tight." I patted her knee. "I'll be right back."

She nodded and went back to looking out the window at the traffic passing by. Here, in the country, were many more horses and wagons than motorcars or even carriages. That and the little village must have helped with her delusion that she was someplace in her past.

I climbed down to where Oscar was sitting and whispered, "I'm going to check on the men. Don't let her out of the cab."

"Yes, ma'am," he said.

I took one last look at my mother, who seemed contented, and then strode down the sidewalk toward Cass Street. Turning up the road, I saw Chief Struble's automobile parked on the shoulder a few houses down from Lindsay's. I checked in my purse to be sure my pistol was loaded and the safety was on, and then picked up my skirts and ran.

I stopped at the edge of Lindsay's property. The curtains were still all drawn. It was silent other than the traffic sounds coming from Grand Street behind me and the rumbling of a train off in the distance. I crept up to the side of the house and peered through the curtains at a bedroom with an unmade bed and a whiskey bottle on the nightstand. Not surprising. I couldn't see anyone, though I thought I could make out the buzz of conversation inside the house. I tiptoed around back and saw that the next room was also a bedroom, also unoccupied. I continued along the house and looked in through one of the back door's little windows. No one was visible in the kitchen or hallway, though the sound of conversation was louder.

I hurried down to the next window. The curtains, dark and thick, were pulled tight. I listened. A man—Lindsay—was talking.

"—ask you one more time. Where are they?"

No response.

I heard a thud, like a piece of wood striking a rock, followed by a guttural grunt.

"This could all be over for you. Just tell me where they are."

No response.

My mind raced. I crept around the corner of the house and looked into the next window. The curtain was also closed, but with a small gap in the middle. It was another bedroom. Lindsay stood, breathing heavily, a baseball bat held loosely in his hand. I could just see Chief Struble's jacket. He was lying on the floor. I couldn't see Detective Riordan, but it seemed clear that Lindsay had taken both of them prisoner. He was probably trying to get them to divulge the location of my mother and me. He expected to have a full garden by the end of the night.

I pulled the gun from my purse. Shoot him? I could see him well enough. He wasn't fifteen feet away. I couldn't miss—but . . . was the situation as I thought it to be?

Lindsay gripped the bat with both hands and took a big swing. It connected with something, sending a shock up his arm. A man grunted, and another tried to talk, though it was muffled. It sounded like Chief Struble.

Lindsay was beating Detective Riordan. I switched off the safety and leveled the pistol at Lindsay through the crack between the curtains. With no hesitation, I pulled the trigger. The gun went off with a loud crack and the shattering of glass. I reached in through the window and jerked the curtain open, the gun still pointed toward Lindsay.

Except now he sat against the wall, a hole through his cheek. His eyes were closed, and a smear of blood and gray matter slid down the wall behind him.

# Will

I pushed myself to my feet, keeping my eyes on Ty, trying to figure out how to fight with my wrists and ankles shackled together. My only hope was to somehow wrap a chain around his neck and choke him. I wasn't going down without a fight.

He stood there, leaning against the wall, smiling at me. "That's a mighty nice set a duds you got there. I'da thought you was one a them, I didn't know better."

I just watched him.

"What'samatter, pahdna?"

I didn't reply. My knees were bent, and I was leaning over slightly at the waist. I held the chain loosely in my left hand, ready for his attack.

He slid down the wall until he was seated and stuck his legs out in front of him. "Take a load off. We might be here a while."

"I'll stand, thanks." I stayed near the door, eyeing him.

"You know, I hear they gonna let niggers into the league one day. What you think of that?"

"I don't know." Negroes had moved from slavery to a remarkable amount of freedom in the last fifty years, but it seemed a stretch they'd be playing baseball with white men anytime soon.

"I got nothin' against 'em, understand," Ty said. "Some a them boys can play. Just don't seem right, though." He shook his head.

After a few moments, I said, "So . . . you're not going to kill me?"

He looked surprised. "Why wouldja think that? I saved your ass from that big sumbitch. He was getting ready to bust ya one."

"You were protecting me?"

He nodded. "Got to say, ain't many men stand up to me, 'specially one all busted up and such. I admire your stones. 'Sides"—he winked at me—"you might choke me with that chain."

I thought to placate him. He didn't seem predisposed to murdering me, and I wanted to keep it that way. "What's the rest of the season look like for the Tigers?"

With a wicked smile, he looked at me from under his brow. "Tell you somethin'?"

I shrugged. "Sure." I sat on the cold concrete with my back against the door.

"I ain't Ty Cobb."

"Yeah, I kind of knew that. I've seen the real one."

"Now that's one nasty sumbitch," Ty said.

"Would you tell me your real name?"

He glanced up at the eye-level door before whispering, "Roper. Joe Roper."

"Why are you pretending to be Ty Cobb?"

"My brothers is lookin' for me. You think I'm crazy? Just hope you don't see them."

"Why don't you want to see your brothers?"

Joe shook his head. "I kilt their daddy."

"That would be . . . your daddy, too?"

"Yup. The old bastard done teached me one thing. You don't let nobody disrespect you. He taught me that by whippin' my ass ever' time I mouthed off to him, and I did that plenty. Last year I couldn't take it no more and I kilt him. If they find me . . . well, let's just say some fur's gonna fly. I don' wanna kill them, too. So"—he spread his hands in front of him—"this here's my vacation spot."

We sat in a companionable silence for a few minutes before, with his eyes on the door, he whispered, "Got sumpin' for ya. I think you can use it more'n me." He was palming something.

"What?"

He nodded me over. I crawled to him and sat at his side. He dwarfed me in every respect. Even his head was half again the size of mine. He slid his hand over toward me. Something scraped on the floor. "I don't think they want me dead. You—they ain't no doubt." He lifted his hand to show me a piece of angle iron about six inches long by an inch wide. One end had been filed down to a sharp point. "Got me a piece of the window frame from my room 'fore they stuck me in here. Put it in your shoe."

"Thanks, but I think I'll just put it in my pocket."

"No. They gonna search you again. You got to hide it."

I picked up the knife and slid it into my shoe. It stuck out a few inches. The white trousers were too short to cover it.

"No," he said. "You got to take it off. Stick it down the side. It'll hurt, but it'll be there when you need it."

I unlaced my shoe, slipped it off and shoved the piece of iron in, then tried to slide my foot in with it. Not surprisingly, it didn't fit.

"Get that sumbitch on," he said. "'Less you wanna shove it up your ass."

I winced at the thought, loosened the laces, and crammed my foot in the shoe. The knife dug into my skin, and I tried a few positions before I finally got it so I could stand the pain.

"Go on back over there," Joe said, "'fore they come back and think we're a coupla nancies."

I scooted away until I was against the opposite wall again. He told me about his life. He'd been brought up in a hardscrabble backwoods Georgia town, picked cotton from the time he was three, and spent the last year on the road, always staying one step ahead of his brothers, who had vowed to avenge the murder of their father.

The eye-level door opened and closed a few times over the hours, but no one came in, and no one brought us food or drink.

"How long has it been since you had food or water?" I asked him.

"Just 'fore they hauled you in here."

"Huh." My throat was so parched I could hardly swallow. "I think they're going to kill me any way they can. I guess since you let them down, thirst is the next method."

"Well, if it gets to it, you can drink my piss," Joe said. "It won't kill ya." The offer was made with complete sincerity.

"Thanks," I croaked. "Hopefully it won't get to that."

I finally remembered that Robert had been in the cell next door. I felt like slapping myself. He was why I was here in the first place, and I'd been jabbering with Joe and hadn't even thought of Robert. I explained to Joe that I knew the man in the next cell, then stood and leaned against the adjoining wall. "Robert! Can you hear me?"

Nothing.

I shouted louder. "Robert? Are you there?"

"Who's that?" I heard the voice through the wall.

"It's Will Anderson," I yelled back. "Elizabeth's friend. I'm going to get you out of there."

"When?" he shouted.

"I . . . I don't know yet. Just be ready."

"'I don't know' is not an acceptable answer," he shouted back indignantly.

"Well then, how about tomorrow?" I yelled.

"That would be acceptable," he shouted.

"I'll see you then," I said.

When I turned back, Joe was chuckling to himself. "Crazy bastards. This place cracks me up."

"Yes," I agreed with a straight face. "There are some crazy men in here."

Footsteps scuffled in the hallway and stopped outside our door. Men spoke in low voices, too low for me to make out the words. A key turned in the lock, and the door swung inward. Four cops swarmed in. The first two grabbed me while the others kept their pistols leveled at Joe, who sat there grinning at them. They dragged me out of the room and down the hall, where they gagged me with a handkerchief, tied my hands behind me, and searched me. As Joe had suggested, they checked my pockets but stayed away from my shoes. I still had the knife when they pulled me out the back door.

It was dark out. *It must be around midnight,* I thought. The cool of the night hit my sweat-slicked body. They threw me in the back of a wagon, and both men climbed up with me. Another was at the reins. He snapped them, and the wagon started up with a jerk.

I tried to control my breathing and my heart. Both were racing. This was a trip from which I would not likely return. These men would kill me and bury me in an unmarked grave in their cemetery, where I could lie forever, no one the wiser.

# Elizabeth

I stood there in a daze watching the baseball bat roll across the floor. The scene was more horrific than anything I had ever imagined. Thomas's wrists were chained to a hook anchored in the ceiling, and the toes of his boots just touched the floor. His face was so bloody I couldn't see the wounds. Chief Struble lay on his stomach, hogtied wrists to ankles, a handkerchief stuffed in his mouth and tied around his head. Lindsay sat against the wall splay-footed.

I probably stood there motionless for only a few seconds, but time slowed down. The bat rolled to Thomas's boot, where it stopped, shiny with blood. Chief Struble was shouting, but the handkerchief obscured his words. Lindsay just lay there dead, what was left of his miserable life leaking out onto the floor around him.

My brain started working again. I ran around to the back, smashed a pane of glass in the door, and unlocked it. I threw the door open and sprinted down the hall to the bedroom, where I untied Chief Struble while watching Thomas. His eyes were closed, and he wasn't moving.

Lindsay had tied a dozen knots, and my hands were shaking too much to get them loose. I ran back to the kitchen, pulled a sharp knife from a drawer, and used it to cut the rope and free the chief. I glanced at Lindsay, sitting not five feet from me. His mouth was open, and a small line of blood, like drool, ran down his chin, stretching like a string to his white undershirt.

Chief Struble jumped to his feet, and together we lowered Thomas to the floor. I felt his chest. His heart was beating, and he was breathing. The chief took hold of my arm. "Go to a neighbor's house. Have them get a doctor here. Right away."

I stood and, still feeling shaky, hurried to the front of the house, unlocked the door, and ran directly across the street to a large Queen Anne. A servant answered the door, a Scandinavian woman without much English, but she got the gist of what I was saying. She let me in, and the gentleman of the house phoned a doctor. He came back to Lindsay's house with me and helped us attend to Thomas, who had come around, though he was still lying on the floor.

I knelt down next to him. "How are you?"

"Oh, peachy," he whispered and gave me a little smile through swollen lips. He grimaced, and I could see that there was something badly wrong with him. "Chief told me," he whispered, ". . . what you did . . . Thanks."

"The doctor's on his way." Tears ran down my face.

He closed his eyes, but a second later they popped back open. His hand felt around for mine. I clasped it with both my hands.

"Tell Anna," he whispered, "I . . . I love her." His eyes closed again.

I held on to his hand and leaned down so I could speak into his ear. "You're going to be all right, Thomas," I whispered. "Just hang on."

Finally the doctor arrived. After one quick look, he told the neighbor to phone for an ambulance and then went to work on Thomas, who was now unconscious. I stood and watched the doctor, who bandaged the cuts on the detective's face and examined his torso.

He looked up at Chief Struble. "He's got some broken ribs, likely has some internal bleeding. I don't know how extensive the damage is. The ambulance will be here soon, and we'll get him to the hospital."

All of a sudden, I remembered my mother. She and Oscar were still waiting for us. I looked at my watch. I'd been gone more than an hour. "Where will you be taking him?" I asked.

"Franklin Memorial in Vicksburg. It's only a few miles away."

"All right. I'll meet you there."

A motorcar squealed to a stop in front of the house. I got up and hurried to the door. A pair of firemen ran toward me, carrying a stretcher.

I opened the door and headed for the back again. "It's this way."

They followed me into the room and, with all of us helping, lifted Thomas onto the stretcher. I walked alongside him, holding his hand. When they loaded him into the back of the ambulance, I called, "I'll see you in a few minutes." One of the men stayed in the back with him while the other slammed the door shut, ran around to the driver's side, and drove off. I watched the ambulance go, drained, feeling like I had just run a marathon. The doctor climbed into his automobile and followed behind.

Chief Struble arranged with the neighbor to keep an eye on Lindsay's house until the marshal arrived, and then we jumped into his Model T. He dropped me off by the taxi. I leaned in the window and told Oscar we had to follow the chief's automobile. The cabbie climbed out of the jump seat and ran to the front of the motorcar, where he turned the crank and started the engine, then pulled out his lighter.

I noticed for the first time the long shadows cast over the street, and the light that had dimmed to early dusk. Oscar lit the wicks on the headlamps. I did the same for the taillamps, and we both jumped into the car.

"Theo!" my mother exclaimed. "What happened?"

Chief Struble drove off, and Oscar stepped on the gas. The engine knocked and pinged, but we sped toward the hospital.

I took a deep breath and looked at my mother. "A man's been hurt. He—" I stopped. "He was beaten. With a baseball bat."

"Oh, my goodness," she said.

Oscar crossed himself.

"And . . . I shot the man who did it." It hit me full in the face. I had just killed another man. My hands began to shake as the image of Lindsay's mouth, the line of blood spilling out, branded itself into my mind again.

"You shot him?" My mother gripped my hand. "Is he . . . ?"

"Yes."

"He's dead?"

I nodded, not trusting my ability to speak.

"Oh, my Lord, Theo. You killed a man?"

"It was the only way to stop him. He would have killed Thomas."

"Are you all right?" She turned me toward her and looked into my eyes, her face full of love and concern. She may not have known who I was, but all the same I was looking at the face I'd seen after I skinned my knee, the face I'd seen after my first boyfriend had found another girl, the face I'd seen after I woke to discover I'd almost killed myself aborting Will's child.

She was still my mother. I burst into tears and fell into her arms.


Had there not been a sign in front, I would have thought Franklin Memorial Hospital was nothing more than a nice house. It was a redbrick two-story, nicely kept, with huge oak trees gracing the yard. Flood lamps lit the arched sign and the grounds around the building.

Chief Struble was waiting in the lobby when we arrived. He hurried up to my mother and me. "He's in the operating room. Last I knew they were still waiting for the surgeon."

"How was he doing?" I asked.

"He was still unconscious, but he's a tough man. He'll make it."

"I hope you're right," I said. We slumped onto three of the wooden chairs in the lobby.

"They said they'd let me know as soon as they had word," he said.

I nodded. My mother bowed her head, clasped her hands together, and closed her eyes. She began mouthing a prayer. Chief Struble left to use the telephone. I was impatient, fidgeting, looking at magazines, but my mother remained at her prayers. After a few minutes, Chief Struble returned and we continued our vigil.

We hadn't been there an hour when a policeman walked in, conferred with the nurse at the desk, and walked over to us. He was a very young man with a protruding Adam's apple and a long beaked nose. "Are you Charles Struble and Elizabeth Hume?" His brass badge read VILLAGE OF SCHOOLCRAFT and CONSTABLE.

"Yes," we replied.

"You've got to come with me."

"What do you need us for?" the chief said.

"A man's been killed. You were there. We need your statements."

"Well, listen," Chief Struble said. "You can take our statements here. That dead man almost killed a police detective who is undergoing an operation right now. We still don't know if he's going to make it."

"I'm sorry, sir," the young man said, looking away. "I've got orders."

"Oh, Lord," Chief Struble said. "All right. Will you bring us back here after?"

"I'm sure we can do that," he replied.

"I'll need to bring my mother," I said.

"She can't ride in my wagon."

"Wagon?"

"Yeah, wagon." His mouth twisted to the side as he said it. He was embarrassed.

"Listen, son," Chief Struble said. "We've got perfectly good motorcars here that will save us a lot of time. Why don't you let us drive to the station?"

"I've got orders," he said again.

"But don't you think—"

"I don't get paid to think. I follow orders." His hand slowly rose until it rested on the butt of his pistol. "Is this going to be a problem?"

"Good Lord, boy—" Chief Struble began.

The constable pulled the pistol from his belt. "Hand over any weapons. Now." His eyes shone. He was scared to death.

"Do it," I said. "Give him your gun. We don't need anyone else killed." I took my pistol from my purse and handed it, butt first, to the boy.

He took it. The chief followed my lead. "Mother," I said, "have Oscar drive you to the Schoolcraft police station."

"No, dear," she said with a beatific smile. "I'll tell him to come inside. We'll wait here for now. I'm praying for this man. And for you."

"Thank you."

The constable walked us out to a Black Maria, of all things, as if we were common criminals. The vehicle was essentially a delivery wagon, except that the passenger compartment was painted black and had barred windows. A pair of black horses stood at the front.

Oscar, sitting in the cab, gave us a puzzled look.

"Go in with my mother!" I shouted. "Stay here! And stay with her!"

"Yes, ma'am," he said, fumbling to open the door.

The boy opened the back door of the wagon. "Inside."

Chief Struble shook his head but complied. I followed him in. We took seats on the wooden benches on either side. Night had fallen, and the only light was that that bled in through the barred windows on the sides and back. The wagon rocked as the boy climbed on and then started up with a jerk, heading back toward Schoolcraft. We drove through the village of Vicksburg. Most of the inhabitants had gone home for the night, but a few gawkers remained, trying to see who was in the wagon so as to have some good gossip for the morning. The streetlamps were bright here, and I hoped that no one recognized Chief Struble.

He pointed to a row of iron rings screwed into the floor of the wagon. "I suppose we should be grateful he didn't chain us up."

"I'm having a hard time feeling grateful for much of anything right now."

He sat back and smiled at me. "Well, I'm grateful you came looking for us."

"What happened?"

"Thomas and I split up. I went around back, and he went to the front. The back door was unlocked, so I sneaked in, only to have Lindsay's gun at my temple. He was waiting for me." Even though the night was chilly, Chief Struble wiped his brow with his handkerchief. "By the time Thomas kicked the door in, Lindsay already had me tied up and was lying in wait for him. We never had a chance."

The lights dimmed, and the wagon tipped down onto a dirt road.

I thought back to what Lindsay had been saying when I shot him. "What was Lindsay asking Thomas when I . . . when I got there?"

"He wanted to know where you and your mother had gone. You two were loose ends. Once he killed us, he was going to kill you, too."

Thinking about it, I was incredulous. "Was this over a pension? He killed his partner and was going to kill all of us over a few dollars a month?"

"Two of them would make the difference between poverty and living decently. Still . . ." He shook his head. "It doesn't seem like enough, does it?"

"You said you didn't think they were ethical, but it didn't sound like you thought they were out-and-out criminal."

"I guess I was wrong."

I just couldn't comprehend this. "Yes, but . . ."

"But what?"

"I agree with you. It doesn't seem like enough."

The marshal's office was on the first floor of the village hall, just outside the downtown area. It was a brick building, which, though only two stories, had been designed to emulate the great city halls. A small granite cupola with a belfry rose from the center. Most of the windows were dark.

The boy brought us inside. The station was actually nicer than the one in Kalamazoo, though only by a little. The tiny lobby had a plank floor with half a dozen chairs lined up against the wall. A long counter separated that from a pair of cells on either side of the back. One of them held two men, who eyed us as we walked in.

A huge man, in all directions, dressed in a pair of dungarees and a red flannel shirt, sat at a desk in the back. He looked like a giant sunburned orangutan, with a flat face and nose, bright red and peeling.

Pushing himself to his feet, he lumbered over to us as the boy walked us around the counter. "Chief Struble." The big man held out his hand, and the chief shook it.

"I'm glad you're here, Marshal," the chief said to him and gestured to the boy. "I'm sure this was a mistake."

"Well, now, not so fast," the man said. "We've got to get some questions answered."

"Of course, but can we make this quick? There's a Detroit detective over at Franklin who that good-for-nothing Lindsay may have killed."

"First you tell me what happened."

"Fine," Chief Struble said. "Let's just get to it." He pointed toward me. "This is Elizabeth Hume. She was working with Detective Riordan, the man Lindsay beat."

"Ma'am." The huge man nodded at me. "I'm Phillip Magnan, Schoolcraft marshal. We'll make this as quick as possible. First I'm going to talk to the chief, then I'm going to ask you some questions."

"Fine." I just wanted to get it over with. I needed to get back to my mother . . . and Thomas.

"Billy," he said, "just let her sit out here."

"Sure thing, Marshal," the boy replied.

I took a seat in the lobby while Marshal Magnan took Chief Struble into a room in the back. The boy settled in behind a desk, and the men in the cell lay down on the benches. A train went past, close by, blowing its whistle repeatedly. I wondered how anyone slept in this town.

After twenty minutes or so, the marshal and the chief walked out, and Marshal Magnan asked me to come back. I passed Chief Struble on the way. "Just tell him what happened, Elizabeth," he said. "You'll be fine."

"Call everybody, Billy," Marshal Magnan said. "We got some digging to do, and I'd like to get it done before everybody in town knows about it."

"Yes, sir." The boy picked up the telephone.

I followed the marshal into his office, again a little nicer than Chief

Struble's, which I thought must really irritate him. Kalamazoo was a real city, with tens of thousands of citizens, while Schoolcraft probably didn't have five hundred residents.

The marshal asked me to explain what happened, and I told him of our initial visit to Lindsay's and my return, including shooting him. He asked a few questions but was largely content to let me talk.

"All right," he said when I finished, "I think that will do for now."

"Thank you. Can we please go back to the hospital? My mother—"

"Sorry, miss," he said. "We need you here just a bit longer. See, we need to corroborate your story. Right now, what I've got is a man shot in the head in my village. I need to be sure what you've told me is true."

"Why would we lie about this?"

He smiled. "I don't know, miss. That's why we need to be sure. Look at it from my point of view—how can I let someone who just killed one of our citizens walk out of here until I know exactly what happened?"

"Chief Struble told you the same thing I did, right?"

"He did."

"Then I don't understand why—"

He leaned forward, put his palms on the desk, and pushed himself to his feet. "We've got some cots in back if you want to get some sleep. I hope it won't take too long."

"I—I don't . . . all right, fine. Could I phone the hospital first, though?"

"Sure," he said with a grin. "We give everybody one phone call."

# CHAPTER ELEVEN

*Friday, August 16, 1912*

## Will

The wagon turned for the back of the grounds. *Quieter back there,* I thought. *Fewer potential witnesses.* The horses clopped along on the pavement, their shoes tapping out a slow rhythm.

I flipped over on my side, knees up near my chest, and slipped my fingers down into my shoe. I tried to get hold of the knife, but it was stuck in too far, and I couldn't get a grip. I took a quick glance at the cops next to me. One of them was looking toward the road in front of us. The other stared out the side. I could tell from the lights ahead and the distant sound of coughing that we were coming up on the tubercular sanatorium. I reckoned we would pass it by and go out the back of the complex to somewhere quiet they could kill me, which meant I had a little time.

Even though it was a cool morning, sweat dripped off my forehead onto the wagon's wooden floorboards. I strained back to reach the laces and loosened them, and again reached in for the knife. I had my thumb and forefinger around the end of it when the wagon stopped.

The coughing that had begun in the background was loud now. I looked up in surprise. We were at the back door of the sanatorium. The cops stood, pulled me off the wagon, and dragged me inside to a toilet, which I had enough sense to use. The next thing I knew, I was lying on my back in a brightly lit room, with straps holding me to a bed.

I lay there, listening, watching. I could detect no one in the room. A train whistle blew somewhere far away, and I thought about how much I wanted to be on that train right now, heading away from Eloise for the last time, Robert in tow, Elizabeth at my side. That result didn't seem very likely at the moment.

But this wasn't over, I told myself, trying not to admit I was beaten. They hadn't removed my shoes. I still had the knife. I knew the truth, though. Dr. Beckwith couldn't risk me leaving Eloise. He had to kill me.

I'd been heading in this direction ever since I'd forced Elizabeth to make love with me. Oh, I'd made progress here and there, winning some level of redemption, but something inside kept pushing me to the brink, putting myself in harm's way, tempting death. I knew now that I hadn't beaten the dead man inside me. A few years ago, he clawed at my rib cage every day, trying to tear his way out, to take me away from the grief that had defined my life, that I had brought on in one incredibly stupid, drunken moment.

I deserved death. Nothing I had done since could change that fact. The dead man had bided his time, but he kept working on me. He knew that I knew. I didn't deserve to live. Why else would I have taken on this insane quest?

Judge Hume's face appeared in my mind. He would be alive if it weren't for me. I didn't give a damn about him for his own sake—he was a cheat and a liar—but he was Elizabeth's father. I was responsible for taking him away from her. What would happen to her if I disappeared? She would tear this place apart looking for me, but I had no doubt that Dr. Beckwith would create records that showed me being released or transferred elsewhere, or even committing suicide. Who in a position of authority would doubt him? No one that mattered, who could do anything about it.

The thought of Elizabeth grieving me filled me with rage. Yes, I deserved death—but Elizabeth deserved happiness. She had earned the right to live a happy life, had paid for it in tears and sweat and blood.

I had to escape.


The door swung open. I tensed, peering down my body to see who it was.

Dr. Beckwith walked into view and stood over me. His face glistened with sweat. "I am going to continue with the radium therapy. Perhaps it will help."

I was shocked. Therapy?

He walked out of sight. Drawers opened and closed. Something metal fell onto a metal surface, and another, and another. Finally he came back into view with a shallow pan. "We'll try a few more this time, see how that goes."

I tried to say, "Take off the gag," but all that came out was groans.

Whether he understood it or not, he ignored me and began removing slender metal rods from the pan with a pair of forceps, placing them inside the shiny tubes, and taping them onto the sides of my head. The tubes were cool, but by the time he finished taping half a dozen of them to each of my temples, they were getting warm.

"This might burn a bit," he said, "but I think with your case, a little more radical therapy is required." He pulled up a chair and sat next to the bed. I couldn't turn my head, but I cut my eyes over to him. "I wish I had an alternative," he said, "but Francis can't go to jail any more than Robert could. It would kill him. He's my boy. And I know my therapy is working. He'll get better." He patted me on the shoulder. "Would you like me to give you something for the pain? Morphine, perhaps? I think I ought to. This is going to hurt." He stood and disappeared from view again, returning a minute later with a syringe, which he injected into my arm. Almost immediately, I felt the warming peace of the opiate coursing through my veins. I took a deep breath and held it. Then another.

Dr. Beckwith sat again. "I haven't tried this before, nor has anyone else that I know of. It will be interesting to see what such an intense dosage of radium will do. Of course, it would eventually burn through your skull, but I'm hoping this level of contact will simply rearrange things a bit in your brain, perhaps lesion off a bit of memory. You should be proud. You're serving medical science."

The morphine swirled into my brain, painting beautiful colors. I wasn't sure whether he had given me a particularly heavy dose or, through lack of use, I'd become more susceptible again to its effects. My eyes grew heavy. I let them close.

Peace.

I luxuriated in the ecstasy of the drug. Morphine unlocked a door

I hadn't even known was there, a door that opened to a world of joy and beauty and . . . peace.

The heat continued to build at my temples, but I didn't mind. I heard the *click* of a door closing, and I looked to where Dr. Beckwith had been sitting. He wasn't there. I wondered if perhaps he had left the room.

I lay there for a long time, long enough for the morphine to leave my head dull and heavy. As time passed, the sides of my head became warmer. I began to sweat. I tried to shake my head to dislodge the radium, but I could barely move and it was securely taped in place.

The heat built. I tried to calm myself. After all, if Beckwith wanted me dead there were a hundred easier ways to do it, including just overdosing me with morphine.

After perhaps another hour, I began to smell scorched hair.

## Elizabeth

My sleep was washed in blood, red-tinged nightmares of gray matter sliding down dirty walls and crimson torrents pouring from gore-spattered bodies. When the door creaked open, flooding the room with light, I saw nothing but red. I shielded my eyes with my hand.

"We found him," the huge man silhouetted against the hall light said. "Just where you said we would."

"What?" I pulled myself from that bloody world inside my head. They'd found someone? "Oh, Lindsay's partner?" I tried to blink the sleep from my eyes.

"Yep," Marshal Magnan said. "Loeb. Well, we think it's him. It's somebody."

"Now can we leave?"

"Yep. I'll just need your particulars so we can talk again."

I sat up and scrubbed my face with my hands. "What time is it?"

He pulled out a pocket watch. "Four in the A.M."

At least I knew my mother was all right. Before I had gone to sleep, I'd phoned the hospital and asked the nurse to keep an eye on her. She said she'd find her a bed in one of their vacant rooms. She also said that the cabbie was being a perfect gentleman. By that time, Thomas was out of surgery but was still touch-and-go. The nurse said she'd call if the situation changed. Before she hung up, she mentioned that Mrs. Riordan was on her way from Detroit.

I followed Marshal Magnan back into the lobby, where Chief Struble already stood waiting for me. "The marshal has agreed to let us look through Lindsay's home, if you're game. We might find out why he did this. Heck, we might find the rest of the file."

I agreed with him but phoned the hospital again before we left. The same nurse I'd spoken with previously said that both my mother and the cabbie were sleeping. There was going to be a whale of a tip in this for Oscar. I hoped he took checks.

The marshal returned my gun to me, then fit a cowboy hat on his head, and we all climbed into Chief Struble's Model T, which someone had driven to the station. Most of Lindsay's neighborhood was still dark, though a few of the neighbors had lights on, likely having been roused by the brightly lit house and backyard. We walked around back, where three men stood staring into a deep hole in the ground. We peered in.

A skeleton lay at the bottom, partially covered by rags that presumably had once been clothing. It was large, a man. "Sorry, Walter," Chief Struble said. "Too bad you got hooked up with a louse like Lindsay."

"Let's look around," I said. "I want to get back to the hospital."

"Yes'm." He touched the brim of his derby and gestured for me to lead the way. Chief Struble, Marshal Magnan, and I entered through the back door.

"There's a safe in his bedroom," the marshal said. "We're waiting on our locksmith."

"Key or combo?" Chief Struble asked.

"Combo."

"Let's take a look."

We continued to the room with the unmade bed I'd seen earlier. Dirty clothing lined the floor. The room smelled of man: sweat and stale beer and other things I didn't even want to think about. The closet door was open. Inside was a green combination safe, about two feet square.

Chief Struble strode to the dresser, pulled out the top drawer, and flipped it over. He tossed it aside and did the same with the next drawer and the next. A small piece of paper was taped to the bottom of that drawer. "Right thirty-four, left six, right fifty-two. Try it."

Marshal Magnan knelt down on the floor and began spinning the dial. "How did you know?"

"He taped everything to the bottom of his desk drawer at work. Everyone knew. It's our luck he wasn't aware of that."

The marshal pulled the safe door open. Half a dozen bundles of cash lay atop a pile of papers. The bills ranged from twenties to hundreds. We all gaped at each other.

Chief Struble let out a low whistle. "I guess there was a little more than a pension at stake. Here. Let's see the papers."

Marshal Magnan reached in, pulled a one-inch stack of papers from under the money, and looked it over. "This is it," he said. "Your missing file."

We hurried out to the kitchen and spread the documents across the top of the table. Each of us grabbed a handful and began perusing it. The coroner's report was on the top of my pile. His opinion was that Peter Hamlin had either been hanged, having been dropped no more than one foot, or strangled. Either way, strangulation with a rope was the cause of death. Hamlin had catgut fibers embedded in his neck from the rope, which the coroner admitted never having seen before.

I knew about it, though.

"Look at this," I said, waving the report in front of them. "This is the same murder weapon that's been used at Eloise Hospital." I explained to them about the Phantom and the Punjab lasso.

They shared a glance. I couldn't interpret their expressions. Both the men looked a bit worried, and I was afraid they thought I was the crazy one.

"The Phantom of the Opera?" Marshal Magnan asked. "The Punjab lasso? Seems a bit silly to me."

"Be that as it may," I replied.

He shook his head, and we went back to reading. A minute later, the marshal held up a document. "Listen to this. 'Must question Francis Beckwith. According to informant, he was accused of lighting fires at the state hospital and killing and dismembering animals.'" His eyes scanned down the page, then popped up to meet mine. "Oh, Lord. His father was the administrator!"

"Yes, and now he's at Eloise Hospital," I said. "Where my brother and friend are."

Marshal Magnan shook his head. "It says that Francis and his father both tried to duck them." He looked up at me. "I'd say your boys are in serious trouble."

We kept sorting through documents. It was nerve-racking. I wanted to get to Eloise and sweep Will and Robert out of there. Instead I kept reading. Chief Struble and Marshal Magnan were going nowhere until they knew what conclusions they could draw from the file, and who knew what crucial bit of information was hidden in these pages of dense type?

I dug through lab reports and statements of police officers. Perhaps another fifteen minutes passed before I found something that shocked me. "Wait," I said. "Francis's whereabouts were accounted for. He was in Bronson Hospital at the time getting an appendectomy." I flipped through the pages. "The surgery was the day of the murder. There are a half dozen witness statements to that effect." Looking up at Chief Struble, I said, "Francis couldn't have done it."

"What? Are you sure?" He took the papers from me and looked them over. "You're right. If these are real, Francis isn't the killer."

How did we know they *were* real? I asked the men what they thought.

"Why would they fake them and then steal them?" Chief Struble asked. "If they wanted us to believe the Beckwith boy was innocent, they'd have left these at the station. No . . . They were saving them for some reason, blackmail probably." He stood and stretched his back. "Keep reading. I'm going to see if I can find any mail."

He started opening kitchen cabinets while the marshal and I kept digging through the file. A stack of paper slapped against the counter, and Chief Struble looked at the letter on top. "Oh, Mother Mary. What have we got here? A telegram sent to Lindsay yesterday from the Western Union office in Nankin Township, Michigan. Listen to this.

"'Being investigated. Detroit dick Thomas Riordan. Elizabeth Hume. Will Anderson. Have they contacted you? Take measures.'" He looked up at me. "It's signed 'BM.'"

"I can't think of anyone with the initials *BM*," I said, "but Nankin Township is where Eloise Hospital is."

"We could try to get a roster of their employees," Chief Struble said.

I looked down at the table, and my eyes happened to sweep over one of the documents the chief had read. It was the testimony about Francis's history of arson and animal killing.

The informant's name was typed in and signed at the bottom.

*Clarence Morgan.*

I read further. Two years ago Clarence Morgan was an English teacher at State High School, which, the file at the Kalamazoo police station had said, was just on the other side of the forest from the state hospital.

The same forest in which Peter Hamlin had been found.

According to Morgan's testimony, he was tutoring Francis in literature as a favor to Dr. Beckwith. His duties required him to go to the asylum twice a week, for which he received a small stipend. In his opinion, the report read, "Francis was delusional and violent, possibly homicidal."

Farther on: "Morgan says he's friends with Dr. Beckwith. He wants us to keep his testimony secret unless the case comes to trial." Next to that were a circled question mark and a dollar sign. Possibly a note of communication between Lindsay and Loeb.

A note was scrawled at the bottom of the page and underlined:
*Check Morgan's alibi.*

I scanned the next few pages and the ones preceding it and saw nothing about an alibi for Morgan. I looked up at the men. "Have you come across anything that states what Clarence Morgan's alibi was?"

They shook their heads. "Did he need one?" Marshal Magnan asked.

"The detectives seemed to think so." I showed them the scrawled note.

"Hmm." Chief Struble looked at Marshal Magnan.

"Who's Morgan?" the marshal asked.

"He's the killer," I said. "Clarence Morgan is the Phantom."

# Will

My temples felt blistered. Worms wriggled around inside my head. I shouted into the gag. My voice was hoarse, my cry a raw scrape of vocal cords.

"John," a voice said from far away.

"Help me!" I shouted into the gag.

"Be quiet!"

A second later, I felt a prick in my arm, and a soothing wave of morphine coursed up my shoulder into my brain, cooling the worms, slowing them. Fingers fumbled at my temples, ripping off the tubes.

Francis's face swam into my view. He unstrapped my head, untied the gag, and pulled it off me.

"Wha-what are you doing?" I croaked.

"I am taking out the radium." Metal clicked against metal and rolled around in a pan.

"Why would you do that?"

"He should not kill you. It is wrong."

"I thought . . . you wanted me dead." The morphine reached inside me and washed me in peace. My temples still burned, but the opiate blurred the sensation. I took a deep breath.

He retaped an empty tube to my temple. "I do not want you to be here. You do not belong."

I didn't understand. "Aren't you the Phantom?"

His eyes flashed. "You believe I am killing people?"

"I . . . I don't know."

"You are the same as the rest of them!" he shouted. His fists balled up. "I am trying to help you, and you are just a . . . an imbecile!" He spun around and headed for the door.

"Wait! Francis, please."

He stopped. His body seemed to swell and then contract as he inhaled and exhaled deeply.

"Please, Francis. Could you get me a drink?"

He turned around, his mouth set in a tight line. "Would a killer get you a drink?"

"I'm sorry, Francis." My mind danced in time with the morphine. "You're not a killer. I was wrong."

He strode past me, returning half a minute later with a beaker full of water. "There," he said in that tight voice. "The person who does not kill people has gotten you water."

I gulped it down, apologized again, and had him get me another drink. When I finished my third, I said, "Will you help me?"

"Will I help you do what?"

My eyes were heavy, and he was wearing me out. "To escape."

He didn't answer.

I could see him processing the question. Since he hadn't said no, I asked, "Can you get me off the grounds of the hospital?"

He thought for a moment. "I can research it."

Even through the haze of the morphine, I couldn't imagine Francis pulling this off. We would need help. Clarence Morgan was the only one I could ask. His help had landed me here, but Alice made it clear she wouldn't break hospital rules. There was no one else. "Could you ask Mr. Morgan to help us?"

Francis just stared at me.

"The three of us ought to be able to figure it out, don't you think?"

After gazing at me for a long moment, he nodded.

"What time is it?" I had completely lost track of the hour and, for that matter, the day.

He pulled a watch from his trouser pocket. "Eleven fourteen and twenty-seven seconds."

"Day or night?"

"A.M. Eleven fourteen and"—he looked at his watch again—"thirty-five seconds. A.M."

"Thank you."

"You are welcome."

"Francis? Who is the Phantom?"

He pulled a notepad from his pocket. Running his finger down a page, he said, "I have been investigating, too. I record people who are not where they are supposed to be. I caught Mr. Dill the most—seven times in the last seventy-three days, but . . ."

"But he didn't strangle himself," I said. "Anybody else?"

He leaned toward the notepad until his face was only a few inches from it and scanned through the pages. "The doctors and nurses are always moving around. I do not know where the staff is supposed to be all of the time, even when I look at their schedule. My father says they have to go different places to help out."

"What about Mr. Morgan? Have you ever seen him out on one of the nights someone was murdered?"

"No."

"All right. Talk to him. Ask him to help us."

Francis agreed. His eyes cut to the door before he looked back to me. "I will come back for you tonight." He tied the gag around my head, strapped me to the bed, and left the room.

Assuming Francis really wasn't the Phantom, I was incredibly lucky he had decided to help me. Still, without Clarence Morgan, I had little chance of escaping.

I prayed that Clarence would deliver me from this place.

# Elizabeth

I told Chief Struble and Marshal Magnan about Clarence Morgan and that I was sure Will trusted him. "And the money. Somebody was paying off Lindsay and Loeb. Look at this." I showed them the question mark and dollar sign next to Clarence's statement. "Maybe it was Morgan."

"Do you know whether he has that kind of money?" Marshal Magnan asked.

"No," I admitted. My head throbbed. "But he said his parents owned a ranch when he was a child and that all of his family was dead. Maybe he got a large inheritance." A thought struck me. "Wait. Why couldn't Morgan be in on it with Lindsay? If Dr. Beckwith thinks he's protecting Francis, he might be the one paying Lindsay."

"Makes sense," Chief Struble said. "If Beckwith believes his son is the killer, he would think he was protecting him, when in fact he was protecting Clarence Morgan."

"Clarence is bright enough to pull it off," I said, "and Dr. Beckwith seems to believe his son is capable of murder. Morgan could be facilitating the blackmail for Lindsay—and probably pocketing some money along the way."

"Could Morgan be BM?" Chief Struble asked. "Does he have a nickname or something?"

"He doesn't seem like the type for a nickname," I replied, "but who knows if Clarence is even his real first name? Regardless, I've got to get Will out of there. Now. I need to phone his parents and have them go identify him."

We raced back to the Schoolcraft marshal's office to make the call. On the way, I explained Will's situation to the men, telling them why he was there and how he had gotten in. Even in the dim light of early morning, I could see they didn't approve. I didn't blame them. I didn't either.

At the station, I sat at one of the desks, picked up the phone, and, when the operator finally came on the line, asked for Will's parents' number. After a ten-minute delay, during which the operator made the long connection, the telephone started ringing.

The Andersons' new cook (well, new since we'd been engaged and I spent time at their home) answered the phone. "Anderson residence." She had a strong accent: Spanish, I thought.

"This is Elizabeth Hume. May I speak with either Mr. or Mrs. Anderson, please?"

"They are no here." She tried to pronounce the words carefully.

"When will they be back?"

"Miss Heu, they say I tell you they go to look for Mr. Will."

I thanked her and told the policemen Will's parents were unavailable. "I need your help," I said. "Is there any way you could get him out?"

"Well," Chief Struble said, "do you know what police department has jurisdiction out there?"

"They have their own police department, and they're hiding the murders."

The chief grimaced. "That's not good news."

"What about the county sheriffs or the state police?" I asked.

"I can phone them," Marshal Magnan said, "but I'd guess it's going to take a couple days."

I cursed and rubbed my temples. "We've got to get him out."

"Let me call the Eloise police," Chief Struble said. "I'll tell them we need Will to testify in an investigation. If they know we're aware they have him, they won't let anything happen to him."

"What about Clarence Morgan?" I asked. "Can you get them to arrest him?"

"Not without some proof, Elizabeth," the chief said. "We've got solid evidence for an investigation, but nothing you could arrest him for."

I shook my head with frustration. "Okay. If that's all we can do." I told them that Will had been committed as an amnesia patient, so he was known as John Doe, but that he would be easily recognizable by his burned hand. Chief Struble made the call, he and the marshal having decided that a Kalamazoo investigation, while certainly not something to arouse fear in the heart of a Detroit-area policeman, would at least have more power than that of one from Schoolcraft.

When the phone was finally answered, Chief Struble explained what he wanted and who they were looking for. The Eloise policeman agreed to look into it and phone him back. The chief left the phone numbers for both of their departments.

"Is there anywhere around here we could get a telegram out this early?" I asked.

"Not until eight," Marshal Magnan said. "Write down what you want, and I'll take care of it for you."

I wrote a message for Will's parents along with their address and handed it to him. "All right. I have to get back to the hospital."

Chief Struble looked at his counterpart. "If you're done with me, Phillip, I'll drive the young lady."

The marshal nodded. "I'll let you know if I hear back from Eloise."


Thomas was still unconscious when we arrived at the hospital. My mother was asleep. Oscar sat in the lobby reading a magazine. Chief Struble and I joined him, and we sat in silence. While we awaited word from the doctors and Marshal Magnan, I wracked my brain for ideas on how to free Robert and Will. None were forthcoming, which should not have surprised me given my current exhaustion and shock, but I was frustrated, afraid, and so nervous I was barely able to remain seated. I needed to rest my body and mind, I knew that, but it was impossible.

The marshal phoned for Chief Struble just after nine. I listened in on the call.

After a minute, the chief said, "Really?" He put his hand over the horn on the candlestick. "They told him there's no record of any patient fitting that description."

My hand rose to my mouth of its own accord. "Oh, my God."

He listened to the marshal again. "All right. I'll tell her. Thanks."

Before they rang off, I said, "Ask him if he sent the telegram."

Chief Struble relayed the question, and Marshal Magnan said he had. The chief thanked him, hung up, and turned to me. "They asked if the inquiry was coming from Elizabeth Hume. If so, they wanted him to arrest you for trespassing and fraud."

"What?"

"Obviously, the marshal didn't listen to them. I'm going back to my station. I'll send a telegram to the state police to raid the hospital. It may take a day or two, but with the evidence we have they'll do it. Now you need to stay away from that place."

I started to protest again, but he held his hand up in front of him, silencing me, and told me he had to get to his office. He said he would make sure to stay informed about Thomas's condition. I gave him our telephone number and address, and he said he'd keep me posted if anything major broke. I went back to the lobby and asked Oscar if he would stay a bit longer. He agreed.

I knew I should be exhausted, but my mind wouldn't stop—and I was dying for a cigarette. I opened my case to see that I was down to my last one. After looking at it for a moment, I decided to wait until I had a real emergency. I tiptoed into my mother's room and sat in a chair next to her bed.

I didn't know what to do. I couldn't wait until Monday to get Will and Robert out of Eloise Hospital. They were already denying that Will was even there. No one with any authority was willing to help me. I would have to get them out myself.

I hurried to the lobby and sat down next to Oscar.

"Would you like to leave now?" he asked.

"Soon . . . but I have to ask you something first. Would you drive us to Detroit?"

Even though this had to be an extraordinary request, he just shrugged. "Sure."

"How much would you like to be paid?"

"Ten cent a mile. Quarter per meal."

"That's fine."

Standing, he said, "I'll get the car ready."

I ran back to my mother's room and softly shook her arm. "Mother? We've got to go."

Her eyes opened. "Oh, good morning, dear." Her voice was thick with sleep. She stretched and looked around the room. "Where . . . oh, Lord." She sat up. "How is he?"

"He's still unconscious. But we've got to get back home. Now."

"Why? How can we just leave Thomas?"

"We can talk about it in the taxi. Right now we've got to go."


I couldn't have foreseen the problems we'd have getting back to Detroit. The cab started sputtering a few miles past Battle Creek, the engine coughing and wheezing. The automobile moved forward with a jerk and a pause, a jerk and a pause. Oscar pulled onto the grassy side of the road under an oak tree, took out his tool kit, and opened the engine compartment. I asked my mother to wait in the shade of the tree and joined him.

Inside I was beginning to panic, but I tried to maintain a calm exterior. Fixing automobiles was an integral part of owning them. It seemed that motorists spent more time tinkering in their engine compartments than they did out on the road. Oscar tried a few things, none of which changed the situation a bit. We both stood staring down at the engine with our hands on our hips.

"What do you think?" I asked.

He cupped his chin in his hand. "Never had a problem like this before. Think I might need a real mechanic this time." He grimaced at me. "Sorry. Know you're in a hurry. Tell you what. I'm going to head back to Battle Creek, find me somebody who can work on this thing. You ladies can come along or wait here. Your choice."

I thought for a moment. "We need to get to Detroit. I think we'll look for a ride."

He tried to talk me out of it, saying the roads were dangerous places for ladies, but, feeling the reassuring weight of the Colt in my purse, I told him simply that I knew how to defend myself. "Before you go," I said, pulling my checkbook from my purse.

"Hell, no," he said.

I looked up at him, startled.

"Sorry for the language, but I ain't taking money for leaving you stranded." I argued with him, but he would not relent. He bid us farewell and started up the road, heading back to Battle Creek. My mother shocked me by running over to him and giving him a hug. She hurried back, one hand on top of her hat. Once Oscar was out of sight, I wrote him a check for three hundred dollars, enough to cover our entire trip, his repairs, and a generous tip. I folded it in half and set it on the driver's seat of the motorcar.

My mother and I stood at the side of the road, just past the cab so it would be apparent to passersby that we were stranded. We had been there an hour before the first vehicle that might have accommodated us, a lumber truck, crawled up. The driver, a sketchy-looking character, stopped. He was only going another mile down the road but would be happy to drive us that far, he said. I thanked him and waved him on. Another half hour passed before a farmer in a wagon full of watermelons rolled by. Later, a man flew past on a motorcycle.

I was beginning to lose hope when a Michigan Stove Company truck drove up. I stepped out onto the road, waving my arms. The driver stopped, and I walked around to his side, hoping he was returning to their factory, which was only half a mile from our home.

In fact, he was. He was a heavy fellow of perhaps forty years, with a round, friendly-looking face and a tiny nose. Once I explained that we had to get back to Detroit today and that our taxi had broken down, he was happy to accept some company for his drive home. I sat next to him, though fortunately the cab of the truck was large enough to accommodate all of us without touching.

He was a pleasant man, but I couldn't keep my mind on the conversation. The officials at Eloise said they had never had a patient fitting Will's description. That could mean one of two things. The first was that they were incompetent, which was entirely possible, though I couldn't make myself believe that was the real reason. The second explanation was that they had rid themselves of Will in a way that guaranteed he wouldn't turn up again. Possibly, that meant locking him up in some dank cell away from prying eyes, but it seemed more likely they would kill him.

Will and I had always shared a connection. Ever since we'd met, at times he came to my mind suddenly, and I feared for him. Most often I discovered that he had experienced something frightening or painful. What carried his thoughts to me from across the cosmos, I don't know, but something did. I didn't believe he could die without me feeling it.

The chains linking us together were too strong, the connection too sure, for Will to die while I remained ignorant.

No. He was alive. I just had to get him out of Eloise before it was too late.

I was very poor company on the drive home. My mind careened from thought to thought. Though I couldn't do anything now for Thomas, I couldn't help but think about him. Yet I couldn't afford to do that. I had to concentrate on saving the men inside Eloise Hospital. My first problem would be getting inside the gates. The second would be finding Will and Robert. The third, getting them out of the asylum.

First, getting in: If Clarence Morgan was the Phantom, Dr. Beckwith could become my ally. However, I still didn't know whether Clarence was blackmailing the administrator. If he was, then confiding in Dr. Beckwith could be fatal . . . for me as well as for Will. Obviously, I couldn't trust Clarence. I wasn't sure of Bessie or Alice either.

That left me with one person: perhaps the most abhorrent person in the hospital, whom I could trust only because he was completely untrustworthy. Dr. Davis might respond to the promise of romance. Would that be enough to get him to open the gate for me? I shuddered. The thought of voluntarily seeing that reptile again was almost too much to imagine, but he might let me onto the hospital grounds.

He would likely also be able to help me with problem two: finding Will and Robert. Either he knew where they were or he could easily find out. I was certain I could provide him the motivation. So long as I could keep him on a tether, he'd be able to help us with problem three as well: getting out alive.

I would phone him when we arrived in Detroit. What happened next was in God's hands.

# Will

The pain in my head settled to a mild burn. Some of the relief, I knew, was from the morphine, but there was no doubt that Francis, by removing the radium, had prevented further damage.

Sometime later, Beckwith entered the room. He spoke to me, but I feigned complete unresponsiveness. I did it well enough that he checked for a pulse. He stood close to me and touched the tubes a few times, apparently making sure they were still well attached, but he didn't remove any or check inside them. After only a few minutes, he left again. At some point I actually fell asleep, waking to another shot in the arm, this time given by Dr. Beckwith.

He saw me open my eyes. "How are you feeling?"

The morphine coursed through me. I stared at him as though uncomprehending. I opened my mouth and then closed it.

"Good," he muttered. "Just a bit longer."

## Elizabeth

While I waited for someone at Eloise to answer the telephone, I flipped open the book Alberts had left out for me. *The Phantom of the Opera* had finally arrived.

The telephone clicked. "Eloise Hospital," a woman said.

I shut the book. "Dr. Davis, please." Ghostly voices buzzed in the background of hum coming through the telephone receiver. I'd turned on only the desk lamp, so other than the top of the desk, which was bathed in the bright white glow, the rest of the room was pale and gray.

"He's not on duty."

"This is a personal call."

"Please wait."

I sat back at the desk, resting the candlestick on my thigh, the receiver pressed to my ear. Somewhere in the ether, a man laughed, long and hard, his guffaws like the sound of distant cannons. Alberts had already called the Baker Electric garage for our automobile, which would be arriving any minute. Bridie was still with her parents. He hadn't heard from her all day.

I heard someone fumbling with a telephone. "Davis." His voice was flat, impatient.

"Dr. Davis, this is Elizabeth Hume. May I speak to you for a moment?"

"I'll not discuss your cousin—"

"No," I said quickly. "He's not why I phoned. I have to admit . . ." I paused. "This is very awkward for me, you understand."

"What is it?" He sounded ready to hang up on me.

"I want to see you," I said, in as meek a voice as I could muster.

"You want to see me?"

"Yes. I've been thinking about . . . about the other day. In your office. I can't stop thinking about you."

"Really, Miss Hume," he said. "This is most extraordinary."

"I know, and I'm so sorry. I've never done anything like this—but I've never felt this way. Please. Give me a chance."

"Why should I believe you?"

"Dr. Davis, I've met hundreds of men, but never a man who so completely takes charge. I won't deny that I was taken off guard the other day, but I think you and I were . . ."

"Were what?" he asked.

I hesitated, as if it were difficult for me to admit. In fact, it was. "That we were meant to be together."

"Hmm." He sounded hesitant. "Well . . ."

"Dr. Davis, I must see you. I'll come there. To Eloise. Please."

He was quiet for a moment. "Well," he finally said. "All right." His libido had won out over his common sense.

"I'll be there within the hour."

"Yes, well. All right, then."

"Dr. Davis?"

"Yes?"

"May I ask what your first name is?"

"Christopher."

"Can I call you that?"

"Yes, certainly." He was starting to warm up.

"I'll be there as soon as I can, Christopher." With a shudder, I hung up the phone. I reloaded my pistol and put it back in my purse, fixed my hair and threw on some makeup, and put on the lowest-cut dress I had, a royal blue eye-catcher made of silk. It was my most risqué but showed only a modest amount of cleavage. Before I left, I strapped the holster with the little Mauser .22 to my thigh.

I walked out to the parlor, where Alberts and my mother waited for me. "I'm going to Eloise," I said.

My mother was sitting on the sofa. Alberts stood near the fireplace, one hand on the mantle. He looked as tired as I felt.

"Elizabeth." My mother stood. "Are you sure we can't help you? It's just too—"

"Too dangerous, I know." I looked out the window to see our Baker Electric parked at the curb. "I know it is, and it's too dangerous for either of you. I'm armed. I have two guns, and I'm not leaving that place without Will."

Alberts crossed the room to me and gave me a stiff hug. He'd never done that before. "I'll watch over your mother. Always keep a hand up in front of your face. It will keep the lasso . . . from tightening." He gave me a sheepish smile. "I read the book while you were gone."

"Thank you, Alberts." I kissed him on the cheek and did the same for my mother. "If I'm not back by dawn, call the state police and tell them I've been abducted by Dr. Davis at Eloise Hospital. That ought to get them moving in the right direction."

I fixed my hat onto my head with a pair of hatpins and ran out to the automobile before they could argue. I drove off, heading west on Jefferson into downtown and then out into the country. My hands began to shake. I'd been brave with Dr. Davis on the telephone, but I didn't know how I would react when he was in the room with me. I had never let myself fall so completely into another person's power. If I did that tonight, he would rape me.

He was not going to rape me. I had killed a man only last night, and, though my intention was not to kill Dr. Davis, I would pull the trigger if provoked.

Ahead of me, the sun had dropped behind the trees, painting the horizon in a rosy glow. I switched on the head- and taillamps and drove cautiously, keeping a close eye on the road. By the time I pulled up to the hospital's gate, the sun had set. The majestic buildings of Eloise were lit by floodlights and streetlamps, an island fortress in a sea of darkness. The floodlights were angled upward, creating murky shadows above the parapets, ledges, and balconies, obscuring large swaths of the buildings.

I stopped just down the street from the gate, made sure again that the Colt was in my purse, checked the load in it and the little Mauser, then tucked them both away and drove the last fifty feet. The guard was in his little house and, perhaps because of the Baker's silent electrical motor, didn't notice me. I called out the window, "Hello!"

He looked up, startled, before throwing down a magazine, picking up a clipboard, and walking out to the gate. "Yes, ma'am?" He was an older man, thin and jug-eared. I didn't recognize him.

I leaned out the window. "I'm here to see Dr. Davis, please."

"Is he expecting you?"

"Yes, sir, he is."

He asked my name and checked it against the clipboard. "All right, come on in." He pulled the gate open, and I drove inside, parking at the far end of the lot. I needed to get Robert and Will inside the automobile without being noticed. I walked back to the guardhouse and leaned in the door. The guard hung up his telephone and glanced at me. "He's on his way."

I nodded and gave him a tentative smile. Feeling a sudden dizziness, I steadied myself on the doorjamb. The dizziness passed. I had to get hold of myself. All it would take was a single slipup, and Dr. Davis would have me. I sat on the bench outside the guardhouse and tried to relax. Step one complete. I was inside now. Only two more to go. I smiled at my attempt at bravado. I had accomplished the only easy part of my plan.

The sound of Dr. Davis's footsteps, shoes tapping against the sidewalk in a quick rhythm, preceded him. He came into view, wearing a gray houndstooth suit with a gray homburg and a cane. I wondered if he'd brought that for defense. If so, it would be no match for my hatpins, much less my pistols.

He slowed as he approached, appraising me as he did. I smiled at him, glad for the darkness that would hide the hate in my eyes. My hands began to tremble again.

His eyes were narrowed, and his smile was tight. "Good evening, Miss Hume."

I stood. "Good evening, Dr. Davis." I ducked my head and glanced up at him shyly. "Christopher."

"Would you care to take a little stroll?" he asked.

"Certainly."

He held out his elbow, and I took his arm. His suit was made of wool, soft to the touch, but I would have preferred touching a porcupine. We began walking down the sidewalk that led between the Administration Building and Building B.

He glanced over at me. "So you had a change of mind, did you?"

"Yes. I . . . well, sometimes a person just has to take a chance, don't you think?" I looked at him. He just gazed back at me. I couldn't read his face. "When Mr. Morgan interrupted our meeting the other day, I was . . . disappointed."

"You were disappointed." We passed the buildings and continued down the road, heading toward the river. My heart quickened.

"Yes." I still wasn't sure if he was buying my story. "I have to admit you took me a bit by surprise. I hadn't dared hope that . . . you would . . . be interested in me."

"What about your boyfriend?"

"Oh, Will?" I laughed. "He's not my boyfriend. Well, perhaps he likes to think so. He courted me a number of years ago, and we had planned to get married, but that all fell through. We've remained friends, but that's all we'll ever be."

He stopped and turned to face me. The streetlamp behind me lit his face a ghostly white, shadowy, indistinct. "I saw the missing person advertisement in the newspaper. What happened to him?"

"I don't know. His parents asked me to place the advertisement because they were going out of town."

"If you aren't courting, how did he happen to be with you the night your cousin murdered that man?"

"I phoned him and asked him to come with me. I was too frightened to come here by myself. My father is, well, he's passed on. Will is still fond of me, so he came along for moral support."

"And that's all he provides?"

"Yes."

He gave my elbow a squeeze, hard enough that I stiffened. "Tell me what you want."

I took a quick look up and down the sidewalk. No one was in sight. "I have something for you." I reached into my purse, pulled out the Colt, and shoved the barrel up into the hollow under his chin.

His eyes widened, and he let go of my arm.

"You are going to help me, aren't you, Dr. Davis?"

# Will

Hours later, Francis returned for me. He unbuckled the heavy canvas straps, threw them back, and said, "Come. Now."

I pushed myself up to a seated position and swung my legs off the side of the bed. My head swam. I stayed there for a moment while the dizziness passed. The morphine daze had faded, leaving me with a heavy head and thick tongue, and nothing to block the pain. "I've got to get these damned things off," I said and started peeling the tape off my left temple.

"'Damned' is a bad word," Francis said.

"You're right." I kept peeling off the tubes and throwing them on the bed. I felt the skin where a tube had been. My temple was syrupy to the touch, but surprisingly, almost all the pain was inside my head, not outside. I stayed at it, getting more and more depressed at seeing the blackened and singed hair stuck to the tape. When I'd finally removed the tubes, I slid off the side of the bed and stood. The movement sent a shock wave through my brain, and I nearly collapsed to the floor. I grabbed the side of the bed and waited for it to pass. My foot stung, and I was reminded of the knife Ty had given me. "I have to bandage my head," I said.

"Come," he said again. "Now."

"Get me a bandage first. Please."

He glared at me for a moment before running to the drawers at the side of the room, pulling out a long bandage, and handing it to me. "Hurry," he said, his voice rising on the last syllable. His forehead glistened with sweat.

I wrapped the bandage around my head, moving slowly so as to keep as much of the pressure off my temples as I could. Staying hunched over, I walked to the sink, where I downed two beakers of water before following Francis to the door, trying to move my head as little as possible.

He opened the door and hurried out into the hall. I glanced out first and, seeing no one, followed him. His footsteps, rapid paced and frenetic sounding, and mine, staggering as I bounced off the walls, competed with the distant hacking and coughing of the sanatorium. Francis cut down another hall and sped down a staircase. At the bottom he scurried to a door, threw it open, and ran inside.

It was a tunnel, similar to the first one Dill had taken me down—perhaps five feet wide and seven feet tall. I followed him in and closed the door behind me. "Where are we going?" I whispered.

"The storage room under the amusement hall."

"Why?"

He stopped and looked up at me. "Mr. Morgan said I should bring you to the subbasement. He will be there to help us escape."

"Us?"

"I am going with you."

"Just show me where I'm supposed to go, then you run home."

"No. I am leaving, too."

"Francis, you can't—"

"I am nineteen years old." He glared at me. "I can leave if I want. He cannot make me stay."

I wasn't going to have this argument. I'd humor him—for now. *But wait,* I thought. "The amusement hall is on the other side of Michigan Avenue. How are we going to get there?"

"There is only one way." Francis took a rectangle of paper from his pocket, unfolded it, and braced it against the wall. It was another hand-drawn map, this one with narrow paths, rather than roads. Tunnels—it was a subterranean map of Eloise Hospital. "We need to go here." He pointed to a building near the bottom left corner of the map. "The amusement hall. Right now, we are here." He slid his finger to the top left corner. "The sanatorium."

I braced myself.

"We go through this tunnel"—his finger ran about four inches right on the map—"to this one"—a foot down—"and then a long pipe." His finger snaked down the last ten inches diagonally, under Michigan Avenue to the amusement hall.

A lead weight dropped in my gut. I was desperately hoping I had heard him wrong. "What do you mean, a pipe?"

"A pipe runs from the river, here"—he pointed—"to the lake, there." He ran his finger down the page past the amusement hall. "It is the pipe that feeds water to the lake."

"We can't swim through a pipe that long."

"No. It is usually dry."

"Do you know it's dry now?"

"No, but the water level in the lake looks high enough. I do not believe it will fill."

"You do not believe."

"Correct."

"But if it does?"

"If we are inside the pipe, we will be pumped to the lake by two three-hundred-horsepower steam pumps."

"And drown on the way."

"I do not believe that will happen."

"Why?"

"The water will push us through the pipe in seconds. I believe we would reach the inlet to the lake long before we drowned."

"So we'd have a chance."

"No. The water flows through the pipe at thirty miles per hour. We will hit the grate at the lake inlet at that speed. I believe the impact would kill us immediately."

I sighed. "You're just full of good news, aren't you?"

He gave me a look of utter confusion.

"Is there any other way?"

He shook his head.

"How would we even get inside the pipe?"

"There are access hatches in the tunnels underneath Building B and the amusement hall."

"Have you ever been in it?"

"No, but I have a flashlight." Francis pulled a light, perhaps six inches long and two inches wide, from his coat pocket. He switched it on. The beam was so weak it was barely visible.

"How old is that?"

"My father gave it to me for Christmas when I was seven."

"Shut it off, then. Please. Until we need it." It had been only the last five years or so that flashlights had stopped living down to their names. New battery technology had given them the capability to do more than "flash." Francis's, however, was more than ten years old.

It just kept getting worse. Still, it was my one chance. If I couldn't make it through the pipe, there was no doubt: I was a dead man.

Francis led me about a hundred feet down the tunnel. I hurried after him, holding my head, as if to keep my brains from sliding out the sides. I had only the slightest trepidation at being in the tunnel, so powerful was my desire to leave this place.

He turned right down an intersecting tunnel and hurried along in his curious fashion. This tunnel continued straight for perhaps four hundred feet. My temples throbbed like they were being pounded with hammers. My foot was torn, and blood squished in the toe of my shoe. Francis consulted his map along the way, apparently finding landmarks, because when he opened another door, he peered in and walked through into a boiler room.

"Building B," he whispered.

So far, so good.

A siren cut through the night above us, howling through the building.

Francis put his hands to his ears and screeched, "It's too loud, too loud!"

"Francis." I took hold of his hand and pulled it off his ear. "Francis." His eyes were screwed shut. "Look at me, Francis. It's all right. It's just a noise."

His eyes opened. He winced but looked at me.

"It's okay."

He tentatively moved his hands back and, with a look of determination, let them drop to his sides. The room was lit only from the hallway, but it was bright enough to make our way through. The boiler was huge, with a dozen massive pipes thrust through the ceiling, a six-foot coal pile in front of it. Francis crossed the room, looked through the doorway, and disappeared down the hall. I followed. After a couple of turns, which, given my diminished mental state, I could never have repeated, he opened a door to another tunnel. A huge red pipe, perhaps two feet in diameter, cut across the tunnel about four feet off the floor. An iron ladder scaled the side. At the top was a hatch with a wheel above it, similar to the mechanism that opens a bank safe.

*Oh, my God.* "Is this the pipe?"

"Yes."

I looked back at the door we'd just come through. I could still get out.

"You go first," Francis said. His eyes were wide. He was afraid.

I wiped my palms on my trousers. "You're sure there's no other way?" My skin was crawling.

"Yes."

"Okay." I stepped up on the ladder and looked down at the hatch. "You're sure it goes across the street and we'll be able to get out the other side?"

His cheek twitched. "I . . . yes. This pipe runs to the lake by way of the amusement hall."

A string of curses fired through my head. "Are there any intersecting pipes or tunnels?"

"No."

"How will I know we're at the hatch?"

"The flashlight."

"Could I use it?"

"No. It is mine."

"But you want me to go first."

"Yes."

*Lord.* "Well, could you keep the light pointed ahead of me?"

"Yes."

Trying not to think, I took a deep breath and grabbed hold of the wheel atop the hatch. It was tight, and with one hand I wasn't able to turn it. Francis climbed up and helped me, and together we got it open. I ducked my head down into the pipe. The smell was loamy soil and mud, with a component of rot. About four inches of water sat at the bottom of the pipe. It wasn't moving. I listened carefully—no sound of running water.

I looked back at Francis. "How far do we have to go?"

He consulted the map again, using his fingers to judge the scale. "Two hundred ninety-eight feet. Approximately."

"Through here." My head and heart both pounded in my ears.

"Yes."

My eyes welled up, but I ducked again into the pipe and wriggled inside. The water was cold. "Come on, Francis." I tried to keep my voice calm, but it shook as bad as I could ever remember. I crawled forward, splashing along. My shoulders touched both sides of the pipe. The top was only an inch or two above my head. Beads of sweat dripped down my face. I stopped about ten feet in and ducked to look back at Francis. All I could see was the light from the tunnel illuminating a circle in the darkness.

"Come on, Francis," I said again. If I didn't get him in here, I would have to go back. I would never be able to convince myself to climb in again. "It's not so bad," I added. I was amazed at how calm I sounded. My heart was nearly bursting through my chest.

"All right." He climbed in. The top of the hatch closed, plunging me into instant darkness.

"Wait," I said. "Leave it open."

"No," Francis replied. "Guards patrol these tunnels."

I heard the wheel turn and Francis drop into the water at the bottom of the pipe. He switched on the flashlight. The pipe in front of me turned a deep gray. My head was swimming, and I was finding it increasingly difficult to stay focused. I moved forward with elbows and knees. After about fifty feet, the light faded to black. We were enveloped in perfect darkness. In my mind, I saw the trunk lid closing on me. A whine echoed through the pipe. It took me a moment to realize that it wasn't me. It was Francis.

"You have to let it rest," I said. "Switch it off." I heard the click of a switch. I blindly crawled ahead. If his flashlight failed, we'd never find the hatch. The darkness was closing in on me. When I could wait no longer, I said, "Try it again," with near panic in my voice.

He switched on the light, and a meager glow lit the inside of the pipe, just enough to see. I crawled faster. Another twenty feet and the light failed again.

"My flashlight won't work!" he cried. His voice echoed all around me.

"Francis?" I said. "Switch it off. We're going to be fine."

"It is too tight! I feel like it is going to crush me."

"I know, Francis. We just need to keep moving. We'll be there in a minute." *Assuming he's right*, I thought. *Assuming he knows where the drainpipe leads*. I could see nothing. I crawled along, feeling the pipe constricting, seeing and feeling the lid of the trunk closing on me. I ran straight into a wall. The shock rattled my brain, sending a wave of pain through my head. I had to fight the urge to vomit.

I felt ahead of me and to the sides. The right side was open. "The pipe turns to the right, Francis." There were no turns on his drawing. I started crawling again. Still nothing but blackness and the oppressive weight of the ground above me. I had to be more than a hundred feet in, dozens of feet underground, with hundreds of tons of dirt between me and the surface. The pipe squeezed my shoulders. My head grazed the top again and again. I couldn't breathe. I had to get out. I started crawling faster, scrabbling ahead, panic-stricken.

"John?" Francis wailed. "I am afraid!"

I stopped. I had to get control. It would be impossible to turn back. I focused my mind on Elizabeth's beautiful face, tried to imagine her waiting for me at the end of the pipe. I had to see her again. "It's all right, Francis," I said. "I'm right here."

"John!" I heard him crawling toward me, his arms and legs pumping, until he ran into my feet.

"We're going to be all right, Francis. It can't be much farther. Take a deep breath."

He gasped for air.

"Deep and slow. Do it again."

This time, his breath came a little easier.

"Again."

He breathed.

"Is it all right if I go now?"

I heard him swallow. "Yes," he said quietly. I could hear him clicking the flashlight on and off, but no light cut into the darkness. He was controlling himself remarkably well under the circumstances. I crawled forward, talking to him the entire time, soothing him and soothing myself in the process.

The pipe began vibrating. A deep hum rumbled in my ears.

# Elizabeth

"N-now," Dr. Davis stammered. "N-now, you don't . . . that is, you . . . please, no, please." His eyes glistened with tears.

I stepped in closer and brought my face within inches of his. "Tell me this," I said in a low voice. "How many women here have you raped?"

"No. You misunderstand, that's—"

I pushed the gun barrel harder against the hollow under his chin. He rose up on tiptoes, trying to escape the bullet he expected to blast into his brain.

"How many?"

"None. Why, I . . ." His eyes, wide, found mine, and his voice faded. My finger was tightening on the trigger. I wanted to shoot him, to end the machinations of his sick brain. He saw it on my face.

Closing his eyes, he muttered, "Four."

I marveled at the calm flooding through me. "Tell me about them."

"One . . . was . . . a nurse."

"What is her name?"

He told me. I didn't know her. "Does she still work here?"

His head gave a tight little shake. The gun barrel moved with it. "N-no, she's gone."

"Who else?"

He gave me the name of a volunteer: another woman I didn't know who he said no longer worked at the hospital.

"And?"

"A, uh . . . two . . ."

"Two what?"

His eyes darted about like a spooked horse's. "Two . . . patients."

I smiled at him. It didn't calm him a bit. "There," I said. "That wasn't so hard, was it? I'd guess there are more, but I'll let you stop there. You know these crimes are worth your life, don't you?"

He gulped and nodded.

"Well, I'm going to give you the opportunity to earn it back. Listen to me carefully, because if you don't do exactly what I say I'm going to shoot you tonight and dump you in a trash bin, which is where you should spend eternity."

"All r-right." He was trembling all over, and I luxuriated in his fear and cowardice. I could have stood there for hours enjoying the unmasking of this horrid man. I wasn't proud of it, but I told myself that the other women, the women who never got the chance to gain their own retribution, were the reason I was doing this.

"Your choice tonight is death or prison. Frankly, I hope you choose death. I don't think you are capable of a decent act." I slid the gun up his jawline and held the end of the barrel against his cheek. "I would enjoy killing you."

"What do you want?" His voice was surer now. Perhaps he thought the immediate danger was over. I'm sure his diseased mind was working out a plan.

"The first thing is for you to completely understand that if you cross me, I will kill you. You wouldn't be the first. I won't hesitate."

He lowered his eyes. "I understand."

"The second thing is that you are going to help me get Robert Clarke and Will Anderson out of this place. Right now. We all leave together."

"What's Anderson doing here?" He seemed genuinely shocked. Hopefully, that meant Will's identity had remained completely undiscovered.

"He's here as a John Doe," I said. "An amnesia patient. Where would he be?"

"Building B, I suppose."

"What about Robert? What did they do with him?"

"He's in the Ho—in solitary, at the police station. I can't get him out. Only the chief or Beckwith can do that."

"Then I suppose we'll find out how creative you can be. I will be driving out of this place before sunrise. Either I'll be leaving here with Will and Robert, or you won't have the chance to take another journey of any kind. Have I made myself clear?"

With my pistol in the small of his back, I guided Dr. Davis toward Building B. If Will was there, gaining his release into the doctor's custody would be much easier than freeing Robert from the police station. I made it clear to Dr. Davis that my gun would always be trained on him, and the least deviation from my orders would result in his death.

I stayed a pace behind him, and we walked down the sidewalk to Building B. My purse was large enough to fit my hand and gun, and the strap was long enough for the bag to be slung over my shoulder so I could keep the gun aimed at him from the inside. "How are you going to find him?" I asked as we climbed the steps on the side of the building.

"I'll ask the duty nurse where her John Does are," he snapped.

"Dr. Davis, I don't think you want to irritate me further."

He swallowed a retort before flinging the door open and hurrying inside. I followed, keeping the gun leveled at him. He walked to the main hallway, where there was a minimum of activity, the patients now in bed. Only a few orderlies stood in the hall. I watched their eyes carefully as we passed, to see if Dr. Davis was trying to communicate with them, but they merely said hello to the doctor and continued down the hall.

He stopped at the desk near the men's wards and asked the nurse where he'd be able to find her John Does. She checked her roster, told him they had three in residence, and gave him ward and bed numbers. We checked them all. Will was not one of them. I scanned the faces of the patients as we walked through the wards. He wasn't there. Dr. Davis eyed me a few times, as if he were looking for an opening, either to attack or run. Each time I caught his eye and smiled, as I imagined the bullet bursting through the fabric of my purse, plowing through his waistcoat into his abdomen.

He couldn't get his eyes off me quickly enough. I believe I had impressed upon him the sincerity of my desire to shoot him.

When we returned to the hall, I whispered, "Go back to the duty nurse. Have her check for a Will Anderson."

His mouth flattened into a disapproving scowl, but he did as I said without comment. The nurse told him they didn't have anyone by that name.

I caught Dr. Davis's eye and nodded down the hallway from which we'd come. He turned and strode down the hall to a side door, which he unlocked and held for me. I nodded him forward and followed a pace behind. "Where else could he be?"

"Perhaps he was released."

"Perhaps he wasn't. Where else could he be?"

"Solitary, if he was violent. Outside of that, he's not here."

"Then let's go to the police station."

Turning around, he shook his head and whined, "They won't let me take either of them."

"Sunrise, Dr. Davis. Either we are all out of this place or you will be dead."

His mouth opened, but he thought better of whatever he was going to say and turned toward the Administration Building. We'd only taken a couple of steps when a siren cut through the night, a long wail that seemed to come from all around us. We both jumped.

A moment later, a number of policemen ran out the door of the station and climbed into a black coupe, which roared from the curb, bouncing up on the lawn while the driver turned it around, and then flashed away, heading toward the back of the complex.

"Go, now!" I shouted to be heard over the siren. I pulled my hand from my purse and fit the gun barrel into his spine just below his skull. "Do as I say."

He started up again. Fortunately, the police station was no more than a hundred yards away, so it didn't take long to get there. We entered and walked into the dark, cramped lobby.

A bucktoothed young policeman stood behind the small counter. The top two buttons of his coat were missing, and either a gravy or blood stain ran down the left side of his breast. "Yes, Doctor?"

"This is an emergency. I need to speak with a couple of your prisoners. Dr. Beckwith has me working on a case—"

The young man's face lit up. "Is it about that John Doe?"

"Yes." Dr. Davis sounded stunned. I know I was.

"Who do you need to see?"

I stepped up nearly to Dr. Davis's side, my hand poking the gun into his kidney from inside the purse. "Excuse me. I'm Dr. Davis's secretary. What's going on?" I gestured above me toward the siren.

"We got an escape," he said, "and a kidnapping."

"Who escaped?"

"This patient with amnesia, a maniac, busted out." He looked at Dr. Davis in confusion. "That's why you're here, right?"

"Right, right," Dr. Davis said and put a hand on the young man's shoulder. "I just hadn't filled her in."

"He kidnapped somebody?" I said.

"Beckwith's kid. We got orders to shoot on sight."

# Will

"Francis!" I shouted. "As fast as you can!" I scrambled ahead, slapping at the top of the pipe as I went, feeling for the hatch. Air rushed past me in a maelstrom. The water underneath me trickled forward, then flowed. Around me, nothing but black. The water rose to six inches, then eight, pushing at me, rushing through in a torrent.

Francis screamed. I kept feeling the top of the pipe, but now I was being carried along by the current. I rolled over, floating, and braced both hands against the metal, trying to slow myself.

For a split second, the top of the pipe was gone. My hands shot up and caught the wall of the hatch. My fingers scrabbled for purchase. I felt a rung and grabbed hold with both hands.

Francis slammed into my chest, the rush of water turning him into a projectile.

My feet slipped out from under me, but I clamped my hands tighter around the rung. "Hold on to me, Francis!" I shouted over the roar of the water. His arms wrapped around my torso. I felt above me for the next rung and pulled myself up. Another rung and I felt the hatch.

I was high enough off the bottom now to brace myself against the hatch wall, but the water had nearly reached the top of the pipe. In seconds it would completely fill. Francis pushed himself above the water and screamed again, in my face. He squeezed me so hard I could barely breathe.

I felt above me for the wheel. There. I tried to turn it. The water battered me, crashed into me. I couldn't get any leverage. It rose to my neck. I pulled against the wheel. To my mouth. The wheel gave a little. Lifting my face up to the hatch, I took a deep breath just before water completely filled the pipe. Francis's hands tore at me.

I spun the wheel a quarter turn, and another. My feet slipped out from under me. Francis began to slip away. I reached down with my right hand and held on to his shirt with all my strength while steadying myself and straining at the hatch wheel. It turned, and more.

Water exploded upward, bursting the hatch open. In the geyser that followed, I was blown out of the pipe to the floor of a tunnel. Water gushed out, hitting the ceiling and spraying to the floor all around me. Almost immediately, the geyser began to shrink, and after a few seconds, the water only spilled through the hatch and over the sides of the pipe.

An avalanche of pain from my right hand made me realize I was still holding on to Francis's shirt, and he was still in it, lying next to me on the floor of the tunnel, crying and shouting out curses. I let go and rolled over. Now I did vomit, river water mixing with stomach acids. When I finished retching, I climbed to my feet and stood, looking down at Francis, who had pushed himself back into a corner.

Tears squeezed through his closed eyes. "Goddamn you!" he shouted. "Goddamn you!"

I couldn't tell if he was talking to me or if this was some internal struggle. It didn't really matter. "Francis?"

"Goddamn you!" His voice caught on the last word, and he sobbed. "Goddamn you!"

"It's okay, Francis," I said. "We're safe."

"Goddamn!" His eyes opened. "Goddamn you!"

"Come on, Francis." I held a hand down to him. "We've got to find Mr. Morgan."

"Goddamn. Goddamn!" He sprang to his feet and thrust his face into mine. "That was your fault! Goddamn you! That was your fault!" His face contorted with anger. "I will tear you to pieces!"

I stood my ground, though I have to admit that, in his fury, Francis was nearly as frightening as Ty. "We're safe now," I said again. He grabbed the front of my shirt and slammed me against the tunnel wall. I held my hands up, palms out. "We're safe now, Francis. It's okay."

Tears streamed down his cheeks. His eyes dropped from mine to his hands, and he released me, shouting, "Goddamn!" He turned away and hurried back to the corner, facing the wall. "Goddamn. God . . . damn you."

I let him be for a minute, perhaps two, and stood there freezing in the cold tunnel, water dripping off me to the floor. Finally I walked over to him. "Francis? We have to find Mr. Morgan."

He turned and looked at me. His face twitched and contorted, but he'd stopped crying. "I lost my flashlight."

"I'll buy you another one," I said. "A brand-new one. Okay?"

He nodded.

We splashed through the water pooled on the floor of the tunnel to the first door. Francis looked back at the hatch. My eyes followed. The water had completely stopped.

"Automatic pressure shutoff." The words shot from his mouth rapid-fire. It occurred to me that we could have avoided all this simply by leaving the first hatch open, but I didn't mention it.

We walked through the door into a short, narrow hallway. Water dripped from us onto the concrete floor, the sound hollow, like a dripping faucet. I wanted to stop, to take out the knife that was shredding my foot, but I knew we were far from safe.

Francis stopped in front of the only other door. "This is it. The subbasement of the amusement hall."

I had done it. I'd beaten the trunk. Now I needed to get the hell out of here.

He opened the door, and we walked onto the stairway landing of a large room. The only lights on were one above us, on the wall above the base of the stairway, and another inside a room on the far side of the subbasement, perhaps a hundred and fifty feet away. Between them I could just make out a dirt floor punctuated with piles of horse tack and old wagons.

"There you are." Clarence Morgan walked out of the lit room and waved us over.

We stepped down from the landing onto the packed dirt and walked toward him. My head thrummed with pain and pressure. Just before Morgan disappeared into the room, he turned back and said, "Quickly now."

Francis bolted into the room behind him. It took me much longer, not out of caution, but because I couldn't move at any other rate. When I stepped inside, dirt clinging to my wet shoes crunched like grit on the planks of the wooden floor. Francis stood, motionless, just inside the door.

I looked to see a forest of unimaginable size before us, the trees stretching as far as I could see. I stepped around Francis and walked over to the trees. They seemed to move as I did, shifting as I got closer. In front of them, I saw the three of us a thousand times. Mirrors—but placed so cleverly that, had I not seen the men, I would have walked right into one. A single tree stood, endlessly reflected to create this massive forest. A coil of rope lay on the floor. A shiver went through me. I touched the tree. It was cold and hard. Iron. A sculpture.

Morgan looked from me to Francis and back again. "You look like a couple of drowned rats. What happened?"

"A little mishap in a water pipe," I said.

He gestured toward the bandages on my head. "What did you do?"

"Dr. Beckwith was trying to get rid of me permanently." I looked around us. "What is this place?"

Morgan closed the door and stood in front of it. "I imagine this was part of a set once upon a time, but it was already this way when I first found it." He pulled his handkerchief from the inside pocket of his coat and mopped his forehead.

"How are we going to get off the grounds?" I asked.

"That's not going to be a problem."

"No?" I cocked my head at him. "Why?"

He reached inside his suit coat, put away the handkerchief, and pulled out a pistol. "You won't be leaving."

# Elizabeth

The young policeman explained to us that they were searching the surrounding area, on the chance that "the maniac" had gotten over the fence, but they believed he and Francis were still on the grounds. They were now conducting a building-by-building search. The siren screamed, infiltrating every crack of the building with its urgent shriek.

"How did the John Doe get away?" I asked.

"They had him out for therapy."

I eyed him. "Had he been a prisoner here?"

The policeman nodded.

"Is that normal? For prisoners in solitary to leave for therapy?"

He shrugged. "No—but you never know what to expect around here, know what I mean?"

Nodding, I said, "Where was he when he escaped?"

He shrugged.

Dr. Davis, perhaps sensing my frustration, asked the young man to take us back to Robert Clarke. The policeman seemed conflicted but, having no one to ask, apparently decided a doctor had seniority over him. He led us down the hallway past a number of wooden doors with heavy black iron hinges and handles. Behind one of them, a man cried. Behind another was a mix of dark mutterings and shouted curses. The policeman took us through a door and into another, identical hallway.

About halfway down he stopped and gestured toward a cell. "Clarke's in here."

I nudged Dr. Davis in the back with my gun.

"Uh, unlock the door," he told the policeman. "Dr. Beckwith wants to see him."

"That's . . . too dangerous." His eyes jumped from the doctor's to mine.

"He's not dangerous at all, is he, Dr. Davis?" I asked.

"Oh, uh, no, no, not at all," he blustered. "Docile as a baby."

The young policeman stared at him. "I really can't . . ."

"What's your name?" I asked. "Dr. Beckwith will want to know who is obstructing his investigation."

"It's, uh . . . well, I . . ."

"Do as she says, son," Dr. Davis said. "Every minute is precious. This is my responsibility."

The young man stared at him for a moment before pulling out a set of keys and unlocking the door. "All right, here you go."

He swung the door open, and I saw Robert. He was lying on his side in a back corner, wearing nothing but a nightshirt. The cell stank of urine, feces, and body odor. His eyes were open, but he wasn't moving at all. I thought he was dead.

Then he saw me. "Lizzie," he said, one arm stretching out for me.

I had to suppress the urge to rush to him. No doubt Dr. Davis would lock me in the cell. Instead I stayed where I was, with my gun pressed through the purse into his back, and said, "Dr. Davis and I have some questions for you. Just come with us now."

"Lizzie," Robert said again. He was struggling to stand.

"Help him," I said to the policeman.

He gave me a short bewildered glance before obeying my order. Putting Robert's arm over his shoulder, he walked him out of the cell and down the corridor. Dr. Davis followed, with me bringing up the rear, always with the gun trained on the doctor. The closer we got to the lobby, the louder the siren sounded. The young man unlocked the door for us. "I can't leave the station," he said. "Everybody else is gone."

"That's fine," I said. "Dr. Davis will help him from here."

"Yes, yes indeed." With a look of extreme distaste, Dr. Davis took Robert's arm and led him out into the night.

As soon as the policeman closed the door, Dr. Davis shoved Robert away and wiped his hands on his handkerchief. Robert was crying, and I took him in my arms, shushing him and stroking his back, all the while keeping my eyes, and my gun, aimed at Dr. Davis. "It's going to be all right, Robbie," I said. "I'm going to get you out of here. You've got to be tough for a little bit longer, and I guarantee you'll be all right."

He sniffled and wiped his nose on his sleeve. "I knew you would come for me."

I almost burst out in tears. He had faith in me: the one who had abandoned him. Now, though, I had to think about Will. Where would he have gone if he managed to get away? The only answer was the most frightening: to Clarence Morgan. As far as I knew, Morgan was Will's sole ally among the staff.

I turned to Dr. Davis. "Where does Clarence Morgan live?"

He pointed behind me to a row of buildings a couple of streets over. "The last one. Dr. Beckwith lives on the right side; Morgan lives on the left."

I took my gun from my purse and gestured with it toward the house. "Let's go."

He just looked at me. "You're going to wander around here with a patient in tow? That might get you noticed a bit more than you'd like."

"Shut your mouth and move."

He headed off down the road. Robert and I trailed behind

"Are you going to shoot him?" Robert asked. I glanced up at Dr. Davis and saw him stiffen.

"Perhaps," I said. "I haven't decided yet."

Dr. Davis speeded up a bit. Robert filled me in on his last few weeks, mostly stories of maltreatment by the guards and policemen. Just before we turned up Morgan's street, we passed the schoolhouse. No lights were on, nor was there any hint of movement.

At Morgan's house, the porch light was on, and a light shone in the parlor. The other side of the house, Dr. Beckwith's, was dark. I told Dr. Davis the three of us would be going into Morgan's. He would distract Clarence to the extent that I could get the jump on him.

We climbed the front steps, and Dr. Davis knocked. We waited. I tried the door, but it was locked. Nodding toward the side of the house, I said, "Let's go around back."

The doctor turned, walked down the steps, and moved around the house to the back door. To my surprise, it was unlocked. "After you," I said to him. Dr. Davis walked inside, and I searched the house, room to room, with Robert and the doctor in tow. No one was there. I tried not to feel discouraged, though it was a difficult task.

"Robert," I said, "would you find me something I can use to tie up Dr. Davis?"

He grinned and immediately began rummaging through the closets.

With the doctor nearby, I had to constantly be on my guard, and I had no doubt that he'd kill me, or worse, if he got the chance. I was finished with him.

"Dr. Davis," I said, gesturing toward the kitchen table, "have a seat."

He smiled as he sat. "Every policeman in southeast Michigan will be looking for you."

"Eventually." I sat in the chair opposite him, the gun resting on the table, pointed at his heart. "Where else would Morgan be?"

He shrugged. "I haven't the faintest."

I raised the gun barrel so it was pointing at his forehead. "Think about it."

"He's a teacher, so he could be at the school."

"We passed the school on the way here. It was deserted."

"Lizzie!" Robert shouted from the basement. "I found some rope!"

"Bring it here, Robbie," I called back.

His feet pounded against the steps, and a second later he ran into the kitchen with three lengths of clothesline. I thought they would be fine for our purposes.

I took out my handkerchief, folded it, and again, and stepped behind Dr. Davis. "Open your mouth," I commanded. He did. I pulled the handkerchief across his mouth and around his head and tied it off. "Stand up." I nudged him with the gun barrel and walked in front of him, looking from him to Robert.

Dr. Davis was slow but did get to his feet.

"Now take off your clothes." Robert needed clothing, and though we could have taken something from Clarence's wardrobe, this felt more appropriate.

Dr. Davis's eyes widened, and he tried to speak, but the handkerchief muffled the sound.

I stuck the gun barrel up under his chin again and stepped in close. "Now."

Leaning back, eyes even wider, he dropped his derby on the table, shrugged off his coat, and followed it with his shoes, shirt, and finally trousers. I handed them to Robert and instructed him to put them on. Underneath Dr. Davis wore a graying one-piece undergarment that had to have dated from the last century. I let him keep that on. My gag reflex was already activating.

When Robert was dressed, I looked him over and nodded. "Very nice, young man." I turned back to Dr. Davis. "All right. We're going downstairs. Once again, remember that I will not hesitate to shoot you."

He walked down the hallway to an open door on the left. The wooden plank steps led down into darkness, but in the murky light at the bottom I saw an electrical switch. I followed Dr. Davis down the stairs, my gun pointed at the back of his head. He didn't try anything, and in fact even switched on the light.

The room was a "Michigan basement," perhaps twenty feet square with a dirt floor and a ceiling barely six feet tall. The boiler, a great iron octopus with arms jutting out in all directions, took up nearly half the room, with a pile of coal under the chute next to it. A little tool bench stood near the stairway, the tools hanging squared up on the wall.

"Behind the boiler," I said to Dr. Davis. He complied with no reaction at all. He had accepted his fate.

A steamer trunk lay in the corner behind the boiler, taking up a lot of the space. Dr. Davis wouldn't fit all the way behind the boiler as it was, so I asked Robert to move the trunk. He dragged it out of the corner, and I ordered Dr. Davis to go where it had been. "Robbie, are you good with knots?"

"Yes, Lizzie," he replied. "There are bend knots and binding knots and coil knots and hitches and—"

"Robbie," I said, interrupting him, "just choose the best one for tying him up."

"I could use the bowline knot. But the square knot also has merits."

"Which is more secure?"

"Bowline."

"Use that one. Tie him to the boiler. Very tightly. We can't have him escape."

I watched Robert tie up Dr. Davis, arms behind his back, ankles together, and lash him to the boiler. When he finished, I made sure the knots were secure. "Perfect," I said.

"Thank you." Though he didn't smile, pride radiated from him.

I knelt down in front of Dr. Davis. "I hope you realize how lucky you are."

He looked away. I saw the tracks of tears glistening on his cheeks. I felt a surge of sympathy for him—but he wouldn't see it. Just before I stood, I said, "I'm giving you a chance to change your life. I suggest you do."

I pulled the trunk back as far as it would go, covering up the opening to Dr. Davis's hiding place. It occurred to me that this was a strange place to store a trunk, all the way back behind a boiler, completely out of sight. On a hunch, I tried to open it. The top was locked shut.

"Robbie, is there a hammer down here?" I hoped to find a clue inside the trunk.

A few seconds later, he turned up at my side with a sledgehammer. "Can I try?"

"Sure," I said. "Get this thing open."

He looked down at the trunk. "Oh. That. Do you have two pins?"

I removed my hatpins and held them out to him. "Will these work?"

"Yes." Taking them from me, he knelt and manipulated them in the lock for only a moment before I heard a click. He threw the trunk's lid open.

Inside were piles of clothing, old tuxedos and evening dresses. It made no sense that Morgan would go to the trouble of hiding old clothes, so I dug around inside, throwing the clothing to the floor. Only when a tightly folded ruffled shirt hit the floor with a thud did I realize that something was inside it. I shook it out and a large envelope fell onto the dirt.

I picked it up and pulled out the contents: playbills and newspaper articles. The playbills on top were for various vaudeville shows around the Midwest.

Each show had a single act in common with the others, sometimes buried at the bottom of the list, other times in the middle. I wouldn't have even noticed it had I not been looking for the name Morgan. And there it was.

The act wasn't Clarence Morgan, though.

It was the Magnificent Morgans, Masters of the Lasso.

# Will

Morgan told Francis and me to back up.

"Clarence, you can't be serious," I said. "This isn't you. You're not a killer."

He pulled out short lengths of thin rope from his coat while keeping his eyes—and the gun—trained on me. "You don't know anything about me, Will."

"I know you can't entirely be a phony. There's something good about you."

"Bea is what's good about me."

"Bea? Then you need to speak with her, work this out. Clarence, listen to me. You work in an asylum. You know irrational behavior. That's what this is."

"You don't understand," he said, pointing the gun at my face. "I love her." Sweat poured from him. "Stand up." I did. "Now go stand with your nose against that mirror." He gestured behind me.

I did as he asked and stared at my face in the mirror. The expression I saw was not reassuring.

"Francis, tie him up," Morgan said.

"No." Francis's voice was emphatic.

"Tie him up, or I'm going to kill both of you."

A low moan came from Francis. Though I couldn't see him, I could picture his face working through his fear and anger. He was ready to explode.

"Go ahead, Francis," I said, turning around to look at him. "It's all right." I had to keep us alive until I could turn the tables or someone came along to rescue us.

Francis took the rope from Morgan. I turned around again, with my hands behind my back, wrists together. I clenched my fists, hoping Francis tied me so that I could loosen the rope. I tried to ignore the pain that shot up my arm from my burned right hand. "Clarence," I gasped, "why are you killing these people?"

Francis began wrapping the rope around my wrists. His hands were cold and clammy.

"I—I don't . . ." Morgan began. "It's not me," he finally said. "These people are sick, in pain. Every one of them."

"So you are God's appointed Angel of Death while you flounce around pretending to be the Phantom?"

"Oh." He let out a nervous laugh. "No. I'm not the Phantom. There's only one Phantom." A pause. "Tighter, Francis."

"I am tying it." Francis's voice was strident. He pulled the rope tight and tied it in a double knot.

Morgan pulled a chair from a corner. "Francis, back up and sit here."

Francis didn't move.

"Now!"

He took a stiff step backward, and another.

"Four more big steps," Morgan said.

Francis, peeking behind him, complied and sat on the edge of the chair.

"Good boy," Morgan said. I watched him in the mirror. "Francis, put your hands behind your back."

I tensed. As soon as he put down the gun . . .

"Will?" Morgan said. "Listen carefully, or I will shoot you. Rest your forehead on the mirror and then step back a foot."

I did it, but didn't move my feet far enough back so as to lose my balance. I shivered, my wet clothing clinging to me in the cold.

"Feet back," he said.

*Shit!* He'd noticed. I had no choice but to comply. Now my weight was resting squarely on my forehead, leaving me unable to spring back at him. I couldn't see behind me either.

I heard a little shuffle in the dirt; then Francis said, "No," his voice tight. "Do not touch."

"God damn it, Francis," Morgan said. "Stay still."

I wiggled my hands, trying to get them loose, but Francis had done too good a job, and I was weak.

"Noooo!" Francis's voice rose to a shriek. "Do not touch!"

I pushed off the mirror with my head and spun toward them. Morgan was trying to tie Francis's hands behind the chair, but he was squirming too much. Morgan raised the pistol and brought it down sharply on top of Francis's head. He slumped in the chair. I'd barely taken a step toward Morgan when he aimed the gun at me. "Don't. Now back where you were. Forehead on the mirror, feet back."

I didn't move, other than to wrestle with the rope on my hands.

"Will," Morgan said, "I'll shoot you if I have to. Turn around."

I didn't. "What's the difference? You'll shoot me or you'll strangle me. You might as well shoot me."

"You've got me all wrong," he said with a funny little smile. "I don't strangle anyone."

"Then who does?"

He glanced into the mirrors. I followed his eyes.

Standing in a doorway was a figure in black: black trousers, shirt, cape, fedora, and mask. The only things that weren't covered in black were thin, cruel lips, the white skin of the Phantom's cheeks and jawline—and the lasso that dangled from a black-gloved hand.


Morgan tugged at his collar. We both stared at the Phantom, who stood in the doorway, mute. The only noise I heard was a creaking of the rope when the Phantom shifted it to the other hand. I realized the siren had stopped.

"I have everything ready for you," Morgan said. A bead of sweat slid down the side of his face.

The Phantom glanced at Francis and then at me before turning back to Morgan. "But they're not trussed properly, are they?"

My mouth fell open. "Alice?" I took an involuntary step toward her. Morgan knocked the gun against my temple. I saw stars, and the pain brought me to my knees.

"You are both sick men," Alice said in a soothing tone. The Phantom's mouth was moving, but I couldn't believe it was really her behind the mask. "Nothing will cure you. The only thing you are guaranteed is a lifetime of pain. And that's not fair, now, is it?" She was gazing into my eyes, tenderness peeking out from under the mask.

"There's nothing wrong with me that hasn't been caused here," I said, gasping from the pain in my head. "Look, my name is Will Anderson.

My father owns the Detroit Electric Automobile Company, and he will stop at nothing to find out what has happened to me."

Alice took a step forward and squatted so she could see my face. "The story I hear is that you escaped from the sanatorium, kidnapped Francis Beckwith and took him hostage, and then disappeared. The police will keep looking for Francis, so we'll have to be careful disposing of your bodies, but no one will be looking for *you*."

Trying to move as little as possible, I struggled with the ropes binding my hands together. "You say you want to help us. I'm not sick. Francis's father loves him. He's trying to cure him."

Alice walked over to me and set a gentle hand on my head. "I can hear how much pain you're in. I only want to make that stop."

"Then why the Phantom getup and all this nonsense?" I asked. "Surely it would be easy enough to overdose your patients with morphine?"

"They need to die in a way that draws attention to someone else," Alice said, her voice still quiet, sincere. "If they overdose, the nurses will all be scrutinized. Besides." She smiled. "Nobody believes in the Phantom except Dr. Beckwith, and he's certain it's Francis. He would have covered up these mercy killings indefinitely." She stood and took another step back, looking at Morgan. "The sad part is that now I'll have to stop helping patients. The Phantom must disappear with Francis."

"It will be all right, honeybee," Morgan said, his voice shaking. "You'll be all right."

"Of course I will," Alice replied. "It's the patients I'm thinking about."

"You'll find a way to . . ." Morgan trailed off, his eyes lost in Alice's.

"Where's Bessie?" I asked. "Have you got her lining up more victims?"

"Bessie?" Alice's mouth set in a frown. Then she laughed. "Oh, you think she's got something to do with this? No, she's my friend. She thinks I'm sweet on Clarence. It's nice, isn't it, how she tries to protect me?" She turned back to Morgan. "And we still need to talk about that woman."

"You know you're the only one for me, Bea," Morgan said, his voice trembling.

*Bea?* I thought. *Alice is Beatrice.*

She gave him a patient smile. "Finish tying Francis. Then bring—" She looked at me. "What did you say your name was?"

"Will," Morgan said.

"Fine—Will. Clarence, when you're done with Francis, bring Will out here, please." She turned and vanished into the main room.

Morgan finished tying Francis's arms behind him. He was still unconscious. I tried to get to my feet, but I couldn't use my hands. I fell to the floor.

The rope rasped as Morgan tightened the bonds around Francis's wrists. A few seconds later, he took hold of my arm and helped me to my feet.

"Clarence, this is insane. You can stop this now."

"She'll only be helping you, something not too forthcoming in this institution."

"Help? This is murder."

"Listen, Will. The boy in Kalamazoo is the only person she's really killed. He found out Bea was doing exactly what you suggested—overdosing the patients who were most in pain. His aunt was one of them."

"I don't know anything about a boy in Kalamazoo," I said. "I just—"

"The others were simply a release—like it will be for you."

"What are you talking about? I don't want to die."

The corners of his mouth turned up. "Don't you?" Patting my shoulder, he said, "Why are you here, then? To save Robert Clarke? Please." He shook his head. "You want this."

I couldn't free my hands. The rope binding my wrists was too tight. I tried to knee him in the groin, but I hit his thigh, and not hard enough that it would have hurt him had my aim been better.

Clarence slapped the side of my head with the gun. My knees buckled, and I collapsed to the floor.

# Elizabeth

"Morgans" . . . plural. I dug deeper into the pile and found a photograph of a very young Clarence, dressed in a shiny tuxedo, with a woman in black—skirt, shirtwaist, and cape. Both of them held coiled lengths of rope. She was a tall blonde who looked older than he, though still beautiful. Her skin was pale, hair long.

Alice.

I stopped and stared at the picture. Alice. They were . . . brother and sister? Married?

She'd been here about two years, she said, the same as Clarence. She could have worked at the state hospital in Kalamazoo, down the road from Clarence's school. She could be the killer. They were in on it together. They must be.

I leafed through the newspaper articles. Those on top were reviews for vaudeville shows in St. Louis, Louisville, and Hot Springs, with favorable mentions of the Morgans: Beatrice and Clarence.

Beatrice? Then I saw an article with a large picture of the troupe, all their names listed at the bottom. The picture of Alice aligned with the name Beatrice Morgan. I looked back at the previous article, which was the most effusive with praise for the Morgans. They were listed as Beatrice and Clarence. Beatrice was the performer, Clarence her assistant. She did rope tricks: lassoing various objects and volunteers from the audience.

No wonder she changed her name. Or that they posed as unattached people.

A thought struck me. After Clarence saved me from Dr. Davis, he called Alice "honeybee," the same nickname he'd used for his wife when he told me he'd lost her.

Of course. Beatrice. *Bea*. Honey*bee*.

Farther down were articles of a different sort. The first, from the *Kalamazoo Gazette*, was about Peter Hamlin's death in 1910. The next three were obituaries from the same newspaper, with names circled: two from 1910, the other from 1908. All had been patients at the state hospital. I kept digging and found two more obituaries, one from 1905 and another from 1903, both for men in the vaudeville troupe who had died from "natural causes."

At the bottom of the pile was an old clip from the *San Francisco Examiner* regarding the mysterious death of the lead actor in a Shakespearean company; he'd been garroted in his dressing room. He had to be the man whose advances Clarence claimed to have rejected.

I looked up, thinking. Where would they have taken Will? Bessie told me that she and Alice lived in the women's dormitory. I started for the stairs. "Come on, Robert. We've got to hurry."

He followed me up the steps and out the back door of Morgan's house, where we crept around to the front again. Something was different. It took me a moment to realize the siren was no longer blaring. I wondered if that meant Will had been caught. It didn't matter. I wasn't stopping until I found him.

The dormitory was past the women's asylum building. We hurried down the sidewalk, but I stopped before it was in sight. "Wait." Would she bring him to her dormitory? It shared the same problem as Clarence's house, multiplied many times over: It was too likely someone would discover them. I racked my brain for clues either of them had given me.

"Robert? If Clarence Morgan and Nurse Jensen were going to hide somewhere together, where would they go?"

"Mmm." He thought. Finally he said, "Every building has hidey-holes."

I already knew where they would take him, though. It was away from the other buildings. It was completely private. It would be a perfect place to make Will disappear. A shiver went through me. I didn't want to go there, but it made too much sense. Clarence had wanted me to meet him at the gazebo—for privacy. When I first met Alice, she said something about the place. She liked to go there. It was quiet, she said.

If they hadn't already killed him, Will could be only one place.

The amusement hall.

My heart skipped a beat. I grabbed Robert's arm and began running down the sidewalk. We passed the main buildings and clambered inside my automobile. I drove toward the gate. "Robert, keep your face down and in my shadow." He complied. Rolling down the window, I smiled and waved to the guard, who glanced inside the car, saw me with a man he had to assume was Dr. Davis, and opened the gate. I drove out and turned right. Once I was out of the guard's sight, I pulled to the side of the road and turned to Robert. "Will you do something for me?"

He didn't reply.

"I need you to guard the automobile for a few minutes."

"Can I drive it?"

"I will let you drive tomorrow, in the light. You need to do that before driving in the dark. Tonight, I need you to stay here and wait for me. Keep the doors locked and don't let anyone inside until I return. All right?"

"Yes, Lizzie. I will guard the automobile."

Gun in hand, I opened the door and started to hop down. I stopped as a thought occurred to me. If they were in the amusement hall, they would be down on one of the lower levels, probably in the subbasement. There was only one way to get down there.

That I knew of.

"Robbie, do you remember when you brought me out of the amusement hall when I was a little girl?"

"Yes."

I shivered. "The door of that room was locked, wasn't it?"

"Yes."

"How did you get in there?"

"The stairs."

"There's . . . another stairway?"

"Yes."

"Does it go into that room?"

"Yes."

"Where is it?"

"On the other end of the basement."

"Opposite the main stairway?"

"Yes. The stairs are behind the first door, near the front."

"Thank you." I leaned over and kissed him on the cheek. It startled him, and he squirmed away. "Sorry, Robbie, I just . . . I'm sorry." I stepped down onto the pavement. "I'll be back as soon as I can." I took the key with me, in case Robert had any ideas about driving, and hurried across the street to the walk. I glanced back at him and saw that he was still seated in the car, his head swiveling back and forth.

I ran down the sidewalk around the lake, away from the street. When I saw the outline of the amusement hall against the darkness, beads of perspiration broke out on my forehead, and I shivered. *No. Not there* . . . but . . . somehow I knew this was where I would find Will. Swallowing my fears, I hurried to the door and twisted the knob. It turned. I pulled the door open a few inches and peeked into the lobby. I saw and heard nothing. I stepped inside. It was quiet. Moonlight streamed through the windows, coloring everything dark gray.

I tiptoed to the storeroom doors and tried them. They were locked. No lights had been on up in the hall. I was sure they would be downstairs. Screwing up my courage, I crept to the basement door, twisted the knob, and pulled the door open an inch. A light was on below.

My heart was beating out of my chest. I hurried down the stairs, holding the gun out in front of me, up near my face, fearful of the Punjab lasso. I tried to keep my footsteps from echoing, but they sounded as loud as the crack of a rifle. Halfway down, just below the basement's ceiling, I ducked to look into the room. It had been cleaned up since I'd been here, with long rows of cabinets replacing the theatrical set pieces I'd seen before. I ducked out and looked over the railing. A light was on in the subbasement, but I couldn't see anyone. I took a step down and froze.

Below me was a murmur of voices, just loud enough to hear. I thought one of them might be Clarence Morgan. I leaned over the railing again but saw no one. Very carefully, I stepped back up onto the wooden floor.

Below me, footsteps scuffled on cement, probably on the landing at the bottom of the stairs. I unlaced my shoes and removed them, then crossed the plank floor between a pair of large cabinets, my feet nearly silent against the wood, my gun held in front of my face. I heard nothing and saw no one. I crept to the end of the room, senses on full alert.

*A voice?* I looked back. At the farthest range of my hearing, I thought I heard a woman's voice. It wasn't close, could be above or below. I stopped and listened. It was silent.

I started moving again. Finally at the far wall, I thought I heard something from the other end of the room, near the stairs, but it was so faint as to seem a part of the background; the building shifting, or the wind blowing above us. I opened a door and ducked into the room.

A small wooden staircase, barely wide enough for two people to pass, ran both above and below this floor. I strengthened my grip on the pistol with clammy fingers.

The room below me was lit. I shook my head and wiped sweat from my brow.

I didn't want to see those girls.

I didn't want to hear them scream.

I didn't want to face my insanity.

But I willed myself to walk down the stairway all the same.

# Will

I was freezing cold, lying in the dirt, my wet clothes clinging to me. Clarence had bent me backward, tied my ankles to my wrists, and disappeared up the stairs. My head throbbed. I was on the dirt floor of the subbasement's main room. Beatrice was nowhere in sight. I listened. Nothing. Most of the room was filled with an inky blackness. A single bulb lit a twenty-foot semicircle near the stairs.

*The knife.* I could nearly touch my shoes with my fingers. I stretched back. Something popped in my shoulder. I shouted out from the pain, but I kept stretching and managed to push off the heel of my shoe. My fingers scrabbled around the inside, trying to hold on to the bloody knife. I got it and began scraping the edge against the rope binding my wrists to my ankles. The knife was better suited for stabbing than for cutting, but the fibers began giving way. I kept hacking at it, and finally the rope tore in half and my body straightened, the pressure off my shoulders and back. Now I began sawing at the rope binding my ankles, though it was difficult to keep my body bowed back so I could reach. I had to stop and rest every minute or two.

Upstairs, a door opened. I redoubled my efforts, cutting and hacking at the rope. Footsteps scraped on the concrete stairs to a landing, another set of stairs, and then thudded onto the dirt floor.

I looked toward the sound. Clarence Morgan, with a large burlap bag over his shoulder, walked across the floor to the outside of the mirror room and dropped the bag to the ground, propping it against the wall.

Quicklime.

He turned and looked at me, and saw me staring at the bag. "This isn't something we've spent much time on," he said. "We haven't needed to make bodies disappear before."

"Clarence, remember how you told me that we all have a *belle dame sans merci*?" My voice trembled from the cold. "Beatrice is yours. You are not this person. You know she's insane. You're not. You have to—"

"Now, that's not nice," Beatrice said quietly, only a few feet behind me. She walked around into my field of vision. She'd been watching me trying to escape from her trap the way a little boy watches a fly after he's ripped off its wings.

My despair gave way to anger. These people had no right. No right to kill these poor men who were just trying to live their lives in whatever peace they could. No right to take me from Elizabeth. This place was supposed to be dedicated to helping the insane, not fostering the sickness. Yet these lunatics did that and more.

Beatrice walked around in front of me, her arms folded across her chest, tapping the Punjab lasso against her arm in a rhythmic motion. "You think I'm insane, do you?"

"I think you need help."

"God helps those who help themselves, does he not?"

"Insanity is not something you can help yourself with. You need doctors."

She laughed, a sweet tinkling of wind chimes. "Please, Will. You've been here long enough to see what these doctors do. There isn't a cure for a diseased mind. These people need rest. You see, I have evolved. Everyone else pretends, but I see things as they are. Bessie and the others go around here pretending compassion, but I'm the only one who is truly compassionate. I save these people."

"That's ridiculous." My voice quavered, teeth chattering from the cold.

"What do you know of eugenics?"

"I know what it is."

"Mark my words. The next great leap in medical knowledge will be in culling the sick and weak from our society and replacing them with perfect human beings—strong, intelligent, and, yes, compassionate."

"Which you believe describes you."

She ducked her head in modesty.

I thought I heard the faintest sound—a door being opened somewhere in the building?—then nothing. "You *are* insane," I said.

"No. I'm just ahead of my time."

"Let us go. You don't have to do this any longer."

"Don't you understand, Will? I am going to release you. Really release you."

"Beatrice, you need help."

"You bore me." She looked off into the darkness. "What if I gave you a sporting chance?"

"What do you mean?"

"I'm pretty fair with a rope. Why don't we do this? I'll take three tosses at you. If I can't get the noose around your neck I'll let you go."

"Untie me, then."

She laughed. "I said a sporting chance, not a sure win. Clarence, help him sit up—and gag him. He's giving me a headache."

He walked behind me, grabbed me under the arms, and hoisted me upright. Pulling a handkerchief from his pocket, he shook it out and twisted it before cinching it tightly around my head. My arms were still tied behind my back, my ankles bound in front of me.

He joined Beatrice. They stepped back until they were about twenty feet away. "Are you ready?" she asked.

I nodded. Any chance was better than none. I turned the knife around and began sawing against the rope around my wrists.

Quiet footsteps stole across the floor above us. Someone was in the basement. Both Clarence and Beatrice looked up, tracking the footsteps as they moved across the wooden planks.

She set her hand on Clarence's shoulder. "Be a dear. Go see who's here. Take care of them." Without a word, he nodded, pulled out his pistol, and hurried up the steps. Beatrice looked back to me. "Now we'll play a little game I used to play on the circuit."

I had no idea what she was talking about.

"You must stay seated. If you fall over, the game's over, and I win." She wasn't showing the least concern about the person in the basement. Her confidence in Clarence was strong. The footsteps continued skulking across the floor above us. She twirled the lasso over her head and feinted throwing it, and again. I rocked from side to side, trying to anticipate the throw. When she threw it, I ducked right. The rope hit my shoulder and fell into the dirt. I sawed at the rope on my wrists but didn't think I was making headway.

"Hmm," she said, shaking her head. "Rustier than I thought."

Now I heard Clarence creeping across the floor above. Beatrice pulled the rope back to her, hand over hand, coiling it again. "That's one." Twirling the lasso overhead, she cut the distance between us in half. This time there were no feints. She just hurled the lasso at me. I ducked away, again to the right. The rope hit my head but glanced off, falling to the dirt. I lost my balance and nearly fell over, but caught myself just in time.

Beatrice pursed her lips. "That's two." She retrieved the rope, now looking past me toward the mirror room. Had she heard something? She danced across the dirt to the stairway landing and switched off the lights. Other than the single bare bulb at the base of the stairway, the room plunged into darkness.

I was near the far end of the light's range. I dropped onto my back and began wriggling away, desperate to make it to the darkness. The knife fell from my hands. Beatrice's soft footfalls padded across the floor. In only a few seconds, she stood over me. "Oops," she said. "You fell over. You lose."

She slipped the lasso over my head and began to tighten the noose around my neck. Looking into my eyes, she said, "Third time's a charm."

I twisted from side to side, but Beatrice tightened the lasso, strangling me. She pirouetted and jerked on the rope. I couldn't breathe. My throat was being crushed. I rolled toward her, desperate to relieve the pressure, but she danced away, pulling even harder on the rope.

Behind me, in the mirror room, gunshots roared. The first report was a tight *crack!* followed almost immediately by the boom of a larger-caliber gun, and then more shots by the first.

The rope tightened. My eyes were bulging from my head. Choking, I tried to shout for help, but nothing more than a strained gasp escaped my lips.

I was so tired. I needed to rest. Just for a second.

Red lights burst before me.

Nothing.

## Elizabeth

I looked down the stairs and saw nothing but the wooden floor. The forest and the little girls weren't really there, I told myself. It had been my imagination, nothing more. Not even insanity. I was a child. Children imagine things.

I started down the stairway, my pistol now lower, pointed at the floor. I stopped at the bottom of the stairs. This wasn't even the same room.

There was no forest.

No little girls.

No screaming.

The stairway ended in front of a number of black screens that nearly blocked off the rest of the room. Bright light leaked over the top of them, lighting this cramped area enough to see. I slipped between two of the screens, my gun again in front of my face.

I passed through a dizzying array of light and color, weaving in and out of panels, lights flashing in my eyes. But I kept moving toward the source of the light and soon stepped out into an open area.

Francis Beckwith lay on the floor, gagged, tied hands and feet to a chair that had fallen over backward. He saw me and tried to speak, though it was impossible to make out his words. Other than him, the room was empty. I hurried to him, set the pistol on the floor, and started to remove the gag.

A motion behind me caught my attention. I turned my head.

The forest again lay before me, thousands of trees, just as they had been in my hallucination. Perfect, tall trees with green leaves. All identical. I stared, transfixed. It couldn't be.

Francis was speaking urgently into the gag, but it was as if we were underwater in some psychotic ballet of slurred words and fractured images. He kept repeating a single word. Finally I was able to make it out. "Mirrors?"

He nodded emphatically. I turned and looked. Now I saw planes. Mirrors. There weren't *trees*; only a single tree stood before me, endlessly reflected in the mirrors behind it. The girls in the forest had been me; I'd just been too frightened to realize it.

I untied Francis's gag and pulled it from his mouth.

"They have John Doe," he blurted. "They are going to kill him."

"Oh, my God." *Will.* "Are they still here?"

"Yes."

I got behind him and strained to lift the chair so I could get at the ropes. When I had raised it, I started with his hands. The rope was slick and hard to grip, and the knots were tight.

"I'm going to get you untied," I whispered to Francis. "When I do, leave here as quietly as you can and go tell your father what's happening."

"Yes," he replied.

I freed his hands and was working on the ropes at his ankles when I heard a noise behind me. I looked back toward the mirrors. Clarence Morgan stood in front of the tree, aiming a big pistol at me. "Esther?" He sounded incredulous, but he wasn't so incredulous that he lowered the gun. "Or should I say Elizabeth?"

My gun lay on the floor at my right side, hidden from Clarence. "Oh," I said with a smile. "What a relief to find you here. Help me get Francis untied." I looked back at the knots and started working them with my left hand while my right searched for the gun.

"Stand up," he said, "and back away."

Reaching out slowly for the Colt, I forced myself to look straight ahead. His feet started thudding across the floor at the same time my hand touched the gun. "Just a minute," I said, taking hold of the pistol grip. "Let me finish this." I didn't think he'd shoot me, at least not yet. With the Colt in my right hand, I stood, keeping my profile to Clarence and the gun hidden behind my body. I stepped away from Francis to take him out of the line of fire and waved Clarence over. "Help me out."

"Elizabeth. Put your hands up."

Now I really looked at him. "Clarence," I said with alarm. "You have a gun?" To draw away his attention, I brought the back of my left hand to my forehead, in a pantomime of a swooning woman, and then raised the Colt and fired.

His reaction was immediate. His gun boomed, deafening in this little room. I pulled the trigger again and again, tensing for the shock of his bullet.

There was none. He'd missed.

Some of my bullets, however, had found their mark. His gun clattered to the floor, and he fell against the tree, his right palm held to the center of his chest. Rivulets of blood squeezed between his fingers and seeped down his hand onto his white shirt. I ran over and kicked his gun across the room. Clarence leaned against the tree, his eyes staring past me at his own reflection in the mirrors, watching his life seep out of him a thousand times.

Though his head didn't move, his eyes shifted to me. "Esther, you shot me." His tone was no longer incredulous. He sounded . . . amused.

I stuck my gun against his forehead. "Where's Will?"

He winced from a pain deep inside him. His hand dropped to his side to expose a pair of red blooms on his white shirt. His eyes went back to the mirror, and he stared again at his reflection. "Do you think . . . in there . . . I'll be a . . ." His eyes went glassy.

I cursed to myself and glanced at Francis. He was frozen, staring at Clarence. "Francis," I hissed. "Untie your legs and hide."

He looked at me and blinked. "I will." He started working on the knots. A few seconds later, he stood and ducked behind the mirrors.

I ran to the door. If Alice—Beatrice—was here with Will, my presence was no longer a surprise.

I pulled the little Mauser from my holster and checked the load in the Colt. Two bullets left. Seven total.

Beatrice had the advantage. If she had a gun, I didn't have a chance. Yet I couldn't wait any longer. Will could already be dead. I crept to the door, held the Colt against my side with my elbow, and twisted the knob. Bracing for a shot, I pulled the door open just enough to clear the latch. Outside the room was only silence. I took hold of the Colt again, gathered myself, and raised my left hand, holding the Mauser in front of my face, ready for the Punjab lasso.

I pulled the door open and ran out of the light into the darkness. Nothing happened. Now I stood still in the dark, listening.

A creak. Another. The sound came from everywhere and nowhere. I crouched, preparing to run, and said, "Will?" I ran twenty feet farther into the dark, hoping to throw off Beatrice, who was surely tracking me. I stopped and listened, always certain to keep my gun up.

No one spoke. I heard a chittering somewhere: mice, rats, some sort of rodent.

I began creeping though the room. My eyes were adjusting to the dark. Before me I saw a mass on the floor: a body. I gasped in spite of myself. I could see the white of a shirt and trousers, but it was too dark to make out who it was. Keeping the Mauser up in front of my face, I set the Colt in the dirt and felt along the man's right arm to the hand. His fingers were stunted, the skin rough.

*Will.*

He was cold. My fingers reached across his chest, feeling for a heartbeat.

A rope whistled out of the darkness. The Punjab lasso settled around my neck and pulled tight, jerking me over backward, but my hand was wedged between the rope and my throat. Jumping to my feet, I felt nothing but rage. With my right hand I pulled the Mauser from my left and fired toward the source of the rope. She yanked me this way and that, and I ran toward her, firing the gun until the hammer fell on an empty chamber. Beatrice kept the rope tight, dancing away from me. I tripped over my skirts and sprawled on the floor, but I was up again in an instant, running toward her.

She jerked on the rope, trying to spin me to the ground, but she must have tripped as well, because I heard a thump, and I leapt toward the sound. My knees landed on her chest, knocking the breath out of her. I tumbled off, carried by my momentum. The pressure on my throat slackened. I pulled my left hand out from under the rope and jumped back on top of her, my fingers circling her throat. I squeezed her windpipe with my thumbs, using all my remaining strength.

Beatrice clawed my face, but I hung on. Grabbing hold of my hair, she jerked me off her. She began to stand, but I jumped up faster and, from behind, wrapped my arm around her neck. I leaned back and squeezed, lifting her off her feet, blind and deaf in my anger.

She reached back, trying to claw me, and pulled at the lasso, but her strength was fading.

In my mind I saw Will's dead body . . . My father's . . . My baby's.

I kept the pressure on her throat, squeezing with all I had. Soon she slumped in my arms. I was too tired to hold her up. I fell to the floor with her, but I kept my arm around her neck, squeezing, crying hot tears of anger and sorrow.

My baby. My father. Now Will. They were dead.

They were all dead.

When my mother's mind left her, I would be alone.

I kept squeezing.

# Will

My throat burned, a sharp pain like it had been crushed. I opened my eyes and saw nothing. Black nothingness stretching out in front of me forever. A woman wailed, crying great anguished sobs.

Was this hell?

No.

I knew that voice. I'd heard it cry before. I'd made it cry before.

*Elizabeth.*

I tried to call her name, but only a sorry little croak came from my mouth. I reached up and touched my neck with my left hand, feeling an angry welt all the way around. I rolled over and got to my knees before I collapsed again.

The next I remember, Elizabeth was holding me in her arms, kissing my face, saying, "Oh, thank God, Will. Oh, thank God," repeating it over and over.

# CHAPTER TWELVE

*Wednesday, August 21, 1912*

## Will

Elizabeth walked into my room at Grace Hospital with a book under her arm. She glanced at Silas, the old gentleman in the bed next to me, who was asleep, and tiptoed in.

Leaning down, she kissed my forehead just below the bandage. "How are you?" she whispered.

"I'm fine—better," I whispered back. For me, whispering wasn't being polite. It was the best I could do. Dr. Miller thought I would regain my voice fairly quickly. However, he wasn't nearly so confident the headaches would go away anytime soon. Every few hours the pain would build to an ice pick jabbing at the nerves behind my eyes. He had—very reluctantly—put me back on morphine.

I was equally reluctant, but I needed something.

"How's Detective Riordan?" I asked.

"He's doing better." Elizabeth sat by the bed and leaned in toward me. The three long scabs on her cheek from Beatrice's fingernails had nearly healed. "He's been transferred to the hospital in Kalamazoo. They believe he'll make a complete recovery."

"Thank God," I whispered.

"His wife was very upset I'd left him at the hospital by himself until I explained what happened afterward. As you might imagine, she understood."

"Good. How are Robert and Francis adjusting?"

Elizabeth frowned. Little furrows dug into her forehead. I wanted to reach up and smooth them out. I wanted her to never be sad again. "Robert's having a difficult time," she said. "He's happy, I think, to see Mother and me, but he was in that place for more than a quarter century. He's got a lot of scars."

"I'm sorry."

"Francis has been sullen. He misses his father. Both of them miss the routine."

However, neither of them was going back to Eloise, that much was certain. Even though both Dr. Beckwith and Dr. Davis were now in jail awaiting trial, there was no telling if Robert or Francis would have faced retribution from the staff. Elizabeth had coaxed Francis into temporarily moving in with them, so that he would have at least someone familiar—Robert—around him while he decided what to do.

"Bridie and I have been trying to look after them, although I must admit the election is taking almost all of my time. She's got the patience, but I'm not sure the boys do." She brightened. "Oh, speaking of 'patients,' with the help of an interpreter, Dr. Miller evaluated Herr Zimmermann. It turns out he was newly arrived in this country and was looking for his brother, who lives in the city. Dr. Miller says he's as sane as you and—well, now that I think about it"—she smiled—"he didn't use you as an example."

"I understand," I whispered. "It's hard to imagine anyone else being as completely sane as me."

I could almost hear her think, *Touché*, though she didn't have the decency to say it.

She held up the book in her hand. "I've brought you something to read."

I looked at the cover: *The Phantom of the Opera*. "Haven't you got a *Horseless Age*? Hell, I'd rather read a *Harper's* than that."

She smiled, imagining me reading a fashion magazine. "I think you'll find it interesting. Especially the end. It's not a great book, but the forest of mirrors?"

I nodded, again seeing the endless trees in that amazing forest. "It's in here."

"What? How could that be?"

Shaking her head, she said, "I don't know. It's the same, though. In here it's the Phantom's torture chamber, but this book was first published in France three years ago." She handed it to me.

I looked at the burgundy cover and flipped it open. When Elizabeth had filled me in on her recent experiences, she told me about the first time she saw the mirrored forest. "And you saw it nearly twenty years ago?"

She nodded. "I don't understand."

"The inspiration must be the same. Maybe an old legend?"

"Or Gaston Leroux was at Eloise Hospital."

I handed the book back to her. "I'm not investigating. I'm done with Eloise."

She laughed, and it made my head hurt worse. "I'm in complete agreement." Setting the book on the nightstand, she leaned down and kissed me. "I will never let you do anything like that again. What do you say we go to Glen Springs right after the election, just the two of us?"

"More radiation?" I asked. "I think I've had my limit. I don't care how good it is for you. You can kill yourself by drinking too much water."

"How about going south, then? Or west? What about California?"

"Sure," I whispered. "Just let me get back on my feet. We've got a couple of months to plan."

"I'm not sure how much planning time I'm going to have, to be honest," Elizabeth said. "It was hard just getting over here. Sylvia Pankhurst, the British suffragette, is going to be in Detroit in a few weeks. We've got rallies to plan and speeches to write and . . . well, it's all very exciting, but by November fifth I'll be ready for a few months of the rest cure."

I was more concerned with getting back to work before my father forgot I had an engineering degree and assigned me to the garbage detail, but I nodded and smiled.

We talked a few minutes longer until a nurse shooed Elizabeth out. It was time for my sponge bath. Being treated like an infant was irritating, particularly being sponged everywhere—*everywhere*—by a three-hundred-pound woman, but it gave me more motivation to get healthy.

When that was done, I noticed Elizabeth had left the book on the nightstand. I picked it up and dropped it in the trash can. If I never again heard of *The Phantom of the Opera* it would be too soon.

# AUTHOR'S NOTE

Eloise Hospital was a real place, located in what is now Westland, Michigan, near the Detroit International Airport. It was founded in 1839 and operated continuously until 1984. At one time Eloise boasted seventy-eight buildings on more than nine hundred acres. During the Depression, as many as ten thousand people at a time called Eloise home. (It was the location of the "County House," which served indigent people, as well as the mental hospital and tubercular sanatorium.) Eloise was a self-supporting institution, with a farm, police and fire department, school, and bakery.

Strangely enough, in 1894 the hospital was named for a four-year-old girl named Eloise Dickerson, the daughter of Wayne County's postmaster and governing board president of the Eloise Complex. The name "Eloise" was originally intended for only the post office at the hospital, but it soon came into general use and became the official name until 1945, when it was changed to the Wayne County General Hospital and Infirmary, although everyone still called it Eloise—or the "crazy hospital." Eloise herself passed away in 1982, two years before the hospital closed for good.

Four buildings remain, although all were built after the (fictional) events in this book take place. The Kay Beard Building is the most prominent and at this moment is still used by Wayne County. The others—the powerhouse, the bakery, and the fire department—are in ruins. Much of the property is now part of a golf course, and large sections of the land are bare. The man-made lake from which Eloise got its water and ice (and which was fed via a pipe from the Rouge River on the other side of Michigan Avenue) is much smaller now, really just a pond, but it's still there. I have taken a few liberties with the layout of the hospital in order to serve the story.

The doctors at Eloise were pioneers in some forms of treatment, most of which now seem barbaric, although I'd like to point out that a hundred years from now people will be horrified at the thought of many of the treatments we use today—including radiation, I would imagine, which was one of the treatments pioneered at Eloise. The doctors did early work with radium on inmates with tuberculosis, which has evolved into the radiation therapy still used today.

The treatments Will receives in this book were chosen because of my interest in them and are not necessarily indicative of the treatment amnesia patients received at Eloise Hospital in 1912. While some of the characters in this book are based on real people, those who work at the hospital are all products of my imagination. To the best of my knowledge, Eloise was never plagued with a serial killer, and certainly not one influenced by *The Phantom of the Opera*, which I chose just because I thought it was fun.

The novel *The Phantom of the Opera* was originally published in the United States in 1911. It was not particularly successful as a book but was made into a number of movies and stage plays, some of which you just might have heard about. There are a number of parallels between events and clues in this book with *The Phantom*, though I've mostly limited them to the original novel to make solving the mystery a bit more difficult.

I have borrowed liberally from *Ten Days in a Madhouse* by Nellie Bly, which was published in 1887 and is about her experience as a young investigative reporter exposing the mental health practices of the day. It is a poignant, and surprisingly funny, read.

The story of Eloise Hospital is similar to that of most institutions, whether run by a government, church, or individuals—it was staffed mostly by good people who were doing the best they could under the circumstances. It's always the few that ruin the reputation for the rest, and while doing so provide wonderful material for writers.

# ACKNOWLEDGMENTS

Thanks as always to my early readers—Shelly Johnson, Nicole Cybulski, Grace Shryock, Hannah Johnson, and Yvonne Cooper—and the West Michigan Writers Workshop. I always gain so much from these wonderful people, but I particularly needed their help for this book, since half of it is narrated by a woman. My mind just doesn't work that way—a fact these women were more than happy to point out to me repeatedly throughout the writing of this book.

Thank you to Daniela Rapp, my amazing editor at Minotaur Books, whose insight constantly amazes me, and to Alex Glass for steering me in the right direction and helping me navigate the waters of the publishing world.

Thank you to my lovely wife, Shelly Johnson, for the wonderful map of Eloise, which was a challenge given that she had to channel the spirit of Francis Beckwith.

A big thank you to Jo Johnson of the Eloise Hospital Museum, who shared her memories and research materials with me. Thanks again to the fine folks at the Benson Ford Research Center at the Henry Ford Museum, the Detroit Historical Museum, the National Automotive History Collection, and the Detroit Public Library.

A posthumous thank you to author Nellie Bly for penning *Ten Days in a Madhouse* and Gaston Leroux for the novel *The Phantom of the Opera*, both of which I used for research and inspiration.

All mistakes are mine.

I am a blessed man to have all these people helping me.